Mr Darcy's Persuasion

CASS GRAFTON & ADA BRIGHT

Mr Darcy's Persuasion

Tabby Cow Press

ISBN printed book: 979-8712552504

DEDICATION

We wrote this book throughout the roller coaster journey that was 2020. As always, our friendship and our writing was a balm to our hearts and senses—our escape, our comfort, and a chance to imagine things beyond the daily reality.

Therefore, we dedicate this book to all those friendships around the world—both ours and yours—that helped us all ride out the storm of the past year.

ACKNOWLEDGMENTS

We are grateful for many things during this past year, not least the support of the following:

The readers on Cass's Blog, who followed along with the posting of the opening chapters, despite knowing these would end before the story was completed and—of course—with a massive cliff hanger! Your comments kept us going even when life sometimes felt all too much;

Our amazing editor, Christina Boyd, who kept us on the straight and narrow and, as always, helped guide us in our attempts to create the best possible story for our readers. Her boundless knowledge of the era and her constant support were invaluable;

The Beta-reading crew of Dave McKee, Melanie Jimenez, Debbie Fortin and Diane Zimanski, who offered valuable feedback;

Lee Avison, for the gorgeous cover image, and Steve Scheidler, for making the design 'pop'!

Lastly, but never least, our families for their patience, love and continuous support through a challenging twelve months.

❦

NOTES FROM THE AUTHORS

Mr Darcy's Persuasion is a story inspired by two of Jane Austen's novels: *Pride & Prejudice* and *Persuasion*.

The events follow the timeline of *Pride & Prejudice*, with the story commencing immediately after the Netherfield ball in late November 1811. This is three years earlier than the events of *Persuasion*. Therefore, Anne Elliot is only twenty-four years old, and Captain Wentworth is away at sea.

The timing of one of Caroline Bingley's letters to Jane Bennet has been adjusted to suit the plot.

This tale is set in England, and British English spelling and punctuation have been used throughout.

PROLOGUE

Fitzwilliam Darcy, Gentleman, writes to his cousin,
Colonel Richard Fitzwilliam

Mount Street

Mayfair

Thursday, 28 November 1811

Cousin,

I trust you are conveniently situated in Dorset and that your quarters answer for your immediate needs—do not, I beg you, send me further details on the sanitary habits of your regiment. I am well able to comprehend the truth, without the aid of your explicit illustrations.

Thankful though I am to receive word of your continued good health, I do have a modicum of regret that your hearing was not compromised when you paid a call upon Georgiana last week. Her propensity for indiscretion shows little sign of abating, if she has taken to sharing the content of my correspondence.

Despite your suggestion to the contrary, no young lady has caught my attention. Georgie's imagination is rapid. It leaps from a chance reference to an expression of interest without any justification. (Pray ignore the smudges; my pen blots at will.)

Besides, even with your poor talent for deduction, you will note I have quit Hertfordshire for Town. My friend and his sisters have likewise returned, and I hope this will be the end of Bingley's—and thus my own—association with the county.

I can picture you now, Cousin, brow quizzically raised as you muse upon the reasons for such a precipitous departure, when I had envisaged being bound to attend Bingley for some months. My motives were two-fold.

My friend, you may recall, is of an open disposition and has a propensity for rapidly forming attachments, his admiration for a young lady often turning to love before the introductions have been completed. He had the misfortune to develop such a tendresse in Hertfordshire, concerning a lady of inferior birth and from a most unsuitable family. So marked were Bingley's attentions, a marriage was anticipated by the Meryton populace.

Thus, when my friend was obliged to return to Town yesterday—the day after hosting his confounded ball—our party hastened after him.

Bingley's sisters joined me in expressing a common disapprobation over the lady's circumstances, pointing out the evils of such a match. I feared, nevertheless, my friend would not concede to our plea for him to remain in Town for the winter; thus, I felt it incumbent upon me to further persuade him of the young lady's indifference. In this I am confident, and my assurance carried weight.

My second inducement for leaving so swiftly—be warned, Cousin—is of a far more disagreeable nature.

Wickham is now stationed in Hertfordshire with his regiment! My immediate anxiety was for the county's proximity to London and our charge remaining there unprotected by either of us. What is more, I learned shortly before the ball that Wickham had taken himself off to the Capital.

You can imagine my desperation to return to Georgiana's side directly. I will own this added impetus to my encouragement of the Hursts and Miss Bingley to join me in following my friend (though I did, of course, speak no word to them regarding Wickham).

There is one final matter, which I am obliged to set before you. As well you know, Georgiana has been suffering in recent weeks under a heavy cold, and the impending winter and present damp weather are preventing a swift return to health. She remains wan and listless, with a persistent cough, and though Mr Wilson assures me there is no danger, it keeps her from repose at night; thus, she is also fatigued.

I am taking Georgie west, where the climate and rural situation will provide better opportunity for her to take the air throughout the coming months; as such, I have secured lodgings in Somersetshire, but forty miles distant from your encampment at Blandford.

Sir Walter Elliot of Kellynch Hall has been most obliging in offering a property on his estate for the length of our stay. (Though I suspect his assistance is self-serving. The rumours in Town are of his being strapped for cash). Rein in your alarm, Cousin. I am quite safe from any hopes the gentleman may entertain regarding his unmarried daughters.

We depart on the morrow and shall remain there for the duration of the winter, at the least, and hope to return to Town in the late spring. There is an open invitation for you to pass as much of your liberty with us as you can spare from your parents—you will be a more than welcome sight for your two exiled cousins. I shall send the direction as soon as we are established in the county.

I know you care as deeply for Georgiana as I—indeed, you are as another brother to her. Let us hope this will aid in the improvement of her health, for her spirits, as you know, are still not recovered fully from the events of the summer.

I remain, as ever, your loyal servant.

F Darcy

Miss Elizabeth Bennet writes to her aunt, Mrs Gardiner

Longbourn
Hertfordshire
Friday, 29 November 1811

My dear Aunt,

How are you and the family weathering this inclement season in Gracechurch Street? Be thankful for your pavements; the rains seem never-ending in Hertfordshire, and we have mud and disruption all about.

But oh, dear aunt, if I despaired of only this! When I recollect the catalogue of misfortunes I related in my last—was it but two days ago?—I had no notion matters could worsen beyond my imagining!

How, I hear you say, could they worsen, my disappointment in Mr Wickham not attending the ball being so profound—and all through the insufferable Mr Darcy's influence? How could they worsen more than the ignominy of being obliged to dance the first set with my cousin Collins—his skill in the activity warranting as much respect as his character—and then his having the temerity to propose marriage to me? How could they worsen for Jane, who—after an evening of such delights—knew Mr Bingley's travelling to Town the following day would prevent his calling?

This is how. Word has come, by Miss Bingley's hand to Jane, of the whole party's removal to London and giving no indication of their return. Further, she claims her brother's attention is all upon Mr Darcy's sister—a match she says the families anticipate with pleasure.

I doubt there is truth in what is said about Miss Darcy or that Mr Bingley will not return. His inclination was too pronounced, but Jane will not heed me and has taken this letter in all faith.

And now for the worst of it: my relief at escaping the fate of being shackled to Mr Collins had not long to endure, for the man had the temerity—but four and twenty hours later—to propose marriage to Jane!

In the light of Mr Bingley's defection, and all her schemes for seeing her eldest settled at Netherfield come to naught, Mama is encouraging my beloved sister to accept. To prey upon Jane's sweet, obliging nature when she is so low in spirit is cruel indeed, but Mama will not let up, and Jane is now giving it serious consideration.

Mr Collins thankfully leaves us tomorrow, for he is obliged to return to Kent, but he has avowed his intention of returning in a fortnight to press his case, and Mama is so set upon making it happen, I fear the worst.

I beg you to write Jane and talk some sense into her, for I know there is little point trying to instil any in my mother.

Jane says it matters not whom she weds, with Mr Bingley gone from her life. I hate to see her so disillusioned, but she will not be drawn into my way of thinking. How thankful am I that you will be here within a week of Mr Collins's return to pass the festive season at Longbourn.

May I petition for an invitation for Jane to accompany you and Uncle Gardiner to Town directly afterwards, that you may give her respite from the pressure being brought upon her? If fortune blesses us, she may even cross paths with Mr Bingley.

I beg an early response, my dear aunt. Send me some solace as I try to lift Jane's spirits.

Your affectionate niece,

Lizzy

P.S. Despite the above, I would not have you believe I have kept to my room in a fit of pique at not gaining my point! Indeed, quite the contrary, for I have made a new acquaintance.

A Miss Anne Elliot has come to stay at Lucas Lodge. Charlotte informs me Sir William was introduced to the lady's father, Sir Walter Elliot, at St James's. She seems a genteel lady, a little older than I, but we appear to have much in common. I find I like her very well.

We are to dine at Lucas Lodge this evening, and I anticipate furthering the acquaintance before Miss Elliot is obliged to return to her home in Somersetshire.

CHAPTER ONE

Darcy adjusted his position in the carriage as it gained the turnpike heading west towards their overnight stop between London and the West Country, stretching his long legs but careful not to disturb his sister on the opposite bench. Georgiana Darcy had been asleep this past hour, her head resting against the shoulder of the lady by her side. Mrs Annesley, a sensible woman in her thirties and companion to the young girl, remained engrossed in her book and scarcely seemed to heed Darcy's existence.

The silence suited him; the thoughts in his head did not. With the passing countryside soon providing little distraction, Darcy's mind turned inwards, as it so often did. And as so often of late, only one thing occupied his thoughts: Miss Elizabeth Bennet.

Why? Why could he not free himself from her? Darcy had known his danger, of course. Telling himself he was relieved when she and her sister left after their brief sojourn at Netherfield was mere lip service, and well he comprehended it. Fortunately, no one else was aware of his unfathomable fascination (though Caroline Bingley's hawk-like eyes missed little).

But the ball last Tuesday…was it truly only Friday? It felt as though a lifetime had passed since last he laid eyes upon the lady.

A vision of Elizabeth, attired in her finest, her hair prettily dressed, appeared before Darcy. How he had anticipated standing up for a set with her. How he had argued with himself beforehand, debating the pros and cons of doing so, knowing all along he would be unable to resist the temptation.

Yet the set had not delivered. Instead, it revealed Elizabeth's disapprobation, her disinclination for his company, and worse, her interest in another—in Wickham, of all people. How she defended him!

A tremor seared through Darcy. *Of all people!*

Then he took himself to task, turning to stare out of the window as he forced away the memory.

Be done with it, man.

Elizabeth Bennet closed the door to her sister's bedroom with a snap. She was quite out of sorts, torn between concern for and frustration with Jane. How could someone so sweet natured be so… so *stubborn?* With a huff, Elizabeth hurried along the landing and down the stairs. She needed fresh air and, hopefully, a renewed perspective.

Within five minutes, suitably dressed for the chilly November weather, Elizabeth clambered over a stile into the field situated on Longbourn's western border, thankful for the hard overnight frost and the solid ground.

Deep in thought, she strode resolutely along, hardly heeding her direction. Was Jane truly serious in her consideration of an engagement to Mr Collins? It was nonsensical. What could she possibly do to help her sister see the circumstances differently?

Pausing to draw breath as the terrain began to rise steadily, Elizabeth put her hands on her hips, her brow furrowed.

'There must be an answer,' she muttered.

At least her aunt and uncle would be here soon for their annual Christmas visit, along with their brood. If anyone could talk some sense into the sister Elizabeth once viewed as the most grounded and sensible of them all, it was Aunt Gardiner. There was, at least, that shred of hope to cling to.

Upon reaching the summit of the small mound, Elizabeth paused again to take in the vista of open country. However, it did not deliver the usual contentment as her mind returned to her current concerns.

At first disbelieving Mr Bingley's decampment from Netherfield to be interminable, Elizabeth had dismissed Jane's doubts and anxieties. Now, it was impossible to ignore the facts. She had encountered the gentleman's housekeeper yesterday in Meryton, who confirmed there was no indication her master intended to return. A few retainers would remain through the winter, but rumour was that, come the spring, the property would be sublet to another.

Elizabeth was torn. Keeping secrets from Jane went against her nature, but if she spoke of it, her sister would surely give in to her mother's pressure over Mr Collins.

Anger towards Caroline Bingley and her sister rose in Elizabeth's breast. This was *their* doing. As for Mr Bingley, how could he be persuaded against his affection for Jane? She contemplated the surrounding farmland. There was little doubt in her mind the blame lay with the man's sisters, though another was equally culpable, she was certain.

That man! Setting off at a rapid pace, Elizabeth tried to outrun her thoughts as she descended the slope. Mr Darcy. Mr *Superior* Darcy. He would fail to recognise true affection were it to rise up and poke him in his sardonic eye.

She doubted not he had brought undue influence. After all, had not Mr Bingley himself declared Mr Darcy to be the person he turned to for advice on all matters?

Advice from Mr Darcy on matters of love? *Unfathomable.*

'Eliza!'

Charlotte Lucas was in the lane bordering the field with her guest, Miss Anne Elliot, a young lady of four and twenty years and impeccable manners. She was of a slender frame, average height, and had kind brown eyes, and Elizabeth had enjoyed making her acquaintance over the past week.

With an enthusiastic wave, Elizabeth hurried across the grass to a nearby stile and scaled it.

'We are well met, Eliza.' Charlotte smiled. 'We were on our way to pay a call at Longbourn.'

Elizabeth pulled a face. 'It is well to avoid the place.' She sent a regretful look towards the lady at Charlotte's side. 'Pay me no mind, Miss Elliot. I am attempting to walk off a surfeit of ill temper. How are you enjoying this spell of cold, dry weather?'

'It is welcome, is it not, after the persistent rains of late?' Anne glanced at the sky. 'I am grateful for Charlotte's kind invitation, for the downpours in Town were not conducive to taking the air.'

Charlotte indicated they walk on, and Elizabeth fell into step beside them. 'You were in Town with your godmother, I understand, Miss Elliot?'

'Yes. She is also a dear friend. Lady Russell much prefers the winter pleasures of Bath, and upon that city she is now bent. For myself, I had endured sufficient of hard pavements, bustle, and noise.'

Her recent frustration dissipating with the balm of company, Elizabeth laughed. 'And you have exchanged them for muddy lanes and puddles.'

Anne's expression was wistful. 'It is always my preference over Bath.'

They paused on the verge for a moment to let a horse and cart pass.

'I should so like to see Bath,' Elizabeth mused as they continued along the lane. 'I travel so rarely.'

Charlotte seemed disbelieving. 'You visit your aunt and uncle in London often enough, Eliza.'

'Yes, but that is all. There is much to be seen, and I have experienced so little. I would love to journey as far as the Lakes or the Peak District.' Elizabeth surveyed the all too familiar lane. 'I will own to being generally content with my lot in life, but of late, I have become somewhat disenchanted.'

Charlotte was frowning. 'Is this to do with Jane?'

'Unquestionably.'

Silence fell upon the ladies as they negotiated a crossing on the lane. Longbourn was in sight, and Elizabeth viewed it with mixed emotions. She had not anticipated so precipitous a return. However, she had only recently become acquainted with Anne Elliot, and this was not the time to discuss Jane and Mr Collins.

Elizabeth frowned as she addressed Charlotte. 'I comprehend the connection between your fathers, their having met at St James's, but how is it you are both acquainted?'

'Anne and I met when we attended the ladies' seminary for a twelve-month.' Charlotte waved a hand. 'You recall, Eliza, do you not, my stay in Surrey some years ago?'

'Yes, of course.'

'We maintained our acquaintance through correspondence,' Anne interjected. 'But have rarely met in the interim. I had never visited Hertfordshire before, and Charlotte has never come to Kellynch. That is our home in Somersetshire,' she added.

'And now we are to address the situation!' Charlotte beamed as they made their way down the drive to Longbourn. 'Anne has kindly extended an invitation to accompany her when she returns to the West Country. I shall make a stay of some weeks.'

Knowing of Charlotte's importance to the running of the household at Lucas Lodge, this was surprising intelligence to Elizabeth and sufficient distraction from her present vexations. As such, the three young ladies continued a lively discussion on the charms of home until they were inside the house.

❋

'She is pleasant, is she not?' Jane Bennet was at the window when Elizabeth returned from seeing the callers on their way.

'I find her excellent company. She has an independent air that is much to be admired.' Elizabeth joined Jane by the window, determined to make a point. 'She epitomises the prerogative of a lady's choice to remain unwed.'

Jane raised an admonishing brow at her sister, but Lydia, the only other of the Bennet ladies remaining, snorted.

'I did *not* find her good company. Miss Elliot is far too *piano* for my tastes.' Lydia flounced out of the room, and Jane and Elizabeth exchanged a resigned look.

''Tis a shame Lydia makes so little use of the mute pedal herself.' Elizabeth held out a hand to her sister, and Jane smiled, taking the hand as they crossed the room to settle on a chaise beside the hearth.

'Jane—'

'No, Lizzy.' Jane placed a hand on her sister's arm. 'I beg of you. No more. Let me come to my own decision.' She raised a hand as Elizabeth opened her mouth. 'And in my own time.'

Sensing the swift return of her annoyance, Elizabeth blew out a breath. 'I cannot believe you are even considering Mama's scheme.'

'Dear Lizzy'—Jane turned in her seat, her eyes solemn— 'Mama was quite right. One of us must secure the futures of the others. It is incumbent upon me to at least give the heir to the estate some consideration. Besides, think of the peace of mind it would bring to our parents.'

Elizabeth rolled her eyes. Peace of mind? Never! 'Those are Mama's words! And Papa is not as content as you may believe.'

'I know.' Jane sighed. 'I do not wish people to be at odds, but I am only doing my duty in not dismissing it out of hand, and if it is my choice, you will not talk me out of it.'

'So be it. It shall no more be spoken of.' Neither of them believed it a solemn promise. All the good of Charlotte and Anne's visit faded as melancholy settled upon Elizabeth with a firm hand.

'Do not be sad. Let us speak on pleasanter topics, such as this evening's invitation to dine at Lucas Lodge.'

Elizabeth stayed her sister with her hand as they both rose from their seats. 'Promise me one thing, Jane.

'Just one, Lizzy?'

'I am perfectly serious.' Elizabeth stepped aside as Jane opened the door. 'Will you promise to make no quick decision? After all, Mr Collins has already said he will return in a fortnight.'

Jane held Elizabeth's gaze for a moment, then nodded. 'It is the least I can commit to. The matter is sealed.'

'It is *not*,' Elizabeth muttered as she followed Jane out into the hall.

'Did you say anything?'

Elizabeth shook her head, hope taking a firmer hold. 'Naught of consequence.'

Perhaps it was time to channel Mr Darcy himself? If he could persuade his friend away from her sister, perhaps there would be a way for Jane to be *persuaded* from this ridiculous notion of taking Mr Collins as a husband?

The carriage made excellent progress the following day, though Georgiana slept once again, and Darcy was thankful to note a milestone as they passed by. Their journey neared its end. They had left the turnpike behind some time ago, their speed lessening to accommodate the winding lanes of Somersetshire. Though it was pretty country, predominantly farmland and small villages, the state of the roads reflected it.

Darcy winced as the wheels found another rut, jostling the travellers roughly in their seats. Georgiana, however, did not stir.

He surveyed her with concern. His sister had slept badly of late, her cough troubling her, and it had been no better during the previous night in Andover. It was no surprise the somnolent motion of the carriage when on the smoother roads had lulled her to sleep. He hoped—no, prayed—he had done right in bringing her away.

As the carriage slowed to enter an impressive gateway, rolling in state into the park, Darcy leaned forward and rested a hand on Georgiana's arm.

'Dearest. We are arrived.'

Mrs Annesley closed her book as Georgiana sleepily opened her eyes and straightened. Her wan complexion smote Darcy's heart. Lord, he hoped Wilson's prognosis was sound.

'Forgive me, Brother. I have not been the best of company.' Her voice was hoarse, but Darcy shook his head as he sat back in his seat.

'You need your rest, my dear. I will make your apologies to Sir Walter. Remain in the carriage with Mrs Annesley whilst I establish where the house is situated.'

Relief filled Georgiana's features, and she turned to speak quietly to the lady at her side as Darcy viewed the countryside with growing interest.

The park at Kellynch was extensive, but the Hall soon came into view, an impressive Elizabethan building with an excess of windows. The upkeep must be a severe drain on Sir Walter Elliot's income—the rumours may well be true after all.

Barely had the steps been lowered before Darcy was out of the carriage and striding forward, exchanging acknowledgements with the baronet who had come out of the imposing doorway to greet them.

'My good sir, welcome to Kellynch.' Sir Walter puffed out his chest, and Darcy blinked. He sported a ridiculously ornate waistcoat for the time of day, his hair arranged with more care and precision than a lady of fashion.

'Sir Walter. I trust you and your family are in good health?'

'What? Ah, yes. Capital, I thank you. But you will see for yourself, Darcy. You will join us for some refreshments.'

'With regret, sir, I must decline for the present.'

A frown creased Sir Walter's brow, though it was quickly banished. 'What is this? No refreshments after such a journey?' He passed a smoothing hand across his forehead, as though fearful the frown wrinkled it.

'I thank you sincerely for the kind offer, sir, but my sister has been unwell and requires rest. If your man would be so good as to supply the direction, I will ensure she is comfortably installed before coming to pay my respects.'

Sir Walter's gaze drifted towards the open door of the carriage.

'Of course. Shepherd.' He gestured towards a neatly-dressed man hovering just inside the doorway. 'Furnish Mr Darcy's coachman with directions to Meadowbrook House.' He bowed fussily to Darcy. 'We shall see you directly, sir.'

Darcy was back in the carriage before Sir Walter had disappeared inside the building. His impression of the gentleman had not wavered. He was as much a spectacle at home as he was in Town.

Some minutes later, the carriage drew up on a gravel sweep before a substantial property of much more recent build than the main house. The columns supporting the portico, the tall windows, and the smooth stonework spoke of its Georgian origins. It was, perhaps, in a similar style to Netherfield, only on a smaller scale.

Once inside, Darcy was relieved to see his valet, Raworth, and Mrs Reynolds, the housekeeper from Pemberley, waiting in the entrance hall.

'Welcome to Meadowbrook House, Mr Darcy.' Mrs Reynolds dropped a curtsey as Raworth relieved Darcy of his greatcoat. 'Shall I bring tea to the drawing room?'

'Georgiana?' Darcy turned to his sister and her companion.

'May I go to my room, Fitz?'

'Of course.' He turned to the housekeeper as Georgiana's maid, Tilly, took her coat and bonnet. 'I trust you are all well settled, Mrs Reynolds?'

'Of course, sir. Come, Miss Georgiana, Mrs Annesley. I will show you to your apartments and send up some tea.'

Darcy watched the ladies making their way up the elegant staircase, then walked over to where one of the Pemberley footmen held open the door to the drawing room, and he entered with interest.

It was a well-furnished room, and a roaring fire in the grate made it all the more welcoming. There was a well-stocked bookcase along the far wall, and Darcy walked over to inspect it, only to mutter at the first book he selected. Was not this the volume of poems Elizabeth had been studying during that interminable half hour in Netherfield's library? How he had struggled through those endless minutes, determined to remain in his place, whilst equally committed to ensuring no particular attention to the lady escaped him on the final day of her stay in the house.

'Enough,' Darcy said aloud as he thrust the slim volume back onto the shelf, turning his back on the books.

There was a desk under the far window, and a quick inspection showed it to be well equipped with the necessary writing implements. Taking a seat, Darcy selected a pen, dipped it into the ink and began to write. His cousin could be relied upon for a great deal, providing distraction being a particular talent. The sooner Richard came to visit, the better.

CHAPTER TWO

Saturday and Sunday in Hertfordshire passed much as they generally did, though Elizabeth had taken much pleasure from furthering her acquaintance with Anne Elliot. With Charlotte engaged with her younger sisters and brothers after church, they had taken the opportunity to indulge in the fresh air by walking to a nearby park, where a pleasant hour or two had been whiled away.

The following morning, Elizabeth curled up in a chair by the drawing room window, thankful for the peace, which descended upon the house whenever Kitty and Lydia took it into their heads to walk into Meryton to plague the soldiers.

Until, that is, the door flew open with a crash.

'Whatever is the matter?'

Elizabeth raised startled eyes from her book as her mother came bustling across the room bearing a note, thrusting it at her daughter.

Getting to her feet, she recognised Charlotte's hand, and read it through quickly.

'Well, Lizzy? What is it?' Mrs Bennet flapped her arms. 'The boy insists on waiting.'

'Lady Lucas is taken ill.' Elizabeth raised her head. 'It is not believed to be infectious, but Charlotte requests her guest, Miss Elliot, stay with us until her departure on Wednesday.'

Mrs Bennet's mouth opened, then closed with a snap. 'Miss Elliot? She is the daughter of a baronet, is she not? A lady such as she will expect only the best. I must make some alteration to the dinner course.'

She left the room, shrieking 'Hill! Hill!' and, sinking into a chair at the desk, Elizabeth penned a quick response, assuring Charlotte of Miss Elliot's welcome at her soonest convenience. Once the boy had been dispatched into the December evening, Elizabeth sought out the housekeeper to establish the best room for Anne's brief stay, hoping she would not find life at Longbourn too trying.

In truth, she was confident this development would bring some relief to her own situation (though wishing no ill upon Lady Lucas). Jane's obduracy had somehow placed an invisible barrier between them, and though their relationship *seemed* as usual, Elizabeth felt unable to talk to her in the open way she was used to. Though Anne lacked the familiarity of a sister, she was amiable in every way and would be a comfort.

The lady had also shown herself to be as fond of walking as Elizabeth, and she anticipated them spending much of the remainder of Anne's stay roaming the countryside and continuing to talk about books, plays, and the journeys they wished they could make. Anne seemed to have a particular fascination with the sea, and the places she wished to visit were far more exotic than Elizabeth's choices, and she looked forward to hearing more from her new friend.

'I think Richard is here!'

Darcy looked up from his book. Georgiana, who had been keeping watch at the drawing room window since breaking their fast, shot out of the door.

Putting the volume aside, Darcy rose from his seat and walked to the window. To his surprise, a carriage slowed to a halt on the gravel sweep before the house. Even as he watched Boliver, his butler, make his stately way down the steps, Darcy saw Georgiana hurry out of the doorway and overtake him, hovering as one of the footmen lowered the carriage steps and opened the door.

He turned away, picking up his sister's discarded shawl and went out to join them, thankful for his cousin's prompt arrival. Much as Georgiana's health slowly improved, her spirits remained quite low, and the burst of pleasure she had shown was a welcome sight.

By the time Darcy reached the top of the steps, the colonel and Georgiana had made their way up them, and the carriage had moved away. He tucked the warm shawl about his sister as they entered the house.

'You made good time.' Darcy shook his cousin's hand. 'I did not expect you to come by conveyance.'

'A colleague is on his way to Bristol and offered me a ride. Seemed churlish to refuse the ease and comfort. Hereward should be in the stables, assuming Mackenzie has arrived?'

Georgiana, who still clung to her cousin's arm, nodded. 'Mrs Reynolds mentioned your man was installed in his quarters.' She covered her mouth as her cough made itself known. 'You will find your rooms pleasant, though not as spacious as Pemberley.'

The colonel grinned as Boliver relieved him of his travelling cloak.

'I am accustomed to coping with the hardship of basic accommodations.' He turned to Darcy. 'You are well situated. I had not expected such a modern and airy property.'

'Built but five and twenty years ago as the dower house for the present incumbent's mother. She did not live to see it completed, but I believe the late Lady Elliot furnished it and made regular use of it.'

The colonel smirked. 'Probably hopeful of residing in it herself one day. Shame she did not live to do so either.' He raised a brow. 'So, Darce, how do you find the air of Somersetshire?'

Darcy pulled a face and the colonel laughed.

'Do not tell me. You find the company confined and unvarying.'

'It is like any other away from Town.'

'Including Pemberley, Brother.' Georgiana's impish smile appeared but soon faded. 'I do miss our home, much as we are well settled here.'

'We have a dozen of the Pemberley servants attending us, Georgie.'

'I know, Fitz, but this scenery is so sedate. I miss the drama of the peaks.'

The colonel grimaced as they turned for the drawing room. 'You will not miss the winter weather. Mother's latest says snow is forecast. Ice is forming on the lakes, and the livestock is already quartered in the barns.'

Darcy frowned. 'I have not heard from Peters. I trust he has all in hand at Pemberley. After the wet summer and the poor harvest, the last the farmers need is a harsh winter.'

'Peters *always* has matters in fine shape, Darcy, as well you know.' The colonel studied the charming and comfortable room. 'You are simply feeling the tedium of being a tenant yourself, with no steward to order around.'

'Richard'—Georgiana tried to clear her throat—'How long will you stay?'

'I must return to camp on Friday, but Blandford is not far distant. I have some leave due during the festive season and hoped for an invitation?'

He looked to Darcy, who had resumed his seat.

'Of course. You would be most welcome, for it will be a quiet Yuletide this year.'

'Had you not thought to invite your friend, Bingley?'

Darcy stirred uncomfortably in his seat. He did not like to think of the morose Bingley he had last seen.

'Permit me some leeway before I consider the social whirl of the season.'

'It will be upon us before you know it.' The colonel stretched his legs out in front of the roaring fire. 'And how do you find Sir Walter Elliot as a neighbour?'

'Tolerable, I suppose.' Darcy shrugged. 'I saw him briefly on Saturday to pay my respects, and likewise in church yesterday.'

'And Miss Elliot?'

'Richard.' Darcy's tone held a warning as he studied Georgiana, who listened intently.

Colonel Fitzwilliam merely smirked, so Darcy continued.

'Should you have the opportunity to become reacquainted with Sir Walter during your brief stay, you can be certain he will introduce his daughters to you.'

'All three of them? Is not the youngest married?'

Georgiana nodded. 'Mrs Musgrove suffers with her health, thus, she has not paid a call here, for fear of contracting my cold. They live at Uppercross, two miles across the parkland.'

'Miss Elliot has called once with her father,' added Darcy. 'Though Georgiana did not meet them, and we have not made the acquaintance of Miss Anne Elliot. She has been travelling, we are told, and will return shortly.'

'I shall anticipate the meeting with pleasure.' The colonel settled more comfortably against the cushions. 'A soldier is oft in need of female companionship to soothe his rougher edges.'

Darcy all but rolled his eyes. 'I doubt the daughters of a baronet are quite the right company for such a purpose, Richard.'

'What do you mean, Brother?'

'Some foolish nonsense from your cousin. Would you be so good as to ring for refreshments, Georgie?'

The colonel was interested in exploring the neighbourhood the following morning, and he and Darcy soon enjoyed a fine gallop across the fields.

Drawing in their mounts on a rise of ground, Darcy leaned forward to pat Gunnar's silken neck.

Colonel Fitzwilliam looked around. 'It is fine country.'

Turning in the saddle, Darcy followed the direction of his cousin's scrutiny as it roamed over the scenery. The fields were bordered by a combination of fencing and honey-coloured hamstone walls, which were common to the area, and were scattered with sheep.

To the left lay woodland; and to the right, from their raised position, they could see down the valley to Kellynch Hall in all its splendour.

'Such a charming prospect. Unless one is within, I suspect,' mused the colonel.

'You refer to the inhabitants, I assume, rather than the internal dimensions.'

The colonel laughed. 'How extensive is the estate?' He shielded his eyes from the low winter sun as he took in the vista around them.

'Not dissimilar to Pemberley, but in need of some investment.' Darcy gestured towards a nearby boundary with his crop. 'Many of the walls are in need of repair, there are some fences down, and I have already discerned several trees which ought to be felled before they choose to do so of their own accord.'

The colonel raised a brow. 'The estate is not channelling its resources into where it is required. Is Sir Walter in the suds?'

'I believe he is headed that way.' They both urged their mounts to walk on. 'There seems no shortage of funds for garments, fine dining, and refurbishment of the principal rooms in the house.'

'That would conform to the general consensus in Town.' Colonel Fitzwilliam grinned. 'Sir Walter is as fine a specimen as is ever seen, other than Brummel himself, of course. Quite the dandy and, to be fair to the gentleman, not appearing his age.'

'He may not look his age, but he ought at least to dress it.'

The colonel snorted. 'I can imagine his flounce and fancy would not be to your taste, Darce!'

They reached the bridleway, Colonel Fitzwilliam using his crop to handle the metal gate, and turning their mounts to the right, proceeded in a comfortable silence for a moment.

Then, the colonel turned to Darcy. 'I remain curious about your precipitous departure from Hertfordshire. I admire your dedication to both your friend's well-being and Georgiana's protection but sense there is something you are not telling me.'

'Why, pray, would you speak so?' Darcy's eyes narrowed as they continued along the way. He thought he had successfully silenced his cousin on that score.

The colonel reached over and grabbed the reins from Darcy's hands, pulling both mounts to a halt.

'You are distracted. It cannot be Wickham, for Georgie is safe here with you. I doubt it is Bingley. I suspect it is a woman.' The colonel grinned.

'Do not be so asinine. Why should a woman be the cause?'

'Ha! So, you will own to the distraction of your thoughts?'

Damn it.

Darcy drew in a long breath, trying to pretend Elizabeth had not come to mind in an instant. Where was she now? Would she be out walking if this fine weather graced Meryton or...

'And there you go again.' The colonel's grin widened, and Darcy wrenched the reins from him and set off at a canter, conscious his cousin followed suit.

Trying to outrun his thoughts was futile, and he knew it. It was what Darcy had endeavoured to do ever since the swift removal from Netherfield. Had he not torn himself away rather than gone willingly? And why this ache in his breast even yet? How could he miss a woman who hardly acknowledged his existence; who, what is more, defended his nemesis?

Darcy slowed his mount, and unmindful of his cousin having drawn alongside, the name 'Elizabeth' fell from his lips.

'Good lord, Darce!' The colonel almost choked on a laugh. 'You are aiming high! Setting your sights on Miss Elizabeth Elliot?'

Darcy turned to his cousin. What could he possibly say? He most assuredly would not own to an interest in that lady, and he most assuredly would *not* own to an interest in any other Elizabeth.

But is not Elizabeth Bennet a vastly inferior lady?

The thought whispered through his mind, and he shoved it ruthlessly aside. In fortune and connections, perhaps. In character? Never.

'Darce?' The colonel's amusement faded. 'Hey, old chap, I comprehend the need to secure a mistress for the estate, but Miss Elliot? I may not have made her personal acquaintance, but the word in Town is not favourable.'

He shook his head. 'I am no fool, Richard. That way, madness lies.'

His cousin, of course, knew not the truth of Darcy's words.

CHAPTER THREE

'I shall miss your company when you leave in the morning.' Elizabeth smiled at Anne as they made their way through the lanes near Meryton on Tuesday.

'And I yours.' Anne looked back as a burst of laughter emanated from Lydia Bennet, who walked behind them with her sister, Kitty.

'But not my sisters'!' Elizabeth shook her head as she and Anne turned their steps towards Longbourn. 'No attempt to check them holds sway. Did you ever have such trials from your youngest sister?'

'Mary is quite the opposite, though her younger sisters through marriage are not dissimilar.' Anne paused, then added. 'Louisa and Henrietta Musgrove are away at school, which may tame some of their exuberance.'

Anne preceded Elizabeth through the open gates, and they continued down the drive towards the house. 'Sisters can present many trials, can they not?'

Elizabeth pulled a face, then laughed. 'Aye, that they can. Tell me about your sister Mary. You said she is the only one of you to marry so far?'

'Yes, she wed a Mr Charles Musgrove but a year ago.'

'And is she content?'

Anne did not answer, and Elizabeth stayed the lady with her hand. 'Forgive me. I am too inquisitive.'

'You are not!' Anne's tone reassured. 'I merely reflected. How much do any of us truly comprehend of a married couple's life when all we see is their public face? Mary is with child at present, and some of her ailments make her querulous, so happiness in her present situation is difficult to determine.'

'You are quite the diplomat, Miss Elliot.'

Anne shook her head. 'I speak as I find.'

'Which is why we get on so famously.' Elizabeth laughed. 'Though I will own, you speak with less impertinence than I.'

She flinched at a shout of laughter from Lydia as they resumed their walk. How Anne endured her stay, she had no idea, but there were another four and twenty hours to get through before she would be able to escape Longbourn. How could she help her pass them without excessive exposure to her family?

Reluctant to give up the fine day, Anne and Elizabeth eschewed returning to the house, choosing to stroll in the garden.

'What is through that gate?'

'A pleasant grove. Would you like to see it?'

'Oh yes. I have always had a particular fondness for groves.'

'It is perfect when one wants to escape for a while. My younger sisters are unlikely to consider venturing out here unless they are told red coats might be growing.'

They strolled in the grove in a companionable silence for a while, but Elizabeth felt out of sorts.

'Will you think badly of me, Miss Elliot, if I speak more openly than our acquaintance might warrant?'

'If speaking will aid you, then please do. You can trust in my discretion.'

Elizabeth took Anne's arm, and they resumed their walk.

'I am unsurprised by my mother playing upon Jane's lowness of mood, but I cannot comprehend my sister's lack of faith in Mr Bingley's returning. Her consideration of Mama's proposition is not duty. It is madness of the highest order.'

'Is it truly?'

Anne's soft-spoken question merely confirmed what Elizabeth already knew.

'No, of course not. But my father...' She stopped and faced Anne, conscious of rising agitation. 'If Jane is willing, Papa is not going to dissuade her from her apparent choice.'

'And you feel Mr Bennet should act?'

Elizabeth raised both hands before dropping them to her sides. 'Having been rescued from such a match myself, I find Papa's acceptance of the situation unfathomable. His reasoning is that Jane needs time to reflect, time to see the notion of the engagement from a more rational perspective.' She let out a breath. 'It does have some merit. Jane is caught up in her own misery. She cannot see happiness with any man and thus concludes she may as well make a convenient match to aid her sisters.'

'It is a noble gesture.'

'And I wish I could accept it.' Elizabeth's every thought railed against it; her whole being rejected the notion.

'Come. Let us walk on.' Anne urged Elizabeth into step, and they followed a winding path to their left.

'Jane once said I was not formed for ill humour. Never did I foresee the sweetest, most benevolent of my sisters putting me in one such as this.'

They came to a bench nestled against the hedging and sat.

'Oh, Miss Elliot. How fortunate you are.'

'I?' Anne's kind eyes clouded for a second. 'Yes, of course. Though I struggle to ascertain your present meaning?'

'Forgive me. I am over familiar.'

Anne shook her head. 'Our friendship may be of short duration, but we have already formed quite the bond, have we not? Thus, the boundaries are quite liberal and shall no doubt be infinite in time.'

Elizabeth was warmed by the sincere sentiments. 'I fail to recall a time when I was not conscious of the expectation for all of us to secure a match—and that at least one of us must make a *good* one to protect the future of the others.' She paused, inhaling the chill winter air. 'Though Mr Collins is not a rich man, being heir to the estate would offer protection for us all, but despite this, I cannot reconcile myself to Jane's sacrifice.'

'We have an entailment in common. Kellynch is destined for my father's cousin, William Walter Elliot, Esquire.'

'And has there been no pressure upon your eldest sister?'

Anne released a short laugh. 'I think the pressure might well have been upon the cousin, but it bore no fruit. My sister, from as early as I can recall, meant to marry Mr Elliot—he is the heir presumptive, you see, and a future baronet—and my father had always meant that she should.'

'Was Miss Elliot deeply attached to the gentleman?'

'I believe they only met twice in Town. Both my father and my sister were angered by Mr Elliot snubbing the hand of friendship from the head of the family and then going on to marry a woman of inferior birth.'

'Oh!' Elizabeth frowned. 'So, Miss Elliot and yourself...' It would be indelicate to ask if they were in *need* of a match. Surely they had plentiful dowries and would not fail to secure a situation when they chose? 'You have not been persuaded by your father to settle down, have no desire to follow your younger sister's inclination?'

Anne's features were indicative of some discomfort. 'It is true my eldest sister has, this last twelve-month, seemed almost desperate for a situation, and my father is equally desirous of her securing one. For myself'—she hesitated—'I have never feared being thrust *into* a situation against my wishes, but…'

Elizabeth viewed Anne with growing curiosity.

'It is simply… Well, there is the truth. It is not simple at all, for the grass spreads no greener over the fields of Kellynch than it does elsewhere. Perchance it is simply of a different hue.'

'Is your present situation *not* of your choosing?'

'Yes…and no.'

Elizabeth was conscious how carefully Anne spoke. Her air was indicative of disquiet. Perhaps she ought to redirect the conversation?

Anne, however, continued. 'Choice is a complicated thing for a woman,' Then, she waved a hand. 'Pay me no mind. For the present, I will own to some regrets—regrets that have never left me.'

'You make me curious, but I will ask no more. One day, I hope you will share your burden with me.'

'I am quite content with my lot in life.'

Quite content? Elizabeth knew it would not be sufficient for her, and she doubted, ultimately, it would be sufficient for Anne Elliot.

The lady at her side shivered, and Elizabeth stood. 'Come. Let us walk back towards the house whilst you talk me into a better humour.'

Anne fell into step beside her. 'I wish I had an attachment to either of my sisters as strong as yours. I envy you, Miss Bennet.'

Elizabeth followed her out of the grove, then turned to take Anne's proffered arm.

'Jane is my truest friend and a most beloved sister.' Elizabeth considered this for a moment. 'I have never felt this way about her before, as though we are drifting apart.'

'May I make a suggestion?'

'Of course.'

'A change of scene may bring you some reprieve. Dear Miss Bennet, will you not come, in Charlotte's stead, to Kellynch?'

'Can you be quite serious?' Elizabeth stared at Anne in part disbelief, part wild hope. 'Accompany you to Somersetshire?'

'Why ever not? Charlotte was to make a stay of some duration with us. In her absence, why not take her place?' Anne spoke earnestly. 'I am sorely in need of company—*good* company. Will you not indulge me?'

'I—' Elizabeth cast around for the right words, but they would not oblige, mainly because her head simply shouted 'yes, yes, yes'. Why did she hesitate? Because of Jane.

'Can you not spare a couple of weeks? Your sister has promised to make no decision before your cousin's return. When is that to be?'

'The sixteenth.'

Anne raised a brow. 'The month has barely begun. There is ample time for you to visit and return.'

It was true, and there was merit in the suggestion, for Jane showed no sign of listening to anything Elizabeth said.

She smiled. 'Pay no mind to my dithering. It is not for want of accepting with alacrity. I am surprised, that is all. Would it be acceptable to your family? They are vastly my…'

'They are expecting me to return with Charlotte. Whomsoever I return with will make no difference to my father or my eldest sister.'

'They sound most accommodating.'

A small sound escaped Anne, but Elizabeth was too taken up with the notion of escape.

'I must speak to Papa.' It was a necessity, but Elizabeth knew her father would always take the path of least disruption, and if she made it clear she wanted to go into Somersetshire, then to Somersetshire she would go.

Anne's face was alight with warmth. 'I should so love to show Kellynch to you, Miss Bennet! It is my solace and comfort.'

'You make me envious.' Elizabeth considered the charming walled garden. The golden chimney tops of Longbourn and the rooftops were all that could be seen from here. 'I do like my home, but I would not say it gives me much relief.' She turned back to face Miss Elliot. 'Indeed, of late, I have oft dreamed of escaping its confines for the wider world. Your offer is most fortuitous.'

'Then you will come? And...' Colour crept into Miss Elliot's cheeks. 'Do I ask too much, after so brief an acquaintance...would you give me leave to call you Elizabeth?'

'Oh, thank heavens!' Elizabeth laughed. 'The formality at times is enough to drive one to bedlam.' She sobered, but remained full of her unexpected good fortune. 'And please call me Lizzy, as my friends do. Come. Let us repair to the house. I shall speak to Papa directly. With your carriage due on the morrow, I must make haste to address my packing, and you can advise me on the suitability of my wardrobe.'

CHAPTER FOUR

Darcy dropped Bingley's latest letter onto his desk and leaned back in his chair. Distance from Hertfordshire and a certain young lady had done little to lessen his friend's attachment, and he made it obvious.

With a faint smile, Darcy stood. Bingley was a lot bolder at expressing his opinion when they were not face-to-face. The momentary amusement faded, and Darcy released a frustrated breath.

Damn it!

He felt guilt-ridden once more. Bingley had no patience for writing letters, dashing them off with such speed they were almost unintelligible, but since Darcy and he parted company, he had become a regular correspondent.

His attention returned to the discarded letter on the desk. All too regular. As was the refrain. His friend was unhappy, excessively so, doubting his own actions and, thus, the advice he had been given. Bingley *never* doubted Darcy's advice.

Frowning, Darcy left the room and roamed the hall. He had no misgivings whatsoever.

Or did he? Was he not painfully aware of his own danger when in Hertfordshire? Did Darcy not feel the same anguish his friend so freely expressed, whenever thoughts of Elizabeth passed through his mind?

However, did the lady not come from the same unsuitable family, who displayed little decorum, had no fortune and the weakest of connections? A country town attorney, for heaven's sake, and a businessman in Cheapside!

Once again, Elizabeth appeared before him, her chin raised and her fine eyes sparkling as she traded opinions with him, and something deep within Darcy's breast clenched as he instinctively placed a hand over his heart. Why did she persist in haunting him? Her voice played in his ears day and night, her eyes followed him—intelligent, forthright...

'Brother?'

Darcy stirred, looking towards the drawing room door.

'Is aught amiss?'

Darcy joined his sister, taking her outstretched hands. 'Not at all, my dear.' He frowned again. 'Why do you ask?'

'Your bearing, Fitz.' Georgiana's eyes raked his face. 'I know you are disturbed. We have not been brother and sister these many years without my comprehending a little of your countenance.'

'My habitual dour expression, you mean?' Darcy followed Georgiana into the room.

'You are not dour!' Georgiana took a seat by the hearth. 'You are...'

'Curmudgeonly? Irascible? Cantankerous?' The colonel joined them, and Darcy laughed.

'Quite often.' He turned back to his sister. 'Never with you, dear Georgie.'

'But what is it, Brother?' Georgiana's stare wavered not, and Darcy stirred under its intensity. Where the devil did *this* come from?

The colonel looked from one to the other, then dropped into an armchair opposite his young cousin, a smirk spreading across his features.

'Aha! Caught out, I gather?' He winked at Georgiana. 'What has Darcy been revealing? He has a secret of some sort, though I have failed thus far to discern it. Perchance you will have better luck than I.'

'I have no secret.' Darcy bit out.

You lie, whispered a soft voice, somewhere out of reach.

'I fear he doth protest too much, Georgie.' The colonel grinned at his young cousin. 'How shall we cajole the facts from him?'

'Is it to do with your time in Hertfordshire?' Her curiosity was evident. 'Did some misfortune befall you there?'

Leaning back in his seat, Darcy studied his sister from across the room. If only she knew.

'Your silence is telling, Brother. Is it connected to Mr Bingley?'

Darcy blinked. 'What makes you say—'

'You told me you and his sisters hastened after him, though you did not elaborate on your reasons. And between your return and our departure for Somersetshire, you rarely saw him, even though it is customary for him to lodge with us or Mr and Mrs Hurst rather than in an hotel. Thus, I must conclude, there is a difficulty between you both.'

'I think it is more than that, Georgie.' Colonel Fitzwilliam smirked at Darcy. 'Aside from blotting his letter—unheard of—when writing of Hertfordshire recently, he has already told me of the service he rendered to Bingley in successfully extracting him from a situation in that county.'

Georgiana's expression was filled with concern. 'Had he formed another attachment?'

Darcy nodded. 'He was quickly smitten, but the lady less so.'

'Oh, poor Mr Bingley!'

'An indifferent lady and a besotted Bingley.' The colonel barked a laugh. 'You did the lady a favour, that much is certain, Darce.'

'I merely pointed out the ills of such an alliance. The lady was of inferior birth and the family's situation appalling. Separating them was in both their interests.'

Georgiana's brow furrowed. 'But if you feel thus, why would it plague you so, have you pacing the hall with such a conflicted air?'

'Ha!' The colonel laughed. 'Definitely caught out! I wonder, Georgie, if it has aught to do with this mention of another young lady in Hertfordshire.'

'Be silent, Richard.' Darcy left his seat, weary of the subject. 'Amuse yourselves as best you can. I have correspondence to attend to before we dine.'

Darcy closed the door on his cousin's chuckling. Let them speculate at will. There was no possible chance of them stumbling upon the truth.

Wednesday dawned soon enough, and the trunks were quickly loaded onto the Elliot carriage, but before Anne and Elizabeth left the house, Hill joined them in the entrance hall.

'A letter has been sent up from Lucas Lodge, Miss Lizzy. For Miss Elliot.' Hill handed over the missive and hurried away, and Anne frowned.

'I am not expecting any letters. Oh! It is Elizabeth's hand.' She looked up. 'You share a name but little else.'

Elizabeth smiled. 'Shall we get on our way? You can read it as we travel. Wait, where is your maid?'

'She is to travel with the coachman as the weather holds for now.'

'Is that not a little singular?' Elizabeth followed Anne into the elegant carriage and took a seat opposite her.

'Elise and James are married.'

Elizabeth stared out of the window at Longbourn as the carriage began to move, waving to her sisters, who came to see them off, and feeling little regret at leaving them behind.

It would have been difficult to say goodbye to Anne, for she had been the best of companions. She also talked with such warmth of her home, of Somersetshire, that Elizabeth was all anticipation for her visit.

As the carriage set off along the turnpike towards the West Country, Anne leaned back against the cushions.

'You seem disturbed, Lizzy. Is it leaving Miss Bennet behind?'

Elizabeth settled back in her seat. 'I am astounded at my relief. Ordinarily, when I am parted from Jane, I miss her profoundly.'

'Perchance the separation will do your sister some good, permit her to see a way forward more clearly.'

'I truly hope so.'

Anne's mild, dark eyes met Elizabeth's solemnly. 'Be not so concerned, Lizzy. A disappointment—even one that may not be fully overcome—can be borne. For your sister, it is too raw, too soon, for her to see beyond her immediate sense of loss. I feel for her, I truly do.'

Not for the first time, Elizabeth sensed hidden meaning behind Anne's words, and she responded gently.

'You are kind and compassionate. As is Jane. You would do well together, I am certain.'

Anne merely smiled, turning her attention to her letter. Her eyes skimmed the two sides of the paper, then her hand dropped into her lap.

'You are displeased with its content?'

Anne folded the letter and tucked it into her reticule. 'It is always the way of it. Rarely does my eldest sister write me, and whenever such an occasion arises, she never fails to disappoint.'

'How so?'

'My sister takes much after my father and displays a decided lack of compassion. I must warn you, Lizzy...' Anne leaned forward in her seat. 'They are not like me. Or I am not like them. I know not what I mean to say, but they may not be as welcoming towards you as I would wish.'

It was no surprise to Elizabeth that a baronet and his eldest might be condescending towards her. 'Miss Elliot will object to your bringing an acquaintance to stay who is not of equal social standing.' Elizabeth's tone was matter of fact, but a blush stained Anne's cheeks.

'Regretfully, she and my father are obsessed with rank.'

Elizabeth laughed as Anne sat back in her seat. 'They sound akin to Mr Darcy.'

'That proud, arrogant man you mentioned? The one who has great influence over his friend?'

'The very same. Mr Darcy is full of a sense of his own importance, thinks meanly of anyone of lower rank, and is disdainful of those with a prior claim upon him.' Feeling disgruntled and not liking the sensation, Elizabeth pushed away her memories of the gentleman. 'But tell me more of your sister. Is she much older than you?'

'By two summers.'

'Oh!' Elizabeth was surprised. 'I thought she must be quite the elder, with being so set upon finding an establishment.'

Anne was thoughtful. 'I always believed my sister was content with her circumstances. There was an alteration, and if I recall correctly, it was some months before Mary and Charles' wedding.'

'Perchance she resented a younger sister marrying before her?'

Anne clasped her hands in her lap. 'Perhaps.'

Elizabeth pulled a face. 'It is ironic, is it not, that the need to find an establishment affects all classes of society?'

'For women, certainly.'

Not wanting to dwell upon this, Elizabeth adjusted her position.

'Let us talk of Kellynch. I am curious about how attached you are to your home and would love to hear more about it.'

Thus, they continued on their way, the conversation remaining light and easy, until they reached the first inn and a change of horses.

Although the temperature dropped as night fell, bringing with it a biting wind, both Darcy and the colonel felt the need for exercise after dining with Georgiana and Mrs Annesley, and they set off on foot down the lane. They had only gone but a half mile, however, when a voice hailed them.

'Ah, Darcy. Well met.'

Sir Walter Elliot was about to enter his carriage in front of Kellynch parsonage. Waving away his footman, the gentleman strode towards them in the falling light.

'Sir Walter. Permit me to reacquaint you with my cousin, Colonel Fitzwilliam? I believe you have met before now in Town?'

'Delighted.' Sir Walter bowed in his usual fashion, and Darcy threw the colonel a warning look.

'Likewise.' The colonel exaggerated his own bow. 'It is a fine estate you have here, sir.'

Sir Walter drew himself up. 'Most certainly. Extensive acreage in all directions.' He waved a hand expressively, then patted his coiffure and replaced his hat. 'Regrettably, it is entailed upon a male cousin.'

'As is oft the way of it, sir.'

'The living is under review.' Sir Walter waved a perfunctory hand towards the building behind him. 'You would not generally find me attending to such matters myself, of course, but I wish to ensure my own man is installed. Still, glad to have caught you, Darcy. Wished to extend the invitation to dine with us. The morrow would be convenient.'

Darcy and the colonel exchanged a lightning glance, and the former inclined his head. 'Your attention is appreciated, Sir Walter. Would it not be an imposition?'

'My youngest and her husband will be in attendance, and my other daughter is to return from her travels. Bring Miss Darcy along. We shall make a fine party without need of additional guests.'

Darcy shook his head. 'My sister is…'

'My cousin is delighted to accept, Sir Walter.' The colonel silenced Darcy with a look. 'Miss Darcy is not out, and though her health is much improved, she will be better-served by a warm hearth and her companion to attend her.'

'As you wish. Well, gentlemen, I bid you farewell until tomorrow evening. Shall we say six o'clock?'

They watched in silence as Sir Walter returned to his carriage, then gave them a regal wave on passing by, and they then continued their walk.

'How far is it from here to the hall?'

'No more than four furlongs.'

A snort came from the colonel, and Darcy grinned into the falling darkness. He knew Richard would find the gentleman as ridiculous as he did.

CHAPTER FIVE

The elegant equipage bearing the ladies reached Kellynch by noon the next day, and Elizabeth stared around with avid interest as they entered the great hall. A tall, middle-aged gentleman emerged from a room at the top of a small flight of steps, accompanied by an elegantly dressed young woman.

'I begin to wish I had brought Mama,' Elizabeth whispered to Anne as she was urged forward.

'But I thought you were not close to your mother?'

'Indeed, I am not,' Elizabeth said in a quiet aside. 'She was quite in awe of the splendours of Netherfield, but I believe Kellynch would render her speechless—a rare phenomenon and always worth the witness.'

Anne smothered a laugh as her family joined them. The introductions were swiftly made, and Elizabeth and Anne followed Sir Walter and Miss Elliot to the drawing room, where the new guest was invited to praise the furnishings, the prominence of the marble fireplace, and several portraits of former Elliots before she was permitted to partake of any refreshment.

Anne's sympathy was evident, but Elizabeth was unperturbed. She sought distraction, and it seemed Kellynch and its inhabitants would deliver tenfold.

Later, having been shown to her chamber and allocated a maid from the household servants, Elizabeth stood by the window, feeling redundant as Lottie emptied her trunk and travelling case. She was not used to being inactive and longed to explore the parkland. Two days in the carriage, albeit a conveyance of great comfort, was two too many.

Restless, Elizabeth left her room and peered up and down the landing. Anne had said she would meet her downstairs. Had she returned to the drawing room?

Once in the imposing great hall again, Elizabeth approached the room she had been in earlier. Voices drifted out through the partially open door.

'Who *is* this Miss Bennet, Anne? And why, pray, are we to take her into our home as a guest? Surely she is but a companion and should be treated accordingly.'

Sir Walter sounded out of countenance, and Elizabeth paused, highly entertained.

'When Lady Lucas became ill, I was welcomed as a guest at Longbourn, Miss Bennet's home. Miss Elizabeth Bennet has become my particular friend, Father, and I ask you to be as welcoming to her as you would towards any of Elizabeth's acquaintance.'

Anne spoke firmly, and Elizabeth was grateful for her support but less pleased with the indifferent tone of her father towards her friend.

'Really, Anne,' Miss Elliot's voice interjected. 'How can you compare Miss Bennet with those who count themselves as friends to the eldest daughter of a baronet? We know nothing of these Bennets. What is their position in the world? Who are their connections?'

Elizabeth eased away from the door.

'Mr Bennet is a gentleman, and the estate has been in the family for many generations, and—'

Anne's voice faded as Elizabeth made her way back down the shallow steps into the great hall. She felt for her friend, having to defend her to such people, and Elizabeth walked over to stare out of the leaded glass windows. The absurdity of her own family faded in comparison to Sir Walter, and she anticipated observing more of him during her stay. Perhaps if her letters were full of such folly and nonsense, they would raise Jane's spirits.

※

After tea, Anne took Elizabeth on a tour of the principal rooms, but when she left her guest at her room to prepare for the evening ahead, Anne turned back and hurried down the staircase. Dusk approached; if she did not make haste, she would be unable to fulfil her ritual walk.

She slipped out of a side door, stepping onto the gravelled walk bordering the lawns before making her way along the path.

Turning around, Anne stared at Kellynch Hall, where it loomed before her: tall, immensely handsome despite its age, the malfunctioning roof tiles and ill-fitting casements invisible to the eye.

Though she loved her home, so much of the building conjured gloomy memories, despite the time lengthening since Lady Elliot's passing. Her mother's chamber had lain empty for eleven summers, the small sitting room where she had taught Anne her first letters and later instilled a love of poetry remained a melancholy place. As for the year six…a spasm shook Anne's chest as recollections poured in unbidden.

Commander Frederick Wentworth, as he was then, had never been welcomed over the threshold of Kellynch Hall except by Anne herself.

The drawing room, where she had waited on the outcome of his interview with her father, aroused bittersweet sensations, for she could still recall being held close by Frederick when he finally came to her. Such happiness as they had, despite its brief duration, was not easily forsaken. Sadly, the room also contained the chair into which Anne had collapsed, distraught and broken after ending the engagement.

Frederick's anger, his cold expression, and his boots striking the flagstones as he walked away from her remained Anne's last abiding memory of him.

With a shudder, she continued along the path beside a stretch of ancient hedging, her shawl whipped by strong westerly breeze, seeking the roughly made arch carved in the hawthorn's sturdy branches. Beyond lay Anne's favourite place, a grove where she often lost herself in thoughts of a happier time.

Oft had she strolled there with Frederick. It was where he had offered Anne his hand, his ardent love, and the promise of a wonderful life. Here she had once walked with such joy, her arm tucked securely within his, awash with the anticipation of love, of romance, of their plans for a cottage in the country where they would raise a family.

It had thus become Anne's habit, upon a return from any travels, to go there to retrieve her more comforting memories.

It was not long, however, before the fading light and the increasing gusts of wind persuaded Anne to leave, and she hurriedly retraced her steps, pausing to cast one lingering look back.

No matter whose feet walked there in the centuries to come, the grove would remain forever hers and Frederick's. It never failed to remind her she had once been loved. Perhaps, if she were blessed with good fortune, the day might come when she would love again.

Until then, Anne would keep safe her memories; that was something her father could never take away from her.

Elizabeth was unsure how she felt about her arrival at Kellynch thus far. That Sir Walter viewed her as merely a companion for his second eldest daughter vexed her a little, though she could see amusement in it. Miss Elliot's dismissal of her as unworthy of any notice was as she had anticipated. Thankfully, Anne remained a charming and intelligent friend, and—

A knock on the door roused Elizabeth.

'It is time to go down, Lizzy.'

Anne came into the room, then took in Elizabeth's appearance.

'Lottie has done your hair with such elegance!'

With a laugh, Elizabeth turned to inspect her coiffure, moving her head from side to side and enjoying the effect of the carefully curled tendrils brushing against her neck.

'Indeed. I shall be able to admire it in every looking glass I pass.' She grinned at Anne. 'Though I am unused to such attentions unless I am attending a dance...' Elizabeth paused, as a memory flashed through her mind, of standing opposite Mr Darcy at the Netherfield ball. 'And I suspect there will be little of that this evening.'

'Do you enjoy the activity?'

Anne led the way along the landing towards the stone staircase leading to the main floor.

'Vastly.' Elizabeth laughed as they started down the stairs. 'Though the assemblies at home leave much to be desired. There is little to be had of alteration to our gatherings…'

It was not true of late though. Had not the arrival of the Netherfield party disrupted the neighbourhood, the Bennet household and—if she were honest with herself—Elizabeth too? Again, Mr Darcy came to mind, his mien filled with disdain as he watched Lydia and Kitty's cavorting at the ball, but Elizabeth forced it aside. No tall, proud man could interest her, and certainly not one that had done his childhood friend such a dreadful disservice.

'There you are, Anne.' Miss Elliot's cold voice greeted them as they reached the great hall. 'How tiresome it is when you are tardy.'

Anne said nothing as they walked past her eldest sister and up the shallow steps to the drawing room where Sir Walter waited with a young couple.

'Miss Anne Elliot,' Sir Walter began. 'Must you persist in trying my patience?'

Anne appeared remarkably calm, but Elizabeth had a suspicion this was a frequent lament.

Raising her chin, Elizabeth addressed the gentleman. 'Forgive me, Sir Walter, for delaying your daughter. She was perfectly on time until I forestalled her with my many questions about Kellynch.'

Sir Walter blinked rapidly and smoothed his fingers over the fine lines below his eyes, and Elizabeth tried—and almost succeeded—in concealing her smile.

Ludicrous man!

'I doubt you have ever seen the like of the interiors here, Miss Bennet.'

'They would be impossible to emulate, sir.'

'Quite right. Now, permit me to introduce my youngest to you. Mrs Mary Musgrove of Uppercross, and her husband, Charles. Mary will be mistress of that estate, you understand, when the time comes.'

The man at Mary Musgrove's side seemed a little discomfited at this reference to his father's future demise.

'This is Anne's companion, Miss Elizabeth Bennet from…' He frowned, and Anne stepped forward to address her sister and brother-in-law.

'Miss Bennet lives at Longbourn, her family's estate in Hertfordshire.' Anne turned to her father. 'And Lizzy is my friend, Father, as well you know.'

Sir Walter waved an indifferent hand. 'Friends, companions. What are they, if not interchangeable?'

Miss Elliot joined them. 'Indeed, though there is at least some benefit in a companion. They have their uses, whereas friendship hardly ever does.' She looked around at the gathered company with an air easily as arrogant as any Elizabeth had seen on Mr Darcy. 'I have no use for such acquaintance.'

Ostensibly taking Anne's arm, Elizabeth smiled at Mary and Charles Musgrove. 'It is a pleasure to make your acquaintance.'

'Capital!' Charles Musgrove beamed, and he stepped forward to engage Elizabeth and Anne in conversation, the former only half listening, because Mary Musgrove's plaintive voice had caught her attention.

'And who are these people, Father?'

'An old family from the North. Excellent titled connections, a grand estate and of good fortune. Ah, here they are. Welcome, Darcy!'

Darcy?

Elizabeth shook her head. There had to be more than one family of such name. Calmly, she turned to observe the two tall gentlemen looming in the doorway, her face becoming suddenly warm.

There he was. The very same Mr Darcy, and the last man in the world she had ever wished to become reacquainted with.

CHAPTER SIX

The gentlemen moved forward to greet Sir Walter before Darcy's eyes skimmed over the other occupants of the room, then stalled, his hand instinctively drawn to his chest.

What the devil was this? What strange Fate was at work, bringing Elizabeth Bennet not only to the West Country but to the actual estate where he had taken refuge?

Refuge, Darcy? Come now. Did you not take this step for Georgiana?

A loud drumming filled Darcy's ears as they were led across the room. Elizabeth, *Miss Bennet!*...before him...and so enchanting, eyes gleaming with unknown thoughts, and her chin raised as if ready to spar with him over any manner of subject.

Lord, he was not prepared for this!

'Mr Darcy.'

Her voice. How he had missed her voice. His throat was strangely dry.

'Miss Bennet. How...unexpected.'

Sir Walter, with complete disregard for the smooth skin of his forehead, frowned.

'What is this, Darcy? You are acquainted with my daughter's com—'

'Then introduce me at once, Darcy!' The colonel smiled widely, and Elizabeth returned it. It was hardly helpful to Darcy's current lack of wits.

'Darce?' His cousin nudged him in the ribs.

'Yes, yes, of course.' He turned back to the lady who had assumed an enquiring air. 'May I introduce Miss Elizabeth Bennet of Longbourn in Hertfordshire to your acquaintance. Miss Bennet, please forgive me for introducing my cousin, Colonel Fitzwilliam, to yours.'

She laughed delightfully, and Darcy drew in a short breath, then held it as his cousin regarded him intently before addressing Elizabeth.

'Words cannot sufficiently express my pleasure in making your acquaintance, Miss Bennet.' His eyes slid towards Darcy and back to Elizabeth. 'At last.'

Darcy pressed his lips together, silently cursing his cousin, but before any more could be said, Sir Walter clapped his hands together.

'Yes, yes. Quite, quite,' he blustered. 'Come Darcy, Colonel Fitzwilliam. I shall introduce my other daughters to you.'

Elizabeth glared at Mr Darcy's back. Had that hateful man thought she found him amusing? Unfathomable. It was the shock of seeing him, that was all, a visceral response. And what did the colonel's 'at last' mean? Had Mr Darcy the nerve to share his opinions on the Bennet family with his own kin? How dare he!

The blood rushing in Elizabeth's ears almost muted the exchange between the Musgroves and the new arrivals. How could anyone care how Mr Darcy's journey to the West Country had passed, or where he rode out every day? Why was

Charles Musgrove so particularly interested in the make of rifle the colonel favoured?

Fixing Mr Darcy with a blank stare, she only wished he could hear her far more pertinent thoughts.

'Lizzy?'

Anne had come to stand beside her. 'It is he, is it not? The man you told me of?' She spoke softly, and Elizabeth turned her back on the gentleman.

'Yes. 'Tis Mr Darcy, though how he comes to be here, I cannot think.' The last word came out almost as a squeak, and Anne took her by the arm and led her to where a footman prepared drinks.

'Sherry, please.'

Anne handed one to Elizabeth. 'Drink. It will help with the surprise.'

'I am perfectly well.' Elizabeth raised her chin, but then she downed the sherry in one, emitting a small cough as her eyes met Mr Darcy's across the room.

Anne indicated to the footman to refill the glass, then steered Elizabeth to a sofa in a quiet corner.

Positioning herself so she could not see the rest of the party, Elizabeth tried to heed her friend. The surprise eased, but she was all anticipation to learn how this coincidence had come about.

'I did not know you were acquainted with the Darcy family.'

'I am not. I had not heard the name before you mentioned it.'

'How is it he is here?' Elizabeth's curiosity was at its height, and she tried to curb her impatience. 'I hope he is not long in the country. Perhaps he is passing through…?'

Anne was a little discomfited. 'From what I understand, Mr Darcy and his sister are to reside on the estate for the duration of the winter. Father had merely said he met a gentleman in Town and was pleased to offer him a property. I knew not the name until he was introduced, but then I saw your face and realised it must be *your* Mr Darcy.'

A small sound came from Elizabeth. 'Believe me, he is not my Mr Darcy.'

Anne flicked a glance over her friend's shoulder. 'The gentleman seems unable to keep his eyes from you, Lizzy.'

'Hmph. Only because he cannot believe what he is seeing either.'

'I am not so certain.' The edges of Anne's mouth turned up. 'Did Mr Darcy pay you no particular attention in Hertfordshire?'

Elizabeth could not help but smile. 'He paid me an insult.' A raised brow was the only response to this, and she drew in a breath. 'I had the misfortune to stand up for a set with him at Mr Bingley's ball.'

'A singular attention for a woman he affronted.' Anne eyed Elizabeth with curiosity. 'And did he pay the same compliment to your sisters?'

A small burst of laughter spilled from Elizabeth as she shook her head. 'Heavens, the notion of him dancing with Lydia or Kitty. No, he chose only to plague me for a half hour.' The remembrance of their constrained dances, particularly the second, was sufficient for her spirits to sink once more. 'Perhaps I ought to curtail my visit.'

Anne's face clouded. 'You must do as you see fit, though I shall make a poor few weeks without you, especially with Lady Russell away in Bath. But if his presence so affects you…'

'It does *not!*' Elizabeth's indignation was momentary, and she pulled a face at Anne's amused expression.

'Or course not, dear Lizzy. I meant considering your deep aversion to Mr Darcy and the damage he has done your sister.'

Elizabeth almost emitted a most undignified snort. 'If anyone should go, it ought to be *him*.'

Leaving so soon after her arrival held little attraction. All she would face at Longbourn would be her younger sisters' foolhardiness and more of Jane's obstinacy. Elizabeth was not afraid of Mr Darcy. On the contrary, she enjoyed sparring with him in the past, and she had an added impetus to goad him. Perhaps she could, in some small way, atone for some of the disservice he had done.

'Lizzy? You are frightening me with your stern look.'

Elizabeth roused herself. 'Pay me no mind, Anne. I am happy to stay as planned, and if I am in luck, I shall have few encounters with the gentleman.'

Anne inclined her head towards the door. 'We are summoned to the dining room.' She placed their empty glasses on a side table as they rose from their seats. 'I am relieved, but sorry the gentleman's presence is blighting your first evening.'

They turned their steps to where the others stood, arranging themselves for the parade into dinner, and a momentary tension gripped Elizabeth as Sir Walter offered his arm to his married daughter and Mr Darcy turned to hold her gaze for a second. Then she released a taut breath as Miss Elliot took her place beside Mr Darcy, taking his arm before he could offer it.

'I believe we are to partner each other on the arduous journey from the drawing room to the dining room, Miss Bennet.' Colonel Fitzwilliam was beside her, offering an arm. 'Are you sufficiently brave to navigate the territory?'

With a laugh, Elizabeth took the proffered arm as they fell into step behind Mr Musgrove and Anne.

'I am not afraid of being beset upon by any of the wild beasts the West Country offers, Colonel Fitzwilliam.'

The colonel let out a bark of laughter as they traversed the great hall. 'It would be my duty—nay, my honour, ma'am—to protect you.'

Glancing ahead at their hosts, Elizabeth lowered her voice. 'The resident beasts appear suitably tamed for now. I think we may assume we shall be safe for the duration of a meal.'

'Thank the Lord for that. Being attacked, I fear not, but the notion of expiring on an empty stomach has provoked horrid dreams before now!'

This piece of silliness brought them to the table, and Elizabeth was torn between delight and annoyance at finding the colonel was to sit to her right and Mr Darcy to her left. Literally caught between them, she was thankful her initial interaction with the former proved him a far easier companion.

Sir Walter took his place at the head of the table, with his eldest daughter at the opposite end, and as a footman poured wine into her glass, Elizabeth met Anne's sympathetic look across the table.

The sherry may have calmed her a little, but for the sake of her friend, Mr Darcy and Sir Walter were about to gain a lesson in just how well behaved a poor gentleman's daughter could be.

Darcy stared at the bowl presented to him. He fully comprehended the expectation to pick up his spoon and taste the chestnut bisque, but he struggled with far more simple actions than mastering the soup course.

Breathing, for instance.

Elizabeth Bennet had walked straight out of his intractable thoughts to sit beside him. Far from being out of reach, intangible, invisible other than as a distant memory, she was so close, he could move his hand ever so slightly and touch her.

Darcy tugged at his neckcloth. It felt uncommonly tight this evening.

He viewed his spoon, then picked it up, but the movement of Elizabeth's hand caught his eye. She seemed to be having no such difficulty in wielding her own implement for its given purpose, despite his cousin demanding her attention. Regardless, Darcy had little appetite for the food, longing only to feast his eyes upon the lady at his side.

'What is your opinion of the soup, Elizabeth?' Sir Walter's question was a godsend to Darcy and, knowing she would be turned away from him to address her host, he instinctively turned in her direction.

Only she was not looking away. Elizabeth had twisted towards him instead and he stared directly into her fine eyes as Miss Elliot's plaintive tones drifted down the table to her father.

'It is palatable, I suppose.'

You utter simpleton, Darcy. Sir Walter would hardly have spoken to Miss Bennet by her given name on so short an acquaintance, and you fell—

'Mr Darcy?' Elizabeth Bennet's quizzical expression drew Darcy in more quickly than an expert angler reeling in his catch.

'Er, yes?' He cleared his throat. 'My apologies, Miss Bennet. Did you say something?'

Darcy clenched his hand to quash the urge to reach out and touch one of the dark curls grazing her cheek as she shook her head.

'I merely enquired as to whether or not you like the soup. It is your turn to speak now, Mr Darcy.'

Echoes of their dance at the Netherfield ball swept through him, and he desperately pushed it aside as he sought some common civility.

'I—I trust all your family remain in good health and spirits?'

To his surprise, Elizabeth's face clouded. 'I recall you once saying you abhor disguise, sir.'

He inclined his head. 'I do.'

'Then I will not dissemble and, for the sake of good manners, must decline answering your question.'

With that, Elizabeth turned away from him and immediately engaged his cousin in conversation, and Darcy grabbed his wine glass. This would be one long meal.

CHAPTER SEVEN

The meal passed more pleasantly than Elizabeth anticipated, mainly owing to the amusing and undemanding conversation offered by the colonel and having very few, almost monosyllabic, exchanges with Mr Darcy, and before long, the dessert dishes had been arrayed on the table.

'How are you finding the Somersetshire air, Miss Bennet?'

'I have yet to experience it, Colonel. We arrived just after noon, and I have only seen the house. I hope to explore the grounds on the morrow.'

The colonel glanced at his cousin.

'And you hail from Hertfordshire, I believe?'

'Yes, near Meryton.' Elizabeth admired the delicate glass dish of blancmange before her. 'It is a small enough town. I doubt you would have heard of it.'

'Meryton, you say? On the contrary.' The colonel sounded amused. 'I became acquainted with the name quite recently.'

Elizabeth frowned. Had a word emanated from the silent man to her right?

'How...coincidental, Colonel.'

'Coincidences are only that.' Mr Darcy's clipped tone drew Elizabeth's attention. 'Anyone who deems to read further into them is destined for failure, and not least, a waste of their time.'

'Is that so, sir?' Elizabeth arched a brow. 'I have been prone to wonder whether a coincidence is truly such, or perchance, it is a question of Fate.'

'Ah, the Fates.' The colonel laughed, and Elizabeth turned back to him with relief. Mr Darcy's eyes seemed to be boring into her this evening, and she did not appreciate the notice. 'My cousin has spent some time in Hertfordshire of late, which is, I assume, how you come to be acquainted? I am not incorrect, Darce, if I recall the name Meryton from a letter you wrote?'

'I…er, I do not recall writing to you during my stay, Cousin. It was of short enough duration.'

Elizabeth almost rolled her eyes. It seemed endless to her! 'I believe you were in the neighbourhood five weeks complete, sir.'

The colonel sighed exaggeratedly. 'Despite which, he did not show me the courtesy of a single letter. My sole intelligence arises from my cousin's correspondence with his sister.' He leaned forward. 'Why have you gone so pale, Darcy? Take some wine.'

He indicated Darcy's almost empty glass, then applied himself to his dish of raspberry trifle with relish, and Elizabeth welcomed the silence—

'You…er, I did not know you would be in Somersetshire, Miss Bennet.'

Why can Mr Darcy not remain mute?

'That is correct, sir, you did not.' Elizabeth eyed the gentleman for a moment, then relented. 'To be certain, nor did I until two days ago.'

She picked up her spoon and plunged it into the blancmange but, before she could raise it to her mouth, Mr Darcy spoke again.

'May I enquire how it is you are acquainted with the Elliot family?'

Amused, despite her general dissatisfaction with the gentleman, Elizabeth lowered her spoon.

'I see what you are about, Mr Darcy. You are surprised to discover a person of my station counting the daughter of a baronet amongst her intimate friends.'

The gentleman appeared quite affronted, and Elizabeth faltered.

'Forgive me. It has been a long day, and I am fatigued.' She cast a longing look at the closed doors, wishing she could disappear through them. 'Miss Anne Elliot came to visit my friend, Miss Lucas, recently. When Lady Lucas fell ill, Anne became a guest at Longbourn and invited me to return with her to Somersetshire.'

Mr Darcy seemed unable to devise a response to this, and Elizabeth took the opportunity to attend to her dessert. A minute later, however, she lowered her spoon again as the colonel addressed her.

'Do you intend to stay long at Kellynch, Miss Bennet?'

'As long as is tolerated, Colonel!' Elizabeth's eyes twinkled. 'By either my hosts or my family.'

'I am sure there will be quite the battle between them in due course,' he replied gallantly, and Elizabeth laughed.

'You are generous, sir. I am certain there are some at this table who would disagree. Regardless, I hope to stay for a fortnight.'

A movement caught Elizabeth's eye, but Mr Darcy merely picked up his wine glass, and she was finally at liberty to pay the blancmange the attention it deserved.

So relieved was she, when Miss Elliot finally signalled for the ladies to withdraw, she almost tripped over her own feet upon rising. Colonel Fitzwilliam moved with alacrity, but when a hand grasped an arm to steady her, it was not his.

Mortified, Elizabeth could feel heat stealing into her cheeks, but she raised her chin as Mr Darcy released his firm grip on her.

'I thank you, sir.'

She held his gaze for a second, then dropped a curtsey and hurried to join Anne.

'Mr Darcy has not moved, Lizzy,' Anne whispered as she took her arm and followed Mrs Musgrove and Miss Elliot from the room. 'You appear to have turned the gentleman to stone.'

'If only I could!' Elizabeth laughed as they returned to the drawing room, shedding her embarrassment over stumbling so inelegantly. Not wishing to dwell upon Mr Darcy's coming to her aid, she occupied her mind by strolling around the room and admiring more of the paintings—until, that is, an altercation drew her notice.

Miss Elliot and Mrs Musgrove seemed to be at odds over a chaise longue, upon which the eldest was languidly posed with studied elegance, whilst Mrs Musgrove berated her sister from the middle of the room.

'How can you say such a thing, Elizabeth? A chaise longue does not care for the distinction of rank. Besides, as a married woman, I *out*rank you, even though you are the eldest. My condition surely dictates the use of it. I should not be so surprised if the purpose of a chaise longue was first designed for women who are with child.'

Observing Miss Elliot feign a yawn that was surely as false as the lady herself, Elizabeth turned back to study a portrait of a beautiful Georgian lady with dark, expressive eyes and a decided likeness to Anne.

There was a rustle of fabric, and Elizabeth turned about.

'Who is this lady? She is beautiful.'

Mrs Musgrove scarcely looked at the painting. 'My mother. Did you ever hear of such rudeness, Miss Bennet? That a person in my delicate way should be expected to sit in a rigid position, like a soldier awaiting his orders?'

Elizabeth smiled kindly at the lady.

'I cannot imagine what the French were about, designing such uncomfortable seating as a chaise longue, Mrs Musgrove. You are well relieved of the discomfort.' Elizabeth lowered her voice. 'Do you not see how pained your sister seems in her choice? It is not a position I would covet.'

Anne came to her sister's side. 'Come, Mary, take the red couch. I have oft considered it the most comfortable in the drawing room.'

She took Mrs Musgrove's arm, but her younger sister dug her heels into the rug much as a reluctant mule being led to water might. Pushing away her sister's arm, Mrs Musgrove strode across the room and lifted Miss Elliot's feet up and swung them to the floor, quickly taking the vacated part of the seat.

With a loud tsk, Miss Elliot sat upright but moved no further, and they both stared in opposite directions.

Elizabeth and Anne exchanged a look.

'Would you care for some tea? Or maybe something stronger?'

Elizabeth laughed. 'Do I seem as though I need it?'

'I am grieved the gentleman's presence brings you displeasure.'

Elizabeth waved an airy hand. 'Mr Darcy may do as he pleases. I shall not seek him out, and I doubt he will seek me out either. We are not the best of friends.'

'Just the tea, then?'

'Yes please.' As Anne approached the tea tray, Elizabeth walked over to one of the tall windows, studying her own distorted image and thankful the lingering warmth of Mr Darcy's touch on her arm had faded. Despite her words, she felt out of sorts. That man had put her into an ill humour again, and she would not allow it to take hold.

Anne joined her, handing over a cup. Across the room, the war of words between Miss Elliot and Mrs Musgrove resumed, albeit in hissed undertones.

Taking a sip of her drink, Elizabeth eyed Anne over the rim of her cup. 'I begin to feel I am appearing in a farce on the stage.'

The two ladies exchanged a look encompassing both the ridiculousness of the battle of the chaise longue and the insanity that was Mr Darcy's being resident on the Kellynch estate.

Anne's amusement soon faded, however. 'I feel I should apologise. If I had taken more interest, I might have ascertained the name of the people who had taken Meadowbrook House.'

Elizabeth shook her head. 'Not in the least. None of this is your doing, and what would be gained by my having known in advance? Besides, this may inadvertently turn out to be a balm for my aggrieved feelings. Though I may not be able to voice my dissatisfaction with Mr Darcy directly, being in his company once more is allowing some imaginary confrontations full rein, and I feel all the more masterful for it. If Mr Darcy could but hear my thoughts, he would be begging for atonement.'

'Of that, I have little doubt.'

Miss Elliot's voice carried towards them. 'Do play for us, Anne, and make it something soothing, before Mary has a fit.'

'Excuse me.' Anne placed her cup on a nearby table and walked to the pianoforte, and a moment later, a soft, lilting melody filled the room. Elizabeth let her eyelids drop as the soothing music floated around her, effectively silencing both Miss Elliot and Mrs Musgrove. She would have to order a copy, for she would dearly love to play this piece on her return home.

Elizabeth's moment of peace was not to endure, however, as Miss Elliot's strident tones reached her, and she opened her eyes.

'Miss Bennet, I wish to have my curiosity satisfied. How is it you are acquainted with Mr Darcy?'

Elizabeth approached the fought-over chaise longue. 'A close friend of the gentleman leased a property near our estate in Hertfordshire, and Mr Darcy came to stay with him.'

'I see. It can only have been a passing acquaintance then.' Miss Elliot eyed Elizabeth's simply fashioned evening gown. 'You do not know each other well.'

'Passing acquaintances are oft the best, in my experience, though I believe spending several days in the same house as Mr Darcy contributed a little more to our understanding of each other.'

Miss Elliot's expression was indifferent. 'It is as I suspected, a fleeting connection of little consequence.'

'It is certainly as deep an acquaintance as *I* could ever wish for.' Elizabeth dropped a brief curtsey and joined Anne, who had finished playing and perused some music sheets.

'Shall we play a duet?'

Anne's discomfort was evident. 'I have never done so.'

Elizabeth was astonished. 'Not even with your sisters?' She surveyed the silent women on the chaise. Perhaps not. 'We have plenty of time during my visit for me to teach you, but for now, perhaps you play, and I shall sing?'

With a flourish, Anne placed some more music on the stand, and Elizabeth skimmed through the words.

'I am familiar with this. It will liven our spirits.' She took her place by the pianoforte and, as soon as the rich notes reached their cue, she began to sing.

❧

Darcy's preference had long been for a prolonged separation of the parties after dinner. He had never precipitated the return to the ladies before now, but this evening proved to be interminable.

What the devil had Elizabeth's meaning been earlier? For the sake of good manners, she could not—*would* not—elaborate on the well-being or otherwise of her family? Then, he took himself to task. *What of it?* Maintaining her confidence was the lady's prerogative, should she wish to exercise it.

'Darce?' The colonel nudged him as a footman offered more port.

Darcy declined, his eyes moving from his cousin to the doors.

'Bent upon escape, old man? They will not open of their own accord.' The colonel sipped his refreshed drink. 'Though you are in luck. Sir Walter may be ready to grace the ladies with his presence directly.'

The gentleman had left the table to examine his appearance in a looking glass.

'Musgrove, here, has invited us to shoot at Uppercross, Monday next.'

'Indeed, indeed!' Charles Musgrove grinned affably across the table. 'There is much sport to be had, Mr Darcy. Your cousin says he must leave on the morrow, but I trust you will join us?'

'I am all for the activity.' Darcy flexed his arms. He would relish a little movement *now*, preferably towards the drawing room.

Sir Walter, who had completed his inspection of the fall of his neckcloth, faced them.

'Come, gentlemen.' He waved a hand at the footman, who flung the doors wide. 'Let us join the ladies.'

Charles Musgrove fell into step with his father-in-law as they left the room, and the colonel drained his glass and placed it on the table before he and Darcy followed suit.

'Musgrove is a genial chap, though I suspect his interest lies more with your rifle of choice than your company.'

'There is little enough to occupy my time and attention in the district. A shoot will be a welcome diversion.'

'You surprise me, Darce. You seem sufficiently disrupted as it is.'

Darcy threw his cousin a frustrated look. 'I am in no mood for your nonsense, Richard.'

'No mood, you say?' The colonel grinned. 'I begin to comprehend your distracted air, especially—'

A welcome intervention came when Sir Walter drew their attention to a particularly fine landscape in the great hall, before leading them up the steps to the drawing room.

Darcy instantly sought Elizabeth, as she brought a song to its conclusion. She made a striking picture, so vibrant in contrast to the paleness of her friend. Might he manage some further conversation, and—

'As I said,' the colonel continued in a low voice. 'Especially in the light of Miss Bennet's being from Hertfordshire and, I suspect, the mysterious *Elizabeth*.'

Darcy stood stock still at Fitzwilliam's words, but his cousin marched past him to the ladies, bowing deeply and breaking into applause as the last notes faded.

'Capital, ladies. It is unfortunate we were not privy to the whole performance. Would you be so kind as to oblige us with another song?'

Darcy could not hear Elizabeth's response, but she clearly acquiesced, and he was able to relish the indulgence of not only listening to her performance but also keeping his eyes upon her throughout.

Though Elizabeth's accomplishment at the pianoforte in Hertfordshire had in no way been of the highest standard, Darcy could well recall listening to it with great pleasure. He had also heard the lady sing before, but this evening he was completely entranced.

In his enchantment, however, Darcy remained insensible to his cousin's knowing smirk.

CHAPTER EIGHT

'Come, Darcy, I would have you join us.'

Darcy blinked. Elizabeth's song had ended, and he looked to where Sir Walter pointed: a seat beside Miss Elliot. With little choice in the matter, he reluctantly crossed the room and took the indicated armchair, noting his cousin engaging Anne and Elizabeth in conversation and envying his easy manners as he escorted them to join the Musgroves.

Miss Elliot's smile was gracious. She was a handsome woman, Darcy supposed, if one did not object to the excessive ornamentation of hair.

'Darcy has sound experience with estate management, my dear.' Sir Walter addressed his eldest with a complacent air. 'I am hoping to benefit from his guidance over the winter, to make the most of our assets.'

Stunned, Darcy stared at Sir Walter. Confound the man! He had no intention of getting involved in matters at Kellynch.

'You are too kind, sir.' Miss Elliot spoke as though he conferred some great favour on them. 'Your advice will be invaluable, I am certain, for Cartwright is not the best steward.'

Darcy shook his head. 'I am master of my own estate, ma'am. Of another man's, I can offer little assistance.'

'Yes, yes,'— Sir Walter waved away his words. 'Be that as it may, we shall welcome your presence on the estate these coming months. My daughter, in particular, is gratified by your attendance upon us.'

Uncomfortable with the implication, Darcy was thankful for the entrance of two footmen bearing decanters and a silver pot of coffee, and Sir Walter summoned one of them over.

'A glass of Madeira for Miss Elliot. Darcy?'

'Coffee, please.' He turned to Sir Walter. 'If you will excuse me for a moment, sir? My cousin leaves early on the morrow, and I must speak with him. I shall return directly.' He bowed to them both, and made his way to the colonel, who excused himself from the ladies and the Musgroves and retreated to the other side of the room.

One of the footmen arrived with Darcy's coffee, then turned to the colonel.

'Two brandies.' He smirked at Darcy.

'Thirsty, Cousin?'

'One is for you, dunderhead.'

Once furnished with their respective glasses, however, the colonel fixed Darcy with a profound stare.

'We must join our hosts, but I caution you: do not let your admiration for one lady be noted by the other.' He spoke quietly, and Darcy frowned.

'I cannot comprehend your meaning.' Darcy placed the brandy on a side table and sipped his coffee.

'You can and you ought to heed it.' The colonel took a slug from his glass, but Darcy had no intention of responding.

'You still plan to leave at first light?'

'Indeed.' They both turned their steps towards the company, albeit rather slowly. 'I must be with my regiment by noon.'

'I shall break my fast with you.'

'Excellent!' The colonel smiled around as they took seats within the grouping either side of the hearth. 'An early morning start oft brings fresh perspectives. Do you not think so, Mrs Musgrove?'

As his cousin engaged the lady in conversation, Darcy considered the other occupants of the room. Elizabeth paid him no mind when they approached and appeared deep in discussion with her friend. Charles Musgrove listened intently to the colonel's chatter with his wife, and Sir Walter and Miss Elliot, who—damn it, had her eyes fixed on Darcy—smiled attentively in his direction.

'I trust we shall make this a regular occurrence, Darcy. You are welcome to dine at the Hall whenever you wish.'

Darcy inclined his head. With Elizabeth in residence, the temptation to commit to dining there every evening was fierce.

'You must meet all our acquaintance, Mr Darcy.' Miss Elliot fawned. 'For we are to hold a ball on St Stephen's Day—an annual event—and we would not have you in want of a partner.'

'It would be an honour, ma'am.'

It would be horrendous.

'The Yuletide season will be upon us directly!' Charles Musgrove smiled genially around the room. 'The St Stephen's Ball last year was the highlight of our season, Mr Darcy. How could one not delight in the anticipation?'

'I suspect you will delight more in the following day's shoot, Charles.' Anne was soft-spoken, but her words pleased her brother-in-law whilst drawing a scowl from Mrs Musgrove.

'To be certain, Charles, I do not know how I am to cope.' Mrs Musgrove lowered her eyes. 'I shall be in need of unceasing attention by then.'

Darcy noted the small smile exchanged by Elizabeth and her friend, but Anne quickly attended to her sister, assuring her of any support she may require.

'You will join us, Colonel.' Sir Walter's request sounded more like a command, but the colonel merely inclined his head.

'A kind invitation, sir. I anticipate a return to Somersetshire for Christmas, but whether I am able to stay for any duration, I cannot at present say.'

'I do wonder at Lady Russell always absenting herself at this time of year.' Miss Elliot's voice was plaintive. 'She has failed to attend the ball since Mother's passing. It is eleven years since she died. You would think she might have recovered from the loss of her friend by now.'

A small sound came from Anne Elliot, whose hand was instantly taken by Elizabeth, a gesture which touched Darcy, and he contemplated the lady with pleasure as Sir Walter addressed him again.

'Lady Russell is an old family friend, Darcy.' He stirred in his seat, then took a sip from his glass. 'She has passed the winter in Bath for many years, but she lives at Kellynch Lodge. You will meet her when she returns in the spring.'

'Oh, how I wish it was this time last year.' Mrs Musgrove threw her husband a wistful look. Charles Musgrove's expression was blank.

'Your marriage, Charles. Your wedding day was the sixteenth.' Anne spoke softly again, but all eyes turned upon Mrs Musgrove, who continued.

'It was *such* a wonderful day, for all the stresses and strains in the weeks beforehand.' She turned to Elizabeth. 'I had the most beautiful gown made. The highest quality silk, with a fur-lined cloak of cream satin. It was the envy of the entire neighbourhood, I assure you.'

'And how was the service?' Elizabeth's voice was kind, as was her expression, and Darcy watched her with some complacency. 'Which hymns did you choose?'

'Oh, I dare say I cannot recall.' Mrs Musgrove waved an airy hand. 'But the wedding was talked of for many months. Was it not splendid, Father? No expense was spared.'

Darcy looked towards Sir Walter, then frowned. The gentleman's expression was extremely guarded, and his eldest daughter sent him an almost anxious look at the turn of the conversation. The moment was fleeting, however, and as Sir Walter launched into a panegyric on the finery of his brocade wedding coat, Darcy's mind drifted to more pertinent matters.

Elizabeth Bennet. The woman he thought he had relegated to the past sat across the room from him, as alluring and unattainable as she had ever been, and raising inexplicable emotions in Darcy that he struggled to conceal, let alone comprehend.

※

Darcy and the colonel had walked up to Kellynch, and they welcomed the chance to stretch their legs, despite the bracing wind as they strode back to Meadowbrook House under the light of a full moon.

At first, Colonel Fitzwilliam amused himself with observations on the Elliots, none of which required a response. When silence fell between them, however, he nudged Darcy on the arm.

'You do see the lady's purpose?'

'What do you mean?' Did Elizabeth have a purpose? A strange sensation filtered through Darcy.

The colonel tapped his cane on the ground. 'Methinks I begin to see the lay of the land.'

Darcy threw his cousin a puzzled look. 'What land?'

'Miss Elliot's intentions. Or rather, she and her father's. You may believe yourself not to be their target, but whatever your *belief*, it *is* their purpose.'

'How can you discern such a thing on so short an acquaintance?'

The colonel shrugged. 'It does not take much to ascertain the advantage to Sir Walter in leasing you a property for the winter. It must have seemed as though the best of good fortune had befallen him. *Your* fortune, to be precise.'

'Perhaps Miss Elliot has no desire to secure a situation,' Darcy mused as they continued along the rutted lane. 'As I understand it, she has been mistress since she succeeded to the position when but sixteen.'

'Indeed. There is only Lady Russell who walks before her into all the dining rooms of the county, as the lady was prompt to inform us. After laying down the domestic law at Kellynch these many years, she must be ready—*more* than ready—to be mistress of her own manor, to lead the way, not follow.'

Darcy sensed his cousin's pointed attention upon him.

'Can you pretend not to have considered her?' The colonel paused, but Darcy did not oblige. 'Your silence is telling, old man. Of course, Miss Elliot is the simple solution to your dilemma.'

'What dilemma?' Darcy peered warily at the colonel through the darkness.

'The continuation of the estate at Pemberley. Come, man. Even you must own Miss Elliot to be the perfect candidate for the role.'

'I am not seeking—'

'You are in need of a wife, whether you chose to acknowledge it openly or not. Pemberley needs an heir, and the lady has excellent credentials.'

Unlike Elizabeth Bennet.

The thought swept unbidden through Darcy's mind, and he stopped in his tracks.

Marriage to Elizabeth Bennet had never been a consideration, much as he admired her and was drawn to be in her company. Marrying a woman of inferior birth went against Darcy's upbringing, and when one added in the appalling family... Miss Elliot had all that in her favour, and a considerable dowry.

The colonel came to a halt as he realised he had lost his companion and walked back to stand before his cousin.

'You are eight and twenty, old man. Time to do your duty to the estate.'

Darcy could not deny it. 'I accede. Pemberley is in need of an heir, but—'

'Before that, the estate needs a mistress.' The colonel grinned. 'You do know they go together, Darce? A bit like a horse and carriage? You need both to make it work?'

Rolling his eyes at the colonel, Darcy set off at a fair stride. He may have been raised to do his duty, and Miss Elliot may well seem the perfect fit, but Darcy rebelled against the notion.

'Not so fast, Darce.' Colonel Fitzwilliam stayed Darcy with his hand as they reached the driveway to Meadowbrook House. 'There is another matter we need to discuss.'

'There is no—'

'Regarding Georgiana.'

'Oh.' Relieved, Darcy looked up at the clear sky. The temperature had plummeted well below the mild weather he had sought for his sister. 'Out here? It is sufficient to freeze one's bones.'

'I am willing to compromise. As I shall be on my way to Blandford as soon as dawn breaks, we can continue this by the hearth, if that is your wont.'

It was *not* his wont. Following his cousin into the house, Darcy's head was still swirling with a maelstrom of thoughts, ones that only swelled in their confusion and…yes, he must own, anticipation of what the next few weeks might bring.

Within five minutes, they were ensconced in the room Darcy had taken as his study, each nursing another glass of brandy.

'Your health.' The colonel raised his glass and Darcy followed suit, then shifted under his cousin's scrutiny.

He took a sip from his glass. 'What is it you wished to discuss regarding Georgiana?' Darcy frowned. 'The hard winter was forecast in the North, but I had not anticipated the milder West Country being so affected.'

They discussed the potential harsh weather at Pemberley for a while, with the colonel sharing his father's preparations for their own Derbyshire estate, but then silence fell upon the room. Darcy's eyes were upon the crackling logs in the hearth; the colonel's were upon his cousin.

Draining his glass, Colonel Fitzwilliam stood up and held out a hand for Darcy's. 'Come on. Knock it back.'

Darcy stared into the fire whilst his cousin replenished their glasses. Though he could hear the slosh of liquid as it hit the glass, the clink of the decanter stopper being replaced, his thoughts were some distance away. One mile away, to be precise.

He had not the chance to speak to Elizabeth after dinner, but at least he had learned how she came to be at Kellynch and that her sojourn would be of some duration. How singular was it that the friendship had been formed in Hertfordshire, of all places.

Darcy's mind flew swiftly back to the county, his stay at Netherfield and how it had concluded. Well, he had successfully extricated his friend from a poor alliance, for that he must be thankful.

And does not Miss Elizabeth Bennet fall into the same class of people?

'I know not where your mind has taken you, Darce, but I would advocate closing a door on it. Your countenance has rarely been more conflicted. Here.'

The colonel thrust Darcy's refilled glass under his nose, and he took it, taking a quick sip as his cousin settled back into his seat.

'Speak to me of your concern regarding Georgiana, for I assume it *is* a concern?'

The colonel laughed. 'It is more for you, old man.' Darcy raised a brow, as his cousin continued. 'Despite Georgiana's need for rest and recuperation, she will soon make the acquaintance of the ladies up at the Hall, including Miss Bennet.'

Georgiana meeting Elizabeth!

Darcy sat up so sharply, he almost spilled his drink.

'And there it is. All the evidence I require.' The colonel took a mouthful of brandy before placing his glass on a side table and leaning forward, his elbows resting on his knees. 'So, Miss Elizabeth Bennet *is* the cause of your unrest.'

'For heaven's sake, Richard. What does it signify if we have a previous acquaintance? It was of a passing nature and, as you could see from this evening, we have naught of consequence to speak of.'

'Taciturnity is your staple in company. It signifies naught. It appears quite the opposite for the lady, although interestingly, she had little enough to say to *you*.'

Darcy got to his feet. 'I have had sufficient of your blethering. I am for bed. I will see you at breakfast.' He drained his glass. 'To quote Homer, "there is a time for many words, and there is also a time for sleep".'

The colonel stood up as well. 'And Shakespeare said, "We are such stuff as dreams are made on." I will wager there will be more dream than sleep this night, Darce.'

CHAPTER NINE

Despite her dissatisfaction with Mr Darcy's being in the neighbourhood, Elizabeth slept well and was grateful for the attentions of Lottie as she made haste to dress and join Anne at the table.

Sir Walter was nowhere to be seen when Elizabeth entered the breakfast room, a pleasing space with an ornate domed ceiling and leaded windows through which the weak winter sunshine filtered.

'There you are.'

Anne smiled as Elizabeth closed the door and dropped a curtsey to Miss Elliot, who inclined her head at the new arrival before returning her attention to the letter in her hand.

Anne hastily tucked a small pamphlet under her seat as Elizabeth came to sit beside her, and they exchanged pleasantries as they broke their fast, both seeming conscious of the third party in the room and not falling naturally into their usual way of speaking.

To be fair, Miss Elliot hardly spared them any notice, caught up in her correspondence as she was. The quietness of the table was in stark contrast to the bustle of Longbourn.

Once she finished reading, however, Miss Elliot addressed her sister.

'You will accompany me to Meadowbrook House this morning, Anne. I wish to call upon the Darcys. Father is engaged with his steward, and I cannot go alone.' She considered Elizabeth, then added, 'You may bring your...friend.' She waved a hand in the air and the footman standing behind her leapt into action, pulling back her chair and then darting to open the door.

'But Sister'—Anne rose, and Miss Elliot turned about— 'Do you not think it inappropriate? Miss Darcy has been unwell. We may be considered an intrusion and—'

'An intrusion? Do not be tiresome, Anne. It is an honour, and not one I lightly confer.'

Anne moved around the table to join her sister, speaking with low-voiced urgency, but Miss Elliot would carry her point. Anne would accede; thus, Elizabeth would do likewise.

Elizabeth had no wish to pay a call—especially out of respect—on Mr Darcy, or his sister, whom she could well recall Wickham describing as too much like her brother, very proud, a person he wished he could call amiable but could not.

No, Miss Georgiana Darcy was not someone Elizabeth had any desire to become acquainted with, especially as both Wickham and Caroline Bingley had described her as highly accomplished. How would one find time to display such an array of talents? Perhaps Miss Darcy amused her visitors by playing the pianoforte—exquisitely, of course—with her left hand whilst speaking fluent Italian as she decorated a screen with her right?

'I am simply concerned Miss Darcy may not be up to receiving callers. I understand from her cousin that her recent poor health was the primary reason for their relocating to the

West Country for the winter rather than travelling to their estate in Derbyshire.'

Sickly, too. The girl sounded delightful. Elizabeth's earlier irritation was quashed by her rising amusement at what the call might deliver. Indeed, she began to feel quite reconciled to it, and—

'You are quite wrong, Anne. What could be more pleasing an attention than to present ourselves as thoughtful neighbours on hand to deliver the best of company and care? Miss Darcy was indisposed when last we called, and an introduction to Mr Darcy's sister is long outstanding.' Miss Elliot turned away. 'I wish to leave in a half hour. I do not like to be kept waiting.'

'Nor do the cows at milking time,' Elizabeth muttered.

The lady's eyes narrowed on Elizabeth. 'Did you say something, Miss Bennet?'

'I did.' Elizabeth assumed an innocent expression.

'Anne, a word, if I may?' Miss Elliot turned on her heel and Anne followed her out of the room.

Once the door was closed, Elizabeth sank back into her seat, then noticed the pamphlet Anne had been perusing earlier, and she picked it up.

It was a copy of *Steel's Navy List*, the likes of which Elizabeth had seen once before, when Lydia—who had become quite taken with a young Lucas cousin who had recently joined the Navy—begged Mr Bennet to obtain a copy for her.

Elizabeth much preferred a novel or a book of poetry for her reading pleasure, but she flicked through the pages all the same, though the names and reports of various perils at sea held little interest for her. Then, she frowned, studying more closely a page of naval lists. Was that a pencil mark there, by one of the ship's names?

'Lizzy?'

Anne stood alone in the doorway.

'My apologies. My sister is quite set upon paying this call.'

'I shall bear it as well as I can.' Elizabeth smiled impishly as she stood up.

'Can you be ready in a half hour? We had best make haste if we are not to provoke my sister further.'

Assessing her gown, a smile still tugged at the corners of Elizabeth's mouth. 'I am as ready as I intend to be.' She laughed lightly. 'After all, there is no one I seek to impress.'

They turned towards the door, but then Anne noticed the publication Elizabeth held out to her. Wariness filled her friend's features, but before her curiosity could be satisfied, Anne reached out and took the pamphlet, tucking it into her sleeve and preceding Elizabeth from the room.

'Forgive me, Lizzy, for putting you in such a situation as this. I truly do not mind if you wish to remain here.'

Elizabeth stayed her friend with a gentle hand.

'No apology is needed, dear Anne, and there will be no excuses made. If I am your companion, then I have a duty to accompany you.'

Anne's mild brown eyes widened. 'You are *not* my companion! You are my friend and...'

Elizabeth laughed and Anne shook her head. 'You tease me. Will I ever learn?'

'Mama has yet to do so, even though it has been my way for nigh on twenty years.'

They turned down the passage leading to the stairs, Elizabeth preparing to gain what enjoyment she could from observing both Mr Darcy's discomfort from Miss Elliot's attentions and the absurdities of his paragon of a sister.

'What is amusing you so?' Anne glanced at Elizabeth as they reached the first landing.

'I am assuming my presence is just as distasteful to Mr Darcy as his is to me. In effect, I may take comfort from extracting at least this much revenge.'

Anne did not respond as they proceeded up the next flight of steps, but when they were outside the door to her chamber, she turned to Elizabeth with a small smile.

'I believe you are mistaken, Lizzy. From all I observed last night, I think Mr Darcy finds your presence quite the contrary.'

As was so often the case, Colonel Fitzwilliam had spoken the truth. Sleep had proven elusive and, in those few moments when Darcy had succumbed, his dreams had not been to his satisfaction.

In mixed spirits, he had earlier broken his fast with his cousin and seen him on his way, but Darcy felt the loss of his company the moment he rode out of the gates.

Once Georgiana breakfasted, and Mrs Annesley left to carry out some commissions in Montacute—the nearest of the two estate villages—he repaired with his sister to the drawing room, where he endeavoured to become engrossed in the newspaper. It did not suffice, as Elizabeth quickly returned to the forefront of his mind, as did his incessant speculation over the implications of her presence in Somersetshire.

He stared at the page before him, attempting to read. There was an hour to fill before he must leave for an appointment in Yeovil. He must endeavour to put the lady from his thoughts.

'What were they like, Brother?'

Darcy lowered the paper. 'Who, Georgie?'

Taking a sip of the remedy Mrs Reynolds had prepared for her sore throat, Georgiana peeped at him over the glass.

'You have said much of Sir Walter, but little of his family. Are his daughters much like him, or indeed, like each other? And what of the friend who is currently visiting? If only Richard had not left so early, I could have asked him about it.'

Putting aside the paper and picking up his tea, Darcy cradled the cup in his hands. There was much he could say of the Elliot women, but he had no desire to colour Georgiana's impression of them, and he certainly had no intention of revealing anything about Elizabeth Bennet.

'Richard implied the other day your opinion of Sir Walter Elliot is not favourable. I am anxious to comprehend there are some within the family with whom I would be comfortable.'

Darcy fidgeted under Georgiana's scrutiny.

'Our cousin would do well to keep his own counsel. Any words spoken of the father were said in confidence.' His sister's cheeks grew pink. 'I mean no censure, my dear, but we are beholden to the Elliot family for our present comfortable situation and will be passing many months on their estate. It is important that cordial relations are maintained between our two houses.'

Georgiana coughed daintily behind her hand. 'You know you have my support, Fitz, but I would have my curiosity satisfied if you would oblige?' She looked about. 'Pleasant though these accommodations are, it is not home, and unable as I am to take any form of exercise at present, you ought to oblige me with what entertainment you can offer.' She smiled widely. 'And you did promise, did you not, but yesterday, to put yourself at my disposal once Richard had gone? To do all in your power to make me happy?'

Foolish promise, Darcy.

He summoned a smile. 'As I think you know, Sir Walter has three daughters. Last evening, we were a small party of eight.

The eldest, Miss Elliot, who remains at home, Mr and Mrs Musgrove, Miss Anne Elliot, who had but returned that day from spending some time in Hertfordshire, and her friend—'

'Hertfordshire?' Georgiana sat up in her seat, her eyes more animated than Darcy had seen them in some time. 'Is not that where—'

'Mr Bingley has rented a property. Now, to answer your initial question…' Darcy fixed his sister with a firm eye as she leaned back against the cushions. 'It is true, Miss Elliot does share some similarity of…manners with her father.' Darcy noted his sister's rapt attention. 'All I am prepared to add is that they are not manners I would ever hope to see you emulate.'

'Brother, should it ever transpire, you have my consent to dip me in a pond, that I come to my senses!' Georgiana laughed. He dearly loved when she did, albeit this time it ended with that ever-persistent cough. How Darcy missed her delight in things, absurd or otherwise, in these long months since her unfortunate experience with Wickham.

'Do not think that I would not.'

Georgiana grinned at him. 'I do not doubt it, Fitz. Pray, continue telling me about the ladies, for I am well entertained.'

'Mrs Musgrove is…'

Excruciating and self-absorbed?

Darcy cleared his throat. 'A pleasant enough woman but is soon to be confined.'

'Oh dear! Is she generally in good health?'

'I believe her ailments are trifling though her complaints are significant.'

Georgiana giggled.

'Her husband is a proficient sportsman and has invited me to join a shoot this Friday.'

'I am glad you will have some sport. And the middle daughter? You say Miss Anne Elliot has been in Hertfordshire? Did you know her when you were there?' It was Georgiana's turn to frown. 'You mentioned a lady in one of your letters? I cannot recall her name, but I am certain it began with a *B*, not an *E*.'

Darcy stirred in his seat. 'I—er, I did not meet Miss Anne Elliot in Hertfordshire. She is quiet and unassuming but with pleasing manners. She is also an accomplished pianist. I am certain you will find her to your liking, though she is a little older than you. There, are you content?'

'And Miss Anne Elliot's friend? What is her name?'

Darcy viewed the cloudy day through the window. Perhaps this would be a good time to go for a quick ride, before the rains came?

'Sir?'

Boliver appeared in the open doorway.

'There are some callers from Kellynch Hall. The Miss Elliots. Shall I show them in?'

Darcy's gaze flew to Georgiana's. Her eyes were wide with a mixture of anxiety and anticipation.

'Would you prefer I saw them alone? I can attend them in the library if you wish.'

His sister raised her chin, though her trepidation was obvious. 'I shall endeavour to speak little, so as not to aggravate my cough. I would like to meet the ladies more than anything.'

Darcy turned to his butler. 'Show them in please, Boliver, and could you ask James to ensure the carriage is ready? I must depart for Yeovil shortly.'

He got up and walked over to join Georgiana, helping to arrange the woollen shawl around her as she whispered, 'What if I embarrass us?'

Darcy smiled faintly. 'That is an honour you can leave entirely to me, my dear.'

CHAPTER TEN

Georgiana smothered a laugh as Boliver returned with the visitors.

'Miss Elliot, Miss Anne Elliot, and Miss Bennet, sir.'

Darcy drew in a sharp breath as an urgent tug came on his sleeve.

'I did not foresee my curiosity being so amply satisfied.' Georgiana's voice was a whisper as Miss Elliot swept into the room with an air of familiarity.

Darcy took his sister's hand and placed it on his arm.

'Nor did I.' He straightened as Anne Elliot joined her sister, trying not to seek out the third of their party. 'But be at ease. I will bear the burden of conversation.'

At least, if he could retain coherent thought…

Acknowledgements were exchanged, and no amount of inner reprimand could prevent Darcy's gaze from lingering on Elizabeth Bennet's fine figure and sparkling eyes. The lady, however, seemed vastly interested in Georgiana, and he frowned at the mild surprise upon Elizabeth's face.

He glanced at Georgiana, but she performed her curtsey prettily and waited on the introductions.

'Mr Darcy'—Miss Elliot stepped forward—'I felt it incumbent upon me to call this morning and pay my respects to Miss Darcy, as I have not yet made her acquaintance.'

Darcy, who longed to say the lady would do better to not feel incumbent on their account, did what he was obliged to.

'Miss Elliot, Miss Anne Elliot, Miss Bennet. Permit me to introduce my sister, Miss Georgiana Darcy, to your acquaintance.'

He led his sister forward two steps, and she performed another curtsey, but contrary to her studying the floor, as was her tendency in the embarrassment of making new acquaintances, she stared at Elizabeth with rapt attention. *Damn it*, had she recalled the name Bennet from his letter? How foolish of him to have made such a slip.

Darcy gestured towards the chairs grouped around some small tables. 'Ladies, please, be seated.'

He led Georgiana over to a chaise and waited for the ladies to settle before sitting beside her. He took her hand, and she squeezed it.

'I trust we find you in good health this morning?' Darcy spoke the words instinctively, but a glimmer of emotion passed over Elizabeth's features, recalling him instantly to their exchange the night before.

'As you see, sir, I am in extraordinary good health.' Miss Elliot's smile was condescending.

'The walk was invigorating, I trust?' Darcy skimmed over all three ladies, refusing to linger on Elizabeth Bennet, then turning to his sister as she burst into hurried speech.

'Oh yes. Was the weather obliging? It appears quite dry, though there is a lack of sun today…'

Miss Elliot, however, raised a finely arched brow. 'Walk? The lane is in far too poor condition. Fortunately, the carriage is always at my disposal.'

'Miss Bennet and I chose to walk and found the air quite invigorating, Miss Darcy.' Anne Elliot lifted a hand towards the window. 'It has dropped very cold overnight, so the ruts are quite solid.'

'Though you would question the elegance of our gait as we tottered on the uneven ground.' Elizabeth's eyes sparkled much as Darcy remembered them when she was in conversation with…well, anyone other than himself. 'We held our arms out akin to walking a tightrope. It was a most stimulating exercise!'

Georgiana seemed as though she wanted to respond, but her cough returned to plague her, and Darcy put an arm about her.

'My sister has been a little unwell. I came to the West Country in the hopes of finding milder weather.'

'I am afraid we are in for a bracing winter, sir.' Elizabeth regarded Darcy as he tucked the shawl more securely about his sister's frame. 'There was talk of it in Hertfordshire before we left. I believe we shall see snow before too long.'

Darcy frowned. He had not expected it so far south.

'You do not favour the snow, Mr Darcy?'

Anne Elliot's expression politely enquired, but Darcy smiled. 'As a child, it was my delight. When one has an estate to manage, crops to consider, and stock to care for, it is less desirable.'

There was a small interruption as the tea paraphernalia was brought in, and knowing it would occupy her, Darcy encouraged Georgiana to prepare the beverage and fill several cups before he walked over to offer one to Miss Elliot.

'The tea is a little dark for my taste.' The lady handed the cup back, which Darcy knew would mortify Georgiana.

'Permit me.' Darcy returned to the table and, after a moment, picked up exactly the same cup and offered it again to Miss Elliot.

'Oh, that is quite perfect, sir. Thank you for looking after me.' Miss Elliot looked at Darcy as though he had saved her life, before refusing milk but accepting two generous lumps of sugar into the cup.

Once everyone was served, Darcy meant to sit beside his sister again, but Miss Elliot had taken the vacated seat, and he was left with no recourse but to take the only remaining place, beside Elizabeth.

For some reason, he found he no longer knew how to sit at ease. Though the talk continued at a gentle rhythm around them, Darcy realised, unless they conversed directly, he could no longer look at her without making his attention obvious.

Elizabeth seemed perfectly unaware of his dilemma, her attention all upon Georgiana, and Darcy was puzzled. What did the lady find quite so fascinating in his sister?

'We anticipate with pleasure receiving you at Kellynch Hall, Miss Darcy.' Miss Elliot inclined her head graciously. 'It is reportedly one of the finest Elizabethan buildings in the country.'

Georgiana brightened. 'I am fond of history. I should be most grateful to see it. My brother tells me the building is quite beautiful.'

Darcy had also decried the way it had been decorated, but he knew his sister had better sense than to bring that up.

Miss Elliot straightened. 'Kellynch has been in our family for many generations. We respect the age of its exterior, but I feel it is my duty, as the present mistress, to ensure the interior always reflects the latest fashion.' She sent a complacent look at the company. 'Such grand apartments warrant only the best, of course. My present project is to redecorate the dining room.'

'It was renovated in Mama's lifetime,' Anne interjected. 'I think it quite perfect as it is.'

'Nonsense, Anne.' Miss Elliot waved her folded fan. 'The wall coverings are not in the current style and the table is démodé. I have long disliked it, for it quite taints the food upon it.'

A sound escaped the lady at Darcy's side, but he did not look at Elizabeth for fear he might share in her amusement.

'I have instructed the most prestigious of craftsmen,' Miss Elliot continued. 'The table and chairs are being made from the finest rosewood.'

Silence followed this declaration, and as Darcy could tell Georgiana knew not how to respond, he expected her to make no further contribution to the conversation. He was mistaken.

'Miss Bennet, my brother informs me you are from Hertfordshire?'

'Then it must be true.' Elizabeth smiled warmly at Georgiana. 'The county has been my home all my life.'

'And do you like it there?'

'I like it well enough, and even more so when I am away.'

Georgiana looked confused, and Miss Elliot concealed a yawn behind her hand as Elizabeth elaborated.

'I live with my parents and my four sisters. Whilst there is frequency of companionship, there is also a want of escape.'

'You have *four* sisters!' Georgiana leaned forward in rapt attention.

Darcy was likewise enthralled. What was this effect Elizabeth had on people, no matter the length of the acquaintance? When had Georgiana ever been this loquacious with strangers?

'Do not envy me, Miss Darcy. I can assure you, one sister would be quite ample.' Elizabeth paused. 'Provided I could choose which one, of course.'

Miss Elliot raised a brow. 'Sisters are often surplus to requirements.' She seemed to have forgotten one of her own was in the room.

Colour flooded Anne's cheeks, and Darcy turned to her with a smile. 'Georgiana has long wished for a sister of her own. I fear I do not answer sufficiently.'

'It is not that, Brother.' Georgiana sent Darcy a regretful look. 'I would not trade you for the world. But Miss Bennet—'

'Your home is in Derbyshire, I understand, Miss Darcy?' Miss Elliot interjected.

'I—er, yes it is. At least, I am established in Town, but Pemberley is where I grew up, and we return often each year.'

'And pray tell me, for how many generations has your family owned the property?'

Georgiana blinked. 'There have been Darcys on the land since the 1500s.'

Darcy stepped in. 'We are merely guardians of the estate, Miss Elliot, trusted with ensuring it is passed on to the next generation. I do not consider myself Pemberley's owner. As for how long the family has been there, that my sister and I are able to call it home is all that matters.'

Miss Elliot, however, obviously disagreed, and continued with her interrogation.

'But it is the principal property in the county?'

'It is the principal property of interest to *us*, ma'am.'

'May I be so bold as to request a replenishment of my cup, Miss Darcy?' Elizabeth smiled kindly at Georgiana, who leapt to her feet with alacrity, her relief at being able to leave her place beside Miss Elliot palpable, and Darcy could have kicked himself for not finding a way to assist her.

Before he knew what happened, however, Elizabeth was out of her seat and joining Georgiana by the tea tray, and Miss Elliot patted the vacated seat beside her.

Darcy pretended not to notice, addressing her sister instead. 'Would you care for more tea, Miss Anne?'

'I have not finished my first, Mr Darcy. But thank you. Do you find the house suitable for your needs, sir? There is a small annexe on the grounds, should you require more space.'

'Yes. Willow Cottage. It is perfectly charming.' Darcy smiled at Anne.

'My mother fitted it out for—'

'Had you heard, Mr Darcy, that we are connected to the Dalrymple family?' Miss Elliot raised her chin. 'Our cousins, the Dowager Viscountess Dalrymple, that is, and her daughter, the Honourable Miss Carteret?'

'I believe it is well known, ma'am.' It was also widely understood they were estranged.

The lady launched into a monologue requiring no contribution, and Darcy assumed his habitual mask of inscrutability, resigning himself to his duty, whilst simultaneously wishing he could be privy to the conversation being held behind him between Elizabeth and Georgiana.

Miss Elliot, meanwhile, confirmed precisely why Darcy hated the ritual of morning calls. Much as he wished Elizabeth did not have to go, he had never been so thankful to see the ladies leave.

'Where is the carriage?' Miss Elliot turned to Anne in confusion as the door to Meadowbrook House closed behind them.

Anne and Elizabeth exchanged a look, but just then a stable hand came round the corner of the house.

'You there!'

The lad scurried forward and docked his cloth cap. 'Yes, ma'am.'

'Fetch my carriage this instant.'

The boy was discomfited. 'But the carriage 'as returned to the big house, ma'am.'

'The big...oh, for heaven's sake.'

Miss Elliot all but stamped her elegantly-shod foot as the hapless stable boy continued on his way to wherever he was bound.

'It seems you must join us.' Anne smiled sympathetically at her sister. 'The walk will do you much good.'

'On the contrary. I shall request the aid of Mr Darcy.'

Anne was horrified. 'You cannot ask that he make ready his own carriage for such a short journey! We are only so recently acquainted.'

Elizabeth, on the other hand, was quite taken with the idea of Mr Darcy being plagued to do something he would rather not.

'Let us continue, Anne. I am sure Miss Elliot knows what she is about.'

The lady in question inclined her head to Elizabeth before pulling the bell, and the two ladies walked swiftly down the driveway and turned into the lane.

CHAPTER ELEVEN

The ladies ambled in silence at first, though Elizabeth sensed Anne's intermittent attention upon her. Then, she spoke. 'You are quite pensive, Lizzy. Did the call not deliver to your expectations? For myself, I cannot see your presence caused Mr Darcy quite the level of dissatisfaction you had hoped for.'

'I confess I paid the man scarce mind. That had always been my intention, of course, but I was distracted by how incompatible my expectations of Miss Darcy were compared to the evidence before me.'

Anne raised a curious brow as they continued along the lane.

'How so?'

Elizabeth smiled weakly. 'I cannot comprehend how this has come about. I had heard reports of Miss Darcy from people who are long acquainted with her.'

They reached the corner of the lane, and Elizabeth looked back towards Meadowbrook House, the rooftops and chimneys just visible above the hedge line.

'Lizzy?' Anne nudged her gently.

'Forgive me.' Elizabeth turned and fell into step beside her friend once more. 'Miss Darcy is, in appearance, much as she was described: almost womanly in figure for one so young, and markedly handsome.'

'The latter can also be said of her brother.'

Elizabeth did not want to think about Mr Darcy. 'And she is said to be truly accomplished, though I saw little evidence of *that* today.'

Anne laughed. 'What did you expect? That she would recite poetry to us, or perform upon the harp?'

It was Elizabeth's turn to laugh, the sentiment being so close to what she imagined. 'Even my biased eye can discern Miss Darcy has little.... Another lady of my acquaintance implied they had much in common, but I could not see it.'

The sound of a carriage coming along the lane drew their attention then, and they both stepped up onto a grassy bank.

To Elizabeth's surprise, Mr Darcy's dark eyes met hers as the elegant conveyance slowed to a stop.

'May I offer you both a ride to the Hall?'

Anne shook her head. 'Thank you for the kind offer, Mr Darcy, but as you can see, we are enjoying our exercise.'

He doffed his hat as the carriage slowly moved away, Miss Elliot eyeing them smugly from the opposite bench.

'It seems my sister is more persuasive than I gave her credit for.' Anne stepped back onto the lane, and Elizabeth joined her as the carriage turned the corner ahead.

'Aye, or Mr Darcy keeps a carriage permanently readied, that he might make use of it on a whim.' Elizabeth feigned amusement, but she felt inexplicably resentful. Was Miss Elliot an object with the gentleman? With her own attention fixed on Miss Darcy, she missed their interactions during the visit.

Anne continued. 'Miss Darcy is prone to the shyness not uncommon in someone both so young and not out in society, but she is also undeniably charming.'

They reached a gate set into the wall bordering the grounds of Kellynch and, pushing it open, they walked into the garden. Anne was quite correct, but Elizabeth acknowledged the discomfort this acceptance brought.

'In truth, Anne, the young lady's character resembles my dear Jane's, especially when she was of a similar age.'

'You are so fortunate, Lizzy, to have Jane as your confidante and friend.' Anne shivered as they crossed the lawn, still dusted with the morning frost. 'My sister Elizabeth is so cold. I cannot account for it. Though we are vastly different in nature, why should that not make us friends? You and Miss Bennet are likewise akin to opposites, are you not?'

Elizabeth burst out laughing. 'Indeed. Sweet and sour, and I am sure you can discern who takes which crown!'

'You are far sweeter than you give yourself credit for, Lizzy.'

Smiling, Elizabeth stepped up onto the terrace and they both surveyed the gardens.

'The grounds here are exquisite.' Elizabeth turned to Anne. 'You did not do them justice in your descriptions to me.'

Anne raised a brow. 'Description did not do justice elsewhere today.'

Elizabeth studied her feet for a moment, then raised her head. Anne remained diplomatically quiet.

'So be it. The visit was not unpleasant. Miss Darcy was a delightful surprise. Beyond that, I am unwilling to venture, though I will express some sympathy towards her for having such a brother.'

Anne maintained her silence, though humour filled her countenance, and Elizabeth was goaded into speaking further.

'Mr Darcy may have done little this morning to worsen my opinion of him, and I have shown myself to be wrong in my expectations of his sister, but you must trust me on this, Anne. I have first-hand experience of the harm that man has wrought upon others, of the lives he has ruined.'

'I respect your word, Lizzy. And I comprehend fully your belief in it. All I am saying is that Mr Darcy, for any faults he may have, was on this occasion both a gracious and accommodating host, and his affection for and protection of his sister was evident.'

'I will not argue with you, though you must own there are few that do not extend unconditional love to their own family, however they might perform to strangers.'

Anne did not respond, and Elizabeth immediately wished to retract the words. Sir Walter and his eldest had thus far demonstrated little regard for her friend.

Elizabeth took Anne's arm and turned her about.

'Come, we have had sufficient talk on the matter. Let us continue our exercise and permit our minds to wander in a happier direction. I anticipate a letter on the morrow from Jane, and I am hopeful of a favourable one.'

Relief swept through Darcy as Hartwright—his coachman—closed the carriage door, and he ignored Miss Elliot waving him off from the portico of Kellynch Hall as though they were old friends. The more time Darcy spent in the lady's company, the less he found to admire.

He tried to settle back against the squabs as the carriage found every rut Elizabeth and Anne negated, as though mocking him.

Mocking him… Elizabeth's eyes when they met his, as the carriage passed the ladies, had been assessing, as though she would judge him. What the devil could he possibly be doing wrong by acceding to Miss Elliot's request to deliver her safely home?

It was fortunate the carriage had previously been readied to carry him to his appointment, meaning he only had to leave the lady unattended for as long as it had taken to don his great coat. Thankfully, Georgiana had been spared, having gone up to her room to rest, and Miss Elliot seemed to find plenty to engross her in the book his sister had lately been perusing.

Darcy stared out of the window at the passing scenery. They would be on the turnpike heading east shortly, where the roads would be in better condition, and they would make faster progress. He needed to turn his thoughts to his appointment at the bank, but instead they were firmly fixed on a certain lady.

Had Elizabeth arrived home? Her pink cheeks and bright eyes had been evidence of her pleasure in taking the air.

He frowned. Miss Elliot had made a disparaging remark about Elizabeth's presence at Kellynch as the carriage moved on. It made little impression upon Darcy. He knew full well the situation of her family without it being pointed out to him. He had been more struck by how tightly Miss Elliot appeared to be clutching her reticule. Did she fear he might exact payment for the ride home?

Laughing under his breath, Darcy pulled out his watch to confirm the time. Miss Elliot's disdain for others echoed all he knew of her father, and she had clearly been an attentive pupil.

Unease swept through Darcy. Did he not share this condescension towards those of lower rank? Was it not a significant part of his reservations over Bingley wishing to attach himself to Miss Bennet? Had it not plagued him day and night, both during his stay in Hertfordshire and here in Somersetshire, how far Elizabeth was below him, unworthy of his notice?

It would seem he was not only guilty of looking down upon those less fortunate than himself but also of judging them in the same way the Elliots did. This notion was of little comfort. Darcy was fully aware of his own duplicity and, exasperated by his endless speculation about Elizabeth Bennet, he endeavoured to cull the futile dreams and desires whirling through his mind by forcing it onto the impending meeting.

❧

Darcy returned from Yeovil with a half hour before dinner, and little time to refresh himself but confident in the gentleman who would liaise with his London banker as and when required. The weather had turned even colder, so much so, even Darcy realised the West Country was about to receive an unprecedented snowfall. He only hoped it would not be prolonged or oft repeated. If the roads became impassable and the colonel was unable to join them for the season, he might well go mad.

Georgiana waited for him in the drawing room, and he poured them both a small sherry.

'Is all well, Fitz?' Georgiana sat across from him in the chairs they had taken as their own, either side of the fireplace. She remained pale, but her cough seemed less frequent, and Darcy smiled.

'I am by my hearth with you, my dear. What could possibly ail me?'

She took a sip from her glass and pulled a face. 'I have not acquired a taste for sherry.'

'Then do not take it. I would not presume, but it has seemed to aid your throat of an evening.'

'Indeed, but it seems much clearer these past four and twenty hours.'

'I am glad to hear it. What did you do with your afternoon?'

Georgiana appeared a little evasive, and Darcy frowned.

'Did anything occur to disturb you?'

Now she seemed positively anxious. Darcy put his glass aside and moved over to crouch beside her, taking one of her hands.

'You are cold.' He rubbed the hand between both of his, then reached up to pull her woollen shawl back onto her shoulders.

'I am well, Fitz. It is better my skin feels cool to the touch than feverish.'

Darcy sat back on his haunches. He did not wish to recall the concern he felt when he found Georgiana's illness to be far more severe than he had been told.

'Indeed.' He straightened up and returned to his seat. 'Did anything happen in my absence, Georgie?'

'No. At least, I searched for a letter, but I could not find it.'

Darcy's eyes narrowed, and she stirred restlessly under his scrutiny. Why had he instantly assumed she had been seeking the one in which he recklessly mentioned a Miss Bennet?

He ran a hand through his hair. *Damn it,* why was Elizabeth so easily recalled?

'I asked if *you* were troubled, Brother?'

Darcy shook his head. 'By nothing of consequence. The temperature has dropped very low. I will ensure your fire is well stoked when you retire.'

'I would like it to snow.' Georgiana's voice was wistful. 'I should like to be able to go out in it, like we do at Pemberley.'

'Let us get you to full health first. If the harsh winter that is predicted comes southwards, then you may get your wish.'

'I hope Miss Bennet will decide to tarry longer and pass the Yuletide season here.' Georgiana became more animated. 'I should so like to know her better.'

Darcy drained his glass. As would he, but he must not accede to the temptation.

'Come, Georgie.' He stood up. 'Let us dine, and we can start to think about the entertainments we might be able to offer Richard. We have limited acquaintance in the neighbourhood, but I am certain we can find much to amuse him.'

Georgiana hurried to his side. 'What an excellent notion.' She almost skipped into the dining room as she said, 'He will be certain to want to see Miss Bennet and Miss Anne Elliot again. I am sure he found them good company. We must ask them to dine, Fitz.'

Darcy opened his mouth, then closed it with a snap. This instinctive urge to acquiesce to anything where Elizabeth was concerned had to stop, or he would be in even more danger than he had been in Hertfordshire.

The following two days passed pleasantly, with the Musgroves inviting Anne and Elizabeth to them on an excursion to Muchelney Abbey ruins, and on Sunday after morning service—throughout which she did her best to pretend Mr Darcy was not in attendance—exploring the grounds of Kellynch further with Anne as her guide.

After passing much of her time in the fresh but cold winter air, indulging in a satisfying meal each evening, and enjoying plenty of conversation with Anne, Elizabeth should have slept like the proverbial log, but rest on Sunday night proved elusive.

Even after dawn had broken, Elizabeth tossed and turned in her bed, eventually rolling onto her side and staring at the heavy curtains across the windows. The light filtering in from outside held a strange greyness to it and seemed to flutter. Sitting up, Elizabeth shoved her hair over her shoulder and swung her legs out of bed.

She shivered. The fire in the grate had reduced to embers, and Elizabeth grabbed a thick shawl from a nearby chair and wrapped it around her as she padded over to pull back one of the curtains.

The grounds of Kellynch were white over, and snow continued to fall from a leaden sky that portended no end to the current conditions. Delighted, Elizabeth pushed both curtains aside and reached up to unfasten the clasp and opened the window.

Shivering again, she hugged the shawl closer, but leaned out, stretching her hand to catch the flakes, and laughing as they danced away from her. The world was strangely muted, as though someone had placed a blanket over it, and Elizabeth was filled with contentment. It so rarely snowed in Hertfordshire, and when it did, it drew protests and wails from Kitty and Lydia until the roads were once again passable. Here, she felt wrapped in the embrace of silence.

'Morning, miss.'

Elizabeth spun around. Lottie came into the room, followed by a young servant who headed to the hearth to set a fresh fire in the grate.

'Come now, miss, or you will catch cold.'

The maid helped her latch the window, and Elizabeth submitted to her attentions and soon joined Anne, who was alone in the breakfast room.

'My sister is breaking her fast in her room, as her hearth is more accommodating, and my father has gone to prepare for a meeting with the departing curate of Monkford—a nearby parish—who is due to call at noon.' Anne seemed a little conscious, and Elizabeth observed her with curiosity as she picked up a plate from the console table. Was there a chance Anne was sweet upon this clergyman?

'Is it not beautiful?' Elizabeth waved a hand towards the leaded windows. The room was bathed in the glow of the snow, despite the heavy skies.

'It is indeed. And I suspect you are eager to go out, but Lizzy, I must ask you to wait until the snow at least ceases.'

'Of course.' Elizabeth filled her plate from the array on offer and poured a cup of tea. 'What time do you receive the post?'

'It is usually collected by late morning.' Anne smiled as Elizabeth took a seat beside her. 'Today, of course, there may be a slight delay.'

Despite the roaring fires in every grate, Miss Elliot, once persuaded downstairs, complained as steadily as the flakes fell, of the coldness in the air, the ineffectiveness of the chimneys and the paucity of the neighbourhood for offering any possible distraction in such circumstances.

As the clock struck noon, she settled beside the drawing room fire, refusing to move from its warmth. Sir Walter removed himself to attend the visiting clergyman who, despite the inclement conditions, had managed to arrive on time, and Elizabeth had been relieved when a note came from Uppercross Cottage, requesting Anne to call on her sister, Mary, who suffered from a recurrence of an old ailment.

'You will join me, Lizzy? I am sure you are eager for more fresh air, and it is a good two miles to Uppercross from here.'

'It would be my delight!' Elizabeth, who was sick and tired of Miss Elliot's complaints, suspected she merely traded them for Mrs Musgrove's, but the exercise and fresh air each way would be welcome and well worth the sacrifice.

The door opened and Anne greeted the housekeeper, who handed over the post.

'Here is that which you seek, Lizzy.'

Taking the letter from Anne, Elizabeth viewed the postmark and her sister's familiar hand with a mixture of trepidation and pleasure.

'You wish to read your letter in peace?' Anne took her friend's arm as they left the room. 'Shall we meet at the front door in a half hour and head to Mary's?'

At the appointed time, Elizabeth hurried down the stairs, fastening a thick scarf about her neck and pulling on her warmest gloves. The letter delivered news, but none of it to her satisfaction, for the situation in Hertfordshire had hardly improved. Jane made the best of it, but Elizabeth still feared for her sister's declining spirits. A brisk walk was required to walk off her frustrations, and though Elizabeth regretted Mrs Musgrove's apparent ailment, accompanying Anne to Uppercross Cottage would more than compensate.

Anne awaited her, but as they reached the hall, Elizabeth noticed gloves and a cane on a side table and a cleric's hat suspended on the coat stand.

'The curate from Monkford is with my father.'

The strange consciousness filtered across Anne's features again, but then she took Elizabeth's arm.

'Come. Let us make good our escape!'

With that, they hurried along the passageway and soon stepped out onto the snow-covered terrace.

CHAPTER TWELVE

The blast of wintry weather came as no surprise to Darcy, but despite the snow upon the ground and heavy festoons hanging from the branches of the surrounding trees, the planned shoot at Uppercross had taken place. To his surprise, Darcy passed a pleasant morning in company with Charles Musgrove. Once he had partaken of the traditional refreshments, however, and having sent his man home with his guns, he set out on a circuitous route back to Meadowbrook House.

Striding along, Darcy's boots made no sound in the virgin snow. The skies lightened slowly, and he inhaled deeply of the crisp, clear air, relishing its coolness but hoping for a quick thaw, for there would be little opportunity to encounter Elizabeth if the conditions persisted. He frowned. His hope had been for a moment's conversation with her after church on the previous day, but she was particularly elusive. Then, he smiled, recalling the pleasure he derived listening to her sing. Perchance next Sunday, he would endeavour to sit further back in order to observe the lady.

A strange tightening in his chest—one that frequently made its presence felt before he left Hertfordshire—returned, and he walked for some distance, unclear on his direction, until a sound caught his ear, and he stopped to listen: children playing, their shouts of joy and laughter drifting to him like snowflakes on the wind. Turning a corner, Darcy beheld them, using make-shift sledges to fly down a nearby slope before, pink-faced, trudging to the top again, bent upon repeating the pleasure.

Seeking solitude, Darcy headed away from the children and soon slipped through an opening in the hedgerow, his evasive action proving his downfall. With a resounding thud, something hit him directly in the throat and, as icy slithers of snow began to slide beneath his neckcloth, his gaze met that of a wide-eyed Elizabeth Bennet.

'Forgive me, Mr Darcy, I did not expect you.' Her tone was sufficiently contrite, but her demeanour did not speak of regret. Unless he was much mistaken, the lady struggled to conceal her mirth.

He wiped the snow from his neck, brushing the remainder from his coat. 'You have a sure aim for a lady, Miss Bennet.'

A raised brow greeted this comment. 'For a lady, sir? I will take the credit, begrudgingly though you bestow it, but honesty will prevail. I did not take aim and fire, you merely obliged by walking into my range.' She waved a hand, and he followed its direction.

A low stone wall ran the length of the copse and balanced atop it was a small snowman, albeit minus part of its head. Before Darcy could study it further, Elizabeth spoke from beside him.

'You place yourself in continued peril, sir.'

She gathered the remnants of the snowball and began forming it into shape before returning to the place where she first stood and, sensing she would make no allowance, he quickly stepped aside, just in time to avoid the missile as it struck its target.

Elizabeth made a charming picture, wrapped warmly in a thick coat, a colourful scarf at her throat, her pink cheeks glowing almost as much as her hazel eyes and, despite the lingering dampness about his neck, Darcy's contentment grew.

'You force me to repeat my praise, Miss Bennet. Your aim is true.'

She laughed. 'It is a fine accomplishment, is it not?' Bending to scoop up another handful of snow, she moulded it into a tight ball. 'You are gallant, Mr Darcy.'

'You seem surprised.'

Elizabeth pursed her lips. 'Aye, I had not coupled you and gallantry together before now.'

Shocked by the implication of her words, Darcy knew not what to say. He was the consummate gentleman! How dare she imply otherwise?

Elizabeth, meanwhile, showed no respect for his inner turmoil, releasing the next snowball with expediency.

As she passed Darcy on her way to inspect the damage, he noted the snow clinging in clumps to her boots and the hem of her coat. 'You are a long way from home in these conditions, ma'am. May I not see you safely back?'

Elizabeth adjusted the snowman's body; its head fully dispatched to the other side of the wall and she turned to study him. Though he could not recall saying aught out of turn, her expression did not auger well.

'My home is indeed somewhat distant, but should I wish to return to the *Hall*, I will do so when my desire for solitude is satisfied.'

Accepting the hit, Darcy inclined his head. 'Then permit me to leave you in peace, madam.'

At this, the lady shook her head. 'Pay me no mind, Mr Darcy. I am out of sorts with myself more than any other. I accompanied Miss Anne Elliot on a call to Mrs Musgrove and was urged to take the air whilst my friend attended her sister. You are perfectly at liberty to walk here.'

Glad of the reprieve, Darcy smiled. 'May I be of any assistance?'

Elizabeth failed to conceal her surprise at the offer. 'I doubt you can. I am sorely in need of an outlet for a surfeit of ill temper.' She paused, then added, 'Do not be alarmed, sir; I am merely aggrieved by my cousin…' She hesitated. 'You recall Mr Collins? Your aunt's curate?'

'Indeed.' How Mr Collins, who was indeed his aunt Catherine's clergyman in Kent, could have caused Elizabeth frustration here in Somersetshire was beyond Darcy.

Turning, Elizabeth walked back to a small pile of remaining snowballs and picked one up, weighing it on her palm, before facing him. 'May I ask you a question?'

Did she wish to ask permission to aim the next missile at him? 'I—er, of course.'

She smoothed the snowball. 'Would you always put duty to your family before your own happiness?'

Darcy stared at her thoughtfully for a moment, unsure of the relevance of her words. 'If I thought I had forsaken my duty, I do not think I could find peace or contentment.' He studied her troubled countenance, then added. 'But my resolve has not been tested in earnest.'

What he might have said next, Darcy did not know, for voices drifted towards them on the cold air as two ladies appeared near a stile part way along the wall.

'Come, Lizzy! Mary is somewhat revived since she has eaten, as you see, and requests you join us for some tea.'

Anne Elliot's astonishment at perceiving Darcy would have amused him, but as he bowed in the ladies' direction, he was consumed by the disappointment of the imminent loss of Elizabeth's company.

The lady appeared a little awkward, then said, 'I am sure Mrs Musgrove would welcome your joining us, sir?'

Darcy shook his head. Much as he wished to remain in Elizabeth's invigorating company, drinking tea with the ladies held little attraction.

'I am bent upon exercise, Miss Bennet.'

'Then I bid you good day, Mr Darcy.' Elizabeth curtsied, and he bowed by return. 'I thank you for bearing me company.' She held out her latest offering towards him, and he took it.

'I return the compliment, Miss Bennet.'

Elizabeth soon disappeared over the stile and into the company of her friends, their voices fading, and Darcy stooped to gather more snow, doubling the missile in size.

Though it had been many a year since he had thrown a snowball, Darcy was a keen sportsman with a good eye and a true aim, and the remains of the snowman soon disappeared over the wall in search of its head. How was it he felt such satisfaction from the childish gesture and so revitalised by spending a short time in the lady's company?

Darcy turned to retrace his steps, deep in thought. A few light flakes of snow began to fall again, and he cast a wary glance heavenwards. Then, he shook his head at his own folly.

Whatever the weather chose to deliver, he was caught in a trap of his own making—it was time he owned it to himself.

Anne and Elizabeth walked in a comfortable silence along the snow-covered lane after saying farewell to Mary at Uppercross Cottage, both seeming wrapped in their own thoughts.

Elizabeth had been attempting to recapture her joy from when she awoke to a world of beauty, a memory that had almost sunk under Jane's letter and the complaints of Mary Musgrove. If only the breeze that had arisen could brush away the lady's relentless voice as smoothly as it grazed Elizabeth's cheek.

'I am sorry your letter did not deliver pleasing intelligence, Lizzy.'

'I am becoming accustomed to naught but frustration.'

'Do you wish to share it? You seemed so much better after your solitary walk.' Anne stayed Elizabeth with a hand on her arm. 'All the more surprising for your having met with Mr Darcy, of all people.'

Elizabeth laughed. 'Mr Darcy obliged by taking a snowball in the neck.'

Anne let out a gasp. 'He did not!'

'I will own to its aiding me in releasing some vexation. It was unintentional, of course.' Elizabeth frowned. 'He took it surprisingly well for such a proud man.'

Her spirits reviving at the memory of the gentleman's shocked face, Elizabeth turned to Anne as they fell into step once more. 'And you, Anne? Did your call upon your sister satisfy your concerns over her health? It is a worry in her condition, is it not?'

There was silence for a moment before Anne said: 'Mary is as well as she ever is.'

'A few words speak many.'

'I fear being indiscreet, but you are an astute observer, Lizzy. It will not surprise you to learn Mary has some ailments, which increase or decrease in accordance with how much attention she receives.'

'Yes, when I first left you, she had only just sat upright to take some nourishment and within an hour, you walked out in the snow.'

Anne smiled. 'It is the common way with her. A little refreshment always sets her up. She claims my company is a balm, but I fear I am merely an audience for her in Charles's absence.'

'I was surprised to learn he was out in such inclement weather.'

Anne took Elizabeth's arm. 'It would take more than a few inches of snow to have Charles stand down the beaters. I suspect my brother-in-law is lingering at the post-shoot gathering.' She hesitated. 'Do you believe in happiness in marriage, Lizzy?'

For a moment, Elizabeth knew not what to answer. 'I wish to. I long to marry for love, though I know it is not always possible.' They reached a crossroads and turned towards Kellynch, retracing their own footsteps in the snow from earlier.

'Mary and Charles muddle along. They seem as content as any other couple of my acquaintance.' Anne frowned. 'I am saddened that I have thus far failed to meet a married couple who demonstrate the happiness and contentment I anticipated with… Perhaps it does not exist.'

Elizabeth noted the slip. Anne had never said anything about a past love, but she suppressed her curiosity.

'My experience is equally limited, and my parents are a poor example, though my aunt and uncle Gardiner are entirely happy.' The memory of Mr and Mrs Hurst flashed into Elizabeth's mind. 'Even wealth, prestige, and good connections do not necessarily equate to a happy marriage.'

'I fear they often preclude it.'

Meadowbrook House came into view, and Elizabeth became thoughtful.

'Mr Darcy said he could not be content knowing he had forsaken his duty.' Elizabeth considered his words. 'I doubt he referred to marriage, but it did not surprise me. I have heard he is destined for a cousin.'

'I believe Mr Darcy takes his guardianship of Pemberley extremely seriously and would put it before anything—other than his sister's happiness.'

Musing on Jane's letter, Elizabeth's thoughts on Mr Darcy's sister remained all confusion. Then, she let out a huff of breath.

'You are fairer towards him than I.'

'I do not have a sister whose own happiness he has damaged.'

Elizabeth shivered, thankful that the chimney tops of Kellynch were in view. 'Speaking of which, you asked about Jane's letter. Are you certain you wish me to share my troubles? I believe you bear the confidence of many.'

Anne shook her head. 'Do not deprive me of the pleasure of being your friend, Lizzy.'

'Jane's consideration of Mr Collins continues to be a grave concern with me.' Elizabeth felt all the frustration from earlier return with a vengeance. 'There is no sign of Netherfield being readied for its master's return—and no word in response to Jane's letter to Miss Bingley.'

'Mr Bingley is a distant lover, then, if he remains in Town whilst his alleged amour is here in Somersetshire.'

Elizabeth frowned. 'You are right. If Miss Darcy has been unwell and Mr Bingley is so devoted, why is he not here?'

'Will you say as much to your sister?'

'I shall indeed.' Elizabeth summoned a smile. 'Mr Collins proposed marriage to me before addressing my sister.' Then, she added hastily. 'I refused, of course! If only the man could have reined himself in. He waited but four and twenty hours after my refusal to propose to Jane.'

Anne laughed. 'Forgive me. Your sister's situation is too sad for amusement, but I must confess, Charles Musgrove asked me to be his wife before approaching Mary.'

'Truly?' Elizabeth studied her friend thoughtfully. 'When was this?'

'In the year nine. Lady Russell was all for it, but I would not be persuaded.' Anne's expression was pensive. 'Though I will give Charles praise for waiting a year before offering for Mary.'

Elizabeth sighed. 'To make matters worse, Mr Collins returns to the neighbourhood in but a se'nnight, and he is sure to press his suit.'

'And has your sister implied if her sentiments have changed?'

'Jane generally conceals her feelings from the world, attempting to distract me by relating some of Mr Collins's ridiculousness in his latest to Papa.'

Anne glanced at Elizabeth as they turned their steps along the drive to the Hall. 'In what way ridiculous?'

'He relayed to Papa some of Lady Catherine's advice—which, of course, is the gospel by which he lives. She is the person who instructed him to find a wife in Hertfordshire, and she has had the temerity to suggest his choice must learn to conduct herself in "a manner most befitting the wife of a clergyman with such an honourable benefactress", or some such nonsense.'

Anne was suitably astounded, and Elizabeth laughed, though without humour. 'Precisely. Mr Collins, it seems, is beside himself with gratitude that Lady Catherine would deign to give such personal advice.'

'And how does Jane feel?'

'She seems to have decided it is humorous.'

'Your sister appears a sensible young woman.'

'Far too sensible. I would like to feed Mr Collins his insulting suggestion along with his stupid hat. I have always had great respect for men of the cloth, but my cousin is testing my faith in them.'

Anne smiled, but then it faded, the consciousness returning.

'Mr Wentworth—he is the gentleman presently with my father—is a good man. He has been presented with a living in Shropshire. He departs on the morrow, as I understand it. Though his parish is not under the jurisdiction of the estate, he has called as part of his general farewells to the neighbourhood. My father will not appreciate the gesture, for he does not have much time for the clergy.'

Elizabeth was surprised. 'How so?'

'He does not consider them "gentlemen". Thus, beyond the service they render, Father sees no value in the connection.'

There was little time to speculate on this, as they rounded the side of the house and entered the boot room, but not before tapping their boots on the scraper to remove the excess snow.

'My stockings are quite wet through!' Elizabeth studied her damp toes, as an obliging maid took charge of their boots for drying and cleaning.

They padded along the corridor to the stairs, intent upon finding dry stockings, but before they reached the bottom step, Sir Walter came striding through from the great hall.

'There you are, Anne. Where have you been?'

'We walked over to Uppercross, Father, to call upon Mary. She sent a message to say she was unwell. Did my sister not tell you?'

'Hmph.' Sir Walter turned to admire his image in a nearby looking glass, tucking a newspaper under his arm to inspect his coiffure more closely.

'Your sister is quite out of sorts. The weather is not to her liking.'

Elizabeth raised a brow. 'How remiss of Mother Nature, sir.'

Sir Walter had not heard, having dropped the newspaper, which he bent to retrieve with a frown.

'That Wentworth is a singular fellow. I am not displeased that he has been offered a living elsewhere.'

It was Anne's turn to frown. 'But you had so little to do with him, Father.'

'And thankful am I that it was so.' Sir Walter drew himself up. 'I am of course consulted on many a matter concerning the wider district. Wentworth came to pay his respects, or so he said, but the man left without the courtesy of a by your leave!'

Anne raised a brow. 'How extraordinary.'

'This is what one must expect when lower classes try to raise themselves. Picked up the newspaper, he did. Proceeded to ask me some such nonsense about a report. Then, the oddest noise came from the man, the paper fell to the floor, and he was gone! Preposterous!'

Sir Walter tossed the offending newspaper onto a side table and stalked off, and Anne, sending Elizabeth a small smile, followed her up the stairs.

They agreed to meet again in thirty minutes, and by the time Elizabeth came back down the stairs, she could see Anne perched on a settle in the great hall.

'Come, let us repair to the small sitting room.' Anne rose from her seat, turning back to retrieve Sir Walter's discarded newspaper before joining Elizabeth. 'We shall be undisturbed there.'

The room referred to by Anne overlooked the back terrace and the orderly gardens beyond and had been spared from Miss Elliot's redecorating schemes thus far, remaining much as it was when the late Lady Elliot designed it.

'How lovely!' Elizabeth stood in the centre of the charming room, turning around to take it all in, drawn immediately to a large painting over the mantelpiece depicting a kindly-faced gentleman, a young woman holding a baby, and a small girl sat upon the man's knee.

'Who are these people?' Elizabeth looked over to where Anne was, but her friend stared at the newspaper in her grip—a grip that shook the words on the front page.

'What is amiss?' She hurried to where Anne had sunk against the doorjamb, but her friend merely stared at her blankly. She was white as the freshly fallen snow.

'Come.' Elizabeth placed a firm hand under Anne's arm and led her to a chaise where her friend all but fell onto the cushions, then waited.

Anne remained silent, drawing in shallow breaths, but then she held out the newspaper to Elizabeth, pointing a shaking finger at a passage in the left-hand column.

'*The Laconia is sunk. All hands lost!*'

Elizabeth skimmed the article, then raised her eyes to meet Anne's.

'Someone you knew was on this ship.' Anne said nothing, but the anguished look on her face was sufficient confirmation.

'Do you wish to talk about him?'

Anne shook her head as a solitary tear rolled down her ashen cheek. 'Help me to my room, Lizzy. Please.' She got unsteadily to her feet, tugging a handkerchief from her sleeve and patting her damp skin. 'I wish to be alone.'

Concerned, Elizabeth offered her arm, unsurprised when Anne kept hold of the newspaper even after she collapsed into a fireside chair in her room.

'Shall I give your excuses at dinner, have a tray sent up?'

Elizabeth was not sure Anne heard her. She remained staring into the flames in the hearth, the newspaper clutched in her hands. Leaning down, Elizabeth gave her a gentle embrace, casting one lingering look at her afflicted friend before softly closing the door.

CHAPTER THIRTEEN

With shaking hands, Anne raised the newspaper to scrutinise again the ominous words.

'No,' she whispered, emotion gripping her throat. 'Oh, Frederick, not this…' Her voice broke and tears spilled down her cheeks as she bent over in her seat, her body shaking.

How long the torrent of emotion lasted, Anne was unsure, but eventually, she raised her head.

'Just breathe. Try to breathe,' she intoned, taking small gulps of air, then sinking back into her chair, the newspaper finally falling from her grasp.

Anne stared at her hands, stained with the print from the paper, which was damp from her outpouring of grief. She ought to wash them, repair the damage to her face, but her legs felt as though they would not support her.

Wearily, she stood, holding onto the arm of the chair, then stepped towards her bedside cabinet. Pulling out an old wooden box, which once belonged to her mother, she unlocked it and stared at its contents: a couple of letters bound in ribbon, a faded rose, pressed between fine paper, some lines of poetry, and a small pebble shaped almost like a heart. This was all she possessed of her brief months with Frederick Wentworth.

Anne lifted out the small bundle of letters, pressing it to her lips as the memories made with him replayed in her mind. There were precious few, but she clung to them, forcing out the horror of what his last moments might have been like. To no avail; Anne's heart betrayed her, winging its way towards his own, longing to have seen him just one more time, and wondering—foolish though the thought was—if Frederick held any thoughts of her when the end came.

A knock on the servant's door roused her, and Anne quickly returned the letters to the box as Elise entered with a tray.

'Miss Bennet said you were unwell, Miss Anne.' She placed the tray on a small table, and Anne wiped her eyes on her shawl. She had no appetite and no wish to be seen in her present state.

Elise approached her warily. 'May I fetch you anything? Would you like me to dress your hair? You have become a little…'

'Dishevelled.' Anne tried to pull herself together. 'Thank you, Elise. I will tend to myself. You may go.'

Alone again, Anne approached the looking glass in the fading light. Her reflection stared back: pale cheeks, a pink nose, and clouded eyes, with tendrils of hair hanging about her face. Then, she turned her back. What did it signify?

Ignoring the tray, Anne tried not to notice the discarded newspaper as she returned to the chair beside the fire. Perhaps she ought to try and see the Mr Wentworth on the morrow, before he departed the West Country? They rarely spoke in the intervening years, though he was the actual reason Frederick had even come into the county back in the year six. Did the reverend blame her for his brother's never coming to stay again? Whatever his feelings, he clearly received the intelligence of his brother's demise much as Anne had.

Anne's gaze drifted to the flames in the hearth and, hugging her shawl more closely about her, she curled up in her seat and tried to immerse herself in her happiest memories, those of walking in the grove on the arm of her commander.

Elizabeth was desperate to escape the dining room and, knowing both Sir Walter and Miss Elliot had no time for her presence, her excuse to call in on Anne was welcomed by all.

'Do wish her well.' Sir Walter waved a cavalier hand. 'Should she remain indisposed on the morrow, I shall summon Robinson to attend her.'

Miss Elliot yawned, as she did with annoying frequency. 'I am certain she merely took cold for being so foolish as to walk out in this foul weather, Father. It is her own fault if she picks up a chill.'

Sir Walter was quite appalled at this and held his napkin to his face. 'We do not want it to become a fever. Think of the detriment to one's looks.'

Elizabeth glared at them both, not that they noticed, having returned their attention to their meal. It took all her self-control not to tell them what she thought of their carelessness towards one of the sweetest people she had ever known. Instead, she turned on her heel and left the room, hurrying up the stairs to Anne's chamber.

Anne responded to Elizabeth's call through the door, and she entered to find her friend much as she had left her: wan and listless in the fireside chair.

'Dearest Anne.' Elizabeth hurried across the room to kneel beside her, taking one of her hands in her own and rubbing it to instil some warmth into the cold skin.

'I am so thankful you are here, Lizzy. My family has no comprehension…had no time for…' Anne's voice wavered.

Elizabeth adjusted her position on the floor. 'I suspected there had been someone before now. I am saddened for you.'

Anne lifted a listless hand, which fell back onto her lap. 'It was years ago.'

'And you care yet. Was it—did he not return your affection, or was it never even declared?'

Anne lowered her head and stared at her hands, then raised solemn eyes to Elizabeth's.

'I had a short attachment in my nineteenth year. He… Frederick,' her voice faltered as she spoke his name. 'Captain Wentworth is…*was* the reverend, Mr Wentworth's, brother and came to pass a few months with him. We were soon acquainted and rapidly attached to each other. He asked for my hand.' Anne smiled, her eyes distant. 'I could not speak my acceptance fast enough. We were to be the happiest of couples. No one could have more felicity.' The smile faded, as did the burst of animation.

'And…what happened?'

There was no answer.

'Anne?'

She spoke gently, unsure whether to leave her friend in peace, but then Anne straightened in her seat, her melancholy drawing Elizabeth's compassion.

'I was persuaded against continuing with the engagement, and much to my later regret, I conceded.'

'Oh, my poor dear girl.' Elizabeth squeezed Anne's hand gently.

'My father was disappointed—no, more than that. He was angry, claiming it was a disappointing match, that it was too soon, I was too young to make such a decision, and he would do nothing for us.'

Elizabeth's eyes widened. 'He would withhold your portion?'

'It was all I could assume, from his saying such. As it happens, but a twelve-month ago, I learned my grandfather had made some provision for his granddaughters.' Anne met Elizabeth's gaze. 'Back then, I cared little for the financial implications, but Frederick had yet to distinguish himself in the Navy, only having achieved the grade of commander. My father believes the institution has its utility, but he resents it being the means of bringing people of obscure birth into undue distinction, that it might raise them to a position where they had no right to be.' She sighed. 'If such ascendance was detrimental, imagine how he received the intelligence of Frederick having no distinguished connections to assist him in further climbing the ranks. Lady Russell pressed the point that his career was dangerous, a precarious profession with no guarantee of success or financial return. He was ashore at the time because he had no ship, thus no income. They said it was all too much of a risk, but in truth, they felt he was beneath the family, an unsuitable match for an Elliot.'

'It must have been a heart-breaking decision.'

Anne nodded. 'For us both. Frederick was angry, and I do not blame him.' She held Elizabeth's hand tightly, her expression earnest. 'I could not have rescinded—let him go— if I did not think I acted for his benefit. To attach himself to another at such a time, his future so uncertain…a wife may have become a burden he could ill afford. It may have hindered his opportunities, his career.'

'And did the captain gain all he hoped for in his profession?'

'Yes, ten-fold, though he has not wed.'

Elizabeth was surprised. 'How do you know this?'

'I followed Frederick's progression by consulting the Navy lists—*Steele*'s and the *Navy Chronicle*. At first, I could hardly look, breathless in dread of seeing he had perished or that he was listed newly wed, but beyond his promotions, his name never featured other than when he distinguished himself at sea...' Anne's voice faded, and Elizabeth could imagine where they had gone: to the bottom of the ocean.

There was a long silence, but then Anne inhaled deeply and lifted her head to meet Elizabeth's compassionate look.

'Do not be uneasy for me, Lizzy. It is a shock, and I am saddened for him, will grieve for him and his family, but in all truth, Frederick was lost to me the day I changed my mind, and he stormed from the Hall.' Anne gestured weakly with her free hand. 'We have never been in company since, but had it been so, we would have been strangers to one another.'

'You are stoic. More so than I could be in such circumstances.'

Anne shook her head. 'Though I cannot fault the logic of those who had a hand in my decision, my regret has never left me, and had our paths crossed even within months of our parting, I would have begged him to take me back. I will mourn his loss forever, but I have learned to live with it, built myself anew. I am not the same, nor should I be.'

Elizabeth's heart broke for her friend. 'I cannot imagine the pain of your parting, or the burden you now bear. This is why you comprehend so well Jane's situation. Sense versus emotion.'

Anne stirred in her chair. 'I may understand, but how I wish I had acted differently. My decision has been long repented, and I would not wish that for your sister.'

'So much sadness, when one ought to be the happiest of beings.'

'Some things are simply not meant to be.' Anne summoned a smile. 'But there is hope for you, Lizzy. Have you…did you ever meet someone whom you could consider attaching yourself to?'

Elizabeth's thoughts immediately went to Mr Wickham, a charming, handsome man whose circumstances made him excessively interesting to her. She felt for him, even defended him to Mr Darcy, despite it being a match that would bring little comfort to Elizabeth's family or any promise of security.

'There was someone in Hertfordshire who held my interest, and there is some similarity to your circumstances in that he is in a volatile profession with no connections to further…' Elizabeth drew in a sharp breath. This was not the time to think about Mr Darcy's disservice to his childhood friend. 'But there is an end to it.'

Elizabeth released Anne's hand before getting to her feet, noting the untouched tray of food on a side table.

'Can you not eat a morsel? Sip a little wine? I shall leave you to your rest.'

'Thank you, dear Lizzy. You are a great comfort. We can talk some more on the morrow.'

Darcy walked with Georgiana to the foot of the stairs, where he dropped a kiss on the top of her head, and she embraced him before heading up to her room.

After she disappeared from view, he turned to survey the empty hall. *What now?* It would be days before Colonel Fitzwilliam returned. With no estate to oversee, which kept him fully occupied when in Derbyshire, and none of the social obligations of Town, Darcy had little else to occupy his thoughts aside from the next Uppercross shoot. Other than Elizabeth Bennet.

Darcy blew out a frustrated breath. Little else indeed. Unless…

'No, damn it. You will not contemplate such a thing!' He spoke the words aloud, as though doing so would remove the notion, but his mind was no fool.

Heading for his study, he slammed the door behind him. Then, he crossed to the hearth, grabbed a poker and gave the logs a severe prodding.

It was insufficient to relieve his feelings. Returning to the desk, Darcy flipped open the diary, running a finger down the page to the date of his cousin's anticipated return. How the devil was he to occupy himself in the interim?

Much as Darcy loved his sister, there were many years between them, and though she fast became an adult, they were hardly ideal company for each other. Was that not why he engaged her companion?

No, Darcy. You engaged Mrs Annesley as someone to watch over her. The woman is even older than you are. What could they possibly have in common beyond their sex?

It was true. The lady was old enough to be Georgiana's mother. Should he have engaged someone who was closer to her in age, more like a sister? What young lady would have the wisdom and caring to guide Georgiana where she needed it most and also give her the best of company and amusement?

Elizabeth… The name whispered through his mind, and Darcy closed the diary and dropped into the chair at his desk before lowering his head into his hands.

Whence had it come, this…*obsession* with the lady? No answer came to him, and he straightened. Why was he consumed with when he might next see Elizabeth? What reason could he give for calling at the Hall?

Darcy walked over to the tray of spirits, fully replenished since the colonel's attack upon it, and poured himself a brandy, swirling the amber liquid around the glass as he took a seat by the hearth.

And what of Georgiana? With her health improving, she needed fresh air to aid her recovery. Her introduction to the ladies of Kellynch had taken place, but she had yet to meet the head of the household. Was it not incumbent upon them to return the ladies' call, and were they not already a day late in doing so?

Darcy took a slug from his glass, confident in the scheme as the liquid burned a trail down his throat.

Tomorrow, he was for Kellynch.

CHAPTER FOURTEEN

As soon as Elizabeth awoke, her thoughts were of her friend and all she had revealed the night before, and she only just allowed Lottie to insert the last pin into her hair before hurrying from the room.

Relieved to find Anne no longer in her own chamber, Elizabeth made her way down the stairs and walked through the great hall towards the breakfast room. Voices drifted towards her, indicating Sir Walter and his eldest were at table, and Elizabeth's steps slowed. Was she hungry enough to tolerate their company?

Elizabeth decided she was. Besides, Anne may need her.

'I have told you time and again, my dear. You cannot be too choosy.' Sir Walter's strident voice carried to Elizabeth through the partially open door as she approached.

Miss Elliot's response was muted, but her father continued as Elizabeth pushed open the door. 'It is the perfect solution. After what I did for you a year ago, you are in no position to delay, and the gentleman is—ah, Miss Bennet.'

Elizabeth curtseyed as Miss Elliot spun around in her seat, discomfort apparent on her features, but she quickly assumed her usual indolent air. Anne was not in the room, and she addressed her father.

'Excuse me, Sir Walter. Is there word from Miss Anne this morning?'

The gentleman raised a brow. 'We have not seen her. She must be in her room.'

Miss Elliot completely ignored Elizabeth.

'If you will excuse me, sir, ma'am, I shall seek her out.'

Closing the door with a snap, Elizabeth reflected on where Anne might be. It was good to know she felt well enough to leave her room but breaking her fast had clearly not been the incentive.

Elizabeth clutched her stomach as an ominous growl emanated from it. She would have to do a raid on the kitchens later, finding Anne took precedence.

A search of all the rooms on the ground floor bore no fruit; a passing footman had no answer for Miss Anne Elliot's whereabouts, and Elizabeth was on the verge of heading down to the kitchens to beg for a piece of toast or plum cake before searching further when she saw Anne coming through the doorway leading from the boot room, dressed in her riding habit. Her face was flushed and her hair a little disarrayed as she removed her hat, but when she saw Elizabeth, she raised a hand in greeting.

'I was so worried about you!' Elizabeth hurried her steps to meet her friend. 'Where have you been?'

'Come, Lizzy.' Anne said no more but took Elizabeth's arm and urged her along to the small sitting room they had gone to the previous day.

'You are cold.'

Anne nodded, gesturing for Elizabeth to precede her into the room, and she closed the door and turned around to lean against it.

'I wished to catch Mr Wentworth.'

They each took a seat either side of the hearth where a welcome fire crackled in the grate, and Anne held out her hands towards it. Elizabeth chewed her lip. Her friend spoke in a matter of fact manner that belied the dullness of her eyes.

'Did you sleep at all?'

'I do not feel as though I did, but I had such dreams…and one must sleep to dream.' Anne sat back in her seat, tucking her hands into her lap. 'I had to see Mr Wentworth, to see if he had any further intelligence.'

'And did he?'

Anne shook her head. 'It is oft the way in such cases. Initial reports reach the press before private word can be delivered to the families, the distances being so great.'

'And is the reverend the only family in this instance?'

The colour in Anne's cheeks, borne of the brisk walk in the cold air, receded. 'Frederick had a sister to whom he was seriously attached—he spoke of her often and with great affection. She married a naval man, now an admiral, and they are currently in the West Indies. It will be some time before they learn what has befallen her brother.'

Elizabeth leaned back in her own seat. 'So much sadness to be borne, for the families of each and every man lost on the ship. I am so grieved for you, Anne.'

'The gentleman is now on his way to Leominster, where he is to be wed. His new wife will be his comfort.' Anne extended her stocking-clad feet towards the hearth, wriggling her toes in search of its warmth. 'He had heard rumours of a ship going down in the Irish Sea but had no reason to suspect it was the

Laconia.' Anne drew in a short breath. 'He is full of regret for having only seen his brother twice in the past five years. I cannot help but feel I am to blame. Frederick, as you can imagine, never returned to Somersetshire after we…after he… They met in Southampton, when he was ashore, but he was mainly at sea and…' Her voice trailed away as her mind drifted, and Elizabeth clutched her stomach again as it let out a protesting gurgle.

'You have not eaten.'

'I wished to find you.'

'Dear Lizzy.' Anne stood up. 'I will profess to having no appetite, but I am sensible enough to comprehend I will do myself little service by not eating. Let us see if Mrs Howard can supply us with a little nourishment. I cannot face the breakfast table.'

Grateful though she was to know food would be imminent, Elizabeth took Anne's arm as they made their way back along the hall.

'If there is anything I can do, Anne, anything at all… I know there is no way to heal your immediate pain, but if you wish to talk to me, speak of Captain Wentworth in confidence, you have my solemn vow, never shall a word be spoken to another of anything you wish to share.'

They reached the door to the service areas, and Anne turned to face Elizabeth, her expression solemn.

'Thank you. If I had been here with just my father and my sister, then I do not know how I would have borne the news. I could not share it with them, nor would they understand my loss. They had no time for Frederick, he is… was… of no importance to them.'

'He was important to *you*, and that is all that matters. I will let you be the guide, but I remain at your disposal.'

Anne pushed open the door. 'Of that I shall take full opportunity, dear Lizzy. Let us eat, and then, after I have changed out of these clothes, we will go up to the long gallery for some exercise and conversation. It will be the best possible balm.'

To Darcy's disappointment, only Sir Walter and his eldest daughter were present when he and Georgiana were shown into the drawing room, and once his sister had been introduced to the gentleman, she sat in awed silence and Darcy was left to carry the conversation.

To his further discomfort, Miss Elliot paid Georgiana little attention beyond what was required and came to sit beside him to engage him in inconsequential nothings, to which he responded in a distracted manner, his eye upon his equally uncomfortable sister, and his mind wandering the building in search of Elizabeth.

'Do you not think so, sir?'

Darcy blinked and turned to the lady at his side. 'I—er, yes, of course.'

'There! It is as I told my father only this morning. I was certain your cousin would be as fixed in his purpose as you, sir, to attend the ball.'

He looked from Sir Walter to Georgiana, who seemed suddenly interested in the lady.

'We shall, of course, be inviting only the best company.' Miss Elliot frowned. 'Though we are under duress to have all the Musgroves here.' She did not appear pleased by this. 'A family obligation, you understand.'

Georgiana looked eagerly at the lady. 'And Miss Bennet?'

Miss Elliot trilled a light laugh.

'Good heavens, I think not. Miss Bennet will have long gone on her way by St Stephen's Day.' Miss Elliot moved confidentially towards Darcy, who instinctively leaned further away. 'My sister, Anne, has some singular notions. Her bringing Miss Bennet here was a misjudgement, one I am certain you comprehend.'

Thankfully, she straightened, permitting Darcy to do the same and save himself from falling off the back of the chaise.

He was torn between indignation at her derogatory tone and owning it would have been his exact response, had someone had the temerity to bring someone of the Bennets' station to stay at Pemberley.

'Her connections, Mr Darcy, and the situation of her family! An uncle who is a small town, country lawyer and another in trade! You can imagine how Father and I felt when we took steps to investigate the Bennets' wealth and consequence.'

Elizabeth has more consequence than you could ever dream of.

'Did you say something, sir?'

Darcy shook his head. 'Do please continue. You spoke of the day of the ball?'

Miss Elliot accepted the invitation, but Darcy paid no heed to her words. He had known Elizabeth would only stay for a few weeks, but he had hardly seen her.

Why was he so devastated at the thought of her leaving Somersetshire? He was not prepared for this chance encounter to come to so precipitous an ending.

The door opened, and a butler entered to address Sir Walter.

'Mr Shepherd is here, sir. I have shown him to the study, where he awaits your instructions.'

Sir Walter rose from his seat. 'Darcy, join me, if you will. I must speak with my legal man, but I have recently sourced a valuable painting and it arrived this morning. I am certain you will appreciate seeing it.'

'But Father—'

Sir Walter waved an indifferent hand at his daughter. 'Miss Darcy will no doubt be grateful for your attention, my dear. Come, Darcy.'

To Darcy's surprise, Georgiana nodded as he got to his feet, albeit she eyed Miss Elliot warily.

'I will return directly, Georgie, and we will be home in time for your music practice.'

'Music practice be damned, Darcy. Elizabeth'—Sir Walter turned to Miss Elliot— 'take Miss Darcy to the music room. She can try out the instruments to her heart's content, and you can display your own talents by return.'

A glimpse of Miss Elliot's countenance was sufficient for Darcy to comprehend the lady's view on this, but then she perceived Darcy's eye upon her.

'It will be my pleasure. Do come and find us, sir, when you are at leisure. Come, Miss Darcy.' She offered a hand to Georgiana who, after a fleeting look in her brother's direction, rose to take it, allowing herself to be led from the room.

Elizabeth and Anne completed several lengths of the long gallery, an impressive area in which the two of them were quite lost, but which enabled them to speak freely without fear of being overheard or interrupted.

'I shall, at least, have my memories of the happy times we shared, Lizzy. It is more than some can ever aspire to.'

Anne stared out of one of the many windows along the gallery, and Elizabeth joined her. The colour in her friend's cheeks returned, as did her calm manner.

'I have long mourned the man I loved, and though this is wretched, it alters not my own situation.' She turned to face

Elizabeth with a soft smile. 'There will still be moments of anguish, but I have had five years to accept my lot in life.'

Impulsively, Elizabeth embraced her friend.

'What you had with Captain Wentworth, though it ended in a way you would not wish, was more than many experience. You are quite right. The memory cannot be taken away from you.'

Anne was silent for a moment, then she nodded. 'I have come to realise that Frederick Wentworth was the most important person in my life. So much of who I am today is rooted in the love we shared and lost. I had never connected them until now.'

Elizabeth felt consumed by sadness. She wondered if perhaps the good captain had never quite recovered from his affection for Anne. It was certainly likely he had never come across another such woman.

'The past few months have shown me the many complications pertaining to matters of the heart.' Elizabeth took in the beautiful expanse of land, then leaned against the windowsill beside her friend. 'I begin to understand why so many marriages are founded on business. I do not like it, but it seems finding love is oft insufficient.'

'And sometimes it is entirely too much.'

'It is sadly true. I hear all you have endured, and I think of Jane and Mr Bingley.' Elizabeth turned towards her friend earnestly. 'I know he cared for her, Anne. I *know* he did. But persuasion was the means of separating them, much as it was in your own case, and for similar reasons, no doubt. I do not fault you for your decision. I have struggled not to blame Mr Bingley, but if he truly is intending to wed Miss Darcy, I ought to rail against him for paying such marked attentions to my sister.'

Anne frowned. 'It may explain his being so easily influenced to leave Hertfordshire, particularly if his unguarded attentions had given rise to a general expectation of there being an understanding between Mr Bingley and your sister.'

Elizabeth pursed her lips. 'I had not given such a possibility credence, but now I begin to wonder. Mr Bingley's manners were so open and inviting. What if he is prone to such missteps and has had to be warned before now by his friends of the danger of his paying too much attention to a young lady?' Then, she shook her head. 'But I am certain he was genuinely attached to Jane, that he fell in love with her.'

'Being destined for another does not necessarily prevent someone from falling in love elsewhere, certainly if the prior arrangement is more of a business one.'

'Aye.' Elizabeth's mind struggled with this interpretation. 'Though I did not accept it at the time, with Mr Bingley's settled absence, I must begin to give it some weight. As for Miss Darcy, she had been portrayed by Miss Bingley and'— Elizabeth caught herself before mentioning Wickham's assessment— 'and held up as a virtue, so much older and mature than she is. It seems there was some deception in the case.'

'And what do you think Miss Bingley's motives were in making you believe this?'

Miss Bingley's she could surmise, but Elizabeth was unsettled to realise it was harder to fathom Mr Wickham's purpose. Surely, he had known Miss Darcy all her life, and his interpretation ought to be the most reliable?

'Lizzy?'

'At the time, I told Jane I believed it was more about Miss Bingley wanting Miss Darcy as a sister through her own marriage to Mr Darcy.'

'Mr Darcy?' It was Anne's turn to frown as they both pushed away from the window and walked across the room. 'Is he engaged to the lady?'

Elizabeth laughed as they reached the door. 'Oh, how I wish! Mr Darcy deserves such a life, for all he has done to ruin others! The machinations of marriage are all too much for me. I shall have none of it.'

Anne opened the door, and Elizabeth looked back along the gallery.

'You are fortunate to have such a place for when the weather is inclement.'

'And you would, whatever the elements, prefer to be in the fresh air?'

Elizabeth smiled as she followed Anne down the stairs. 'We cannot always have what we prefer.'

They reached the first floor, and Anne paused. 'Will you excuse me, Lizzy? I wish to take a little rest. My poor night of sleep has made me weary.'

'Of course. May I return to the small sitting room with a book? You are certain you do not wish for companionship?'

At the door to Anne's room, she turned to face Elizabeth. There was a noticeable calmness about her. 'I am quite well. I merely wish to rest. I will join you once I am feeling stronger.'

With that, Elizabeth must be content, and she hurried to her room to collect a book before heading down the stairs to the seclusion of the late Lady Elliot's sanctuary.

CHAPTER FIFTEEN

Ten minutes in Sir Walter's study was sufficient for Darcy to realise why the rumours about the gentleman's finances were probably true. Such extravagance over one painting, when the estate failed to direct funds to more important needs, such as keeping the stock in the fields, was flagrant mismanagement.

Whether Sir Walter was entirely to blame, with both an accountant and a legal representative to advise him, Darcy knew not, but he was thankful when the painting's wrapping was restored, and escape seemed imminent.

'If I could have another moment of your time, Sir Walter?'

Shepherd, Sir Walter's lawyer, sat before a desk full of papers. Darcy had attempted to close his ears to their earlier conversation. Kellynch business was none of his concern.

'What is it now, Shepherd?' Sir Walter gestured towards Darcy. 'I have visitors.'

'If you would just sign the authorisation for the quarterly payments?' The lawyer spoke with quiet confidence. 'I shall not trouble you further.'

Turning away as Sir Walter walked over to the desk, Darcy noticed a large table upon which rested an open book. A quick study proved it to be the *Baronetage* and, unsurprisingly, the pages were opened on 'Elliot of Kellynch Hall'.

Darcy's eyes skimmed the entries, his brow rising as he noted the handwritten additions to the printed entries.

'Ah, I see you are interested in the family lineage, Darcy. Have no fear,' Sir Walter came to stand beside Darcy. 'The family has long been blessed with the baronetcy. Our credentials are exemplary.'

'It is a fine volume, Sir Walter.' Darcy pointed at the entry of his youngest daughter's marriage a year ago. 'I am surprised to see the annotations. Do they not affect its value?'

'Done by my own hand. If anyone has the right, then it is I.' Sir Walter's pride in himself was plainly seen, and Darcy fought the urge to roll his eyes. 'You would be surprised the *value* of a good annotation.' He tapped his nose. 'Needs must and—'

'Are you well settled at Meadowbrook House, Mr Darcy?'

Surprised by Shepherd's interruption, Darcy straightened from his study of the book. 'Yes, quite settled, thank you.'

'Good, good.' The lawyer stepped forward and closed the *Baronetage*. 'I have much to work on. If you will excuse me?'

Amused, Darcy followed Sir Walter from the room. Had the man just dismissed his employer from his own study?

'Hmph.' Sir Walter cleared his throat as they walked back along the corridor. 'Shepherd is my confidential friend, you understand, of many years standing. His father before him was my advisor when I reached my majority.'

'You permit him certain liberties, sir.'

Sir Walter raised a brow. 'When a man knows the intricacies of your personal business, it is well to both keep him close and allow him some perceived power.' He gestured towards a corridor to the left. 'What say you we go in search of Elizabeth, Darcy?'

A smile touched Darcy's lips, even as his heart clenched again in his breast. He would gladly do so, and it was only as he followed Sir Walter towards the music room that he realised precisely *which* Elizabeth he meant. Resigning himself to the inevitable, he at least felt reassured he would relieve his sister from the obligation of Miss Elliot's sole attention.

Even so, Darcy hoped to at least see Miss Bennet, engage her in conversation before he left, and he looked around, half expecting his wishes to have manifested her presence.

Strands of music floated through the air as Sir Walter opened the door to the music room. At least Georgiana would be perfectly content at the piano.

The music room was filled with light, so much so, Darcy felt almost blinded by it at first, but as his eyes adjusted, he realised Miss Elliot was alone in the room.

Elizabeth's book failed to capture her attention, her mind engrossed by her recent conversation with Anne. Happiness seemed to hold no sway over the lives of women, who seemed powerless to be their own protectors, whether they had a dowry or not.

Frustrated, Elizabeth inspected the weather outside. A brisk walk around the gardens was required, and with that in mind, she hurried to collect her stoutest pair of boots and a warm pelisse before emerging from the boot room into the chill of the wintry afternoon.

Striking out along a path cleared of snow, Elizabeth walked for some time, head down and deep in thought, though none were conducive to raising her spirits.

Poor Anne... Elizabeth's breath mingled with the chilly air to form swirls, drifting away from her. It was true, this intelligence of her captain had been a shock, and a painful one at that, but as Anne herself owned, her grieving had been across many years. Her melancholy may never fully loosen its hold, but her immediate distress would be alleviated given a little time to adjust to the news.

Having reached the shrubbery, Elizabeth stopped. There were few sounds beyond the cawing of some rooks in the bare treetops, and slowly she began to walk back towards the house. As she entered the formal lawned area, however, a movement caught her eye, and she espied a young woman on the terrace.

She waved a hand, recognising Georgiana Darcy, who returned the gesture.

As she reached the terrace, however, Elizabeth became concerned. 'Miss Darcy, should you be out here?' She considered the girl's white complexion as she put a hand to her mouth to conceal a cough.

'I have been waiting for my brother, but I could not bear'—Georgiana stopped, the hand flying back to her mouth, her eyes widening. 'Forgive me. I must not speak out of turn.'

'I did not know you were at Kellynch.' Curious though Elizabeth was about what Georgiana had been about to say, she was more interested in how she came to be there.

'My brother'—she cleared her throat—'Fitz felt obliged to call upon Sir Walter, so I begged him to allow me to come too. I had hoped to see you.'

Elizabeth eyed Georgiana with surprise. 'Me?'

'Oh, and Miss Anne Elliot, of course. Only I...did not know where to find you.'

Gesturing for them to walk on, Elizabeth fell into step with Georgiana.

'I cannot approve of your being out in this cold weather, Miss Darcy, but as it is not my place to prevent you from doing so, I shall instead bear you company.'

'Fitz will not be pleased with me, but I could remain no longer in the music room.' Georgiana shuddered, and Elizabeth frowned.

'Was the instrument not to your liking?' Perhaps the girl was as fastidious in her tastes as Wickham implied?

'Oh no! It was exquisite. It is…I was with Miss Elliot.' Georgiana stopped and turned to face Elizabeth. Her expression was conflicted, and colour flooded her cheeks. 'I know I should not say it, but I do not find her good company.'

Suppressing a laugh, Elizabeth laid a hand gently on Georgiana's arm as they moved on. 'She is an acquired taste. We cannot all like each other in the same way. It is human nature and how we are formed. Though I sympathise with your desire to escape, I do not think Mr Darcy would wish you to be out for too long.'

'My brother is protective of me, as he is of those he holds dear. We are but a small family, but Fitz would offer his protection to any of his close friends, or indeed those acquaintances who had need of it.'

Thinking of Wickham, Elizabeth was unimpressed. She liked Georgiana well enough, but she was incredibly naïve. Suddenly struck with a notion, Elizabeth glanced at her.

'May I ask you a question, Miss Darcy?'

'Of course?'

'You are well acquainted with your brother's intimate friend, Mr Bingley, I assume?'

Georgiana smiled. 'Indeed. When we are in Town, he is as much in our house as we are. Fitz considers him almost family.'

That was not what Elizabeth wished to hear! They had few steps to go along the terrace before they were back at the door to the boot room. Ought she to ask more? She was being impertinent...

'Mr Bingley was well liked in Hertfordshire. It is a shame he is said to be giving up the estate.'

'I was surprised when my brother first told me.' They reached the door and Elizabeth opened it, waiting for Georgiana to precede her into the building. 'But Fitz takes care of him where he needs it most, and Mr Bingley is most grateful to him for the service.'

Her dissatisfaction with Mr Darcy growing by the minute, Elizabeth did not respond, hanging her pelisse on the coat stand and sitting down to unlace her boots. The sooner the man was gone from the Hall, the better. Then, she frowned.

'What service?'

The words were out before Elizabeth could think about the appropriateness of them, but Georgiana Darcy hung up her own pelisse and continued to chatter, unwittingly revealing her brother's hand in the separation of his friend from a most unsuitable young lady.

'Damnit!'

Pacing was no aid to Darcy, despite the lateness of the hour. Unable to settle, unwilling to make any attempt at sleeping, he glared at the embers in the hearth, scowled at his reflection every time he passed the looking glass and glowered at the undisturbed bed as though his present unrest was down to them and they alone.

Now, a good half hour after dismissing his rather peeved valet, assuring him that he was quite capable of preparing himself for bed for once, Darcy remained wide awake, his mind in more turmoil than ever.

He strode over to the window of his chamber and stared out into the all-consuming darkness. A crescent of the waning moon stood as a slender sentinel in the sky—just as motionless as Darcy. If his line of sight had been clear of trees, and it was not the dead of night, he might be able to see straight to Kellynch Hall. Did Elizabeth's room face in this direction? Was she, too, awake and unable to settle? Did she think of him?

Resuming his pacing, Darcy's expression became thoughtful. His sister had long since retired, her delight in her first visit to the Hall down purely to time spent in Elizabeth's company.

A sudden image from earlier that day flashed through his mind, Elizabeth's fine eyes meeting his across the music room as she entered, his sister in tow. He could not recall what he said. Miss Elliot had been talking to him, but his interest was all with Elizabeth.

Darcy frowned. She did not seem her usual serene self, and her terse response when he enquired after Miss Anne Elliot confounded him. Was it because her friend was unwell? If it were to be a prolonged indisposition, would Elizabeth's time be wholly consumed by attending the lady?

It was Elizabeth's way to care for others. Had Darcy not seen it for himself when she nursed Jane Bennet through her illness at Netherfield? He saw it too in the way she spoke so kindly to Georgiana when first they met.

Walking to the looking glass, he took in his conflicted air. How could Elizabeth have such a hold on the Darcys? He was bewitched; there was no other word for it.

Georgiana blossomed earlier under Elizabeth's attention as she encouraged her to play a duet. When had Darcy last seen such animation in his sister's face, such rapt attention upon anything, even her music? The sound of her laughter had been a delight, as he smiled gratefully at Elizabeth.

Was her assessing stare borne of a growing interest in him? Darcy had yet to fathom the intricacies of Elizabeth's mind, but she must have detected his in hers, for he had become powerless to conceal it.

Darcy prowled over to the window again, staring once more in the direction of the Hall. How could any woman affect him so? Elizabeth could not possibly understand the effect she had upon him; he could scarce account for it himself.

What was it he had said? A stammered compliment about the music, and, because he was eaten up with longing to take a seat beside Elizabeth, to have her notice upon him and him alone, Darcy had done the opposite. He held out his hand for his sister and, he hoped, made a civil retreat from the room and the house.

Consumed by emotions he knew not how to harness, Darcy turned around and leant against the sill. He had known the danger, in Hertfordshire, not only of paying Elizabeth too much attention, but of wanting more from the lady than a gentleman of his standing should consider or permit. He fully comprehended the truth he battled to suppress. Denial was futile.

Reaching up to unfasten his neck cloth, a faint smile touched Darcy's lips. The battle with himself was over; the war had been won.

Darcy's heart was already Elizabeth's and, God help him, he would marry her.

Pacing in her room, Elizabeth was thankful Anne decided to retire early and relieved her friend seemed more herself. She chose not to relate her conversation with Georgiana, for Anne was sufficiently burdened with her own concerns.

Georgiana Darcy's naiveté could easily be put down to her inexperience in the world, and the cosseted way she had likely been raised...

Stopping in the middle of the room, Elizabeth drew in a short breath. Yes, she wished to blame Mr Darcy for the entirety, even his own sister's gaucheness at times, but honesty forced her to acknowledge that over-protectiveness surely had more merit than the lethargic approach of her father towards his daughters.

Elizabeth dropped onto her bed. She had formerly placed the blame for Bingley's desertion with his sisters—Miss Bingley in particular—though she had not been blind to Mr Darcy's disparaging opinion of her family. Aside from anything he might have said, it was writ clear upon his countenance, tangible in his air when any of the Bennet family was within close proximity.

To learn from Miss Darcy her brother *had* been instrumental in both removing his friend from the district and advising him not to return had been infuriating. The girl seemed little troubled by it. If she had any affection for Mr Bingley, it clearly did not distress her to know he had paid attention to another.

'Poor Miss Darcy.' Despite herself, Elizabeth could not help but smile a little at the recollection of Georgiana's face as she realised whatever she said affected Elizabeth.

It had taken Elizabeth's best endeavours, as they walked to the music room, to assure the girl no harm had been done.

'No harm?' muttered Elizabeth, getting to her feet as agitation returned in full measure. 'What lies we speak to save the innocent.'

Well, she had done her utmost to make the girl easy, had accompanied her back to the music room only to find *him* there already. Oh, how proud her parents would have been at the restraint Elizabeth held over her feelings upon entering the room.

As for Mr Darcy...

The door to the servants' staircase opened and Lottie entered with a pitcher of hot water.

'Oh! Are you ready, miss?'

'As ready as I shall ever be, Lottie.'

The morrow was another day, and if chance favoured her, Elizabeth would not see Mr Darcy until she had herself under better regulation.

CHAPTER SIXTEEN

Darcy never had such fastidious care taken with his appearance. Raworth—though he knew not his master's intentions—seemed to think it more than adequate recompense for his master having no use of his services the previous evening, and fussed around him, knotting his neckcloth three times before he was satisfied and insisting—with due deference—the green stripe waistcoat suited his master best.

Darcy hurried down the stairs on pure verve, belying the sleepless night he had passed as he tossed and turned, fighting the voice of reason, of duty, whenever it made itself known.

This went against all his principles, taking a woman of inferior birth, no fortune, no connections, for his wife. There would be family obstacles to overcome; Darcy would invoke their displeasure by connecting himself to someone whose relations and condition in life were so decidedly beneath his own. Even his own parents would have railed against a match with Elizabeth.

'Then it is a blessing they are at rest,' he mused as a footman assisted him into his great coat. The gratification of having Elizabeth as his wife overruled all sense, all reason. His heart would win out, beyond any rational argument Darcy's conscience could summon.

'Brother? Where are you going?' Georgiana emerged from the drawing room, a book in her hand.

'Up to the Hall.'

She walked over to him, then frowned. 'Is anything amiss?'

Darcy, busy committing his speech to Elizabeth to memory, did not respond, so Georgiana tugged at his sleeve as he held out a hand for his gloves.

'What is it?' He had not meant to speak so sharply, and colour flooded her cheeks. 'Georgie.' Contrite now, Darcy waved away the footman and took her hands in his. 'Forgive me, dearest. I have a matter of some import on my mind.'

Georgiana went into his open arms and he held her close, then dropped a kiss on top of her head.

'And it will be resolved by your visit?'

Darcy smiled, though she could not see it. 'Most indubitably.'

'Then you will return in better humour, Fitz?' Her voice was somewhat muffled by his coat, but Darcy's heart swelled with the joy he soon anticipated. The family in general may not approve, but Georgiana would, and hers was the only opinion he cared for.

He set her away from him. 'I shall. And I hope to bring news.'

Her face brightened. 'What sort of news, Brother?'

Darcy laughed and tapped her lightly on the nose. 'Later, Georgie.' He looked at his watch. 'I must leave directly.'

'You seem a little better this morning, Anne.'

Elizabeth followed her friend into the small sitting room they had taken as their own.

'I did sleep for a while.' Anne walked over to the writing desk against the far wall. 'I am sorry your night was disturbed, though.' She placed a bottle of ink into one of the compartments and turned to face Elizabeth. 'Will you not tell me why?'

Knowing how riled she would become if she began, Elizabeth shook her head. 'Pay me no mind, Anne. Now, I am curious. I was most taken with this painting the other day. Do tell me about it.'

She gestured towards the portrait hanging above the mantel, and they both walked over to stand before it.

'This is my mother.' Anne pointed to the young lady seated in a chair, a baby in her arms. Resting a hand lightly on the figure, she trailed a finger down the canvas to rest upon the baby. 'And this is Mary.'

'It is beautifully rendered.' Elizabeth turned to her friend. 'And the little girl nestled upon the gentleman's lap? She appears perfectly content.'

'She was.' Anne's gaze fell upon the small figure. 'I was all of four years of age and despite appearances, apparently I fidgeted a great deal!'

Elizabeth laughed. 'Who is the gentleman? You are vastly at ease in his embrace.'

Anne's face softened. 'Grandpapa James. My mother's father. We were extremely close.' Her air crumpled, and Elizabeth took her hand.

'I am sorry if my inquisitiveness has brought you pain.'

'It has not.' Anne squeezed Elizabeth's hand gently. 'I miss them both so much. Grandpapa only survived my mother by a year. He was devastated by her death.' She raised her fingers, placing a kiss upon them before touching her mother's cheek and then her grandfather's. 'Mama used to take Mary and I to visit Grandpapa often.'

Elizabeth frowned. 'What of Miss Elliot?'

'My eldest sister preferred to remain here with Father.'

A tap came on the door, followed by the appearance of the housekeeper bearing a salver.

'The post has arrived, Miss Anne.'

Anne took up the letters as the housekeeper hurried from the room.

'There is one for you, Lizzy.'

'Oh, it is from Jane.' Elizabeth broke the seal and began to read, sinking onto a chaise beside the hearth, but within seconds, her hand dropped into her lap and her fingers clenched as she struggled not to screw the letter up and hurl it at the glowing fire.

'What is it?' Anne came to sit beside Elizabeth, who released a frustrated breath.

'Mr Collins has returned ahead of himself, but that is not the worst of it. Here.' Elizabeth handed the letter at Anne. 'Read the first paragraph, and you shall see.'

Anne did as she was bid, then handed the letter back. 'Miss Bennet has capitulated. I am grieved for you, Lizzy.'

'I truly thought Jane would come to view the scheme as nonsensical.' Elizabeth leapt up, though uncertain of her purpose. She took a few steps, turned on her heel, and walked back before sinking onto the chaise beside Anne again. 'How unfeeling of Mr Collins, to return unannounced to press her for an answer? This is Lady Catherine's doing, I am certain. He will heed no one's advice but hers. A curse on that family! I wish they had never been born—*any* of them.'

'Lizzy,' Anne cautioned.

Elizabeth laughed but without humour. 'Mr Darcy will not overhear me from here, Anne, though more is the pity.'

'Read the letter fully, Lizzy. See what your sister has to say on the matter.'

Elizabeth took the letter and tried to absorb Jane's words, striving to suppress her growing despair.

Her sister was resigned, as she expected her to be, and Elizabeth's spirits lowered. Much as she had not approved Jane's decision to do her duty, as she saw it, to detect this slow awakening to the permanence of her situation was heartbreaking. Damn Mr Bingley for deserting her, and damn Mr Darcy for his influence upon his friend.

'A letter from Caroline Bingley arrived, putting an end to all doubt. Her brother is settled in London for the winter with no view of returning to Hertfordshire. The remainder of Miss Bingley's letter—the chief of it—was given over to praise of Miss Darcy and the anticipated union with her brother.' Elizabeth was touched by the compassion in Anne's face. 'At least my father is insisting upon an engagement of no less than three months. Jane claims her acceptance to be the only sensible response, but I cannot abide it. I feel as though I have lost my dearest sister.'

'Oh, Lizzy. I am so sorry, both for you and for Jane.'

Elizabeth stood again. 'Will you excuse me, Anne?' She gestured towards the window. 'I do not wish to desert you, but I fear if I do not walk off this temper, it will consume me. I am so…I am so *angry* with that man.'

Anne bit her lip. 'Is it wise to lay all the blame at Mr Darcy's feet, Lizzy? It seems Mr Bingley's family were equally instrumental in separating them?'

Elizabeth knew what they were both also thinking. Jane put herself in this situation, even if it was a direct result of Mr Bingley's desertion.

Frustrated and saddened, Elizabeth almost wrung her hands. 'None of this would have happened if persuasion had not been brought to bear upon Mr Bingley.'

'Go for a walk, Lizzy. Shed your vexation in the garden.'

'I am doing you a disservice. I promised you company.'

Anne stood up. 'Come and find me when you are refreshed. I shall repair to the music room for a while.'

Elizabeth followed her friend out of the room, and they parted at the foot of the stairs.

Anne, of course, did not know of Mr Darcy's treatment of Mr Wickham. Her mind full of the gentleman's transgressions, Elizabeth headed for the boot room. Hopefully, Anne's advice to take the air would adequately calm her agitation, and if Fate was kind, she would return to the house in better spirits and more able to support her friend.

Relishing the fine wintry morning, Darcy inhaled deeply. He could not stop smiling as he strode down the lane, unaware of the crunch of snow beneath his boots or the chill wind all but freezing the tips of his ears. Elizabeth would be astonished, of course. For all the attention he had shown, she could not expect an honour such as *this*!

Darcy felt invigorated, the smile on his face widening as he rounded the corner and approached the gates to Kellynch Hall. All he needed to do was choose the right words, and then, when Elizabeth's enchanting eyes fixed upon his, her attention fully on him in a way it had never been before, he would not lose the power of coherent thought.

Eying the building's façade as he walked along the driveway, Darcy's confidence faltered somewhat. He had not even considered the practicalities! How the devil was he to find a moment alone with Elizabeth? She was continually at her friend's side, and even if he found them all in the drawing room, extracting Elizabeth from the room would be nigh on impossible, for what credible reason could he give? What if Miss Anne Elliot was still indisposed and Elizabeth attended to her?

The Fates, however, seemed to be in his corner. As Darcy neared the house, a movement caught his eye, and he espied Elizabeth—alone—walking away from him on the terrace bordering the west wing.

Darcy moved forward, trying to recall his carefully rehearsed speech.

'Collect yourself, man,' he muttered. 'You are asking the lady for her hand. It is hardly difficult…just consider all you wish to explain.' To Darcy's consternation, this merely brought the entirety of his arguments against the match tumbling into his head.

'Be done,' he cautioned himself. 'You have made your choice. Just decide where to start. The rest will follow.'

Tell her you love her, you dunderhead.

Though the colonel knew not of Darcy's intentions, he could hear his cousin's voice as clearly as though he stood before him.

Yes, Cousin. That is precisely where I shall begin.

Elizabeth would be so gratified, and all he wished to say—of his struggle, of all he sacrificed for her, of the obligations overcome with such difficulty—would follow quite easily, for his feelings were natural and just in the circumstances.

'Just breathe,' Darcy intoned quietly as he reached the terrace. The thrill of his intentions rushed through him again, filling his ears with noise…

'Mr Darcy!'

His startled gaze met that of Elizabeth's as she turned about and fetched up short in front of him.

'Elizabeth!'

Her name fell involuntarily from his lips, but the lady seemed decidedly out of countenance. Darcy stared at her, entranced by the pretty picture she made; then, he recalled himself.

'Forgive me. Miss Bennet.'

Heat permeated his skin despite the cold.

Speak, you simpleton! Seize the moment!

'In vain have I struggled. It will not do. My feelings will not be repressed. You must allow me to—'

'*Must* I, *Mr* Darcy?' Elizabeth's expression was not encouraging. 'Well, *I* must choose not to listen. If you will excuse me, sir.' She gestured with her hand. 'I wish to continue my walk.'

Her tone was uncompromising, and Darcy's brow furrowed. Had he so affronted her with merely the slip of address? He could hardly help it; it was how he had thought of her for weeks.

'Forgive me, ma'am. I meant no offence and certainly had no intention of treating you with any less respect than you deserve.'

Elizabeth raised a brow. 'Truly, sir? I am curious to learn what level of respect that might be?'

Darcy drew in a short breath. 'The fullest respect, ma'am. Without question.' He ran a hand through his hair. Lord, it was more difficult than he imagined. 'I repeat, forgive me, Miss Bennet, for such a slip. I should have been more circumspect.'

A sound escaped the lady. 'How singular of you to own it.'

Darcy winced. 'I have made my share of mistakes, like any man.'

Elizabeth laughed, but he sensed she was not amused. 'How…astonishing.' She looked around. 'And how unfortunate I am the only audience for this incredible show of humility.'

Something was definitely wrong. Darcy's perplexed eyes met Elizabeth's as she returned her attention to him.

'Have I committed some particular transgression today, Miss Bennet?'

'Today, Mr Darcy? Not particularly.'

Darcy released a relieved breath. 'Then—'

'Your offences, sir, extend far beyond today.'

He almost rolled his eyes as Elizabeth skipped around him and moved towards the house. Surely she would not repeat her defence of Wickham from the ball? Then, he frowned.

'Offences?' He set off in pursuit.

Elizabeth raised her chin as he fell into step beside her, fixing him with her intelligent eyes. How he wished to lose himself in them and—

'You are so consumed with your own consequence, you cannot see worth in anyone not fortunate enough to have your background and upbringing. You may have been raised with good principles'—she did not sound as if she believed it—'but you seem to follow them in pride and conceit.'

She headed for a nearby door, then stopped so abruptly, he almost ran into her.

'You are made of the same ilk as Sir Walter and Miss Elliot. Judgemental, supercilious, and filled with arrogance.'

This was her opinion of him?

'You would tar me with the same brush?'

'No, you are right. I should not.'

Darcy's relief was fleeting.

'Sir Walter and his daughter have slighted me inconsequentially. I find their contempt diverting. You, sir, on the other hand, have brought permanent harm upon people I care for—far greater offences and ones I find no humour in.'

Cut to the quick by this affirmation of her continued interest in Wickham, Darcy drew himself to his full height.

'I will not discuss Wickham's false claims. His word is not to be trusted.'

Elizabeth's eyes flashed. 'His misfortunes are of your infliction. An offence, to be certain, but not what most angers me against you. *That* is the ruin of my sister's happiness by your hand. Your obsession with wealth and consequence should not be imposed upon others, nor should your influence be brought to bear to deny someone the chance of making a marriage of affection.'

Darcy suddenly felt on a surer footing. After all, he had done Miss Jane Bennet a service. 'I do not deny I was instrumental in separating my friend from your sister. Miss Bennet has much to recommend her—'

'But not fortune or connections.'

With frustration, Darcy shook his head.

'Your sister's air was calm, and her manners towards my friend were cheerful and engaging, but I detected no symptom of particular regard, merely a dutiful daughter following a mother's objective. I observed your sister closely, and Miss Bennet received Bingley's attentions with pleasure but did not return them. I acted only to protect him from—'

'*Protect him?*' Elizabeth's frame shook. 'Please do finish your sentence, sir. Your friend needed defending from what, exactly? And what of my sister and the safety of her heart? Does Mr Bingley make a habit of paying his attentions to young ladies when he is expected to please his family and friends by marrying your sister?'

Darcy frowned. 'What has Georgiana to do with this?'

Elizabeth ignored the question. 'I hope they are happy together because I like Miss Darcy. My concern is not with your sister, sir, it is with *mine* and her present circumstances. A dreadful situation for which I hold you wholly responsible!'

Darcy was thoroughly confused, the ache in his breast sharpened at the words falling from Elizabeth's lips.

'I have not the pleasure of understanding you.'

'My father's estate, as well you know, is entailed upon my cousin, Mr Collins. Jane has, in the light of Mr Bingley's defection and her subsequent broken heart, succumbed to persuasion and agreed to marry this cousin.'

Broken heart? *His* was the heart that had broken.

Elizabeth grasped the door handle, then turned around. 'For dear, sweet Jane to have agreed to such an attachment is unbearable.' She glowered at Darcy. 'I have no doubt you will see the fruits of your labour in person when next you call upon your aunt, for the engagement is to last until the spring, after which my sister will be shackled to Mr Collins for eternity. Your arrogance, your conceit, and your selfish disdain for the feelings of others have brought Jane to this.'

Darcy's head reeled, his hopes and dreams collapsing around him. Almost in a trance, he stepped forward to stand beside Elizabeth, who held her ground, glaring at him from the fine eyes he so long admired.

How could he turn this around, speak words that would diffuse the situation?

The silence between them swelled; then, Elizabeth pushed open the door.

'If you will excuse me, sir. I find the air out here quite disagreeable.'

Drawing on every reserve as Elizabeth disappeared inside the building, Darcy turned his back on it. How could this have gone so disastrously wrong? The ache in his breast he tried to ignore; pain and disappointment would overcome him later, but as his head spun with the relentless words falling from Elizabeth's lips and...

The click of the latch as the door opened, roused him. She had come back! He swung around, hope filling him.

'Elizabeth! I must explain my—'

He broke off as Miss Elliot fluttered her lashes.

'Mr Darcy.' She smiled coyly. 'You are a little familiar, but it confirms my hopes. What is it you wish to say to me?'

What?

'No! Forgive me, madam. I meant...' Involuntarily, Darcy's gaze drifted beyond the lady into the house, and the expectant smile was wiped from Miss Elliot's face.

'Miss *Bennet* appeared to be in rather a hurry just now.'

Darcy had no reply to this. After all, what was there to say?

'If you will excuse me, ma'am.' He bowed and turned on his heel, walking rapidly back towards the front of the house, desperate to put distance between himself and the disaster of his altercation with Elizabeth.

CHAPTER SEVENTEEN

Elizabeth's emotions were high as she raced through the house, hurrying as quickly as decorum permitted along the corridor to the great hall, where she stopped and drew in a shuddering breath.

How could she have done that? Colour rushed into her face and she put a hand to her cheek.

Because Mr Darcy deserved it.

All the same, he was Lady Catherine de Burgh's nephew. Did he not have the power to make Jane's life even more intolerable? Elizabeth shook her head. How could it possibly become more so? Would it be wise to remain at Kellynch? Her presence always felt somewhat tenuous, but she had insulted Mr Darcy in every possible way, and perhaps his influence would be brought to bear upon her.

A door slammed somewhere in the distance, and Elizabeth hastened her steps, desperate for the sanctuary of her room.

By the time Darcy reached Meadowbrook House, his head pounded, and he took refuge in his study, closing the door behind him with a resounding thud.

Then, he stood stock-still, the rigidity of his frame belying the incessant thoughts spinning around in his head. What, in the name of the *devil*, just happened?

Be calm, Darcy cautioned himself, but the rapid pounding of his heart and the raw anger filling his being fought against him. How could the world present itself the same as when he had left earlier, determined, fired up by his decision, and *excited* almost in his anticipation of claiming Elizabeth as his own? *Elizabeth…*

Darcy almost shied away from the name. Miss Bennet, possessor of his mind, his senses and finally his heart. For weeks now, the woman had filled his thoughts…but he must think of her no more.

The clock on the mantel chimed, and a momentary anguish gripped Darcy, sweeping aside the anger and disbelief that had carried him back to the house. Had all this taken place in so little time? Far from realising his dreams, the past hour had unfolded into a torment of wretched proportions.

He had no desire to see Elizabeth again, wished he had never come to Somersetshire. Why had they not gone further south?

Then, a flare of frustration shot through him as Darcy recalled her unyielding support for Wickham and her defiance of his assessment of her sister's feelings. The lady was quite liberal with her affections where she chose to bestow them. Her fondness for Miss Anne Elliot was also obvious, even under such short acquaintance. Darcy seethed in silence. The lady held no feelings for him other than hatred and disgust.

He did not wish to dwell upon what his *own* feelings had been; they must be forgotten. Elizabeth Bennet did not deserve such honourable sentiments, and certainly not from a gentleman of his consequence…

Yes, he was a gentleman, of excellent character, family, and social standing, and acknowledged by all for his integrity and honesty. How could the lady question his character? How *dare* she?

Darcy's throat felt tight, and he tugged at his neckcloth, unable to shut out Elizabeth's voice.

'Your arrogance, your conceit and your selfish disdain of the feelings of others…'

Ridiculous! Unfounded, totally erroneous accusations and, what is more, a slur on his honour! His conduct was never questioned——*never*! What did *she* comprehend of his worth?

Darcy leaned back against the door; his heart clenched so tightly in his chest he could scarce draw breath. The unspoken proposal and her harsh words smouldered in his gut.

What a damnable day this was!

Elizabeth cooled her face with a damp cloth as she took herself to task. Her anger had all but faded but she felt out of sorts from a combination of embarrassment at having spoken so candidly and frustration that the gentleman seemed to have no interest in the consequences of his past transgressions. Her head felt almost too full for coherent thought, but as she noted the chimes of the nearby church bell, she left her chamber, intent on seeking out Anne before she wondered what had become of her.

Notes from the pianoforte drifted towards Elizabeth as she approached the music room, and slipping inside, she allowed them to wash over her, desperate to soothe her frayed spirits.

'You are out of countenance. What has happened?'

Elizabeth walked slowly across the room as Anne lifted her hands from the keys. What could she say?

'Lizzy?'

'My taking the air did not deliver the hoped for remedy.'

'You seem flustered. Whatever is the matter?' Anne rose from the stool with a concerned air.

'It is nothing.' Elizabeth tried to push aside a tumult of feelings. Had she not vowed to support her friend? 'I am perfectly well. Shall we find somewhere to sit and talk? You can tell me more of your captain if you wish.'

'I think it best you tell me more of what has happened to *you*. Sit with me.'

They settled into the window seat, and Elizabeth strove to push away her anxieties, but Anne's need of her only emphasised her sense of culpability.

'Tell me what it is.' Anne shifted in her seat to face her friend, and Elizabeth pulled a face.

'I had an...argument with him.'

Anne blinked. 'With whom?'

'Mr Darcy. I—I told him what I think of him.' The words tumbled out in a rush.

'He was here at Kellynch? I wonder what his purpose might have been?'

Elizabeth could not care less. 'He appeared on the terrace, just as I went over in my head all Jane had written in her letter. It was not the most fortuitous timing.'

'Oh dear.' Anne bit back on a smile. 'Forgive me, dear Lizzy. I can sense you are uncomfortable enough.'

'I am, though the man does not deserve it. Mr Darcy's scorn for the feelings of others has long raised my ire.' Elizabeth waved a hand. 'He has done a cruel disservice to a...friend, and coupled with Jane's latest news, my indignation overruled my sense, and out it all came.' It sounded so childish when said aloud.

Anne patted Elizabeth's arm soothingly. 'All, as in your sister's situation and your belief his influence upon his friend contributed?'

Elizabeth nodded. 'He owned his actions with pride and conceit, but he is angry with me, and I cannot say it is completely unwarranted.'

There was silence for a moment; then, Anne sent Elizabeth a searching look.

'What set you off in the first place?'

With a huff, Elizabeth got to her feet. 'I felt goaded. He had the effrontery to claim I *must* allow him to—'

'To what?'

Agitated, Elizabeth walked over to the hearth, then spun around.

'I have no idea. I interrupted him. I tried to walk away, to leave.' She threw Anne a pleading look as she paced back across the room. 'I promise, I did, but...' Stopping abruptly, Elizabeth stared at Anne. A vivid recollection of Mr Darcy's expression, of the unfathomable look in his eyes—one she had no familiarity with—assailed her, as did his opening words.

What on earth had he been about to say?

'Lizzy?' Anne rose to stand before her. 'What is it?'

'He said his feelings would not be repressed, that he must tell me something.'

Anne's eyes widened. 'Good heavens! Do you think he meant—'

Unhappy with indulging her curiosity, Elizabeth summoned a smile. She would *not* spare Mr Darcy any further notice.

'It meant nothing. It is likely I misheard him. Shall we indulge in some music? I believe I was charged with the duty of teaching you a duet!'

The remainder of the day passed in a haze and Darcy kept to his study for much of it, knowing his sister was occupied with Mrs Annesley, but before long the evening descended. Staring out of the drawing room window into the blackness, Darcy strove to keep Elizabeth from his thoughts. His earlier burst of anger towards her had abated, replaced with a despair he feared would never leave him.

'Brother?' Georgiana appeared in the doorway and crossed to stand before him. 'Is anything wrong? You are quite strained.'

Darcy shook his head. 'Pay me no mind, my dear. It has been a rather trying day, that is all.

Judgemental, supercilious, and filled with arrogance...'

Darcy winced as Elizabeth's angry face appeared before him again. Was there some truth in her accusations?

He almost jumped as Georgiana took his hand and kissed it.

'Your face is dark as night. What is the good news you were to share on your return?'

The irony was galling.

'I am afraid I was mistaken. I have no good news to impart. Come. It is time we went in for dinner.'

The food would taste like ashes, but he must maintain a pretence of regularity for Georgiana, even as his world was in tatters.

It was not until his sister retired for the night that Darcy could finally release the tight rein he held upon his thoughts.

Dismissing his valet, Darcy roamed his chamber like a caged beast, then dropped into an armchair near the hearth. For a while, he stared into the flames, but then his frame sagged, and his head dropped into his hands.

Elizabeth's dislike and her damning of his character were sufficiently painful to him, but nothing to the devastation coursing through him at the loss of all his recent hopes and dreams.

Darcy leaned back in his seat, then pressed a palm against his pounding forehead. How foolish of him to assume Wickham's tales would antagonise her more than his influence over Bingley.

Sitting up, Darcy narrowed his eyes. Elizabeth had been fierce in her claim of his being mistaken. *Could* he have erred? Had the lady's affections truly been engaged?

No! He made certain to observe Miss Bennet closely and had thus done both the lady and his friend a great service. How could Elizabeth doubt his good intentions?

Darcy's brow furrowed. And what had been her meaning regarding Georgiana and Bingley?

Getting wearily to his feet, Darcy loosened his neckcloth and unbuttoned his waistcoat. How he was to seek repose, he knew not. And how was he to behave when next he saw her? Elizabeth's departure for Hertfordshire could not come soon enough.

You deceive yourself.

It was a truth Darcy owned as he removed his shirt and tossed it onto a chair. The thought of never laying eyes upon Elizabeth Bennet again brought little consolation to his bruised heart.

More snow fell overnight, and Darcy—who had escaped to his study as soon as breakfast was over, Georgiana having gone on a short walk with Mrs Annesley—viewed the day stretching before him with dissatisfaction. How interminable did time seem now? With little effort at resistance, his thoughts swept along the lane to Kellynch.

What might Elizabeth be doing? Did she spare a thought for him at all?

You are ridiculous, Darcy. Why would the lady think of you? Has she not made her view of your person, your character, plain?

Darcy dropped his pen onto the blotter and got impatiently to his feet. Though his anger had indeed been of short duration, he had no doubt the pain and disappointment would linger. The only saving grace—one he had been haunted by through the long night—was the certainty Elizabeth would have refused him, had he been permitted to speak. How thankful was he that the words had never fallen from his lips.

Rejection! A notion so alien to all Darcy had been raised to expect, he simply could not comprehend it.

A tap on the door heralded Mrs Reynolds, who placed the salver of post on his desk.

'A note has come from the Hall, sir. The boy did not wait for a reply.' She pointed to the folded paper on top of the pile. 'Shall I send in more tea?'

Darcy examined the note, before raising his eyes to his housekeeper.

'No, thank you. I shall be going out directly.'

Anne and Elizabeth had taken to the long gallery again after breaking their fast, the cold wind convincing them to remain indoors.

Although Elizabeth's dissatisfaction with Mr Darcy had not abated in its entirety, Anne's soothing voice and calm demeanour worked upon her vexation much as Jane's was wont to do.

'You are good for me, Anne.' Elizabeth smiled warmly at her friend. 'I will do as you suggest and ask my aunt if Jane can visit them for a few days before they travel to Longbourn for the Christmas season. Thankfully, Mr Collins can ill be spared from his parish at this time of year, so his stay should be of short duration. Distance and Aunt Gardiner's good sense may prevail upon Jane yet, though I fear it is all too late.' Elizabeth sighed. 'I have been selfish, indulging my own low spirits with little regard for yours. You said you still had trouble sleeping.'

'I am a little weary. It is not a new sensation, to have Frederick in mind. Only now, it is sharpened, as though our parting has happened all over again.'

'Do you'—Elizabeth hesitated, welcoming the change of subject from her own obsessive thoughts—'Were you fortunate enough to have a likeness of him?'

Anne shook her head as they turned their steps back along the gallery. 'It was promised, but we were parted before he could have one done.' She stared ahead, and Elizabeth suspected her mind was years away. 'After he left, I was glad I had no permanent reminder. I did not feel I warranted the consolation, so badly did I feel my guilt for being persuaded away from him. I thought perhaps I might forget him, or at least his features, over time. With no miniature to savour, and few letters…' She sighed. 'We were only parted once, for but a few days, during the short months of our acquaintance, so any correspondence was of a trifling nature.'

'You cherish it, all the same?'

'Of course. Yet'—there was a tremor in Anne's voice—'I can see him as clearly in my mind's eye today as I could then. I am comforted by it, that he has not become some faceless memory, but it pains me also.'

Elizabeth put an arm around Anne. 'Let us go to the small sitting room. Perhaps your cook, Mrs Howard, will prepare us a hot toddy, and you shall talk to your heart's content about your captain.'

Darcy had no idea what the matter of business was that had persuaded Sir Walter Elliot to request he call on him at his earliest convenience, but it at least provided him with a purpose. The fact it meant calling at the Hall was hardly conducive to peace of mind, however, for each step reminded him of the walk there on the previous day and how high Darcy's expectations had been, not only of bringing his plans to fruition, but also of the happiness it would have brought, both to him and Elizabeth.

Disgusted with himself for indulging in such false hopes, Darcy marched along, lost in his thoughts until he discerned the sound of a conveyance making its sedentary way along the lane, the clip clop of the horses' hooves, and the rumbling of the carriage wheels muffled by the cushion of snow. He stepped up onto the verge, lifting his hat at the gentleman peering out of the window, but the carriage slowed to a halt as the driver turned in his seat.

'Begging your pardon, sir. Be this the direction for Kellynch Hall? The road markers are all but unreadable.'

Darcy replaced his hat and pointed ahead. 'Around this corner, then a little further on. You will see the gates on your left.'

The driver urged the horses onward, and Darcy continued his introspective march along the lane. If Sir Walter had an unexpected caller, then perhaps he could escape his own meeting?

His desire to avoid seeing Elizabeth wavered as the tautness in his breast intensified. How could he *not* wish to lay eyes upon her? Harsh though her words had been, they could not extinguish his ardent love for her so easily.

Fetching up at the gates to the long driveway, Darcy noted the carriage pulling up in front of the house. Whatever this business of Sir Walter's was, it could be of little importance. He would allow the stranger to enter, then Darcy would present his card and indicate his return the following day.

'I am merely using you as a distraction, you understand.' Elizabeth smirked as she and Anne made their way down the stairs. 'I wish to spare no further thought for Mr Darcy today. Instead, I shall learn all about Captain Wentworth from one who knew him best.'

'And loved him best.'

Elizabeth took Anne's arm fondly as they walked along the corridor. 'That too.'

They were but a few steps from the great hall when raised voices drifted towards them.

Anne and Elizabeth exchanged a look.

'That is Mr Darcy's voice.' Elizabeth's irritation returned. What was his obsession with being at Kellynch Hall?

'I will not have it. He cannot come here.' Sir Walter sounded angry.

'Sir, where would you have me take him?' A stranger's voice this time. 'He has spoken but two words and one of them was Kellynch.'

There was silence for a second, and Elizabeth frowned at Anne. 'Should we find another way?'

Anne shook her head. 'Father is in a temper. He will likely not heed us passing.'

They rounded the corner into the great hall, and Elizabeth followed Anne as she skirted past the three men in the centre of the room: Sir Walter, red-faced and indignant, a stranger who was equally red-faced, and Mr Darcy, whom Elizabeth pointedly ignored.

'Let it be understood! No sailor will cross my threshold, least of all one called Wentworth.'

CHAPTER EIGHTEEN

Elizabeth turned to stare at Anne, whose shoulders stiffened. What strangeness was this?

'Wentworth?' Anne spoke faintly, and Elizabeth put a supporting hand under her friend's elbow as she walked unsteadily towards the men.

'Did you say Wentworth?' Anne's voice hitched, but the stranger looked over with relief.

'Yes, ma'am. A Captain Wentworth. Badly injured, pulled from the ice-cold sea.'

'Alive? I cannot believe it!' Anne wilted against Elizabeth, who put both arms around her and held tight. Involuntarily, her gaze flew to Mr Darcy, but he seemed as bewildered as she.

'Sir'—the stranger turned back to Sir Walter—'I beg of you, as an emissary of the Navy, give the man shelter and a fighting chance. His injury may well do for him, but at least let him die in peace, not on the road.'

'If he is to die, then so be it. He is no loss to me.'

A whimper came from Anne. 'Where is he?' She spoke so distantly, only Elizabeth heard her, or so she thought, but Mr

Darcy took in Anne's distressed state, before turning back to the stranger.

'Take him to Meadowbrook House. It is but a mile back down the lane.' He turned to Sir Walter. 'You will not object, sir.' It was not a request, but the gentleman's colour deepened, and he began a spluttering protest.

Mr Darcy, however, much to Elizabeth's surprise, ignored him, addressing the newcomer instead. 'There is no fever?'

The man shook his head. 'Captain Wentworth suffered no open wounds but took a severe blow to his head. He was pulled aboard another ship, along with a handful of survivors. At first, he drifted in and out of consciousness, which permitted the intake of some fluids, but the captain has not roused once since before the journey here commenced, and if he remains insensible, he will fade rapidly.'

'If you would be so good as to accompany the gentleman. My housekeeper will summon a surgeon. Rest assured, he will be well cared for until…'

Elizabeth held Anne even tighter as a sob escaped her lips.

'Wait. You said he spoke but two words upon his rescue.' Sir Walter glared at the stranger. 'Can you not take him to this other place?'

The man shook his head. 'I would, sir, but it is not a place. He spoke only of Kellynch and a name: Anne.'

Anne swayed in Elizabeth's arms.

'I must go to him.' Her voice was weak, but the emissary nodded. 'Where is he?'

'In the carriage out front, ma'am, but…'

Wrenching herself from Elizabeth's grasp, Anne fled towards the door, and Elizabeth did not hesitate, breaking into a run—propriety be damned—and reaching the carriage standing on the gravel sweep just as the coachman opened the door for Anne to clamber inside.

An anguished cry came, and Elizabeth hurried over and peered into the small space. Anne fell to her knees beside the prone figure lying awkwardly across one of the benches. The gentleman was too tall for it, his legs half off the seat, though clearly, he was unheeding of the fact.

'Frederick!' Anne's voice broke as she grasped his nearest hand. 'You said my name…' Tears began to stream down her face as she lowered her head, her body shaking.

Elizabeth leaned forward and placed a comforting hand on Anne's back.

'Take hope, Anne. You thought all was lost.' Her friend did not answer, continuing to cling to the captain's lifeless hand and weep. 'Mr Darcy will ensure he has the best possible care.'

Elizabeth blinked. Where on earth had *that* sentiment come from?

The words seemed to reach Anne, however, and she raised her head, wiped her tears, and turned to Elizabeth.

'Do you think…Is it possible Frederick may come round in time?'

'Anything is possible.' Elizabeth hesitated, glancing guiltily at ailing sick man, knowing she must be honest. 'You must prepare for the worst, for what you already believed to have happened, but there is hope as long as he breathes.'

Anne raised a tentative hand and brushed a thick lock of hair from the captain's forehead, which bore testimony to the blow it had taken. Leaning forward, she placed a gentle kiss upon it, and Elizabeth felt tears prick her eyes. It was a poignant moment and a far better farewell for her friend than never seeing the captain again.

'Frederick...' Anne's voice was a whisper, and Elizabeth leaned forward.

'Speak a little louder. If you were in his thoughts when last he was conscious, your voice may reach him wherever he is.'

'Er, excuse me, ma'am?'

Elizabeth looked up. The stranger was at the open door.

'You are fortunate in your neighbour. I must get Captain Wentworth to Meadowbrook House as a matter of urgency, that the medical man may be summoned.' He raised a folded piece of paper. 'I have instructions from the gentleman for his housekeeper.'

'I wish to go with him.' Anne clung tighter to the stricken man's hand. 'I cannot leave him. I will not.'

Elizabeth frowned. What was she to do? Anne's determination to withstand any family opposition to following her heart a mile down the road was evident, but Elizabeth could hardly enter Mr Darcy's home uninvited in the present circumstances!

Darcy stepped out onto the portico. His confusion over who this Captain Wentworth might be and why Miss Anne Elliot reacted so strongly had soon been answered by a terse explanation from Sir Walter and his eldest, when she joined them. The gentleman's aversion to accommodating the injured man was thus explained, but his lack of compassion was not. How could anyone be so unfeeling of any human soul in such a condition?

Taking in the scene before him, Darcy assumed his habitual mask as Elizabeth aided her friend from the carriage, determined no indication of his admiration would escape him. His heart was less obliging, clenching in his breast and drawing an involuntary hand.

'Anne Elliot! You forget yourself. Come here at once.' Sir Walter stepped forward to stand beside Darcy.

The lady's skin was pale but her expression firm as she walked up to her father, Elizabeth by her side.

'I am staying with Captain Wentworth, Father, and I shall not be persuaded otherwise.'

Sir Walter looked astounded, his mouth open and closing like a stranded fish. 'You'—he huffed a breath, then blustered on—'you overreach yourself, Anne. The man was beneath you then. He is beneath you now, and undeserving of any particular attention. Besides, why can his brother not care for him?'

'Mr Wentworth has left the district, as well you know, Father.' Anne raised her chin as Elizabeth grasped her hand. 'To send Frederick onward in his condition would be inhumane.'

'For heaven's sake!' Miss Elliot emerged from the building. 'Why must you, Miss Anne Elliot of Kellynch, daughter of a baronet, no less, be reduced to nursing a sick man? There are people paid to do such chores. It will reflect badly upon us. We have a name to uphold, and—'

'Sir Walter.' Elizabeth's interruption drew Darcy's attention almost against his will, and he strove not to admire her fine eyes as they fixed upon Sir Walter. 'If Mr Darcy permits'—she looked to Darcy. Did she seek his approval?—'I can be at Anne's side throughout the duration of...' She hesitated, and Darcy knew she comprehended as well as he the likely outcome for the captain. 'There is no infection in the case, so your daughter's attendance upon the gentleman will affect no one adversely.'

'Gentleman?' Sir Walter all but spat the word. 'He is a sailor, not a *gentleman*.'

Elizabeth's eyes flashed. 'Captain Wentworth is one of His Majesty's naval officers, sir, and it is our Christian duty and our obligation to the Crown to care for him.'

Darcy wished he could applaud. Instead, he turned to Sir Walter.

'Miss Bennet will be the most fitting person to be with your daughter. I will send for medical advice, and my housekeeper is more than competent. Miss Anne will not be required to do anything beyond be present.'

'But a single young woman staying in a room with such a man! It is unseemly.'

'With Miss Bennet in attendance and my sister's companion, Mrs Annesley, also on hand, the lady will be more than adequately chaperoned.'

Sir Walter harrumphed, then turned back to Anne. 'I am vexed beyond measure by your unfathomable behaviour, but never let it be said I am not an indulgent father.'

A small sound escaped from Elizabeth, but Darcy kept his attention firmly on Sir Walter. He, however, turned his narrowed eyes upon the lady.

'It goes without saying, Anne must never be alone. You understand, Miss Bennet? It is time you were the companion I have always believed you to be.'

Elizabeth inclined her head. 'As you wish, sir. You will be unsurprised to know you have likewise, in this time of crisis, shown yourself to be what I always believed *you* to be.'

Anne turned to Darcy, her usually mild eyes deep with feeling. 'May I go to Meadowbrook House directly, sir?'

Darcy looked to the emissary. 'Are you able to convey Miss Elliot?'

The gentleman bowed. 'There is room only for one, but if you will allow me, ma'am?' He offered an arm to Anne, who took it.

'Lizzy?'

'I will follow on foot. Let me first gather our pelisses for the return walk.'

Sir Walter glared at Darcy as the carriage pulled slowly away. 'You have been part of ruining my day, sir.'

Darcy raised a brow. 'I am sorry to hear it, sir.'

'Father!' To Darcy's surprise, Miss Elliot sent him a condescending smile before turning back to Sir Walter. 'You mistake Mr Darcy. Has he not been of the utmost assistance in removing any obligation for us to take that man in? We ought to be grateful to him, do you not think?'

'What? Hmm, I see your point. Well, you can redeem yourself, sir. Let us now attend to this matter of business.'

'You will have to excuse me, Sir Walter. I have a duty to go to Meadowbrook House to ensure all is done for the injured man. I shall return later, if that is convenient?'

Sir Walter scowled, then gestured at the footman who hovered by the door. 'Bring a fresh bottle of brandy to my study! Well, go on, man!'

The footman scurried away and Sir Walter stalked back into the house.

'It is all too disagreeable, Mr Darcy. But at least we may assume the situation will persist for a short while only.' Miss Elliot spoke in her usual languid tone, but Darcy merely bowed. He needed a moment to collect himself, to prepare.

Elizabeth hurried into the house, bent upon retrieving cloaks and gloves for herself and her friend, and Darcy tried to marshal his thoughts.

So much for distancing himself from Elizabeth. She was to spend the remainder of the day under his own roof.

❦

'Oh!'

The involuntary exclamation fell from Elizabeth's lips as she emerged from the front door once more, a laden basket upon her arm.

She hoped—nay, fully expected—Mr Darcy to have left, but there he was, turning from his contemplation of who knew what, his expression uncompromising.

Without a word, he held out a hand for the basket, but Elizabeth merely stared at him. Did he truly intend to walk with her, given all that had occurred the previous day?

'I am perfectly capable—'

'Did I say anything to the contrary, Miss Bennet?' Mr Darcy threw her a frustrated look. 'I cannot allow you to bear the weight of it over such a distance.'

Elizabeth moved aside to take the step down onto the gravel sweep, but with an exclamation from the gentleman, he tugged the basket firmly from her grasp and set off down the driveway.

She glared after him, then followed, taking a small skip every so often in an attempt to catch up. The basket would indeed have become quite the burden, but Elizabeth was in no humour for his acting the gentleman.

Her step faltered. She was accustomed to holding Mr Darcy in little esteem, but in the time it had taken for Elise to fold Anne's pelisse and add further items to the basket, she had been unable to shake a sense of confusion over him. His gallantry and compassion in permitting a sick stranger to be taken into his home spoke volumes, but this conflicted with all Elizabeth knew him to be. Or did it truly?

179

Mr Darcy reached the gates, and he turned to wait for her, so she hurried her steps. They made silent progress along the lane at first, and Elizabeth assumed he preferred it that way. He was, after all, prone to being taciturn, and this was hardly a social occasion.

Elizabeth tried not to dwell upon all that had been said between them, conscious of the gentleman constraining his stride, being merely a pace ahead. Thoughts most naturally fell upon Anne and the implications of the captain's sudden arrival. It was evident his chances were slim, but what if he were to recover?

Whichever direction the Fates took Captain Wentworth, Anne would likely need Elizabeth for the foreseeable future, and with no wish to curtail her visit—a full se'nnight of which remained—she accepted it might be best if she tried to clear the air.

'Mr Darcy!'

The gentleman slowed further, though he did not turn around, and Elizabeth hurried to fall into step beside him, unsure how to begin.

'Miss Bennet? You had something further to say?'

'We have angered each other.'

'And you have more you wish to add?' Mr Darcy's tone did not encourage, but Elizabeth persevered.

'No, sir. It is…in the circumstances, with this new development and my friend needing my companionship, I wondered if…'

'We both know how to conduct ourselves, madam.'

Elizabeth felt she could well contradict Mr Darcy on this, but her situation was precarious enough.

'In the circumstances, it is an imposition for me to enter your home.'

'Is it?'

She raised her brows. Was it not?

'Whatever you may think of me, Miss Bennet'—Mr Darcy's voice was clipped, and he continued to stare ahead—'I do have compassion. This gentleman is in need and unable to ask for help. Providing a safe place for him to pass his remaining days is the least I can do. From the little I have seen and heard, the captain was once of some importance to Miss Anne Elliot. It would be uncharitable to prevent her from being by his side at such a time.' He threw Elizabeth an assessing glance. 'She wished you with her.'

'Aye. And I'll wager you wished me the other side of the country.' Perhaps she should not have spoken so, but surely it must be the truth?

'If it were so, I would hardly be escorting you to my home, Miss Bennet. It is the only *right* thing to do.'

Elizabeth had no response to this, but then Mr Darcy spoke again.

'There is one thing I wish to know. Will you permit me one question raised by our conversation yesterday?'

She almost laughed. 'You are generous, Mr Darcy, in calling it that.' Uncertain where this might lead, however, she clasped her hands together. 'Do, please ask, and I shall endeavour to reply.'

'Your inference of there being an understanding between my sister and my friend concerns me. If there are rumours to this effect, I would be grateful if you would take no heed of them. Protecting Georgiana's reputation is of the utmost importance to me.'

With mixed feelings, Elizabeth studied the chimneys of Meadowbrook House as they came into view above the hedgerows. Thankful though she was that, of all the words thrown about on the previous day, this was what he wished to speak of, she also appreciated her own indiscretion.

'Forgive me, Mr Darcy. I spoke out of turn. I have heard no general rumours, but...' Elizabeth hesitated. Ought she to reveal her source?

The gentleman stopped, and perforce, Elizabeth did too. Mr Darcy turned to face her, his countenance unreadable.

'You would not fabricate such a thing.'

'Never!' Elizabeth drew in a short breath. 'It was presented as almost a fait accompli to my sister, Jane, recently, and with it so intrinsically connected to her unfortunate situation—of which I had but that morning received news—I spoke without caution.' She raised wary eyes to his. 'As you may have noticed.'

Mr Darcy regarded her silently. Then, he resumed walking and Elizabeth did likewise.

'I will not ask you for your source, Miss Bennet, for I believe I can guess. Suffice it to say, my sister is only recently turned sixteen and not yet out. I do not envisage her seeking an establishment for the foreseeable future.'

'I was unguarded, sir, and regret that the words were spoken.'

'We shall speak of it no more.' He paused, then added. 'The entire conversation is to be forgot.'

Elizabeth blinked. She doubted she would *ever* forget it. 'Must you always have your own way, sir?'

To her surprise, Mr Darcy stopped again, his shoulders stiffening. Then, he drew in a visible breath as he looked at her. 'If you believe I have had my own way lately, then you are much mistaken, madam.'

The look upon his features was unfathomable, but Elizabeth could not help but smile. 'You did win the battle of the basket, Mr Darcy.'

The gentleman closed his eyes briefly, the edges of his mouth twitching, before he set off again. 'I believe you would charge me with selfishness again, Miss Bennet.'

Elizabeth winced but persevered as they approached the gates to Meadowbrook House. 'Will you not enlighten me?'

Mr Darcy gestured with his free arm. 'We are in public, are we not? No gentleman would be seen walking empty handed beside a lady bearing a burden. Just think of the damage to his reputation.'

Elizabeth laughed, but then she sobered, assailed by a myriad of emotions as she saw Anne hovering beside the carriage, and she hurried forward as fast as her skirts permitted.

CHAPTER NINETEEN

Mrs Reynolds had done all Darcy had asked of her in his note, sending for a surgeon without delay and deploying a maid to ready a chamber for the sick man.

With the aid of two footmen and a flat board, they conveyed the captain up the stairs, and Darcy left his housekeeper to bring tea for Elizabeth and her friend in the drawing room before seeking out his sister.

He found Georgiana in the small parlour she had taken to using.

'Fitz! I did not realise the time.' She put aside her book, and Darcy indicated they take the chairs beside the hearth. 'How is it we have an injured naval man in our home?'

Darcy briefly explained what had occurred. It was no task to spare the details, for he had so few.

'Poor Miss Anne Elliot.' Georgiana's sympathy was obvious. 'And poor Captain Wentworth. How is it they are acquainted?'

'I believe they were once...' Darcy's voice failed him. Betrothed. Much as he had anticipated being only the day before.

'Brother? Is there anything wrong? You are pale and drawn.'

Darcy shook his head. 'Pay me no mind, my dear. It has been a rather trying day thus far. Miss Anne Elliot was once engaged to the captain. I know not the reasons for their separation, but it is evident the lady is extremely distressed by the gentleman's prognosis.'

'Could she not stay here, to be with him until the end? It seems unkind for her to have to leave, for she may not be there when...' Georgiana stopped. 'How terribly sad.'

His sister was right; it was both sad and cruel, and Darcy ought to be feeling for Anne and her captain rather than wallowing in his own despair.

Your selfish disdain for the feelings of others...

Darcy winced as Elizabeth's words struck him anew. Then, he felt Georgiana take his hand as she came to kneel beside his chair.

'Fitz, your face is alarming me. I feel your sorrow for the poor man and his fate, but you must not dwell upon it.'

Recalling himself, Darcy gave Georgiana's hand a squeeze before releasing it and getting to his feet.

'I am quite well. We must await the surgeon's verdict, but there is little to be done unless the captain awakens soon.'

'I am grieved.' Georgiana followed Darcy as he crossed over to a writing desk. 'Do you require Mrs Annesley to act as chaperone? I am well able to spare her.'

Taking a seat, Darcy was assailed by conflicting emotions over Elizabeth being in his house.

'Miss Bennet attends Miss Elliot, and we can provide a servant to be in the room if need be.' Georgiana came to stand by his side. 'The captain is hardly in a position to compromise a lady, my dear.'

'I know, Fitz.' Georgiana watched him select a pen and dip it in the ink. 'Are you writing to Richard?'

'I promised Miss Anne Elliot I would send word to Mr Wentworth—the captain's brother—of his being brought here. The reverend believes him to have perished but has since left the district.'

'Is there any chance he will discover his brother's situation before it is too late to wait upon him?'

'The news will have to await him in Shropshire, for it is the only known direction. I believe he was to be married today and travelling north to the Lakes before taking up his new living.' Darcy summoned a smile for his sister. 'We must have faith, Georgie. As long as the captain breathes, hope remains.'

As Darcy set pen to paper, his sister returned to her seat, and he penned his missive whilst his mind grappled with the captain's situation. If only the timing had not been so unfortunate, Captain Wentworth would have been able to go to Monkford and have kin around him in these final hours.

Sitting back in his seat, Darcy set the pen aside. Perhaps the man was not so ill-served as he supposed. Despite the separation of so many years, Miss Anne Elliot's devotion could not be questioned.

Darcy reached for the seal, then fell back in his seat as sadness gripped him once more. Would his passion and admiration for Elizabeth haunt him indefinitely also?

Welcome though the tea tray had been, and warming as the brightly burning fire was, Anne's mind remained in turmoil.

'I struggle to comprehend all that has come about. First, Frederick has perished at sea. Then, he has not. In his conscious ramblings, he speaks my name and arrives at Kellynch. Now'—Anne's voice hitched–'even now, he lies upstairs in a stranger's home for what may be his final hours, unaware of *all* of this.'

'It is a great deal to assimilate, dear Anne. It is no wonder you are conflicted.' Elizabeth pointed to the teapot. Would you care for more?'

Anne shook her head. 'I cannot face it.' She willed the door to open and bring intelligence of Frederick's condition. 'Why would he say my name?'

Elizabeth leaned towards Anne and took her hand briefly. 'Perchance you were his last conscious thought?'

'If only it were so.' Anne's cheeks became chalk white as a hand shot to her throat. 'Oh, Lizzy!' She turned frantic eyes on her friend. 'He said 'Kellynch' too. His memories of my home cannot be good ones. He must have recalled an awful time in his life as he felt his own near its end. I do not think I can bear it.'

Elizabeth put an arm about her. 'Take one moment at a time, dear Anne. Be thankful he has been brought home to England and will be assured the best of medical care for as long as he may need it.'

Holding back impending tears, Anne knew Elizabeth was right. She must be grateful for the small mercy of seeing Frederick once more, of having gained her point with her father over attending him.

'You are wise, Lizzy. I shall do my best to take comfort from seeing Frederick again, of being able to hold his hand in mine, and I shall endeavour—'

They both started as the door opened, and Mr Darcy came into the room.

Getting a little unsteadily to her feet beside Elizabeth, Anne grasped her friend's hand tightly.

'The surgeon—a Mr Parker, from Martock—has examined the captain and left. The gentleman is as well as should be expected after such a journey, but he remains unconscious and with no sign of waking at present.'

The tightness in Anne's throat threatened to overwhelm her, and Elizabeth seemed to sense her struggle, picking up the conversation.

'Has he given any indication, sir? Any hint of what we may expect?'

'Mr Parker has made the captain as comfortable as he could but said there was little aid he could offer. He says the blow to the captain's head must have been severe, but he believes there is no fracture and the contusion, though extensive, is already beginning to fade. An apothecary will be best placed to provide the care Captain Wentworth requires.' He smiled kindly at Anne. 'I understand our man is a Mr Robinson, and a note has already been despatched to request his services.'

Anne felt as though she clung to Mr Darcy's words like a drowning man takes hold of a life raft.

'There, Anne. All is as well as we can expect for now.' Elizabeth's spoke gently. 'An apothecary will likely provide a stimulating tincture or some such, it may rouse the captain.' She addressed the gentleman. 'Anne had hoped to sit with Captain Wentworth for a while, sir. Is it possible?'

Mr Darcy inclined his head. 'I will ask Mrs Reynolds to show you to him. I can place a servant at your disposal.'

Anne's grip on Elizabeth's hand tightened. 'Lizzy will be with me.' She noted the strained look Mr Darcy sent her friend before walking over to pull the bell. 'I hope you comprehend, sir, how much I appreciate your taking Captain Wentworth under this roof until...' Anne faltered, then added, 'I shall never forget your kindness.'

'Please, do not speak of it. I take no credit for doing what is right.' The door opened to reveal the housekeeper. 'Mrs Reynolds, would you be so kind as to show Miss Elliot and Miss Bennet to the captain's room? Excuse me, ladies. I must return to Kellynch.'

Mr Darcy turned on his heel and left the room, and Anne and Elizabeth exchanged a quick glance before joining the housekeeper who led them out into the hall.

'May I ask after Miss Darcy?' Elizabeth addressed Mrs Reynolds as they mounted the stairs. 'We would not wish her to be distressed by all this.'

'It is kind of you to enquire, Miss Bennet. She is well and Mr Darcy has explained the situation.'

They were soon on the landing, and Mrs Reynolds pushed open a door into a pleasant room, with ample light streaming in through the windows and a fire crackling warmly in the grate. A servant rose from a seat beside the bed, placing a damp cloth onto a tray bearing a pitcher and bowl of water.

'Greening, you may return to your duties for now.'

As the servant left the room, Mrs Reynolds invited Anne to take the seat beside the bed, and Elizabeth took an armchair a short distance away.

'Ring the bell'—Mrs Reynolds pointed to the pull rope on the wall beside the mantel—'should you need anything or there is any alteration in the gentleman's condition.'

Silence settled upon the room, only disturbed by the arrival of a kitchen maid with more tea, and although Elizabeth placed a cup by Anne, beyond a whispered 'thank you' they did not speak for some time.

Elizabeth was soon lost in her thoughts. Mr Darcy was a conundrum, one moment angering her beyond reason, the next displaying a strong compassion for his fellow man and—

'I believe Frederick's breathing improves. It was weaker when we first arrived, I am certain of it.'

Coming to stand beside her friend, Elizabeth watched for movement of the sheet as the captain's chest rose and fell. In truth, it was barely discernible.

'I cannot believe I am here with him.' With a hesitant hand, Anne reached out to touch the injured man's hair before tentatively running a finger down the side of his face. 'This shadowy growth brings me comfort. It is a sign of life.'

'It is indeed. Talk to him, Anne. Let the captain hear your voice.'

Elizabeth returned to her chair and the afternoon passed with them exchanging a little conversation now and again but with no alteration in the captain beyond the indistinct movement of the sheet.

Anne kept up a low-voiced monologue, and Elizabeth drifted back into thought, her mind grappling with her fluctuating emotions towards Mr Darcy. His anger from yesterday seemed all but gone, but there was a strange mindfulness about him, a constraint to his regard, as though fearful he might display something he would rather not.

Unbidden, Mr Darcy's words seared through Elizabeth's mind.

What on earth had been his meaning? Then, warmth flooded her cheeks. Surely it could not be so simple as it implied?

'No,' she whispered. 'That would be unfathomable.'

Despite the admonishment, however, the memory of the gentleman's expression as he spoke returned, and she—

'Here we are.' Elizabeth started and looked up as Mrs Reynolds swept into the room, a gentleman in her wake. 'Mr Robinson is arrived to treat the patient.'

The newcomer placed a worn leather bag on a table before walking over to study the lifeless captain. Then, he turned around.

'Ladies, if you would be so kind as to leave the room? Mrs Reynolds, if you would assist?'

Darcy felt no real obligation to wait upon Sir Walter, but as he would rather be where Elizabeth was not, it was a welcome reason to escape from Meadowbrook House.

He took himself to task on the walk back to Kellynch. His confrontation with Elizabeth had happened; it could not be undone, and he must stand by his earlier declaration to the lady. It must be forgot; *all* of it. Regulating his mind with the aid of occupation was assumed; restraining his stubborn heart, however, was entirely another matter.

'Damned foolishness,' Darcy muttered as he took the step up to the imposing portico and rapped on the door.

The butler let him into the house, showing him into the great hall just as Miss Elliot sailed into the room.

'Good afternoon, Mr Darcy.' She curtsied elegantly, and Darcy performed a cursory bow.

'Miss Elliot.'

'It was unfortunate you had to leave earlier. My father wished to speak to you on a matter of some urgency.' She waved an imperious hand to dismiss the butler and took hold of Darcy's arm.

He gently but firmly released his arm from her grip, and the lady's gaze narrowed.

'As I am aware. If you will excuse me, ma'am, I shall await your father here.'

With that, Darcy walked over to the bookshelves lining the far wall and began ostensibly perusing the titles, relieved to hear the swish of Miss Elliot's skirts as she swept from the great hall.

She returned directly with her father in tow, who strode over to Darcy.

'Come, sir. We have business to discuss.' Sir Walter reeked of brandy.

'I cannot fathom what possible business could concern us both, Sir Walter.' Darcy replaced the book he held and turned back, but the gentleman already walked away.

'My study, Darcy, if you would be so obliging.'

Obliging Sir Walter was the last thing Darcy felt inclined towards, but the desire for distraction was genuine and his curiosity got the better of him. He would give the gentleman five minutes of his time, and then he would go on an extensive walk before returning to Meadowbrook House.

The apothecary promised to return to pass the night at the captain's side but warned that the next six and thirty hours would deliver one outcome or another. If the injured man did not regain consciousness soon, there was little the apothecary could do to change the inevitable path down which Captain Wentworth seemed destined to tread.

Elizabeth and Anne lingered for the rest of the afternoon in the sick room, but there was no alteration in the gentleman, his shallow breathing sometimes the only sound to be heard when Anne's voice trailed away.

She grew wan and forlorn as the day faded and no further signs of life came from the captain, whose hand Anne clasped unceasingly. It therefore took all of Elizabeth's efforts to persuade her from the gentleman's bedside, but the impending dusk finally convinced Anne she could linger no longer.

It was a solemn walk back to Kellynch, but with Anne wrapped in her reflections, Elizabeth's mind returned to the inconsistency of her fluctuating sentiments towards Mr Darcy and growing puzzlement over his words possibly meaning what they hinted at.

'Will you keep me company until dinner, Lizzy? I do not wish to be alone with my thoughts just now.'

'Yes, of course.' Elizabeth welcomed the proposal as she followed Anne into the house. She had no desire to be alone with her own either, for they did not serve her well.

No sooner had they entered the great hall, however, when Sir Walter appeared.

'Anne. I wish to speak to you. Come.'

Anne exchanged a look with Elizabeth as Sir Walter headed for his study. 'I will meet you in the small sitting room, Lizzy.'

With a troubled heart, Elizabeth watched Anne disappear down the corridor in her father's wake. How much longer could her friend endure this strain?

Dusk had fallen before Darcy could face returning home, though he left Kellynch Hall within a half hour of his arrival. Walking for miles around the estate had done little to shed the feelings assailing him, however, and when he reached Meadowbrook House, he stood for a moment, staring at its benign façade.

Was Elizabeth still within? Then, Darcy assessed the darkening skies. No, she would have returned to Kellynch. Frustrated to feel disappointment instead of relief, he strode towards the boot room. This was no time for such indulgence.

Ten minutes later, Darcy prowled the house in search of his sister. Mrs Annesley had last seen her in the music room, but it was empty, as was the drawing room, the small parlour, and the breakfast room.

Heading upstairs, Darcy hesitated as he reached the door to his sister's chamber, but then it swung open.

'Fitz! I thought I heard a step.' Georgiana raised her cheek for his kiss, and he followed her into the room, wishing they were anywhere but Somersetshire.

What hellish sort of week was this? Firstly, Elizabeth's damning of his character, then...

'Fitz?'

Marshalling his thoughts, Darcy took the chair opposite his sister, fixing her with a keen look.

'Forgive me, my dear, but there is a matter we must discuss. I am going to be brutally candid, and by return, I expect full and open honesty from you. You do understand, Georgie? I would not ask it of you in such a way if it were not of the utmost importance.'

The colour drained from Georgiana's face, but she nodded. 'You are scaring me, Brother. But, yes, I understand, and I promise to speak the truth.'

'Are you still...does your attachment to George Wickham endure?'

A deep pink filled Georgiana's cheeks, and she lowered her head.

'Dearest?' Darcy tried to soften his voice, though impatience for an answer gripped him. 'I do not wish to pain you, but it is imperative I understand the truth. Be not afraid of speaking honestly. Do you remain enamoured of the man?'

Georgiana's head shot up. 'No! How could you think so? I am ashamed of my foolish inclination and could not regret it more.'

Much as he did not wish to distress his sister, Darcy knew he must press on.

'But you keep a letter from him between the pages of your book.'

At this, Georgiana leapt to her feet, and Darcy stood too, stepping forward to take her hands in his.

'Please, Georgie. Tell me the truth.'

Her eyes pleaded, and Darcy's ire stirred. If that scoundrel did still have a hold upon her, he did not want to be accountable for his actions, should Wickham ever cross his path.

'It is not what you think.' Georgiana spoke urgently, holding tight onto Darcy's hands. 'I promise you. I merely keep the letter to remind me, daily, not how much I loved him, but never to fall again for such false promises. I do not attend to its content, it is but a marker for my book, but it is also an abiding reinforcement of my foolishness and gullibility.' Her voice broke on the last word, and Darcy released her hands and put an arm around her, holding her close.

'I know what it cost you to save me, Brother.' Georgiana's voice was muffled against his coat, and Darcy lowered his head to better hear her. 'I have lived with the guilt these past months, learnt a lesson I wish never to forget.'

Georgiana straightened up, and he released his hold on her as she took a step back to peep up at him. Her eyes were no longer full of guilt. 'I have no feelings for George Wickham other than hatred and distrust.'

Much as Elizabeth Bennet feels for me…

He cleared his throat. 'Thank you for your honesty, Georgie. Forgive me for forcing it from you.' He dropped a kiss on her cheek. 'I am immensely proud of you.'

Georgiana sat as Darcy reclaimed his own seat, wishing he felt as at ease as he usually did when sitting there.

'I am so relieved, Brother.' Georgiana gestured towards the small pile of books on her bedside table. 'I could not work out what had happened to it, other than it must have fallen from the pages. I have been searching everywhere for it.' Her relief was obvious. 'I did not realise you had found the letter.'

'I did not.'

A hand flew to Georgiana's throat. 'Oh no! Please tell me it was Mrs Reynolds, not one of the other servants who…' Her voice faded as Darcy shook his head.

How he hated to do this to her.

'It was Miss Elliot.' Darcy spoke through clenched teeth, his recent interview with the lady and Sir Walter burning through his brain.

'Miss *Elliot*? But how…when…?'

'When she paid her call upon us. You had retired to your chamber to rest after the ladies visited, do you remember?' To Darcy, it seemed a lifetime ago. 'Miss Elliot returned with a request for a carriage to take her home. I was bound for Yeovil and bade her await me in the drawing room. I can only assume she discovered it then.'

Georgiana's face reflected her horror. 'She did not…she would not *read* it?' Darcy's expression must have confirmed the truth of it. 'How *dare* she?'

'How indeed.'

'But—' Georgiana frowned. 'Brother, how do you know of this?'

Darcy rose from his seat and strode over to the window. 'When I was at the Hall earlier, I was obliged to meet with Sir Walter. Miss Elliot was there, and she'—he broke off, anger consuming him as he recalled the meeting.

Georgiana came to join him, taking his hand in hers. 'She told you she had seen it?'

Darcy nodded. 'Worse than that, she has passed it to her father.'

'No!' Georgiana's face was all confusion as she dropped his hand. 'But why? Of what possible importance could it be to Sir Walter Elliot?'

'As an instrument to further his own interest.' Darcy turned around. Georgiana's face reflected her despair, and his heart went out to her. 'I am grieved to say, Sir Walter is threatening to expose your plans with Wickham and cause a scandal around us.'

'But you prevented the elopement!'

'He claims it is all in the telling. I do not think he cares if the report misrepresents the facts.'

Georgiana's eyes were full of tears, and Darcy put his arms around her again, holding her close as she wept into his waistcoat.

'They will not harm you, Georgie. I will protect your reputation with everything I have.'

Darcy held her tightly, but then Georgiana raised her head, her forehead furrowed. 'What is his purpose? I cannot see how Sir Walter benefits from making such a threat.'

'His barter for keeping silent is that…' Darcy forced back the bile rising in his throat. 'That I take Miss Elliot as my wife.'

CHAPTER TWENTY

Georgiana stared at Darcy in disbelief. 'Did you agree to this?'

'Not entirely.' He released his hold upon her.

'But you must not! Better I am sent away than you have to marry *her*. Tell me you did not agree to their terms!'

Darcy turned to stare out of the window into the blackness that had fully enveloped the house.

'I said I needed some time. I implied my possible acceptance of the terms merely to keep Sir Walter quiet, but I have no intention of being trapped into a sham of an engagement.' He turned around to face Georgiana. 'My way is not clear, but I intend to overcome this without further pain for either of us.'

Georgiana seemed on the verge of tears again. 'I cannot see how this might be resolved. It is all my fault. Can he not be reported?'

Darcy took her hands and held them gently. 'Not without risk of exposing that which we seek to conceal. Take heart, my dear. It is my duty to keep you safe. I almost failed you in the summer. I will not do so again. No, do not cry, Georgie.' He wiped away a solitary tear as it rolled down one cheek. 'We have no need of tears. What we need is a plan.'

'Have you ever been threatened in such a way before?'

'I have not.'

Georgiana walked slowly back to her chair, then turned around, her expression hopeful. 'Richard will know what to do.'

'Are you insinuating our cousin has experience in such matters?'

'He cannot have been born so mischievous for no reason.'

'I will write to see if he can expedite his arrival.' In truth, though Darcy would be thankful for his cousin's presence and ear, he could not see how it would help free him from this trap.

'What is it? What has happened?'

Elizabeth hurried to Anne as she came into the room.

'You are ashen. Come, sit by the fire.'

Elizabeth coaxed Anne into a chair and hurried to fetch a small glass of wine from the tray on the sideboard.

'Here, take this. What is it? Is there news from Meadowbrook House?' Her throat was taut with anxiety.

'No, that I have been spared. My father says I am not to visit Frederick again.'

Elizabeth stared at her friend. 'You will not conform?'

Anne sipped the wine as Elizabeth resumed her seat. 'I shall not. I chose not to tell him so, for argument with him is futile.' She took another sip from the glass.

Elizabeth sank back against the cushions. 'Why is your father like this—so unfeeling towards you?'

'He has little time for me. Even as a child, Elizabeth commanded all his attention and love.'

'What love he can spare from himself,' muttered Elizabeth, but Anne let out a small laugh. 'Forgive me. I speak out of turn.'

Anne's expression was resigned. 'I was to be the son who would cut off the entail and, to add insult to the offence of my being born a girl, my mother was next brought to bed of a stillborn son.' She raised her hands in a helpless gesture. 'I am a nonentity to him. Mary was much the same, though she gained a little importance with him by marrying the heir to a neighbouring estate. I have not distinguished myself sufficiently, thus he has no interest in me.'

Elizabeth frowned. 'I had not thought upon it, but my own father can be that way towards my younger sisters at times.' Dissatisfied with this notion, she leaned forward in her seat. 'How are you feeling? I worry you will not gain any rest again this night.'

'I shall endeavour to sleep.'

Elizabeth hesitated, then said tentatively, 'Have you considered—should Captain Wentworth awaken—what you will say to him after all this time?'

Anne drained her glass and placed it on a side table. 'I think of little else, whenever I dare to dream of his surviving. It is a vain hope, is it not?'

'But it *is* a hope, and as long as he breathes, it will remain. He has roused before.'

'I fear Frederick will still be the angry man I last saw and will not wish to see or speak to me.' Anne's eyes were troubled. 'It is, after all, our final memory of each other.'

'But he spoke your name, Anne.'

'In his delirium.'

'This is true.'

Elizabeth could not help but smile, and Anne returned it as she got to her feet.

'I have said as much before, but I do not know what I would have done without you these past few days, Lizzy.'

They left the room and walked along the corridor towards the great hall.

'I will continue to do all I can to comfort you, Anne.'

'You have proven it. Such proximity to Mr Darcy in the light of all that went between you the other day.'

'The circumstances of those Mr Darcy has injured may be unchanged, but I have to afford him full credit for his recent actions.' Elizabeth frowned as they crossed the room. 'I cannot understand his kindness.'

They reached the staircase, and Anne turned to her friend.

'I do not know that I can suffer a dinner with my father and sister, Lizzy. I shall ask for a tray to be sent up.'

'Would you like me to keep you company, to be an ear when you wish to talk?'

Anne shook her head. 'I will do better left alone.'

They parted, with Anne taking the stairs under Elizabeth's watchful eye, before she left to retrieve her book from the small sitting room.

She was forestalled before she had gone far, however, by Sir Walter, who peered out of his study as she passed.

'Miss Bennet. If you would be so kind as to join me?'

He held the door wide and, much against her inclination, Elizabeth walked into the room.

It was over-ornamented, fussily decorated and contained a strategically placed looking glass by the desk.

'There has been a change in circumstances here at Kellynch. I am afraid it is no longer convenient for you to remain for the length of your proposed stay. You will depart for home on the morrow.'

Elizabeth stared at him across the desk. Whence had this come?

'Anne is in great need of me at present, Sir Walter. Could I stay but another four and twenty hours?'

Sir Walter seemed disinterested as he examined his neckcloth in the mirror, but a suspicion came to Elizabeth. Was this Mr Darcy's influence? It was likely Sir Walter would accede to such a request, for he had no time for Elizabeth either, but that would be of no aid to Anne.

'Sir, your daughter is likely to be in distress when she returns from Meadowbrook House tomorrow. I would prefer to remain with her until the day after.'

'It is too late. An express has already been sent to inform your family of your imminent return. I will provide a carriage.' Sir Walter seemed proud of this generosity. 'As for my daughter, she will not be going to Meadowbrook House again until I permit it.'

So you may believe.

Elizabeth was confident in Anne's determination, but she had to at least try to sway the gentleman.

'But Sir Walter. The captain—'

He slammed a hand on the desk. 'The captain be damned. I would not have Miss Anne Elliot throwing herself away on him in the year six, and I will not have her hanging around a dying man now. The sooner he is gone, the better for us all.'

If Elizabeth thought her anger for Mr Darcy to be severe, her feelings towards the gentleman opposite knew no bounds. Vexing though it was to be sent packing like some misbehaving child, her fury was all for Anne's treatment at the hands of her uncaring parent. It was, perhaps, fortunate her rage rendered her speechless, or she would likely say something regrettable.

'The carriage will be prepared for ten o'clock. A maid is already seeing to your packing.'

Sir Walter opened the door, and with one last glare, Elizabeth walked with dignity from the room before breaking into a run. If it were not for Anne, she would happily leave and never return to this damnable place.

Darcy encouraged Georgiana to join him in the drawing room before dinner, conscious the last thing either of them needed was to be alone with their incessant thoughts. Mrs Annesley successfully occupied Georgiana by encouraging her to place her embroidery hoop on its stand and do some stitching, but Darcy found it harder to settle and had taken up his usual position at one of the windows.

Determined to keep his anger towards Sir Walter at bay as best he could, Darcy tried to clear his mind as he stared into the darkness, but Elizabeth remained entrenched in his thoughts.

This realisation brought little comfort, and impatient with himself, he turned around. He must make more effort at distraction.

Darcy's gaze fell upon his sister. Despite their upsetting conversation, she appeared brighter than she had in a while, her cheeks bearing a little more colour as she wielded her embroidery hook with finesse.

'You seem in better health, Georgie.'

'I believe I am. My cough troubles me less, and I am sleeping more soundly. Mrs Annesley has suggested we take a longer walk tomorrow.'

'If it remains dry, I see no problem with you doing so, but only for a short duration. Your cough plagued you after your walk with Miss Bennet the other day.'

Georgiana smiled reminiscently. 'It is because I talked too much, Fitz.'

Disquiet filled Darcy, but before he could speculate on what had been said, Mrs Annesley stood up.

'We will remain within the grounds, sir. If you will excuse me. I have a letter I must finish before dinner.'

As soon as the door closed behind the lady, Georgiana put the hook aside and joined her brother by the window.

'How are you feeling, truly, Georgie?'

'I am concerned about you and ashamed of myself, but I passed the captain's door on my way down and it made me realise there are worse situations to endure.'

'Wise words, my dear.'

Georgiana took his hands in hers. 'But what of you, Brother? You are quite ashen.'

'I am perfectly well, Georgie. Perhaps I am need of fresh air myself. Shall I accompany you on your tour of the grounds in the morning?'

'Yes please! Mrs Annesley is pleasant, but I have so little in common with her.' Her expression brightened. 'May I ask Miss Bennet if she will walk with us?'

'Miss Bennet is not at liberty, my dear. She will be here to chaperone her friend.'

'But they are likely to be here for hours, are they not? I cannot imagine Miss Bennet would not wish for a moment's exercise, should the opportunity arise.'

Darcy's eyes drifted to the window again as thoughts of Elizabeth filled his mind. Would this foolish longing ever leave him?

'Brother?'

His attention snapped back to Georgiana. 'Forgive me. I am wool-gathering.'

'Are you thinking of the poor captain?' Georgiana shook her head. 'It is so tragic for Miss Anne Elliot.'

'It is decidedly tragic for Captain Wentworth.'

'Yes, I know. But *he* does not, if you see what I mean? The lady is having to live through the pain of their parting a second time.'

Lord knows how one does such a thing. Darcy struggled to accept his own loss, and Elizabeth had never even been his to lose…

'I should like to further my acquaintance with Miss Elizabeth Bennet, Fitz.'

As would I.

Georgiana turned away, soon resuming her stitching, and Darcy stared at his feet. His sister's eagerness to befriend Elizabeth was a complication he could well do without.

Anne pushed the food around her plate. Her appetite remained poor, and despite her hope of indulging in happy memories of Frederick, she failed miserably.

With Elizabeth by her side, she felt stronger, better able to face what was surely to come.

Laying aside the tray, she took a sip of wine, but then the servant's door opened.

'Oh, Miss Anne!' Elise wrung her hands as she hurried over and panic gripped Anne.

'What is it? Is there news from Meadowbrook House?'

The maid shook her head.

'It is Lottie, miss. Or rather, it is Miss Bennet. Lottie says she was ordered to pack the lady's trunk, that your friend is to depart on the morrow.'

'*What?*' Elise grabbed the wine glass as Anne shot to her feet, confusion flooding her mind. 'I must go to Lizzy.'

She snatched up a shawl from the bed and in no time tapped on Elizabeth's door and entered.

'You have heard. I would have come to see you directly.' Her friend was clearly uneasy. 'I am so sorry.'

Anne surveyed the open wardrobes and the half-filled trunk beside them. 'I do not understand.'

By mutual consent, they both perched upon the edge of the bed as Elizabeth revealed Sir Walter's edict.

Anne stared at her in disbelief. 'But why?'

'I know not. Your father gave no reason, merely saying it was no longer convenient.' Elizabeth hesitated. 'It crossed my mind, perhaps Mr Darcy had made the suggestion, my having angered him so, but there seemed no reason for his word being so influential.'

'Nor can I. It is nonsensical. Let me speak to Father.'

Elizabeth stayed Anne as she made to get up. 'You will not change his mind. My trunk is to be taken down as soon as it is ready, and he has written to my father to expect me.'

'But you cannot leave! I shall need you more than ever once...' Anne drew in a short breath. 'Let me try, Lizzy.'

She hurried from the room, filled with trepidation. How would she cope if Elizabeth were taken away too?

As anticipated, Anne's request of her father, that her friend be allowed to see out the duration of her planned visit, fell on deaf ears, and the two friends talked long into the night, both attempting to provide comfort for each other until exhaustion obliged them to part.

Having barely slept, Elizabeth rose early, her mind full of how Anne would fare throughout the coming day. Though the pain of them parting as friends could not compare to the emotions Anne would experience if the captain finally passed, she was angered by the unnecessary distress brought upon her friend.

Resigned to her fate, Elizabeth picked up the book from her bedside table, adding it to her small travelling bag. With the trunk taken away the previous evening, the room would soon be free of any reminder of her sojourn.

Walking to the window, Elizabeth surveyed the scene. Dawn had broken, and a dusting of snow had fallen, but as the skies cleared, a weak winter sun peeped through the bare branches of the trees bordering the garden. Much as she disliked Sir Walter and his eldest, she would miss the view from her room. To think, she had been here a se'nnight and so much had occurred. Had she remained for the second, what else might have come to pass?

The clock on the mantel chimed the half hour, and Elizabeth, longing for a cup of tea and knowing none of the family would be breaking their fast at this early hour, left the room and headed down the stairs.

Anne paced up and down her chamber. Unable to find sleep after leaving Elizabeth, she rose before dawn, emotion heavy in her breast at what the coming day would bring. How could her father do this? Did he not know the comfort Elizabeth had been to his daughter?

She turned on her heel. Of course he did not. If only her mother were still alive. No one had ever loved Anne as she had. Was there anyone she could turn to for assistance?

For a moment, Anne thought of Charles Musgrove. He was a sensible, pleasant man, and he was kin. He had always been kind to her, but would the gentleman stand up to his father-in-law? She doubted it.

Fetching up in front of the hearth, a notion struck Anne.

'Nonsensical!' She shook her head, resuming her pacing, but once the thought had taken hold, it would not leave her, and she dropped onto the edge of the bed.

Might there be one person who could help her? Help *them*? Had the offer not already been made, should she have need of it?

Loath though Anne was to make the request for herself, could she not do it for her friend? Elizabeth's distress at having to leave at such a critical time had been touchingly obvious. Besides, might that not be an added inducement?

Anne noted the lightening skies and crossed to the dressing room.

'Elise, make haste. Bring my riding habit.'

CHAPTER TWENTY-ONE

Dropping his pen onto the blotter, Darcy leaned back in the chair, closing his weary eyes. Sleep had evaded him as he relived the interview with Sir Walter and Miss Elliot, his mind grappling endlessly with its implications, and he requested a tray of tea in his study long before the breakfast table was made ready.

Notwithstanding the fact coercion was a crime, Darcy's hands were tied—and Sir Walter knew it. If the offense were reported, it would all come out. A baronet in the dock would guarantee the attention of the national press, and Georgiana's indiscretion would be revealed to all and sundry over their morning repast.

There had to be another way!

Raising weary eyelids, Darcy blinked and looked around, taking in the scattered pieces of parchment on the floor, before taking a slug from his cup and getting to his feet. Retrieving the pages, he stared at the lettering, then crumpled them into a ball.

Even with the distraction of the Elliots' underhand actions, the despair and frustration over Elizabeth's ill opinion showed no sign of abating. The dangers of putting private matters in writing were forcibly before him, yet he had been unable to resist attempting a letter to the lady, defending himself against her charges.

Thrice Darcy had made a start. The first two efforts stalled, but as the third began to take shape, and he addressed Wickham's connection to his family, the pen fell from his hand.

It was a damned foolish notion; a risk he could not take.

Darcy walked over to the hearth, his hand clenching the parchment ever tighter. There was no way of justifying his actions towards Wickham or his service to his friend. He would have to live with Elizabeth's condemnation ringing in his ears. Throwing the ball of paper into the flames, he watched it catch and burn, soon fading into ashes, much as his hopes had done.

Flexing his shoulders in an attempt to ease some tension, Darcy consulted his watch. Georgiana would soon be down to break her fast. He would—

The doorbell sounded, and Darcy looked at the clock to see if his watch had erred. It was infernally early for callers!

Admitted to the house by a surprised Boliver, Anne dutifully waited as the housekeeper sought Mr Darcy, curbing the urge to fly up the stairs to the captain's room.

'Good morning, Miss Elliot.' Mr Darcy emerged from a corridor to her right, the housekeeper on his heels. 'There was no change in the captain's condition when I enquired after him earlier.'

The gentleman's gaze flicked towards the door, then back to Anne. 'You are alone?'

'I am. Forgive the untimely intrusion, Mr Darcy. I must speak to you without delay. I did not know who else to turn to.'

'Come with me.' He led her over to the drawing room. 'Mrs Reynolds, would you bring tea?'

Darcy's curiosity was at its height as Anne sat on the sofa and he took a seat opposite.

'You are concerned for Captain Wentworth.'

'No. I mean, yes, of course, but that is not all.' Anne drew in a visible breath. 'In the short time I have known Lizzy, Mr Darcy, she has shown me more kindness, compassion and love than any of my family since my mother was lost to me.'

Darcy inclined his head, his mind racing. Elizabeth was not the subject he thought she would touch upon.

'She is obliged to leave today and—'

'*Leave*?' Darcy struggled to conceal his shock. 'Forgive me, please continue.' His heart reverberated in his breast. What if he never laid eyes upon Elizabeth again, what if their paths never crossed in the future?

'It is an edict from my father, sir. I know not how to explain it, nor does Lizzy, but he sent word to Longbourn yesterday to expect her return, and she is to be on her way at ten this morning.'

Despair tore at Darcy. Whatever Elizabeth's estimation of him, he was not ready for her to walk out of his life! Not yet.

A reprieve came as Mrs Reynolds entered with the tray of tea, giving him a moment to gather himself.

Once furnished with a cup each, Darcy strove to marshal his thoughts. He had a fair notion of why Elizabeth was to be sent away; his careless slip in front of Miss Elliot had not gone unnoticed.

211

'What is it you would ask of me, ma'am? If I am able to do anything to assist, you have my backing.'

'Lizzy was meant to stay for another se'nnight, but it is the next four and twenty hours that concern us. It is cruel to send my friend away when she is desperate to be my comfort, and I shall suffer deeply for the loss of…' Anne's voice cracked. 'The loss of Lizzy, especially if…when…'

Anne seemed to run out of words, and Darcy viewed her with sympathy. He would aid her in any possible way, and not just for Elizabeth's sake.

'Today may be critical, as I understand it from Robinson.'

Anne raised eyes filled with emotion to Darcy. 'Beyond which there can be no resolution. I do not wish'—she stopped, her breath hitching—'I do not wish to be parted from Captain Wentworth again until he must leave this earth. I am come to beg your assistance, sir. May I stay with him as long as is necessary, and may Lizzy remain with me?'

Darcy's keen mind whirled with a possible solution. Ought he to suggest it? The likelihood was, the situation upstairs would not last beyond a day, or two at most. He had no qualms over speaking to Sir Walter about giving shelter to his daughter. Much as the man had his hold upon Darcy, it was obvious he was desperate to have him wed Miss Elliot and would likely consider himself to have the better deal.

'You are—' He hesitated. Was this foolishness of the highest order? 'The cottage in the grounds is at your disposal, Miss Elliot, for as long as you require it. I would not have you leave the captain against your will, and this should enable you to be on hand throughout the night in case of need.'

Anne placed her cup unsteadily onto a side table. 'Willow Cottage? You will permit me to stay there should I need to remain this evening?' She swallowed visibly. 'I had longed for a way of doing so. Your kindness overwhelms me, sir. And Lizzy?'

Darcy drew in a short breath.

'Miss Bennet is welcome to stay with you, if she will agree.' Would she? Could Elizabeth, for the love of her friend, put aside her aversion to him?

'Thank you, Mr Darcy.' The lady's relief was evident as she rose from her seat and Darcy did likewise. 'If I am ever able to repay you for such generosity, you must take it as given. I shall return to the Hall directly. The carriage is due to leave at ten, and we will be here soon after.'

Darcy smiled wryly as they left the room. 'You are assuming Miss Bennet will be amenable to my suggestion. I could never be quite so certain.'

'Lizzy will do anything for those she holds dear, Mr Darcy. Though our friendship was only recently formed, I am confident I comprehend her well enough.'

As the door closed on the lady, Darcy went in search of Mrs Reynolds to give his instructions regarding the cottage. For all the threat of Sir Walter's scheme, his spirits lifted a little by knowing he had done all he could to assist Anne Elliot.

If he was likewise filled with relief at securing a little more time during which he might lay eyes upon Elizabeth, he refused to acknowledge it.

Elizabeth returned to her room with her tea and some toast, but once they were consumed, she resumed her place at the window. The sun had risen a little higher in a cloudless sky. There would be no inclement weather to prevent her leaving, and her thoughts turned instantly to what Anne would face without her.

A tap on the door roused Elizabeth, and her friend's head appeared around it.

'Anne! I would have come to your room.' She noted her friend's attire in puzzlement as she entered the chamber. 'You are riding to Meadowbrook House this morning?'

Anne hurried to join Elizabeth by the window. 'I have already been there.'

Elizabeth placed a comforting hand on her friend's arm. 'I comprehend your urgency for news of the captain. How is he?'

Anne shook her head. 'I have not seen Frederick, though I am told there is little change in his condition. Come. Let us sit.' They claimed the chairs beside the hearth as she continued. 'I went to speak to Mr Darcy. Listen, Lizzy. You do not have to leave immediately. I mean, you need to quit the Hall, but not the estate.'

Elizabeth's confusion deepened. 'How so? My family anticipate my return on the morrow. Besides'—she laughed, though little amused—'it is rather cold for sleeping under the stars.'

'Mr Darcy is offering us shelter for the next four and twenty hours.'

Her mouth a little open, Elizabeth stared at Anne. 'But…why? And how? Surely we cannot be guests in the house of an unmarried gentleman?'

'I do not think Mr Darcy considers us guests, dear Lizzy.' Anne's smile was faint. 'There is a charming cottage standing empty, just across the lawn from the main house. The gentleman sees no problem with us making use of it should the need arise.'

The thought of staying in such close proximity to Mr Darcy unsettled her, but Elizabeth instantly comprehended the benefit for Anne. 'It is a kind and generous offer.'

'You are surprised.'

'A little.' Elizabeth frowned. 'At least, I would have been, had I not seen the compassion Mr Darcy has already displayed. But will your father not protest?'

'I intend to tell him I will return to sit with Frederick, nothing more.' Anne's expression darkened. 'It is unlikely we shall be required to stay long.'

This reminder of the captain and his circumstances was sufficient to have Elizabeth get to her feet and hold out a hand to Anne.

'Then so be it. If Mr Darcy can tolerate my presence, I am certain I can do the same.' Her brow furrowed as they walked towards the door. 'I must get a message home.'

'I will ask for an express rider to come. Write to your father, Lizzy. I shall pack a small bag in case'—she drew in a wavering breath—'in case we need to linger overnight.'

The express to Longbourn dispatched, Elizabeth waited beside the carriage at the appointed hour as James, the coachman, attended to their luggage.

'All loaded, miss.'

'Thank you. I will seek out Miss Anne.'

Elizabeth hurried inside, filled with relief when she saw her friend walking swiftly towards her.

'I thought perhaps your father would prevent your leaving.'

Shaking her head, Anne took Elizabeth's arm as they emerged into the cold morning air.

'My father blusters with words but often fails to act. He remains excessively angry with me.' She eyed Elizabeth as they moved towards the carriage. 'I did not enlighten him to my intention of remaining with Frederick for as long as is necessary. Mr Darcy has promised to deal with my father, should I need to stay through the night.' Anne drew Elizabeth to a halt. 'Nor did I make mention of your staying with me.'

A wave of discomfort swept through Elizabeth as James opened the carriage door.

'Will your father's wrath be brought down upon your coachman when he returns so precipitously?'

'You forget, Lizzy. He is wed to Elise, who is a most loyal maid. Indeed, she will join us if we have to stay beyond the evening. James is already primed to return to the carriage house by a back lane. My father will not notice immediately, if at all, and there is every likelihood James will be back to collect you at some point on the morrow to convey you onwards.'

This sobering thought and all it implied washed over them both, and they observed each other solemnly, but then footsteps approached from behind.

It was Miss Elliot.

'Quick, Lizzy, let us get into the carriage.'

Anne urged Elizabeth forward as James lowered the steps.

'Where are you going, Anne?' Miss Elliot narrowed her eyes at Elizabeth, then turned back to her sister. 'Miss Bennet is for her home. You cannot possibly contemplate accompanying her to Hertfordshire.'

'I do not.'

Anne took the steps into the carriage, but as Elizabeth made to follow, Miss Elliot came to her side.

'My father has forbidden Anne to attend that…that *man*.' She raised her chin. 'I shall speak to Mr Darcy about it, see that he sends him elsewhere. That is, if the captain does not oblige us by taking himself off *permanently*.'

A gasp came from inside the carriage, and Elizabeth removed her foot from the bottom step and faced Miss Elliot.

'You may speak to Mr Darcy, by all means, but do not rely upon his hearing you.'

Miss Elliot raised a brow. 'The gentleman will do anything I ask of him.' She smiled coyly. 'Our acquaintance is more than you might suppose.'

'I suppose nothing,' Elizabeth muttered, turning her back on Miss Elliot and taking the steps into the carriage.

'We send no compliments to your family, Miss Bennet.'

'I am sure they will be delighted, ma'am.'

The door closed, and Elizabeth met Anne's anxious look with a reassuring smile.

'We are free. Do not fret.' Elizabeth patted her friend on the arm as the carriage began to move.

'I thought I would breathe easier once we were on our way, but now I fear what this day will bring.'

'I know.' Elizabeth held her friend's gaze. 'I will stay with you as long as you wish—or at least as long as Mr Darcy permits.'

Anne smiled tremulously. 'If only Mr Wentworth could have arrived in time. Though I am saddened for Frederick, and all his family, I am thankful to have seen him once again.'

Elizabeth settled back into her seat. 'I have not given up hope. I find myself attached to this man I have never quite met, for he had the good sense to fall in love with you and succeeded in winning your heart.'

Silence fell for a short while as the carriage moved into the lane. Then, Anne spoke. 'Your countenance is troubled. Is it for your parents when you do not arrive?'

Elizabeth shook her head. 'Not particularly, now the second express is on its way to them. My overriding anxiety stems from being beholden to a person I have considered the worst of men for some weeks. An opinion I chose to share with him but days ago.' Elizabeth rolled her eyes. 'And here I am, deeply indebted to Mr Darcy for his understanding and kindness towards you.'

'I do wonder.'

'What do you wonder?'

'If it is for me that Mr Darcy has allowed himself to be so imposed upon.'

Elizabeth's brow furrowed. 'For whom else would he do this?'

Anne shrugged. 'Perchance my imagination is at play.'

Elizabeth turned to stare out of the window. They were almost at their destination, and her trepidation rose. 'I suppose you could say he has done it for the captain.'

Anne did not respond, and Elizabeth looked over at her. 'What? Why are you smiling like that?'

'No reason.' She leaned forward and took Elizabeth's hand. 'Thank you for supporting me, and most of all, being my friend, dear Lizzy.'

'I would choose to be nowhere else than by your side.' Elizabeth meant the words, but as the carriage pulled through the gates into the driveway, and she espied Meadowbrook House, her heart faltered.

If she were not mistaken, this would be a day to end all days.

CHAPTER TWENTY-TWO

'Brother? You are quite distracted.'

Of course Darcy was distracted! Elizabeth was upstairs with her friend, watching over the sick man and potentially staying the night. What idiocy drove him to make such an offer?

'Your tea, Fitz. Do not let it cool beyond your preference.'

Darcy turned away from his contemplation of the Elliot carriage as it left the driveway. It took all his resolve to maintain an air of inscrutability on briefly greeting the ladies, that Elizabeth would perceive no hint of the emotions she stirred in him. Thank heavens he never uttered those carefully planned words to her, a proposal she would have—he knew with certainty—refused.

Rejection! Darcy had never, *ever*, contemplated it.

'Fitz!'

'Forgive me, dearest. What did you say?'

'Tea?' Georgiana pointed to the cup on the table beside his chair, and he walked over to resume his seat.

'You have been on tenterhooks all morning, pacing the halls like a caged animal.' Georgiana frowned. 'It is uncommon for visitors to unnerve you in such a way.'

'Georgie.' Darcy's voice was cautionary. 'The ladies are not our guests. Miss Bennet is, as I have told you, on her way home. Should it be necessary for the ladies to linger into the evening hours, they will both stay overnight in Willow Cottage, where they may wish to dine from trays rather than be under any social obligation.'

The notion of Elizabeth leaving so precipitously still tore Darcy apart. Her disapprobation was insufficient in altering his feelings for her, which—since he had acknowledged them—seemed to deepen by the day. How was he to—

'*Fitz!*'

Darcy's head shot up. Georgiana came to stand before him, and he made to stand, but she urged him back into his seat, settling on her knees at his side and taking one of his hands in hers.

'Then your inattention must be down to Sir Walter and his actions. I am grieved over my part in bringing it upon you.'

Her despondent air returned, and Darcy was keen to dispel it.

'Not at all. The blame lies elsewhere. I assure you, my mind was engaged upon another matter entirely.' He summoned a smile.

'Is it the poor man upstairs?'

Shaking his head, Darcy then wished he had not as Georgiana's face became curious.

'Then I cannot understand it, unless it is Miss Bennet's arrival here which disturbs you so?'

Darcy fixed her with a stern eye, but his sister merely assumed an innocent expression belied by the twitch of her lips.

'There is nothing to be said on the subject. Miss Elizabeth Bennet does not view me with favour.'

Georgiana frowned again. 'Why ever not? She must be grateful, at least, for your kindness towards her friend. I am certain she considers you the perfect gentleman, Fitz.'

Darcy almost laughed out loud as he rose from his seat. 'No, dearest, quite the contrary.'

Getting to her feet, Georgiana peered up at him. 'I do not understand. Please explain, lest I make any misstep with Miss Bennet.'

It was a fair request in the circumstances. 'The matter I spoke of the other day, my separating Bingley from an unsuitable alliance. Miss Bennet strongly disagrees with my opinion.'

Quite the understatement.

Georgiana's surprise was evident. 'How would Miss Bennet know of it?' Then, she gasped. 'Of course! She hails from Hertfordshire. Were they acquainted, then? Is she privy to this unsuitable lady's thoughts?'

Somewhat.

Discomfited, Darcy walked over to the window. 'It was her eldest sister.'

'Oh dear!'

At Georgiana's strangled cry, however, he spun around.

'Whatever is it?' Darcy strode back across the room to stand before her.

'I beg you to forgive me, Fitz. I did not realise...I fear I may have caused unintentional upset.'

Darcy studied his sister's face warily. 'For whom? What have you done, Georgie?'

She began to pace, her hands clasped by her waist. 'Miss Bennet. I had no idea the lady concerned was her sister!' She turned aghast eyes upon him. 'What must she think of me? Of you?'

Darcy was well able to satisfy his sister on the latter but chose not to as she resumed her pacing.

'It was an attempt to illustrate your character. I told her what you had said of removing Mr Bingley from a potentially damaging and ill-suited relationship.' Georgiana hurried over to him, but Darcy was not concerned.

Elizabeth had made it plain during their argument she comprehended something of his actions. At least he understood the source.

'Georgie'—Darcy took her hands—'you must think before you speak.'

'Have I angered you?' Her mouth trembled, but Darcy shook his head.

'It was unfortunate, my dear, but it is done now. Miss Bennet disagrees most ardently with my assessment of her sister's indifference.'

Georgiana's eyes widened. 'So, she thinks there *was* interest. Perhaps even more than that?'

He shrugged. 'I studied Miss Jane Bennet carefully on more than one meeting between the lady and Bingley and saw no special indication of regard.'

Darcy stirred beneath Georgiana's scrutiny.

'But Brother, Miss Elizabeth Bennet would know her own sister best, would she not? Both in terms of temperament and her heart?'

A notion that had tormented Darcy for days. *Had* he been mistaken? Elizabeth was convinced of it, had been quite distraught when she told him of Jane's agreeing to wed the obsequious parson.

'I think we have spoken enough on the subject, Georgie. Please remember my caution.'

He observed her sternly for a moment as his sister considered his words, but she must have recognised the unyielding expression on his face, for she smiled.

'Speak of what, Fitz?' Georgiana reached up to kiss his cheek, then hurried from the room, and Darcy returned to the window.

Why could he not rid himself of this growing sense his judgement had failed?

Damn it.

Striving to rid his mind of Elizabeth, and everything connected to her, Darcy moved to the study and immersed himself in his correspondence, his main purpose being the express to his cousin requesting he come to Somersetshire at his earliest convenience but without any mention of why.

It was soon on its way, but the remaining letters lay unread as Darcy's mind grappled with his present situation, the consciousness of Elizabeth being in the house thwarting his every attempt at contemplation.

Tossing his pen onto the blotter, he studied the clock on the mantel. There had been no word from the sickroom, other than Mrs Reynolds reporting the apothecary had gone and would return in a few hours, and likewise, no sight or sound of Elizabeth.

Darcy leaned back in his chair. What if these truly were the last few hours he would spend in any proximity to Elizabeth? What likelihood was there of their paths crossing in the future? This painful prospect was sufficient to propel Darcy from his seat, and he strode over to the door.

He needed activity, some distraction before he had to call on Sir Walter again; a fast gallop on Gunnar would be the solution.

Anne continued her painful vigil, reading aloud from a book of poems, with Elizabeth keeping watch from her chair by the hearth. The captain remained ashen and still, and sadness hung over the room in a veil.

'Is there no alteration?' Elizabeth spoke softly.

Anne shook her head. 'Sometimes I think I hear a change in Frederick's breathing, but as I am reading aloud, I cannot be certain.' She placed a hand on the captain's arm. 'He has become warmer.'

'Mr Robinson did warn of it being a complication of a lack of fluids. He did not seem confident he had succeeded in dropping much barley water into the captain's throat overnight.'

The door opened and a maid came in with a tray of tea, and Anne rose wearily to her feet, stretching her back as she joined Elizabeth, who handed her a cup before they both moved to the chairs beside the hearth.

'I confess I had almost forgotten we are not alone in the house.' Anne sipped her tea. 'It is so quiet.'

Elizabeth cradled her cup. Unlike Anne, whose entire attention was upon Captain Wentworth's lifeless form, she heard a few sounds. Mr Darcy and his sister must have been walking down the landing at one point, for she detected Miss Darcy's voice and her brother's answering rumble.

Elizabeth took a sip of her tea, relishing the hot, refreshing taste. 'Mr Darcy surprises me sometimes.'

Anne raised a brow. 'In what way?'

'I did not expect to find him such a caring and attentive brother. He and Miss Darcy appear to spend much time in company, despite a considerable age difference.'

'Does age affect your level of intimacy with all your sisters, Lizzy?'

Elizabeth laughed quietly. 'No, indeed it does not, and we *are* near in age. I take your point.'

'I suspect you are surprised any time you find a positive in Mr Darcy's conduct. You are so decided against him, it is an uphill struggle for him to appear in a good light.'

There was some truth in Anne's observation, but Elizabeth did not want to think on it.

'I have been considering of late how different we all are, my sisters and I.' She smiled. 'I believe we have very little in common beyond our family name.'

Anne assumed a thoughtful expression. 'I could say as much myself. At least you have a dear friend in your eldest sister, even though you may be opposites. I have never been close to either of mine.'

'We were all born in quick succession. Perchance it is the proximity of our ages which draws Jane and I together.'

Placing her cup on a nearby table, Anne glanced over at the unmoving figure in the bed, then turned back with a sigh.

'My old nursemaid spoke of there being difficulties around my eldest sister's birth. The baby came earlier than anticipated and had to be delivered by Mattie—my mother's personal maid. It is said Mama did not emerge from her chamber for some days after Elizabeth's arrival.' She sighed. 'I wonder if it made my mother wary of another confinement. I cannot imagine the anxieties, her own parents having struggled to have a child.'

Elizabeth drained her cup and placed it beside Anne's.

'Do you know if she suffered upon your birth?'

Anne smiled mistily. 'Mama always said Mary and I came into this world with all the ease of lambs in the fold.' The smile faded. 'I miss my mother so very much.'

Elizabeth got to her feet. 'Sadly, I do not miss mine! Would you care for one of the pastries?' She fetched the plate, offering it to Anne, who shook her head.

'I fear I shall never be hungry again.'

Elizabeth was concerned. Anne hardly consumed a morsel in the past four and twenty hours. Her energy would be sapped before this day was out. She returned to her seat, but before she could select a pastry, the faintest whisper of sound came from the other side of the room, and the hairs on the back of Elizabeth's neck raised.

'*Anne…*'

Elizabeth leapt forward to take her friend's cup as she shot to her feet, tea sloshing over its rim.

Then Anne sped over to the bed, and Elizabeth hurried to join her.

'Frederick? Can you hear me?' Anne looked frantically over her shoulder. 'You heard it too, Lizzy, did you not? He spoke…' Her voice broke. 'Frederick said my name again.'

There was definitely a change, though it was hard to define what it was.

'His breathing has altered. Lizzy?'

Anne's plea for confirmation was heart-wrenching, and Elizabeth put an arm about her friend, praying this was not a reflex as the end neared.

'Talk to him some more. I will ring for Mrs Reynolds.'

Anne sat on the side of the bed now, one hand grasping the captain's, the other smoothing the hair from his forehead.

'Frederick? It is I—Anne.'

Elizabeth tugged the bell fiercely, then ran to the door and pulled it open, in hopes of seeing a servant nearby, but the landing was empty.

No further sound came from the man in the bed, however, and with Anne insensible as to whether Elizabeth was in the room or not, she flew along the landing and down the stairs, only to meet Mrs Reynolds hurrying towards her.

'Oh, Mrs Reynolds, please can you ask Mr Robinson to return as a matter of urgency.'

'Of course, Miss Bennet. Is it time?'

'I do not know.' Why did she wish Mr Darcy were there? 'But the captain uttered a sound—a word.'

Mrs Reynolds put a hand to her mouth, then hurried away, and Elizabeth ran back to the room.

Anne still clasped Captain Wentworth's hand in hers, but a steady flow of tears fell down her cheeks.

Elizabeth walked slowly across to her friend. Was it over? She placed a gentle hand on Anne's shoulder, but she did not move, nor remove her steadfast gaze from the man's face.

'The apothecary will be here directly.' Elizabeth spoke quietly, and Anne raised a teary face to her friend.

'If he would just once more say my name, if I could see his mouth speak the word, then I—'

'Look!'

Anne's head whipped around. The captain's eyelids fluttered, the first time there had been any movement at all.

'Frederick? Please, wake up.' Anne placed a hand on the side of his face. 'You can hear me, my dearest. I know you can hear me. Open your eyes. Oh!' Her voice came out in a squeak. 'I felt his hand move in mine!'

They both stared at the prone figure, willing him to come round. Elizabeth did not know how long they waited, with Anne whispering continual encouragement, but eventually Captain Wentworth's eyelids fluttered once more, then slowly lifted.

CHAPTER TWENTY-THREE

'What the…where…?' The captain's words were barely discernible, and Anne leaned closer.

'Frederick?' A low sob escaped her. 'You have been injured, but you are safe now.'

It was clear Captain Wentworth struggled to keep his eyes open. 'I—thirsty.'

His voice was rough, and he winced, trying to raise a hand to his head, but Anne took it in hers as Elizabeth hurried to fetch the flask left by Mr Robinson.

'Only small sips at first, Anne.' Elizabeth unfastened the stopper and poured the barley water into the feeding cup, handing it to her friend.

'Come, Frederick, you must drink.'

His eyes stared at the canopy. 'I heard your voice…you called for me…'

'Yes, I called, and you came.' Anne's voice broke on the last word, and tears pricked Elizabeth's eyes.

'Get him to drink,' she whispered.

Lifting the captain's head, Anne held the spout to his mouth, and he took a little of the liquid.

'More,' he croaked.

'Slowly, Frederick.'

Anne aided him in taking a few small gulps, then lowered his head to the pillow, and Elizabeth took the cup from her, offering a wet cloth in return.

A soft groan came from the gentleman. 'I do not understand...'

'You took a blow to the head, Frederick.' Anne sent Elizabeth a frantic look as the captain's eyes closed, and he became very still again. 'Will he stay with us?'

Elizabeth had no answer to that. 'Moisten his lips and just keep talking to him.'

Anne turned back to the captain and pressed the wet cloth to his mouth. 'We are at Kellynch, Frederick. Well, on the estate, at least. They brought you here because you mentioned it, and you also spoke...' She swallowed hard. 'You said my name.'

'Anne.' The sound was barely a whisper, but it gave them hope, and a few moments later, Captain Wentworth's eyelids lifted a little. Then, he made a guttural sound, and his arms began flailing, his face distorted. 'The water! So cold...My men...I cannot breathe. I cannot help them...' Just as suddenly, his arms dropped heavily onto the bed, his breathing ragged.

'What shall we do?' Anne's voice was frantic. 'He is in distress!'

Elizabeth placed a hand upon her friend's back. 'He is coming to life. Can you not hear his breathing?'

Anne's frame shuddered under her hand, but she nodded, her attention fixed upon the man in the bed. How long they remained like so, Elizabeth was unsure, but then, the captain's eyes opened again, more fully this time.

'Need…a drink,' he rasped.

A suppressed sob came from Anne. 'Yes, yes. I have more of the barley water.'

Captain Wentworth pulled a face. 'Brandy.'

Elizabeth pursed her lips to keep from smiling, as she handed the cup to Anne again before going over to the box of supplies left by the apothecary—supplies no one expected to need. She returned with a small bottle of cordial, which Mr Robinson asked them to administer if the sick man came around, watching as Anne helped the captain drink some more, then offering the bottle to her.

'You must take a little of this now, Frederick.'

The captain spluttered as the liquid hit the back of his throat. 'What the…?'

'It is a restorative cordial.'

He pulled a face again. 'I cannot stomach the stuff.'

'This is on the apothecary's orders.' Anne persevered, then slowly lowered his head to the pillows.

'My men…the water closed over my head and I could not see them. Blackness…' The captain closed his eyes again, but his brow was furrowed.

'What do I tell him?' Anne whispered to Elizabeth, but she shook her head.

'Do not speak of it, for we know so little and you can say naught of any comfort.'

Before Anne had need of words however, the captain spoke again.

'I had such…dreams.' His voice held hardly any timbre, and Anne leaned in closer to discern it. 'Lost…' He turned his head from side to side on the pillow. 'Thought…lost…'

'You were saved, Frederick. They pulled you from the sea and brought you back to land.'

The captain's frown deepened, then he pouted like a little boy, and Elizabeth had to bite her lip. It was not a laughing moment, after all.

'Not *me*. Lost…*you*…I thought…' He tried to raise his head in his agitation, and Anne placed a hand on his arm to calm him, leaning in closer so that he could hear her.

'Now is not the time to worry about dreams. You must get well.' Her eyes were clouded with anxiety. 'Does he not recall? I must—'

'What I must have is a kiss.' The captain's voice was plaintive, and Anne stared at Elizabeth, who was torn between tears and laughter at the expression on her friend's face.

'Humour him,' she whispered, tapping her cheek, and Anne turned back to the bed.

'There'—she placed a gentle kiss upon the captain's whiskery face. 'Now you must rest whilst we await the apothecary.'

Captain Wentworth's eyes remained closed, but the hint of a smile graced his features.

'Again.'

Anne hesitated, then leaned forward, but as her mouth neared his cheek, the captain turned his head on the pillow and pressed his lips to hers.

Elizabeth looked away for her friend's sake, adding, 'He is disorientated.'

'Who…who is there, Anne?'

'It is my friend, Miss Elizabeth Bennet.'

'Then…' He attempted to clear his throat. 'I trust she will forgive me.'

'She will, but all the same, you should not—'

The captain made a weak movement with his arm, which then dropped heavily onto the coverlet. 'Why should I not? A man'—he cleared his throat again—'may kiss his betrothed if he so chooses.'

Anne gasped. 'Oh, but you and I are not—'

'Alone, remember?' Elizabeth finished, though the captain's eyes had closed and he was probably unheeding of their words.

She took Anne's arm and persuaded her away from the bed. 'He needs peace and comfort just now.' Elizabeth spoke quietly. 'Follow what his dreams have told him.'

Anne shook her head. 'How can I? It is *my* dream he is lost in.'

'You will not aid the captain by revealing the truth just now. He is too weak to even turn his back, never mind stalk out of the room. Just bear with it for now.'

'Do you think…' Anne's attention was fixed on the captain. 'He is not unconscious again?'

Stepping closer, Elizabeth studied the face upon the pillow and the rise and fall of the sheet on Captain Wentworth's chest. 'I am no expert on such matters, but I believe he sleeps of his own will. I must inform Mrs Reynolds.'

She turned to leave, but Anne grasped her arm. 'You cannot go!'

Elizabeth embraced her friend. 'Do not fret so. The man has received a severe blow to his head and received no sustenance for days on end. He certainly cannot be held accountable for a little delirium on first waking.'

She walked over to the door. 'I shall leave this ajar and send a maid to wait with you. And keep talking to him, Anne. Your voice will bring him comfort.'

Anne did as she was bid, and Elizabeth, unable to locate a servant nearby, headed down the stairs, a myriad of thoughts whirling through her mind.

Captain Wentworth's rousing was both unexpected and a blessing. Whether it would sustain should be swiftly determined, she assumed, but the implications for Anne were profound, especially if the gentleman persisted in his belief that they were still engaged.

As she reached the hall, Elizabeth stopped, a disturbing thought encroaching upon her speculation. Mr Darcy could not have anticipated this, much as he might wish for the captain to recover. He had been more than gracious, but that had been when the prognosis implied no more than a night's inconvenience. What now?

Elizabeth turned around in a circle. Where should she go? She had only seen the drawing room. Then, she noticed the door to the service areas, and as there was as much chance as any that Mrs Reynolds would be down there, she set off towards it.

'Miss Bennet?' Georgiana emerged from a door to Elizabeth's left. 'Is all well?'

'Good morning, Miss Darcy. I trust your health continues to improve?'

'Indeed. Beyond a trifling cough, I am quite well. How is...Mrs Reynolds said there was some change and has sent for the apothecary.'

Elizabeth smiled as Georgiana approached her. 'We may have turned a corner. The captain has awakened and seems a little confused but is now sleeping.'

Clasping her hands together, Georgiana returned the smile. 'Oh, that is news I dared not hope for!' Her expression sobered. 'Are you looking for my brother?'

'In truth, I sought word of when Mr Robinson might arrive. With reflection, Mr Darcy ought not to be the last to know of this alteration.'

'Then we had best seek him out.' Georgiana gestured along the hall, and Elizabeth fell into step beside her. 'Fitz has been in his study since coming back from his ride.'

'You and your brother have been most accommodating, Miss Darcy. I do not think I, and certainly, Miss Elliot, can thank you enough.'

Georgiana stopped, and through necessity so did Elizabeth. 'My brother…' She hesitated. 'He has been brought low with worry and concern of late.'

'I am sorry to hear it.' Elizabeth hoped the young girl would not blurt out words Mr Darcy would wish she had not.

She was clearly uncomfortable. 'There are matters I cannot…I must not speak of.'

Elizabeth was unsure this warranted an answer, but Georgiana seemed to labour under some anxiety.

'You are a good sister, I think.' To Elizabeth's dismay, this did not bring comfort.

'I am not. I do not deserve Fitz. He is the best of men, and the most attentive of brothers.'

The latter was true. Elizabeth could not fault anything she had seen in Mr Darcy as a brother. 'It is quite natural, Miss Darcy, to feel for our loved ones when we are powerless to aid them.'

Georgiana seemed thoughtful as they resumed their walk.

'Do you experience this also, Miss Bennet, with regard to your own sister?'

Elizabeth slowed to a halt, and Georgiana turned to face her, colour filling her cheeks.

'Forgive me. I know now I spoke out of turn the other day, about Mr Bingley. My brother explained, but I…'

She fell silent as a door opened behind them.

'Georgiana?' Mr Darcy emerged from his study, frowning. 'Miss Bennet? Is there a problem?'

'No, Fitz. Miss Bennet has news.' Georgiana threw Elizabeth a conscious look. 'I will advise Mrs Reynolds.'

With that, she hurried back along the corridor, leaving Elizabeth trying to decipher what Georgiana might have been about to say. She had a strong suspicion she comprehended something of the disagreement between herself and Mr Darcy.

'Miss Bennet?'

'Oh, yes! There was a change in the captain's condition, a positive one, and Mrs Reynolds has sent for Mr Robinson again.'

Darcy gestured along the hall and they walked back in the direction Elizabeth had just come. 'Then he should be here directly.'

As they reached the main entrance hall, Elizabeth came to a decision.

'Mr Darcy, should the captain recover—and I pray to the Lord he does—you may be obliged to extend your kindness in sheltering both the gentleman and Miss Anne Elliot a while longer.' Elizabeth's gaze raked his face, trying to discern his feelings but his habitual mask was firmly in place. 'I appreciate my being here has been difficult in the light of our...' What on earth could one call it? 'Our discussion the other day. You will wish me to leave for Hertfordshire at the earliest convenience.'

Did he glare at her? Elizabeth cast around for other words.

'Not content with revealing what you think of me, Miss Bennet, you now wish to put words in my mouth?'

'No! I did not mean—'

Elizabeth stopped as Mrs Reynolds came into the hall with Boliver, who assisted Mr Darcy into his great coat.

'You will have to excuse me, madam. I am due up at the Hall.' With that, the gentleman took his hat and gloves from his butler and strode towards the door.

Confused as to why her words raised Mr Darcy's ire, Elizabeth's puzzled gaze followed him. What was his meaning? How could he *not* want her to depart as soon as possible?

Unable to justify such a notion, Elizabeth summoned a smile for the housekeeper. She would dwell upon Mr Darcy another time.

For now, all her interest must be with her friend and the prompt return of Mr Robinson.

Anne had been staring with rapt attention at Captain Wentworth. Though five years had passed, he was as handsome as she remembered, despite the facial hair and the bruise upon his forehead. Full of thanks as she was for his awakening, however, Anne's head was a complete muddle.

Frederick speaking her name in his delirium she discounted, for it could be accounted for by all manner of things, but this! How could he think the engagement persisted, when it could not be farther from the truth?

Wary of touching him since he awoke, Anne eased away from the edge of the bed, then got to her feet and walked over to stare out of the window. The sky was a heavy grey, indicative of further snow, and she shivered. What would happen now?

If Frederick recovered, he would soon realise his mistake, remember the angry words exchanged between them, judge her once more with the disbelief and disfavour of five years ago. Though it was a memory Anne had been unable to expunge, she had no desire to revisit it.

A sound came from across the room, and Anne flew back to Captain Wentworth's side. She watched him carefully as his head moved restlessly on the pillow, grateful for these returning signs of life, then glanced over at the open door before retaking her seat.

Anne caught her breath as his eyelids fluttered, then slowly raised. His face bespoke confusion but then the corners of his mouth lifted.

'I did not dream it, then.' The captain's voice remained distant, and Anne retrieved the barley water, doing her best to administer it, before he fell back against the pillows, his brow furrowed.

'What happened to me? My ship, the men.' Captain Wentworth sighed. 'I cannot recall, though I suspect the dear old Asp is gone to her watery grave.'

Unready for this inquisition, Anne knew not how to respond. The Laconia was indeed sunk. The Asp was the sloop he had taken command of back in the year six, soon after their acrimonious parting.

'I know only what the papers reported and the little supplied by the naval emissary who brought you here from the port. At first, we thought all hands had been lost, and—'

'We?'

Anne drew in a short breath. 'My friend. Miss Bennet. She was here earlier when you first awoke.'

The captain did not speak, his eyes closing once more, and assuming he had drifted back into sleep, Anne remained quiet, but then his hand gripped the coverlet tightly.

'Tell me. I must know, however little.'

Despite its hoarseness, Captain Wentworth's voice commanded much as she recalled, and Anne closed her own eyes briefly, simply relishing a sound she had long thought lost.

'Anne?'

'Your ship was caught in a monstrous storm off the coast of Ireland. I am so sorry, Frederick. I believe only a handful of men survived.' She lowered her head, imagining those terrifying moments as the freezing waves crashed over them all, as they fought with all their being for survival, thoughts of their loved ones most prevalent in their minds as life was brutally forced from their bodies.

There was silence for a moment, but then the captain drew a shuddering breath and his eyes opened. Though Anne did not wish him to know she could see his distress, the moisture on his lashes was sufficient to have her reach for her handkerchief, which she held out to him.

'Take this.'

Turning his head on the pillow, the captain took the square of linen, a strange consciousness filling his face. 'You made me such an offering before. I kept it with me always as a token, but I fear it is now lost.'

Tears welled in Anne's eyes, and she dashed them away. She recalled the moment, in one of those happy days before they had parted. Did Frederick speak the truth in that he retained it?

The captain pressed the linen to his eyes, then held it to his nose. He tried to raise himself but fell back against the pillows.

'I am ashamed to appear before you like this, dearest Anne.' He weakly indicated his state of undress. Then, his frown reappeared. 'How long have I lain thus?'

'You have been here in Somersetshire a mere four and twenty hours, but you were brought into Plymouth a few days ago.'

'I am so weary. My eyes persist in closing against my will.' Captain Wentworth's hand fell open upon the coverlet. 'Stay with me. Take my hand.'

Anne reached out to take it, just as footsteps could be heard approaching, and Elizabeth entered the room with Mr Robinson.

❊

Shepherd was once again at the desk when Darcy was shown into the study, his attention with the papers before him.

Sir Walter, who had been adjusting his cravat in the looking glass, greeted Darcy, then turned to his lawyer.

'You may leave us, Shepherd.'

'But Sir Walter, you have yet to deal with the...' The man flicked a wary glance in Darcy's direction. 'The Northamptonshire problem.'

Sir Walter waved a hand. 'I will deal with it later. It is not your business.'

With a disgruntled air, Shepherd left the room, and Darcy wasted no time in informing Sir Walter of his daughter's intention of remaining at Meadowbrook House until she felt able to leave. He chose not to mention the captain's awakening, or Elizabeth's continuing in the neighbourhood. Besides, if the lady had her way, she would be homeward bound as soon as the horses could be harnessed on the morrow.

Darcy pushed away his feelings on the subject. It was no time for such indulgence.

Sir Walter, in the meantime, eyed Darcy with displeasure, but then he brightened.

'Well, doubtless the man will soon be gone, and there will be an end to it. You will have heard I sent the Bennet girl onward? Anne's choosing to bring her here was most ill-judged.' He gestured towards the tray of spirits on the dresser. 'Shall we drink to the departure of those who are naught but an obstruction?'

Darcy kept his tongue under good regulation, shaking his head as Sir Walter poured himself a large brandy.

'That is better.' He sipped at the brandy, waving Darcy into a chair and taking his own behind the desk. 'She was harmless enough, I will warrant, but Elizabeth took it into her head Miss Bennet was some sort of threat.'

Sir Walter laughed, and Darcy gripped his hands together, his ever-present anger towards the man and Miss Elliot stirring in his breast.

'Had some odd notion she had set her bonnet at you.' Sir Walter continued. 'Nonsensical. Ladies can be irrational in matters of the heart can they not? I had no such fear, the lady's circumstances being so decidedly beneath your own. You would never deign to stoop so low.' He drained his glass. 'But my daughter would not have it. What we do for those we love, eh, Darcy?'

Darcy stood up, almost choking on his words. 'That we can agree on, sir. I will do all in my power to protect those who are dear to me.'

'Capital. A father could not ask for finer sentiments.' Sir Walter rose from his seat and gestured towards the door. 'Let us find Elizabeth.'

'You will have to excuse me, sir. I came merely to advise you of your daughter's wishes.'

'Nonsense, Darcy. A good turn deserves one in return. If I am to cause no fuss over Anne defying me and making a fool of herself in your house, then you will humour me. There is much to be decided.'

CHAPTER TWENTY-FOUR

On his return to Meadowbrook House, Darcy slammed the door to the study and flung himself into the chair behind his desk. He was annoyed with himself for permitting Sir Walter and his daughter to rile him so and frustrated likewise for them pushing him into such adolescent behaviour.

For a second, Darcy thought longingly of Pemberley. If only they had gone north... Then, he gathered his thoughts. Much as the Elliots may feel they had a hold over him, he managed a stay of execution. Pushing him for settlements to be drawn up and the engagement to be announced, Darcy stated firmly he would agree to neither until he informed his uncle, the Earl of Matlock, of his possible intentions. As the head of the family, it was essential he went in person to see him; he also added that he must advise his aunt, Lady Catherine de Burgh, as she laboured under the illusion he would marry her own daughter.

Darcy smiled bitterly to himself. Neither Sir Walter nor Miss Elliot seemed at all put out by the delay once he named some of his more illustrious connections. How Aunt Catherine would have relished being of use, even in her absence! Darcy groaned. She would throw all manner of fits over this.

Leaning forward, Darcy studied the unopened letter on his desk and, recognising Bingley's hand, he broke the seal, his thoughts still wrapped up in the interview at Kellynch.

Miss Elliot bemoaned once more Darcy's lack of title, when so many of his family seemed to own one, and he almost offered to step down before he recalled all that was at stake. It was lowering to realise the lady's obsession with rank and connections was on a par with his; or rather, what his had been before he met Elizabeth Bennet.

The hand holding the unread letter dropped into his lap, Darcy's mind drifting back, as it so often did, to Hertfordshire. Was Elizabeth's family, and their behaviour, any more palatable for his having fallen in love with her? Were her connections more acceptable—a country town attorney of small means and a man of business in Cheapside?

If Darcy were to own the truth, he would say not, but the lady was so much more than her lack of wealth, lowly station, and influential relations. It was Elizabeth who had shown him the veracity of such principles.

With a sigh, Darcy opened Bingley's letter and read it through, a notion swiftly forming as he lowered it to his desk. As soon as his cousin arrived, he would head to London, ostensibly to see his uncle, the earl.

Willow Cottage, which had been converted to accommodate any excess of guests, had been as elegantly furnished as the main house, and consisted of a spacious sitting room and a smaller parlour on the lower floor, with two comfortable chambers with dressing rooms above. There were even well-equipped servants' quarters in the attic, suitable for

Elise, and both Anne and Elizabeth found themselves well-pleased with their new abode.

As evening drew near, Elise put the finishing touches to their appearances, and they donned thick shawls for the walk across to the main house.

'I cannot believe we are being summoned to eat with the family. Why can we not dine from trays in our rooms? Mr Darcy even said as much.' Elizabeth had been surprised by the offer but found it somewhat unnerving.

'It was an invitation, Lizzy, not a summons.'

Anne sounded amused as they stepped up onto the terrace running along the back of the house, and Elizabeth could not help but smile.

'You are quite right. I must learn to be less peeved whenever Mr Darcy acts nobly. Besides, I would not wish his servants to have the additional trouble of waiting on us elsewhere.'

They soon entered the building through the garden door, with Anne's attention immediately drawn to the stairs as they crossed the hall, and Elizabeth took her arm and urged her on.

'It was good of Mr Robinson to stay the night in the captain's room to oversee the intake of fluids, I am sure he is in the best possible hands, Anne.'

'I still cannot take it in, that Frederick woke, that he spoke my name and...' Colour flooded into her cheeks.

'Kissed you? Thinks you and he are still engaged?' They fetched up by the drawing room, where they had been instructed—Elizabeth caught herself. Where they had been *invited* to attend before dining. 'It is your turn to support me. This is likely to be one of the most uncomfortable dinners in memory.'

To be fair, Mr Darcy did not join the ladies until just before it was time to dine, and Elizabeth was vexed by her own confusion. Why was her eye drawn repeatedly to the door, and what was this inexplicable disappointment when it did not open? What on earth did she do, wasting a half hour thinking about where the man was when Mr Darcy clearly had no intention of joining them until he must?

The meal began as Elizabeth feared, with the weather heavily canvassed as the first course was served, and when this subject had been exhausted, an awkward silence falling, but then Mr Darcy spoke.

'Miss Elliot, in the light of today's developments, I would like to propose a toast. To Captain Wentworth's continued recovery.' He raised his glass, and the ladies did likewise, Elizabeth observing her friend.

Pink washed Anne's cheeks, and Elizabeth could surmise which development was foremost in her mind.

'I was so relieved to hear the captain had awoken!' Georgiana looked expectantly at Anne.

'Thank you, Miss Darcy.' Anne smiled. 'The captain is a little disorientated, but his returning to consciousness is a blessing.'

The conversation moved on to the forthcoming season, with Mrs Annesley being quizzed by Georgiana over a Christmas she had once passed in Belgium, and Anne recounting a memory from a childhood sleigh ride across Kellynch's snowy fields, during which she had toppled out, thankfully unhurt, and begged instantly to be overturned again.

Elizabeth was gratified to see Anne's animation and that her eyes no longer drifted towards the dining room door every five minutes as if expecting news from upstairs. Mr Darcy contributed little, but as Elizabeth found his stare unnerving whenever she faced in his direction, she decided to pretend he was not in the room.

When the second course was before them, however, Elizabeth—spurred on by a glass of fine wine—launched into the tale of a Yuletide gift she had once made, when just a child, for the wife of the incumbent of Longbourn church. It had been a cushion embroidered with what appeared to be a five-legged horse—until more closely inspected.

'Good heavens!' Georgiana's astonishment was profound. 'What did your parents do?'

Elizabeth took a sip from her refilled wine glass. 'As is my father's wont, he did little, for fear his culpability might be revealed, for how else could one explain my understanding of animal anatomy at my young age.'

'And you were but nine years of age, Miss Bennet?' Mrs Annesley was clearly fascinated, and Elizabeth laughed.

'I am a poor example for you, Miss Darcy.' She turned to Georgiana. 'It is as well you are grown, for my influence upon your younger self would have been detrimental.'

'But what happened?' Anne's voice was amused. 'Did you receive no reprimand?'

Elizabeth smirked. 'My mother was assailed by an attack of nerves, leaving my punishment to my father.'

Georgiana bit her lip. 'And was it quite awful?'

'I do believe it was to help Papa choose the next book we should study together.'

'You sound as though you were quite fearless as a child, Lizzy.'

Elizabeth assumed a thoughtful expression. 'One might call it foolhardiness. I am afraid I have long leaned towards it, though as a young child, it was generally considered charming.' She laughed. 'Now I am grown, there are few of my acquaintance who find it quite so endearing, least of all Mama.' Elizabeth took a sip of her wine. 'Which is all the encouragement I need.'

A sound came from Mr Darcy, and Elizabeth flicked him a glance. He cleared his throat and picked up his own glass, and she turned back to the ladies. Did he attempt to conceal a smile? The gentleman had been at the receiving end of enough of Elizabeth's pert opinions to know she was not in jest!

'But what of the vicar's wife?' Georgiana's voice was eager, and Elizabeth laughed.

'Oh, Mrs Hart never hinted at wishing for a new cushion again. Her own children learned entirely too much about horses that day.'

In the general laughter, Elizabeth chanced another peek at Mr Darcy. He attended to his plate, but she had a feeling his attention had just been removed from her.

'Would you tell this story again, Miss Bennet? For our cousin? He is to return directly and will remain for some days.'

Elizabeth opened her mouth, then hesitated, glancing back at Mr Darcy again. 'I am not sure I will still be—'

'Colonel Fitzwilliam will be quite diverted.' Mr Darcy placed his knife and fork on the table. 'It would be unfair upon your friend to leave before the captain has fully recovered, after all.' He raised a brow, as though there was no question in the matter.

Elizabeth held his gaze for a moment, an unspoken agreement passing between them. So be it. She inclined her head. 'Thank you, sir.'

A lighter mood settled over the party at table for the remainder of the meal, with much talk of family. Georgiana could not speak highly enough of the colonel, and Elizabeth was amused at Mr Darcy's contradictory asides.

'Richard will be full of anticipation for his return here, Miss Elliot.' Georgiana smiled mistily. 'We see little enough of him. It is nice to have him not far distant.'

'And are you well settled in Somersetshire, Mr Darcy?' Anne turned her attention to their host. 'For myself, it is rewarding to see the house occupied.'

'It is a charming property.' Mr Darcy's gaze drifted around the room, then back to Anne. 'We are very comfortably settled, thank you.'

'My mother oversaw the fitting out of the house. She was inordinately fond of it and spent much time here, when her late mother-in-law was unable to take up residence.'

Both Mr Darcy and his sister expressed a great deal of interest in the late Lady Elliot and a discussion of the proportions and furnishings of Meadowbrook House, and this conversation carried the meal to its conclusion.

To Elizabeth's surprise, she felt disappointment when the time came to leave the table, and under the bustle of the party getting to its feet, she approached the gentleman.

'Mr Darcy.' She spoke quietly, that the others might not hear. 'I thank you for your considerate words. It was—'

He raised a hand. 'Please, Miss Bennet, speak no more of it. You are welcome to remain as long as Miss Elliot needs you.'

Surprised by the rush of gratitude she felt towards him, Elizabeth's eyes raked Mr Darcy's features for an indication of what he thought—to no avail.

'I trust you have all you need over at the cottage?'

'Perfectly so, sir.' She hesitated, then added. 'I have already written to my father, but would it be permissible for me to give this address to my friend in Hertfordshire, and also to my aunt Gardiner in Town? I fear any post which arrives at the Hall will either be returned or simply disposed of.'

'Of course. Leave any letters you wish posted on the salver in the hall. They are taken daily.'

'I thank you again, sir.' Elizabeth walked out of the room, then looked back. Mr Darcy remained by the door, and disturbed by his intense scrutiny, she hurried after Anne and Georgiana, unsure why she suddenly felt unsettled.

Though no further snow fell, the skies were heavy with the threat of it on Saturday morning, and Darcy hurriedly broke his fast ahead of the ladies, knowing he ought to allow Elizabeth as much freedom from his company as possible.

His valet reported on the captain passing a troubled night, the apothecary remaining with him for the time being, and as the clock in the hall chimed the hour of nine, Darcy walked down the hall into the small library.

The tasteful arrangements of Meadowbrook House, including the well-stocked and varied bookcases in the library, made so much more sense. It was no wonder the late Lady Elliot passed much of her days here.

Be honest, Darcy. She likely wished to spend as little time as possible in her insufferable husband's company.

If only he felt calm enough to simply peruse a book! He picked up the newspaper, read the headlines, then tossed it aside. Was Elizabeth on her way over to the house yet? He knew he had done the right thing by her in avoiding the ladies' company but having her at such close proximity tested his fortitude. Perhaps he could just return to the breakfast room shortly to collect a cup of tea?

Or perhaps you could just pull the bell like you generally would?

Frustrated with himself, Darcy studied the laden clouds and the stiff breeze bending the trees. There would be little chance for exercise today. Then, he became lost in a memory of the previous evening's dinner. Georgiana gave all the signs of being as smitten with Elizabeth as—

Darcy turned around as the door opened and Colonel Fitzwilliam strode in. Never had he been more pleased to see his cousin, and Darcy greeted him with a shake of his hand.

'This weather is sufficient to chill the nether regions of an old nag, Darce!' The colonel rubbed his hands together and crossed to the hearth, holding out his hands to the roaring fire.

'You are timely, Cousin.'

'The early bird catches the worm. Fortunately, my superior is supportive of the need to attend to family matters. You may have been evasive about the purpose of your summons, man, but I know you well enough to comprehend there is something serious afoot.'

Serious indeed. Darcy walked over to reach for the bell pull, but the colonel put his hand up.

'Saw Mrs R just now. She is sending refreshments. I suggest we do not speak until they have arrived, and we are unlikely to be undisturbed.'

Darcy nodded as they both took a seat by the fire. 'How is it you are here so soon after the day began?'

'Came on horseback whilst the roads remain passable. Mackenzie is following on with my things.' He eyed Darcy. 'Mama was most put out I would not be joining them for Christmas this year, but I have promised to visit them soonest.'

'It is good of her to spare you—' Darcy broke off as the door was tapped and opened to reveal Mrs Reynolds and a maid bearing a tray, which she placed carefully on the side table.

'Ah, Mrs R. A sight for sore eyes.' The colonel beamed at her. 'And tea. Just the thing.'

'It is good to see you safely returned, Colonel,' said the housekeeper. 'Shall I pour, Mr Darcy?'

'Thank you, no. We will cater for ourselves. You have sufficient with our…' Darcy hesitated. 'You have enough to do.'

'As you wish, sir.' Mrs Reynolds headed for the door, but then turned back. 'The ladies are lingering over their breakfast, and Miss Georgiana asked me to tell you they intend to repair to the music room thereafter. Mr Robinson remains upstairs with the captain.'

She left the room, and a heavy silence took her place. Darcy lifted the tea pot and poured two cups, waiting for—

'We have guests this early in the day?' The colonel blinked. 'And who is the captain, and why is he upstairs with a chap called Robinson?'

Amused by his cousin's perplexed expression, Darcy handed him a cup before picking up his own and resuming his seat, and the colonel grabbed a couple of biscuits from the plate before joining Darcy beside the hearth.

'Explain, Darce.'

The colonel bit into one of the biscuits with relish, and Darcy stirred in his seat.

Where to begin?

CHAPTER TWENTY-FIVE

'The ladies concerned are Miss Anne Elliot and Miss Elizabeth Bennet, and they are not paying an early call, Cousin. They are staying here.' Darcy hesitated. 'In Willow Cottage, that is.'

Almost choking on a piece of biscuit, the colonel took a gulp of his tea. 'How the devil has such a thing come to pass?'

'If you will apply yourself to your victuals and keep silent, I will tell you all.'

The colonel smirked at him. 'Well done, Darce! I did not think you had it in you to be so…ingenious. I may only have seen you once in company with Miss Bennet, but it was obvious to anyone who chose to notice, you were quite smitten.'

'That is not the reason they are here! Do you think me a simpleton?' The colonel pretended to muse upon the point, and Darcy shook his head at him. 'Keep a rein on your tongue, Cousin. There is more to come.'

Placing his cup on the side table, the colonel settled back into his seat. 'I am all ears, Darce. This is promising to be quite the tale!'

Indeed.

Darcy cleared his throat, then swiftly related how Captain Wentworth came to be in the house, along with the ladies.

The colonel frowned. 'But why are the ladies staying *here*? Kellynch is but a mile up the road, and if the reports are true, running more carriages than the King's entourage. Surely they could come from day to day?'

Putting his cup down, Darcy got to his feet and walked over to the window to stare out, though seeing little of the scene before him. Then, he turned around. If he wanted his cousin on side, he must reveal all.

'Sir Walter threatened to prevent his daughter from attending the man, and he banished Miss Bennet from Kellynch. Willow Cottage stood empty. There were no guarantees the captain would survive, but Miss Elliot was desperate to remain at his side and also in need of her friend. To have sent Miss Bennet home rather than allowing her to wait upon Miss Elliot would have been cruel.'

The colonel rose from his seat. 'Cruel upon whom, I wonder?' He picked up another biscuit. 'So, this explains why the ladies are here, and the presence of a captain and this Robinson—a medical man, I assume—but does not account for all the situation's singularity.'

He came over to where Darcy stood. They were of similar height, and the colonel studied his cousin intently. 'What could Miss Bennet have possibly done to provoke Sir Walter into expelling her from his home?'

Darcy raised his hands, then let them fall to his sides. How did he begin to explain *this*?

The colonel popped the biscuit into his mouth and munched for a moment, his astute gaze still on Darcy, who released a pent up breath.

'I…I have…'

'Cousin, if you do not tell me, I will be tempted to sit on you until you repent. I am not averse to employing the means I used in our youth.'

'Fine!' Darcy strode over to the fireplace, then swung around to face his cousin. 'It seems I must take Miss Elliot as my wife. Miss Elizabeth Elliot.'

If the situation were not so dire, Darcy would have laughed at the expression on his cousin's face. It was probably the first time in his life he could effectively recall silencing him.

The colonel ran a hand through his hair, then walked slowly across the room to stand in front of his cousin again.

'Are you out of your senses, man?'

'Circumstances arose, leaving me with little choice.'

The colonel's eyes widened. 'What possible reason can you give for considering such an unfathomable step?'

As succinctly as he could, Darcy laid before his cousin all that had befallen him in the last eight and forty hours, from his arrival at Kellynch determined to offer for Elizabeth, the proposal that was not a proposal, the argument with the woman who held his heart, and Sir Walter and Miss Elliot's actions over the discovery of Georgiana's secret, resulting in his present situation.

To be fair to the colonel, he held his tongue, though it was clear it cost him, and when Darcy's tale drew to a close, a heavy silence fell upon the room, permeated by the ticking clock and the crackling of the logs in the grate.

Then, the colonel released a huff of breath. 'How the *hell* could Georgie have been so damned careless?'

Darcy shook his head. 'I know not, but do not bring any anger down upon her, Richard. She suffers enough as it is.'

'Not as much as she will when that woman is her sister. Or as much as you will when she is your wife.'

'I have no intention of letting that happen.'

'As you say, but we have yet to find a way out.'

Darcy was comforted by knowing he was not in this alone. 'There has to be a solution. My instinctive thought was the law. Coercion is a crime, after all, but although it would release me, a baronet on trial would guarantee it being a high-profile one. The thought of the *ton* pouring over the newspaper reports, which would recount the full history…' Darcy's skin went cold. 'It cannot be done in such a way.'

'And what of Miss Bennet?'

Darcy's gaze snapped to his cousin's. 'What of her?'

'You intended to ask for her hand. You were…*are* completely enchanted by the woman, despite her circumstances. I know you, Darce. Only the most ardent of affections could have overruled your principles in this.'

Darcy did not wish to dwell upon what his intentions had been. 'You will not be surprised to learn, now I have revealed recent events, I am thankful I did not offer for Miss Bennet. She would have refused me.'

'And therein lies another conundrum. What could you possibly have done to raise the lady's ire to such an extent?'

'She believes I interfered in separating her sister from Bingley.'

'As you did. Is that all?' The colonel raised a brow.

'At the time, I believed I acted in my friend's favour, not to his detriment.'

'And now?'

Darcy hesitated. 'I may have erred. I have written to Bingley, promised to call upon him in Town.' Shame filled him. 'Miss Bennet accused me of'—Darcy swallowed hard—'of arrogance, conceit and a selfish disdain for the feelings of others.'

The colonel released a slow whistle, then rested a hand upon Darcy's shoulder. 'I am grieved, old man. You have had one hell of a few days.' He frowned. 'Is that truly all of Miss Bennet's complaints against you?'

'No. She has fallen victim to Wickham's lies, and I was in no position to refute the claim beyond saying she should not trust him.' Darcy winced, remembering. 'That seemed to incense her even further.'

They both sat again, and Darcy waved a hand. 'Miss Bennet is the least of my worries right now. I have to find a way of silencing Sir Walter and his daughter over what they perceive as Georgiana's ruin, and I need your help.'

The colonel leaned forward, offering his hand and Darcy took it. 'You shall have it.' They shook on it and then both turned their attention to their tea, but Darcy grimaced as he took a sip. Cold again.

❦

Elizabeth and Anne had all but finished their breakfast by the time Georgiana joined them, so they each had another cup of tea to keep her company, as Mrs Annesley had a day off and would go into Yeovil.

The conversation centred mainly around the impending festive season, reminding Elizabeth of its proximity.

'It is so much more enjoyable to spend Christmas with you and your family, Miss Darcy, than at the Hall with my own.' Anne smiled kindly at Georgiana.

'Oh, that is so sad!'

Anne laughed. 'Not for me. There is too much formality at Kellynch. Did you know my father has even begun a tradition of placing a live tree from the grounds in the entrance hall?'

Georgiana's eyes widened. 'I had heard of the aristocracy emulating Queen Charlotte's preference, but I have never seen one of these indoor trees. It must be a sight to behold.'

Exchanging an amused look with Elizabeth, Anne nodded. 'Quite the spectacle. What is Christmas at Longbourn like, Lizzy?'

'Oh, much as any other day, but with an excess of mayhem and noise!' Elizabeth laughed. 'I will own to not missing it at all, other than Jane's company. It is not often we are so long apart.' She looked over to Georgiana, keen to take advantage of the opportunity to satisfy a recent curiosity.

'Would you generally be in Derbyshire for the festive season, Miss Darcy, or do you remain in Town?'

'It varies. If the weather is dire, the Derbyshire roads can easily become impassable, but if we can journey safely, Pemberley is where both Fitz and I prefer to spend Christmas.'

'And do you fill the house with people, host parties and play parlour games?' Elizabeth could not imagine Mr Darcy in such a situation, and she awaited the answer with great expectation.

Georgiana, however, laughed. 'It is not my brother's way to indulge in games, though he has no objection in general to the activity. We tend to have family to stay. My aunt and uncle live in Matlock and often come for a week or so, and Richard will join us if he is able to. His elder brother is now married and spends Christmas with his wife's family, but we are merry enough. St Stephen's Day is my favourite of all, though.'

Anne smiled. 'As it should be.' Her face sobered. 'My father does not observe the traditions as well as he ought.'

With a frown, Georgiana looked from Anne to Elizabeth and back again. 'But how so? It is only fair, is it not, to give the servants the day to themselves after working so hard all year? And what of the boxes for the poor and needy?'

Elizabeth could detect discomfort in Anne's expression, but her friend nevertheless replied. 'He is hosting his annual ball on that day. What does it tell you of his intentions to give his household a day of rest? And when Mama was alive, there was charity in abundance, but the boxes have dwindled in number, along with their contents. I am quite ashamed of it.' She shrugged her shoulders. 'I can do little about it, but for a man who is obsessed with the reputation of himself and his family, it is contradictory behaviour to be certain.

'The inconsistencies of human nature,' mused Elizabeth. 'I once found them such a source of amusement.'

Anne looked over at the clock. 'Do you think we could pay a call upon Captain Wentworth?' She turned to Georgiana. 'Would you mind, Miss Darcy, if we joined you in the music room in a short while?'

'Of course not.' Georgiana beamed at them both. 'I look forward to hearing a good report.'

Mr Robinson responded to Elizabeth's knock on the door to the sickroom, coming out onto the landing and closing the door behind him. He seemed weary, as well he might, but not despondent.

'The captain has experienced a disturbed night, but he is still with us and although he lapses in and out of consciousness, I am confident the periods of sensibility will lengthen.'

'May we see him?' Anne almost took a step towards the door.

'You may but he is sleeping at present. The captain has been troubled when conscious, at times in some distress, and must rest as much as he is able.'

Elizabeth placed a gentle hand on Anne's arm. 'You said how upset he became as he comprehended the loss of his men. It is not an easy burden to bear.'

Mr Robinson inclined his head. 'It is clear his mind is conflicted. He seemed confused over his rank when I called him captain.' Elizabeth and Anne exchanged a lightning glance. 'Some amnesia is to be expected in such a case. Excuse me, ladies. I must refresh myself and shall return directly.'

The apothecary set off along the landing, and Anne tapped on the door before they walked in.

Captain Wentworth was propped up on his pillows, his complexion pale but without the ashen hue of before. His eyes were closed, and they walked over to the window on the opposite side of the room.

'He was a commander when we parted.' Anne spoke quietly, her eyes on the sleeping figure in the bed. 'He gained the rank of captain in the year eight and was posted to the Laconia.'

'You know this from that list you study?' Elizabeth was careful to speak equally softly.

'Yes, *Steel's*.'

Anne's gaze drifted out of the window. 'It is how I knew he had never married.'

'Neither have you. There must be a chance for you both.'

There was no response for a moment; then, Anne looked back across the room. 'Though we parted in acrimony, I have never stopped loving Frederick. And whatever happens, I know now I never will.'

'Then he is a fortunate man.' Elizabeth peered over at the bed, then turned to stare out of the window too, but as she did so, a sound came from the sleeping captain, and they both swung around.

'Does he awaken?' Anne whispered as they edged towards the bed.

Captain Wentworth slowly opened both eyes, his expression blank. Then, he smiled.

'Perhaps you ought to introduce me, Anne?'

The captain, dressed in a freshly laundered shirt, had more strength to his voice, though he clearly had little recollection of the previous afternoon.

'This is my good friend, Miss Elizabeth Bennet, sir. Lizzy, this is Captain Wentworth.'

He turned his head on the pillow. 'Forgive me for not getting to my feet, Miss Bennet. I tried earlier and almost landed upon Robinson. My sea legs are much sturdier than my land ones.'

Elizabeth smiled as she and Anne settled into the chairs placed beside the bed. 'I am sure you will soon be restored to full health, Captain. It is a relief to know you are improving.'

His brow furrowed as he looked from Elizabeth to Anne. 'When was I made captain? Where my memories end, I was a mere commander.'

'It was the year eight, Frederick.'

'What *is* the damned year? Robinson claimed it to be the year eleven. How can that be?'

Anne threw Elizabeth an anxious look before turning back to him. 'It is indeed 1811.'

'Then how are we not wed?'

Colour flooded into Anne's cheeks, and Elizabeth took her hand and squeezed it.

The frown deepened. 'We have been engaged for *five* years?'

'I—er—we—' Anne hesitated. 'That is to say, you—'

'Were at sea, sir.' Elizabeth kept a firm grip on Anne's hand. 'You have been at sea for some years since you gained your ship.'

'My ship…I thought it was the Asp, the dear old sloop, when first I awakened, but I am told it was a frigate.' Captain Wentworth's expression darkened. 'Whichever, it is no longer…nor are my men…' His eyes closed, and Anne looked anxiously to Elizabeth, but she shook her head.

They waited anxiously, but the captain's even breathing indicated he had fallen asleep again, and they crept from the room to find Mr Robinson outside, along with a servant.

'I will return this evening, Miss Elliot. Provided the gentleman continues to take the medicine I have left and maintains his level of fluids, he should be much improved within the next four and twenty hours. It will take a while for him to build up his strength, but his former vigour should soon return.'

'Thank you, Mr Robinson. We are so grateful.'

The gentleman bowed, then turned to give instructions to the servant, and the ladies set off along the landing, but as soon as they reached the stairs, Anne dragged Elizabeth aside into an alcove.

'What am I to do? He is convinced we are still engaged!'

'I think you will do the captain more harm than good if you confess the truth just now. He is comforted by your presence, by his faith in your attachment. Would you disappoint him in his current condition?'

Anne put a hand to her head. 'No! But I will have to disappoint him at some point, and having done it once, how can I bear to face it again?'

It was a dilemma indeed.

'Think carefully. If you tell him right now, it might affect his recovery. What damage might a broken heart do him in his present precarious condition? Besides, if you are not engaged, you will be unable to visit him.'

With obvious reluctance, Anne nodded. 'I am not happy with the deception, but as it is more in Frederick's favour than my own, I can bear it for now.'

'You could just beg him to take you back.'

'It is true. I have longed for such an opportunity.' Anne's voice was wistful, and Elizabeth rested a comforting hand on her shoulder.

'All will be well.' She gestured towards the staircase. 'And we are to attend Miss Darcy in the music room, so we had best make haste.'

'It was a genuine plea, dear Lizzy, not an order.'

Elizabeth bit her lip, feeling guilty, as they made their way down the stairs. 'Forgive me. Old habits are hard to shed. I must learn to be less censorious of the Darcys.' Then she smirked. 'Especially when they do not deserve it.'

CHAPTER TWENTY-SIX

Darcy and the colonel discussed all possible angles for putting a muzzle upon Sir Walter, but eventually they both fell silent, for they could think of no approach sufficiently strong to silence him.

'I am more than proficient with a rifle, Darce. That might work.'

'It would effectively silence you as well, by putting a noose around your neck.' Darcy rose from his seat and stretched. 'Much as I wish to extract myself, I will not do it to the detriment of any of my loved ones.'

'Then let us think on it later with clearer heads.' The colonel rose from his seat and gestured towards the window. 'It is not the weather for a gallop across the fields, which makes it opportune for paying my respects to the ladies.'

Darcy followed his cousin to the door. 'Unsurprising, Richard.' Was he not relieved, though, that he had not had to make the suggestion to head to the music room himself?

'I must make the formal acquaintance of the captain. I have not seen him when conscious.'

The colonel's steps slowed as they neared the music room door. 'Should I accompany you?'

With a short laugh, Darcy shook his head. 'The man has only just come round, Richard. I think he may need a day or two before he is fit for your exuberance.'

The colonel grinned. 'When do you propose travelling to Town?'

'On Monday, if you have no objection?'

'None whatsoever. You have left me ample entertainment.'

Colonel Fitzwilliam pushed the door open and they stepped inside. Anne Elliot was at the instrument, and Georgiana sat next to Elizabeth, looking extremely content, and the ever-present ache in Darcy's breast increased as once again his loss was emphasised. The notion of Elizabeth Elliot being sister to his own over Elizabeth Bennet did not bear thinking of.

'Darce,' the colonel hissed. 'Lighten your countenance. You will scare the ladies.'

Darcy threw him a speaking look as they took a seat, and they listened whilst Anne completed her performance.

'Your playing is delightful, Miss Elliot.' Darcy smiled at her as the applause faded. It was far easier to pay attention to Anne than Elizabeth. Whenever he did the latter, his mind would fill with how she might next judge or misinterpret his words. 'Would you be so kind as to introduce me to Captain Wentworth?'

'Of course. Shall we go directly?'

Darcy turned to his cousin. 'I trust I can leave you to amuse the ladies, Richard.'

The colonel bowed. 'How could they want for anything more?'

Elizabeth laughed, and Darcy quashed a sudden urge to postpone his meeting with Captain Wentworth and stay right where he was.

Thankfully, sense overruled his heart's wishes, and soon they were outside the captain's room.

'I hope he is not sleeping.' Anne stared up at Darcy. 'Frederick seems to spend much of his time asleep, and when his consciousness lapses, I always fear he will not wake again.'

'It is perfectly understandable in the circumstances.'

Darcy tapped lightly on the door and opened it. A servant was seated in a chair near the bed.

'You may leave us, Greening.'

The captain was slightly propped up in the bed, and he eyed Darcy warily, but then he saw Anne and smiled.

'Frederick, this is Mr Darcy, who is presently leasing this house. He wishes to become known to you.' She turned to Mr Darcy and said, 'Sir, this is Captain Frederick Wentworth.'

Darcy bowed, then took a step nearer. 'I extend my best wishes for a speedy return to full health, sir.'

The captain shifted in his bed, wincing with the effort. 'Words are insufficient to express my gratitude, Mr Darcy. I believe you may well have saved my life.'

Darcy shook his head. 'Please, think nothing of it. I would not have disturbed you so soon, but I head to Town the day after tomorrow and will be gone for a few days.'

The captain's gaze flicked to Anne briefly. 'I wish I could be of service as the ladies' protector, sir, but I fear I could ill-fight off a moth at present.'

Darcy smiled. 'I shall appoint you in charge of your own welfare, Captain. My cousin—Colonel Fitzwilliam—has arrived and will be here for the duration of my absence. I trust you do not feel passed over for the position.'

Wentworth laughed quietly. 'Thoughtful of you, Mr Darcy.'

'I do what I can. I hope to find you much improved on my return.'

'I cannot trespass upon you further.' A frown formed upon the captain's brow. 'Where is my brother? How is it I am not at Monkford?'

'Your brother recently left the district, Frederick.' Anne took a step closer to the bed. 'Mr Darcy kindly sent word to him of your being alive, for he believed you to be lost.'

'Another debt I owe you, sir. What of my sister?'

'She is at sea with her husband.' Anne raised her hands in a helpless gesture. 'I did not know how to send word.'

The captain leaned further into the pillows as his energy drained again. 'I must write to the Admiralty, for I am told they conveyed me into Somersetshire.' He was clearly struggling to keep his eyes open. 'Forgive me, sir, for my poor display.'

Darcy shook his head. 'There is no need for apology. I have the emissary's direction and will inform him of the change in your condition. Take some rest, Captain. If there is anything I can do to assist you further, let Miss Elliot know and it will be taken care of.'

Captain Wentworth nodded but his eyes were closed, and exchanging a glance, Anne and Darcy left him to his slumber.

The lively banter between Georgiana and the colonel should have been diverting, but in truth, Elizabeth's thoughts were in the sickroom, wondering how Mr Darcy would be with the recovering captain who had been all but thrust upon him.

That is unjust.

She could not fault Mr Darcy's kindness towards both Captain Wentworth and Anne. Elizabeth frowned. She must admit the gentleman had been fair towards her in a way she did not deserve.

And why was she so increasingly mindful of Mr Darcy's presence in the room when she had so profound a disinclination for his company?

'Is aught amiss, Miss Bennet?'

Elizabeth pulled herself together. 'Forgive me, Colonel. My attention wanders.'

He grinned. 'You did not seem at all engaged by its direction. Our conversation needs to be more stimulating, Georgie, than speculating upon whether the bookshop will deliver your order in a timely fashion.'

Elizabeth eyed them both kindly. 'I assure you, my distraction is not related to the company.'

Georgiana smiled impishly. 'Richard mainly speaks nonsense.'

Pretending affront, the colonel got to his feet. 'I am much maligned and must take solace from some music. Come, Georgie. I believe it was your turn, and with a smaller audience, you can make no complaint.'

For a moment, the young girl did not move, colour seeping into her cheeks.

'Your cousin is quite right, Miss Darcy. You have heard me play before and have ample evidence no talent of mine will overshadow yours.'

The colonel made a fuss of choosing the music and arranging it on the stand, making his cousin laugh, and Elizabeth settled comfortably into her seat, welcoming the respite from her incessant thoughts.

A beautiful melody soon filled the room, and Elizabeth closed her eyes, allowing herself to be carried away by it, for the colonel did not cause her any stress, and Miss Darcy... She furrowed her brow. Miss Darcy continued to undermine her prior assumptions by being sweet-natured, completely likeable, and modest. If only she could overcome this predilection for disliking anyone approved by Mr Darcy. She was disturbed to realise she found more to like than not. Miss Darcy, the colonel, the Pemberley servants attending the family here in Somersetshire... Even Mr Bingley, weak-willed though he may be, was likeable. At least his sisters helped balance the scales.

By the time Georgiana had played two difficult pieces without fault, Elizabeth felt much more at ease. Wickham's impression, of Miss Darcy's being so like her brother, she understood. He admitted to rarely having seen her once she was grown, and with Georgiana's natural shyness, it was no wonder he felt she was no longer the child he had known before. If Mr Darcy had not treated him so badly, he might have been able to regain the footing he had known as a boy, and then he would have seen the charm of Georgiana, much as Elizabeth saw it now.

Though both the colonel and Mr Darcy were protective of the young lady, she seemed to be growing into a charming woman, and Elizabeth had been delighted with how any natural reserve she first displayed disintegrated between them. How her brother felt about this, she knew not.

'What say you, Miss Bennet?'

Realising she had lost the sense of the conversation again, Elizabeth gave a regretful smile. 'To what, sir?'

'Georgie is questioning the sense of my keeping a gift bestowed upon me.'

'I do not see how a soldier can properly care for such a beast.'

'What, would you have me abandon him?'

Elizabeth laughed at his indignant expression. 'Pray, Miss Darcy, what animal is this?'

'A donkey. Richard says it was given in reward for some assistance he gave a farmer near the camp in Dorset.'

'Donkeys are beasts of burden, much like those of us in service. No point in rejecting such a token when they can take on some of the work for you. Besides, I gain an inordinate amount of joy in addressing him by his name.' The colonel gave a mock bow from his chair. 'Why good day to you, sir and madam. No, please do not let my ass bother you. George is not the brightest four-legged creature, but a handful of carrots and a few compliments to the army, and he will do anyone's bidding.'

Elizabeth laughed, but Georgiana seemed quite put out.

'You did not name him after me!'

'What? No, of course not, precious. I neglected to tell you his full title.' The colonel stood up, grinning at his cousin as he gestured at some unseen thing. 'Allow me to present, Mr George Wick—'

'Richard!'

The colonel stopped, a culpable look filling his features, as he seemed to recall Elizabeth's presence. 'Ah, yes. Forgive me, Miss Bennet. A—er, a family jest.'

She stared at him, then at Georgiana, surprised the girl had gone so pale. Did he truly refer to Mr Wickham? Was she so mistaken in her judgement of the colonel? No, of course not. Mr Darcy would have tarred his former childhood friend's reputation within his family as well as without.

'Come now.' The colonel leaned down and patted Georgiana's arm. 'I apologise, Georgie. I should not joke about the scoundrel.'

Indignation rose within Elizabeth's breast, but then the door opened, and Anne preceded Mr Darcy into the room.

'There you are.' The colonel spoke heartily. 'And how is the patient?'

Anne smiled. 'He is doing well, thank you, Colonel.'

Elizabeth stood as Anne approached, longing to escape the company and be alone with her friend.

'Shall we make our way to the drawing room, Darce?' The colonel headed for the door. 'I could do with some refreshments. I am parched.'

'If you talked less, your throat would require less lubrication.'

Elizabeth bit back on a laugh; Mr Darcy did not deserve any sign of approval from her.

They filed from the room, the colonel leading the way, Georgiana on his arm as he spoke urgently to her and, conscious Mr Darcy was behind them, Elizabeth took Anne's arm and walked in silence to the drawing room. How could she excuse herself and find the space to indulge her thoughts?

Once inside the room, however, Anne tugged on Elizabeth's sleeve. 'Take a turn with me?'

'Of course.'

They walked away from the end of the room where the company settled. 'I have seen Mr Robinson just now, and we spoke of the amnesia.'

Pushing aside her own frustrations, Elizabeth took Anne's arm, speaking as quietly as she had. 'Oh, and what did he say?'

'That head injuries could be erratic. A law unto themselves. A temporary amnesia is all too common after a severe concussion.'

Elizabeth threw Anne a sharp look as they turned about and walked back towards the centre of the room. 'Temporary? How long is temporary?'

Anne's face filled with trepidation. 'Precisely. He was unable to say. Patchy spots in the memory were not uncommon, depending on the nature of the blow.'

Drawing to a halt, Elizabeth released Anne's arm and faced her. 'And his prognosis in this case?'

Anne shrugged lightly. 'Mr Robinson says such ailments usually resolve themselves within a few days.'

'Usually? And when it's not usual?'

'There is a chance he will never regain all his memories.'

Elizabeth comprehended Anne's worried visage. 'If that is the only lasting effect, we must be thankful.'

Anne smiled, but it faded quickly. 'Yes, of course, but…what if Frederick's full memory does not return for months?' She spoke urgently. 'And if it does, he will be as angry as he was when first I broke off the engagement or worse, disgusted by the ruse and my going along with it.'

'All will right itself in a matter of days, Anne. Surely the captain's brother has received word by now?'

Anne frowned. 'Perchance Mr Darcy's letter sits unopened, awaiting his return from the Lakes?'

They both turned around as the door opened and Mrs Reynolds and a footman entered with the tea.

'Speculation will not resolve the matter. Besides'— Elizabeth tried to reassure her friend as the others rose from their seats—'we shall cross that bridge when we come to it. Captain Wentworth's improvement is the most important thing for the present and any distress could be detrimental.'

'As you say.' Anne sounded quite uncertain.

'You are not motivated by selfish gain; you seek only to aid him. Let it rest for the present.'

'You are mistaken, Lizzy. I do gain, for I am experiencing once more the knowledge I am beloved to him.'

The ladies joined the others, Elizabeth wishing for something stronger than the tea on offer, and what with her confusion over Mr Darcy, her indignation on behalf of Wickham, and her concern for Anne, she felt completely justified in the notion.

Captain Wentworth was asleep when the ladies entered the sick room the following morning. Anne was pleased to see he had received the attentions of a manservant, his face freshly shaven and his hair more tamed, though she was less content to hear he had again been in distress during the night.

When he gradually awakened, to blink at the canopy above him, Anne spoke his name softly, and he swallowed visibly before turning his head on the pillow.

'I am plagued by bad dreams.'

Anne shook her head. 'It is to be expected, Frederick. Did you...' she hesitated. 'Was your night much disturbed?'

The gentleman released a long breath. 'I do not wish to speak of it.' Then, he frowned. 'I wish to remember.'

'It will take a little time.' Anne bit her lip, conscious of Elizabeth's comforting hand on her shoulder.

'You have all my letters?' The captain turned his head again, and his eyes were intent upon her.

'Le...letters?'

'I must have written to you over the past five years.'

'I... I promise I have kept all you ever wrote me.'

The captain stirred restlessly against his pillows. 'Then seek out those whilst I was at sea since the year six. If you read them back to me, perchance the intervening years will return.'

Anne stared at him. 'I—I cannot.'

'How so?'

'They are not here.' Elizabeth smiled at the captain. 'They are at Kellynch, sir.'

'Yes, indeed, Frederick. My father has twice written to order me home. I shall not cross the threshold until I am confident he would not attempt to prevent my return.'

The burst of interest seemed to fade from the captain as Anne spoke, and his eyelids began to droop again.

'Of course. Forgive me. I had hopes…'

Anne threw Elizabeth a frantic look. How difficult had *that* been?

'Let him rest,' her friend said quietly, raising her book. 'I shall read for a while to give you some privacy.'

Elizabeth took a chair by the window and barely minutes later, the captain opened his eyes again, and Anne was thankful his thoughts were with his family.

'Your brother was offered a living of his own in Shropshire. He was already committed to leaving the day after learning of your ship's fate, believing you lost.'

Captain Wentworth released a long, slow breath. 'Such pain I have caused.'

'But through no fault of your own.' Anne spoke earnestly, desperate to ease his inner turmoil. Glancing over to see if Elizabeth remained lost in the pages of her book, Anne took his hand. 'Surely, the reverend will receive Mr Darcy's letter as soon as he returns from the Lakes.'

'The Lakes?' The captain's brow furrowed. 'Since when were the Lakes in Shropshire?'

Anne smiled, relishing the warmth of his hand in hers. 'Since you ask, there are lakes in Shropshire, some quite large, but you misunderstand me. Your brother left here for Leominster, where he was to be married, before he and his wife travelled on to the Lakes for a few days before taking up his living. He had left his new direction with the incoming incumbent at Monkford, and as we had no notion of his address whilst travelling, the intelligence of your being brought here had to go there, where it is likely awaiting his return.'

There was silence for a moment, the captain staring at the canopy, and Anne chewed on her bottom lip. Once Mr Wentworth did return, he would doubtless be on the next post to Somersetshire and these precious moments would be over.

'And Sophy? I cannot recall...what did you say of my sister?'

'I suspect the Admiralty will have notified her, if she is, as we believe, at sea with her husband. You told me often of her delight in sailing to the Indies with him. The news may not reach them for some months.'

The captain sighed heavily. 'I feel as though I am floundering. In the year six, Sophy lived in Southampton. I can even recall the direction.'

'If it were so, then she would have been here before now. At least the news of your loss will be followed swiftly by that of your rescue—indeed, they may even arrive together.'

'Of course.' Captain Wentworth's solemn gaze met Anne's. 'I would not have her sadness endure a moment longer than it must.'

'These circumstances, Frederick, you are powerless to alter. What you can do is rest and become whole again.'

He said nothing for a moment, and then a frown puckered his forehead. 'What day is it? I do not even comprehend *that*!'

'It is a Sunday in mid-December.' Anne eyed the clock on the mantel. 'They will be bringing you some nourishment shortly. We will leave you to eat and then you must try to sleep a little.'

She made to get up, but the captain retained a grip on her hand.

'Kiss me,' he whispered, casting a fleeting glance to where Elizabeth sat.

Her friend raised her head, but she simply smiled, turning back to her book as the captain tugged on Anne's hand again.

'I promise to be a good patient and rest, but at least bid me a proper farewell.' He closed his eyes and pursed his lips comically, and Anne could not help but laugh quietly.

'There.' She placed her lips gently on his, felt the responding pressure, an almost new sensation coiling around whispers of memory, then pulled away.

'Thank you, my love,' he murmured.

If only it could remain that way. Anne tried to conceal her growing trepidation, getting to her feet and turning towards her friend, who put aside her book.

'Is it time we left the good captain in peace?'

Captain Wentworth made a dissatisfied sound. 'The good captain is accepting the peace begrudgingly.'

Anne turned back. 'I believe, sir, we had a bargain. It is time you honoured your part.'

The anxiety that at any moment he might recall what truly happened between them rose again, and Elizabeth took Anne's arm as they left the room and gave it a comforting squeeze.

'What if that is the last time Frederick stays within the haze of his lost memory?' Anne could feel tension stretching across her frame like an iron bar.

'And what if it is not?'

Anne shook her head as they came to a halt at the top of the stairs. 'That is as much a problem too.' She turned to face Elizabeth. 'One thing *is* certain. *I* must be the one to tell him the truth if he does not naturally recover his memories in the next day or so. Should his brother arrive, not only will all disguise be over, but to hear of it from another will make it more cruel than ever.'

Darcy strode through the house with purpose the following morning, having earlier broken his fast with his cousin. Even had he not considered this journey to Town a necessity, a break from the colonel's teasing over Elizabeth would be welcome—though the loss of her company would not.

Company... Darcy shook his head at his own foolishness. He could hardly call the formal exchanges he and Elizabeth managed during the previous evening's dinner and afterwards in the drawing room any such thing. Their words rose like a barrier between them unceasingly.

Darcy's helplessness in defending himself plagued him, but what could he say to the lady? He could not speak of Wickham's degenerate behaviour without incriminating his sister, and with the impending threat from Sir Walter, he would take no further risk of exposing Georgiana. As for Elizabeth's sister...well, that was a topic best avoided too.

Having reached the hall, Darcy turned down the corridor towards the library. A book would help pass the interminable hours.

And you will not read a single page...

'Enough,' Darcy muttered, closing the door to the small library firmly on the sentiment.

CHAPTER TWENTY-SEVEN

Having finished letters to Charlotte, and to Jane—who would arrive in Gracechurch Street later that day—Elizabeth hurried over to the main house to exchange a book, her mind engrossed in thoughts of her sister and wondering when they would be together again.

At least Mr Darcy had gone away. To be certain, by the time he returned, Captain Wentworth may have recovered. Perchance all would be settled between Anne and the captain, and Elizabeth would be free to return to Longbourn—after all, when first she came to Kellynch, this coming Thursday had been set for her departure.

Recalling the expression upon Mr Darcy's face at dinner the night before, Elizabeth paused outside the library door. Why did his eye fall so often upon her, and what was its purpose? She was certain there was not hatred in his...

'Oh!'

Warmth flooded Elizabeth's cheeks as the door opened to reveal the gentleman himself.

'I thought you were for London.'

'I depart directly. I wish to read on the journey.' Darcy raised the book in his hand.

Elizabeth held up her own book. 'May I exchange this for another, sir? I thought it might help me sleep.' It had not, despite burning her candle until the wick expired.

To her surprise, Mr Darcy took it from her and studied the title before handing it back. 'You are not sleeping?'

Elizabeth was amused at his surprise. 'No, but the frustration of being powerless to resolve my dilemmas is all that ails me. It is not a feeling I am unfamiliar with.' This was true, but perhaps never to such a confusing extent.

'I am grieved to hear of it.'

She stepped into the small library as he moved aside.

'I will leave you to enjoy your solitude, Miss Bennet, before another day as chaperone begins.'

'I wish you a pleasant sojourn, sir.'

He held her gaze for a moment, and Elizabeth stirred under its intensity. 'I foresee little pleasure in it. It is a matter of duty.'

'Oh.' What was she to say to that? The gentleman continued to regard her keenly, setting Elizabeth's insides tumbling like leaves on a breezy autumn day. 'Then, I hope it is a successful one.'

Mr Darcy did not speak for a moment, then said, 'I will let you be the judge.' He turned away. 'Good day, Miss Bennet.'

Confounded by the gentleman's cryptic words, Elizabeth stared after him as he strode down the corridor until he was out of sight. What was his purpose in employing such a turn of phrase?

'Elizabeth, are you ready? Have you found a book?'

She looked up to see Anne coming towards her. 'Not yet. I shall make haste.'

Surely *any book* would help banish thoughts of Mr Darcy from her head—for as long as her mind would permit. Grabbing a random book, she joined her friend, and they fell into step together.

Then, Anne cast Elizabeth a curious look. 'Did you happen to see Mr Darcy just now?'

'Yes, he left the library as I arrived. Why do you ask?'

Anne smirked. 'I cannot help but wonder about the gentleman, standing stock still in the middle of the entrance hall, his attention on naught of consequence. One might assume he has been assailed by an excess of feelings.'

Elizabeth laughed. 'That or he has forgotten where he left his—'

'Heart?'

'Anne!'

Much as Elizabeth was taken by the daily improvement in Anne's spirits, she was not quite ready to be teased about Mr Darcy.

'I meant to say, his pride.'

Anne's smile widened as they too reached the empty entrance hall.

'Of course you did, Lizzy.'

Elizabeth expected to derive comfort from Mr Darcy's absence. After all, the comprehension she could not encounter him by chance in the corridors should have been a relief. The lack of his presence at table ought to have enhanced her enjoyment of each meal, but for some inexplicable reason, by the morning after the gentleman's departure, she felt quite the contrary.

Frowning as she closed the door to the sickroom, Elizabeth paused. How had the gentleman managed to become such an object?

Shaking her head—for she had no answer—she set off down the stairs, intent upon distraction. The patient had rested well throughout the previous day and been far more awake than asleep, and this morning Anne's attention had been fixed upon the captain as the apothecary aided him in taking his first unsteady steps. It proved to be a surprisingly intimate moment, and Elizabeth felt, had she been in similar circumstances to her friend, she would have appreciated some privacy.

Intent upon losing herself in a melody, Elizabeth opened the music room door with relief, thankful to find it empty. She took the stool before the instrument and began to play an air she knew by heart, recalling fondly how the learning of it once plagued her so. By the time the last notes faded into the air, she felt much more composed, but then she frowned as she detected voices outside the door.

'…to ever feel the fault lies with *me*.' It was Georgiana, and Elizabeth waited expectantly for the door to open, but a man's voice—the colonel's—responded, the words too quietly spoken to be discerned.

'If you say so, Richard.' There was a pause, the rumble of the colonel's voice and a small laugh from Georgiana. 'I shall do as you bid. I promise. You know practising my music always soothes me.'

For a second, Elizabeth felt conspicuous sitting on the lady's stool and at her pianoforte—an interloper—and she considered the nearby window. No, it would not do to be caught climbing out of it, but all the same—

'Oh! Miss Bennet. Forgive me. I did not mean to disturb you.'

Elizabeth rose from the stool, smiling warmly as the young lady came into the room. 'I have finished. I will leave you to your practise.'

'Please do not go!' Georgiana stepped forward eagerly. 'I would appreciate some company, and Richard has some letters of business to attend to before he is at liberty to entertain me.'

'Then I shall do as I am bid, for my friend is also occupied in aiding the captain and the apothecary.'

They walked by mutual consent over to a chaise near the fireplace. 'It is pleasing to hear the captain makes progress.'

'He is awake more than asleep now and is currently being put through his paces in an attempt to ensure he is upright more than he is prone.'

'Miss Elliot seems truly devoted.' Georgiana's eyes were upon the hands resting in her lap. 'How fortunate they both are to have found each other, to share such a reciprocal respect and admiration.'

Elizabeth's heart warmed even more to the young girl at her side, and she tried to catch Georgiana's lowered gaze. 'You are full young, Miss Darcy. Certainly not of an age to be yearning for something as though it had long been unattainable.'

Slowly, Georgiana raised her head, then summoned a smile. 'Perhaps. I thought not of myself, though. My brother has long admired—' She stopped, a hand shooting to her mouth.

Elizabeth did not know what to say. Did she imply Mr Darcy had developed a *tendresse* for someone? To her surprise, the notion did not please her, but she pushed it aside only to discern the disquiet upon Georgiana's features.

'Do not speak of it, if it pains you.'

Georgiana shook her head. 'I cannot. I should not have spoken so unguardedly. It is…a matter, a situation relating to my brother of which I am not at liberty to speak.'

Elizabeth's brow furrowed. Why did it unsettle her? What did it matter to her if Mr Darcy finally found someone to become his wife? Was he not already to marry his cousin?

'Miss Bennet, please do not mention this to my brother!'

Elizabeth settled back in her seat. 'I can assure you, I shall not. Besides, you have not spoken out of turn. I cannot imagine you have ever given your brother a moment's unease.'

To Elizabeth's discomfort, this did not seem to appease Georgiana, who leapt to her feet, her hands clasped together.

'You do not know...you cannot comprehend...it is...oh!' Sinking back into her seat, Georgiana's head dropped into her hands, and Elizabeth stared in confusion.

Then, she leaned forward, gently removing the hands from Georgiana's face, disturbed to see tears forming in her eyes.

'There now, Miss Darcy.' Elizabeth pulled a neatly pressed handkerchief from her sleeve, offering it over. 'Do not be distressed. I am mortified to have touched on a matter that brings you such despair. Please consider my words unsaid. My mother often says I would do better to forego attempts to embroider a sampler and sew my own lips together instead.'

Georgiana stopped patting her eyes and stared at Elizabeth in astonishment. 'She did not!'

Elizabeth almost agreed. What Mrs Bennet said had been far worse, but Georgiana was too innocent for such words.

'I seem to have been born with a propensity for impertinence. Suffice it to say, it has not endeared me to Mama.' Relieved her confession seemed to have returned some animation to Georgiana, Elizabeth smiled. 'There, let us put it aside and speak of other subjects.'

'Small, inconsequential nothings?'

To Elizabeth's surprise, Georgiana stood again, this time pacing over to the pianoforte, then back again.

'Though our acquaintance is of short duration, Miss Bennet, I have already grown to admire your confidence and candour.' She stopped, then drew in a breath. 'I would aspire to the same, though I suspect I shall never quite achieve it.'

'At the risk of repeating myself, you are, as I understand it, but sixteen years of age?' Elizabeth felt all of her twenty years as she spoke, but Georgiana merely nodded as she stepped to the window.

'As wonderful as my brother and cousin are to me, I fear they see me as a child still, and more so, a foolish and weak one.' Georgiana spun around to face Elizabeth. 'No one would think that of you, Miss Bennet. If only I could have been more like you when…' Colour seeped back into her cheeks.

Her curiosity at its height, Elizabeth joined Georgiana at the window.

'I am flattered you believe me a person worth emulating, dear Miss Darcy, but I do not think there are many who would agree.' Elizabeth studied the young girl before her. Anxiety was writ clear upon her countenance, and Elizabeth's heart went out to her. 'Have you no female friend, a confidante upon whose trust and discretion you can rely?'

Georgiana shook her head. 'My companion is a kind lady. She is vastly older than I, and though I find her good company, I would not be easy discussing something so personal.'

Elizabeth frowned. 'And have you no friends of your own age? No female cousins?'

'I was tutored at home, and my only female cousin is of an age with my brother. She is not in the best of health and lives with her mother—my aunt Catherine—in Kent. I have not seen her in recent years.'

The faceless cousin intended for Mr Darcy, no doubt. This was delicate ground, and if the gentleman knew she offered a confidential ear to his sister, he would likely drag her by the scruff of her neck to the nearest post carriage and send her packing.

What should she do?

CHAPTER TWENTY-EIGHT

Once the captain exerted himself as best he could for Mr Robinson, he collapsed heavily onto the bed, and Anne eyed him with concern. He had taken but a half dozen, unsteady steps, and they had drained all his strength.

As the apothecary rummaged in his bag, Captain Wentworth sent Anne a resigned look.

'What will you think of me? I am weak as a kitten.'

Anne shook her head. 'You are incredibly strong. Days of rest and nourishment will soon bring improvement. Besides, I have a particular fondness for kittens. You must be patient.'

The captain raised a brow. 'Do you ever recall me being patient?'

'Not particularly.' Anne smiled as Mr Robinson turned around, a phial in his hand. 'But you must try.'

'If you would excuse us, ma'am.' The apothecary raised the phial. 'I must complete my ministrations.'

Anne left the room and took a seat on a settle, her head so conflicted, she knew not what to think.

The novelty of being able to speak to Frederick after all this time, of the resurgence of her love for him and the intimacy of being beside him in his borrowed clothes, informal out of necessity, felt overwhelming.

Much as she knew the truth must come out—and opposed as she was in general to deception of any kind—Anne shied away from telling him. These stolen days were too precious and would be over soon enough. Her head comprehended the foolishness of delaying, but her heart begged for just one more day…

The door opened and Mr Robinson came out.

'The patient is all yours, Miss Elliot.'

'Thank you.' Anne stood, and walked over to the open door, then hesitated upon the threshold. She ought to find Elizabeth first.

Anne took a step forward. The captain was in bed once more, the sheet draped across him and his eyes closed. Perhaps she would leave him to sleep and—

'Are you coming in or not?' The captain opened one eye and peered over at her. 'I am in need of comfort.'

'I should wait for—'

'Chaperones be damned! I am hardly in a condition to do you any harm.' He had both eyes open and held out a hand to her. 'I have lost five years. I do not intend to waste another minute.'

Unable to resist him, Anne left the door wide open and crossed the room to take his hand. 'Is Mr Robinson pleased?'

Captain Wentworth scowled. 'Pleased as one can be with a man who is incapable of supporting his own weight.'

'Frederick,' Anne cautioned as she sat on the chair beside the bed.

'I know, I know. I must be *patient*.' He gestured to the far wall. 'I have been left a stick. I shall be able to stagger about like an old man before long. How capital is that?'

'It is excellent.' Anne eyed his disgruntled expression. 'And think how happy you are making the walking cane by giving it a purpose.'

A reluctant smile tugged at the captain's lips. 'I recall well your ability to see the good in all situations, dearest Anne.' He ran a hand through his hair. 'I wish I did not feel so weary. I do not want you to leave, but I fear I may be overcome with fatigue.'

'I will not tarry, for rest will surely be the best possible aid.' She made to get up, but he held onto her hand.

'Wait.' Captain Wentworth pushed himself up from the pillows. 'I must speak whilst opportunity presents.'

'What is it?'

'A recollection from the year six. Your father...he was opposed to the match, was he not? And your godmother, Lady Russell. She did not regard me with favour.'

Anne's throat felt tight with emotion. Had the captain only recently remembered that? Unable to speak, she nodded, her eyes fastened upon him.

'Then, promise me this, we will be married as soon as I am able to stand for the length of time it takes to say our vows.'

Her heart thundering in her chest, Anne stared at him. What should she do? To refuse would require a world of explanation she simply was not ready for. To accept would only enhance the deceit.

Where, oh, where is Elizabeth?

'Anne?'

She drew in some air. 'Frederick, you know how much I love you, do you not?' Her voice hitched in her throat as his eyes filled with the warm regard she well remembered.

'That I shall *never* forget! We vowed all those years ago, my love, that no one would be happier than us. I can well recall a period of exquisite felicity.' He raised the hand he held and kissed it. 'Come, Anne. Your father considered me beneath you, and vowed he would not aid you financially, but he did not withhold consent. Now you are of age and able to act accordingly.'

Anne could deny none of it. Had she not long regretted being persuaded to let him go? But how could she deceive him further?

'I promise—' Her voice broke and Captain Wentworth's gaze softened as tears filled her eyes. 'All I can promise is the constancy of my feelings for you. Our time apart has not altered that.' Anne's skin grew warm under his intense look. 'I wish you to comprehend this: nothing would make me happier than to be your wife.'

There. It was all the truth she could speak.

Captain Wentworth reached up a hand to wipe a tear from her cheek, then kissed her quite thoroughly before falling back against his pillows.

His eyes closed and Anne, her heart still racing from the intimacy of the moment, drew in a shallow breath.

What now?

'Miss Darcy'—Elizabeth took the lady's hand—'as someone surrounded by females of a similar age, I have honed my listening talents. You can trust in my silence.'

Georgiana did not speak, and Elizabeth was about to retract her words. After all, what did she know of her, beyond this short acquaintance?

'I am burdened by my own doing. There was…' Georgiana waved a hand. 'An incident occurred in the summer. I am ashamed of my part in it, accept fully my responsibility, though both my brother and my cousin…' She broke off. 'You know the colonel is my co-guardian with Fitz, yes?'

Elizabeth nodded, and Georgiana continued.

'They are of the conviction I was taken advantage of, persuaded away from my natural inclination. There is some truth in it, but are there not consequences to all our actions, consciously done or otherwise? I wish to own my part, and I took steps to ensure I would never forget the mistake I made in believing…'

Feeling deeply for her, Elizabeth squeezed the hand she still held.

'Dear Miss Darcy, I am a firm advocate of owning one's actions, but I cannot believe you consciously did anything worthy of such self-blame as this. From what you have said thus far, I suspect you have been betrayed by someone you considered a friend?'

Georgiana hesitated, and Elizabeth continued. 'And, if that someone was a man…' Colour flooded the girl's cheeks, and Elizabeth placed a comforting hand on her arm. What must she have been through? 'Even the most confident and mature of women can struggle to discern a rogue from a gentleman; such is the former's talent in their art. You will learn from the experience, but do not live under its cloud.'

'I have striven not to do so, I swear. But my brother—' Georgiana's voice hitched, and Elizabeth took her hand and led her back to the chaise. What had Mr Darcy done? Had he been unfeeling?

They resumed their seats from earlier, and Georgiana raised troubled eyes to Elizabeth. 'My brother rescued me, saved me, and paid the cost of it. That much is true. And it is *he* who continues to pay it, and that is all my fault.'

Elizabeth frowned. What had this poor girl experienced, and at whose hands? As for Mr Darcy…she regretted her first instinct had been to think negatively of him. As a brother, he could not be faulted.

With a gentle smile, Elizabeth took Georgiana's hand in hers again. 'I do not mean to demean your brother's heroic deeds in the least, but that is the mark of a good and honourable man, acting as he should for his loved one. It is not a weight he would wish you to suffer under.'

'Fitz would not. He does not. Forgive me, Miss Bennet, for putting on such a poor show. What will you think of me?'

'I think extremely highly of you. It is time you began believing your brother's words.'

'I had almost begun to do so.' Georgiana's troubled air increased. 'Until my latest blunder. I cannot see how he is to recover from it.'

Elizabeth had no notion of the lady's meaning, but before she could say anything further, the door opened, and the colonel breezed into the room.

'Well met, dear ladies.' He looked between them. 'There is a decided air of despondency in the room. My presence was more sorely missed than I had anticipated.'

Georgiana got to her feet. 'Miss Bennet has been a good friend to me, Richard, and an excellent listener.'

Her reassurance seemed to carry little weight, and Elizabeth noted the narrowing of the colonel's eyes as he assessed his young cousin. Nor did she miss the sidelong glance he gave her.

'If you will excuse me, sir. Miss Darcy.' Elizabeth rose from her seat. 'I must find Miss Elliot.'

Closing the door firmly behind her, Elizabeth paused for a moment, trying to assimilate all she heard. Some rogue had clearly preyed upon Georgiana, and Mr Darcy had come to her rescue; that much was clear.

But what had been her latest blunder, and how was it her brother was unlikely to recover from it?

Captain Wentworth improved rapidly and was able to leave his chamber the next day to take a small amount of exercise on the landing, but once this was over, Anne was determined to spend a few hours with him. Elizabeth had several letters to write, and when Mrs Annesley offered to sit in the room in her stead, she left Anne reading a book to the captain and repaired to the cottage so that she could write at the comfort of a desk rather than with her slope resting on her lap.

She soon completed a letter to her Aunt Gardiner, followed by a shorter one to her father—who knew she had moved residence on the estate but not precisely whose home it was. Afterwards, Elizabeth wandered back to the main house to leave them on the salver in the hall, but found it difficult to settle to anything else. She did not wish to intrude upon Georgiana again, especially if she enjoyed her cousin's company and she wandered along one of the corridors to a conservatory, shown to her by Mrs Reynolds the other day.

It was rather cold as there was no hearth, and Elizabeth tugged her woollen shawl more tightly around her middle as she fetched up by one of the tall windows. Dusk would fall shortly, and the skies were laden once more; would more snow come? If so, might it impede Mr Darcy from returning when he was due?

Turning slowly on her heel, Elizabeth hardly noticed the room as the image of the gentleman's face formed before her.

Had she become interested in him?

'Never!'

'I beg your pardon?'

Startled, Elizabeth turned towards the glass doors to the garden. The colonel had come into the room.

'It is cold enough to freeze the—ah well.' He grinned at Elizabeth as he tugged his gloves from his hands and removed his great coat, tossing them onto a settle before walking over to join her.

'I thought you were with Miss Darcy, Colonel.'

'As indeed I was, until I was called on to visit the stables to assess my mount. A problem with his fetlock.' The colonel studied Elizabeth where she remained in the middle of the room. 'I would say, forgive the interruption, ma'am, but I suspect I do not disturb you?'

Elizabeth shook her head. 'Not at all. You are a welcome distraction from my thoughts.'

'A man likes to be of service.' His countenance sobered. 'Miss Bennet, I wonder—or do I ask too much—if I might have a moment of your time?'

'Yes, of course. How may I assist?'

He gestured towards one of the comfortable-looking armchairs facing the gardens. 'Please, be seated.'

They settled opposite each other, and Elizabeth waited, as the colonel seemed to be organising his thoughts.

'I am not blind to the fact I interrupted a conversation of a delicate nature yesterday. Georgie would not oblige me when I asked if anything troubled her, and I did not wish to press her. I do not wish to press *you* either, against your confidence, but there is a reason why I wish to at least ask. Is there anything I, or Darcy, ought to be aware of, with regard to our charge?'

Though Georgiana revealed little enough, Elizabeth could understand the colonel's concern and was thankful she had no need to be evasive.

'Far from it, sir. Miss Darcy was incredibly discreet and told me nothing of substance. I have no reason to suspect there is anything troubling her, beyond what you or Mr Darcy already know. I was only grateful she believed she could talk to me.'

The colonel stretched his legs out in front of him, nestling back into the chair.

'She is learning, but still has a tendency to be indiscreet. It is unfortunate Georgie has so few females around her, even less so near her own age. Had that been the case, she might well not have—' He stopped and cleared his throat. 'I would not have you think badly of her, Miss Bennet.'

Elizabeth's eyes widened. 'I, sir? I could not think more highly of Miss Darcy. You'—she hesitated—'you and your cousin have done an admirable job in raising her so well.'

'And yet two grown men could not protect her when the time came.' He spoke almost under his breath, but Elizabeth got the gist of his words.

'You cannot blame yourself, Colonel. You must know, even more so than I comprehend, there are those with sufficient charm to disguise their intentions.'

The colonel seemed unappeased. 'It is even more of an affront to one's blindness when the scum once nestled almost within the bosom of one's own family.'

Elizabeth's mind swiftly made the connection.

Surely it was not Mr Wickham who had...

'You surmise correctly.'

Her gaze flew to meet the colonel's. 'I—I am not sure I comprehend your meaning.'

'Wickham. George Wickham, to be precise. You are acquainted, are you not?'

CHAPTER TWENTY-NINE

Elizabeth eyed the colonel warily. 'I—er, yes. I met Mr Wickham in Hertfordshire but two months ago.' Her mind was in turmoil. This could not be true! 'How do you…how could you…?'

'Darcy told me where the scoundrel had reappeared, wrote to me soon after to say he had returned to Town, not wishing to leave Georgie unattended with Wickham in a neighbouring county.'

'I am shocked.' It was an understatement. 'I am pained for all Miss Darcy must have suffered.'

The colonel threw her an assessing look. 'You seem disturbed by this intelligence, Miss Bennet. Would I be right in surmising you perceived him an honourable man?'

The same coldness swept through Elizabeth as had come over her when Colonel Fitzwilliam mentioned Wickham's name the previous day.

She drew in a measured breath. 'Are you at liberty to tell me what happened? You may trust upon my discretion.' When the colonel hesitated, Elizabeth felt compelled to confess further.

'I begin to fear I have been fed falsehoods against your family. I would like to know the extent of my own naiveté.'

'Darcy said as much. You know of Wickham's past association with this family?'

Elizabeth wished she did not. 'Mr Wickham spoke of it.'

The colonel's expression darkened. 'One of his favourite tales. Distorted, of course. Like the whole story of his life.'

Swallowing on a sudden restriction as disgust rose in her throat, Elizabeth leaned forward. 'Were they engaged?'

'Georgiana believed they would be.' The colonel waved a hand. 'Oh, Wickham can be excessively convincing, appearing genuine and sincere, so much so, she believed the family would be happy for her. But she was merely a pawn in his evil game. Wickham's interest was two-fold: Georgiana's dowry and to bring pain upon Darcy.'

Elizabeth closed her eyes. The shame of having been taken in by Mr Wickham! How could she have believed him so easily and on so brief an acquaintance? So convinced had she been, she defended the man to Mr Darcy!

She opened her eyes to encounter Colonel Fitzwilliam's concerned expression.

'And Mr Darcy rescued her from him?' The colonel nodded. Elizabeth's mouth had gone dry. 'And Mr Wickham's promised parish?'

'You know of that too? You are not the first he has regaled with tales of being robbed of his inheritance. When the time came, Wickham professed no interest in taking up the living, requesting a pecuniary compensation, that he might take up law as a profession. He was granted the money—a substantial sum—and swiftly squandered it. I am privy to these matters as I am not only Georgiana's co-guardian but also an executor of the estate.'

Elizabeth got unsteadily to her feet, and the gentleman did likewise.

'You can trust in my discretion, Colonel.' She cleared her throat. 'If you will excuse me. I need to…'

Colonel Fitzwilliam took Elizabeth's hand and squeezed it lightly before releasing it. 'Forgive me for any distress I may have caused. It is important you know the truth.'

The truth? Elizabeth left the conservatory with relief. This was sufficient to keep her mind occupied for days, despite having heard but half a story. What troubled Georgiana was clear, but this blunder in her past was not all. What had she said? That her brother continues to pay the price for her indiscretion, and that it was all her fault… What on earth could she mean?

And why did it suddenly matter to Elizabeth that she find out?

Dinner passed without incident, though Elizabeth was conscious of the colonel's thoughtful scrutiny. He need have no fear. She would take all she knew of Georgiana to the grave before she would divulge it to any other living soul.

Elizabeth was relieved to hear from her aunt the following morning, confirming Jane was well settled in Gracechurch Street and determined to enjoy the few days between then and when they travelled to Longbourn for Christmas.

After the ladies breakfasted, Anne begged Elizabeth to attend her. The captain was to venture out of his room for the first time and this exploit would consist of walking up and down the landing with the aid of his walking cane, the stairs being a little beyond him at present.

'You are doing so well Frederick.' Anne spoke encouragingly from his side.

'I am walking like a drunken goat.'

'Do not speak so! The description is not totally without accuracy, but you should not say it.'

Elizabeth longed to enquire how either of them ever encountered an inebriated goat but did not want to intrude upon them. The couple's endearing interactions were the only thing thus far to distract her from what she learned about Wickham, Miss Darcy, and her complex brother. How much of what Elizabeth thought of the latter was because of what Wickham told her?

Too much.

'I shall topple you over.' Captain Wentworth came to a halt. 'Let me sit for a moment.'

Anne helped the captain towards a nearby seat, and he retained his hold on her hand as she sat beside him.

Elizabeth pointedly stared out the nearest window. The skies were grey with low-lying, thick clouds, and a few flakes of snow drifted down, spiralling towards the ground and disappearing from sight. Would it snow heavily again, and if it did, would Mr Darcy reach home as anticipated on the morrow?

For what seemed like the hundredth time, Elizabeth replayed all she could remember of her acquaintance with the gentleman. Though Mr Darcy was not entirely blameless in causing her offence, Wickham and his false words added significance to the prejudice she already held. The man would also have it that his former childhood friend was proud, but was it misplaced or simply misinterpreted?

With the truth before her, would she see Mr Darcy any differently?

Though the gentleman had not hidden his disdain for those he considered beneath his notice, Elizabeth could well comprehend how far he would go for those he loved, for those in need. Had she not seen it for herself in Mr Darcy's kindness towards an unknown, defenceless man? Was she not reminded daily of his value as a brother and of the warm respect he was held in by his household?

His image formed before Elizabeth—a memory from the other day, a warmth in his eyes she never detected before as he addressed her. What was it he intended to say before she stopped him the other day? What feelings did he intend to speak of—was it possible a man who once declared her as not handsome enough to tempt him had—

'What is it that fascinates you so about the grounds, Lizzy?' Anne joined her at the window, and Elizabeth tried to free herself from her tangled thoughts.

The captain walked slowly with the aid of his cane at the far end of the landing, and Anne eyed his progress fondly. 'Frederick wishes to try independently for a while.'

Elizabeth smiled. 'I am so happy for you. To think this seemed impossible not a week ago.'

'Believe me, I feel my luck.' Anne watched the captain's progress. 'Not just for Frederick's survival, though.' She faced Elizabeth. 'For your friendship, dear Lizzy. Without your kindness and fair counsel, I might well have gone mad. I fully comprehend I must own the truth to Frederick, and soon.' She hesitated. 'Even so, I would not…'

'You would not have it undone?'

Anne did not answer for a moment. 'No. No, I would not. Brief though this interlude might be, these last few days have been more than I ever dreamed possible. I will hold them dear all the rest of my life.'

Elizabeth turned back to stare out of the window. Would she hold these days dear too? She almost gasped at the notion. Whence had it come, and to what might it pertain?

'You are still deep in thought.'

Anne's words did not require an answer, but Elizabeth spoke all the same.

'Have you ever discovered someone to be vastly different from what you thought them to be?'

'You speak of Mr Darcy?'

'Yes... and no. Not entirely.' Elizabeth's acquaintance with Mr Darcy had endured for three months but felt as though it had lasted forever. Her acquaintance with Wickham was of even shorter duration.

'You are being mysterious! What is troubling you?'

For a moment, Elizabeth's mind drifted back to those few weeks in Hertfordshire, when Wickham's arrival in the room was sufficient to lift her spirits and the presence of Mr Darcy raised only her hackles. Yet she had erred without discerning it. Wickham claimed he would never expose the son for love of the father, but no sooner had Mr Darcy left the district, the tale was told to all who would listen.

'I considered myself a good judge of character. Indeed, the study of those around me has long been a habit of mine, but recently, I have found my talents falling short.'

Badly!

Captain Wentworth reached the end of the long corridor and took a moment to rest against the wall, and Anne sent Elizabeth a curious look.

'And what has it taught you?'

'That one person may have all the goodness, and the other merely the appearance of it.' Elizabeth sighed. 'Pay me no mind, Anne. I am perhaps left a little too much to my own devices. I am used to being in a household bustling with noise and activity—though the peace of Meadowbrook House brings some blessings, having so much time to think is not always beneficial.'

A sound drew their notice: Captain Wentworth testing out his cane again.

'His vigour is returning, Anne. He will be back to his full strength in no time, I am certain.'

'Then perhaps it is fortunate I have never felt more infused with liveliness than I do right now.'

Elizabeth burst into quiet laughter. 'Anne, for shame!'

Anne smirked. 'You must not judge me. Though Frederick has yet to regain his whole memory, I retain all of mine. There is no mystery about him for me. Whatever he says or does, it brings back poignant recollections. Daily he grows even more dear to me.' Her voice throbbed with the love behind her words, and Elizabeth sighed.

'You make me envious. I seem to be perpetually wrong-footed over the men I encounter.'

Anne frowned. 'What makes you say so?'

Elizabeth shook her head. 'Nothing. Truly, naught of consequence. I am—'

'Prepare yourselves, ladies. I am coming back.'

Captain Wentworth resumed his progress along the landing.

'Not before we are to be called away for tea,' whispered Elizabeth, and Anne swatted her arm gently.

'Stop it. He will think we are laughing at him.'

'We are, but I swear he will not notice, nor would he care.' Elizabeth moved away to prevent a second swat at her arm. 'Captain Wentworth thinks only of you, Anne.'

'And you think only of Mr Darcy,' Anne said archly as she walked away to meet the captain, praising him on his progress.

Conscious of warmth in her cheeks, Elizabeth turned back to the window. Curse the man for taking possession of her thoughts and dreams these past few days.

And it will only get worse.

The unwelcome thought was quickly quashed, but Elizabeth knew it was true. After all, was not the gentleman due to return on the following day?

Worsening weather forced Darcy to break his journey earlier than he hoped, and his conveyance pulled into a coaching inn just outside Marlborough soon after midday. Thankfully, there were few people travelling in the increasingly poor conditions, and Raworth soon secured more than adequate chambers and placed an order for an evening meal, such as it was.

Darcy put his eagerness to reach Somersetshire down to his concerns for his sister. If any thought of Elizabeth would intrude, he ignored it. There was little point in anticipating their next meeting. He knew full well the lady's opinion of him, and he doubted there was aught he could do to alter it.

'There is talk of another storm following on from this one, sir.' Raworth offered Darcy a newspaper, courtesy of the landlord, and a mug of ale.

Darcy took a swig, wiping his mouth on the back of his hand. It was palatable, as good as one could expect on this secondary turnpike—the coachman having foresworn the upper road. Although faster in good weather, it was far less direct a route, and the hope was to circumvent the worst of other carriage mishaps by making the diversion.

'We must leave at first light to avoid it then. Can you let Hartwright know to have the carriage ready?'

His valet set off to do just that, and Darcy leaned back in the chair, his attention ostensibly on the flickering flames in the hearth but truly many miles distant.

CHAPTER THIRTY

The snows came overnight, quite as deep as the previous fall, and as Elizabeth followed Anne across to the main house, she stepped carefully along the snow-covered terrace. Conscious she had slept better, her spirits rose, though she could not comprehend why. It must be the improvement in Captain Wentworth's condition and the pleasure it brought to her friend.

'Good morning, Miss Darcy.' Elizabeth smiled warmly at Georgiana as they entered the breakfast room. 'Is your cousin not joining us this morning?'

The young lady shook her head. 'Richard broke his fast early and has been out to help with clearing the paths. He said he would then call upon the captain. I believe he plans to put him through some drills.'

The conversation flowed comfortably, with Georgiana's spirits rising in anticipation of her brother's arrival.

'I hope he is not delayed.' Georgiana's gaze was drawn to the wintry scene through the window. 'I miss him a vast deal when he is away.'

Anne sipped her tea. 'Your mutual affection is pleasing to observe. Such fondness amongst sisters is a rare thing in my experience.'

'Fitz is the best of brothers.' Georgiana's admiration was almost palpable, and Anne threw Elizabeth an amused look.

Elizabeth held her tongue. It was not the time to point out that it was easy to be the best of anything if you were the only one. Then, she frowned and picked up her cup. Did she not judge Mr Darcy again, out of habit?

'Is your tea not to your liking, Miss Bennet?'

Elizabeth shook her head as she got to her feet. 'I shall fetch a fresh cup, for it has cooled beyond my preference.'

'What are your plans for the day, Miss Darcy?' Anne patted her lips with a napkin, as Elizabeth returned with a fresh cup of tea.

'I wish to practise a new piece of music, thus—'

She stopped as the door opened to reveal Mrs Reynolds.

'Pardon me for the interruption, Miss Georgiana.' She held out a note to Anne. 'The cart could not make it down the lane when it called at Kellynch Hall first thing this morning. The mail for Meadowbrook House and two other properties on the estate was left there for collection.'

Elizabeth looked to her friend as the housekeeper left, and Anne waved the note, which bore a scrawled line.

'My father orders me home again.'

'You will not go?'

Shaking her head, Anne put the note on the table. 'I doubt he will ever exert himself beyond the wielding of a pen. I shall be safe here.'

As shall I.

Elizabeth pushed the thought away. This was no time to develop an attachment to… anything.

Despite leaving at first light, the further west Darcy's carriage came, the more difficult the roads were to pass. They persevered with caution, however, and despite having to stop occasionally for Hartwright and his groom to dig the wheels out, they finally crossed the Somersetshire border by early afternoon.

Once they reached the smaller country lanes of the Kellynch estate, however, it was evident the conveyance could proceed no further, and pulling into the stables of a farmstead on the Stoke-sub-Hamdon road, Darcy stepped from the carriage. Inhaling deeply, he took a moment to assess his bearings, then addressed his valet.

'The road is impassable, Raworth. I shall proceed on foot. Do not attempt to bring any of the luggage this evening. See if the tenant of this farm will house the carriage in his outbuildings overnight. Everything can be fetched on the morrow.'

'But, sir, you cannot—'

Darcy raised a hand. 'I insist. I shall manage perfectly well with what is already at Meadowbrook House. Follow on as soon as you can. Mrs Reynolds will have a warming cup awaiting you.'

Trying not to think about Elizabeth—a futile pretence, as well he knew—Darcy set off down the lane. It was slow going, and his boots were hardly proof against the freezing conditions, but he had been determined to reach home today and the weather would not stop him.

Darcy's breath formed into swirling mist as he strode along, relishing the exertion after the confines of the carriage and conscious of his spirits rising and falling in turn.

It was a strange sensation, with his eagerness to be home tempered by the distaste he felt for being back at Kellynch.

How much longer could he keep Sir Walter hanging whilst he sought a way out?

With clumps of heavy snow clinging to the hem of his great coat, Darcy finally reached the driveway to Meadowbrook House, pleased to see a pathway had been cleared to the door, and he soon rounded the corner of the house and approached the door to the boot room.

There was no one about when he emerged into the hall, his discarded great coat and boots set out to dry by a passing footman, and he walked quickly into the entrance hall, not wishing to be seen in his unshod state.

About to put a foot on the bottom stair, however, a movement caught Darcy's eye, and swinging around, he came face to face with a startled Elizabeth.

Despite his embarrassment at his state of dress, Darcy bowed.

'Good afternoon, Miss Bennet.' He studied the colour filling Elizabeth's cheeks as she dropped a hurried curtsey.

'Good afternoon, sir. I trust you had a pleasant journey.'

'I did not. It was in all ways abominable.'

Elizabeth fleetingly observed his dishevelled hair, then his unshod feet and the icy droplets still clinging to his breaches. 'Yes, I suppose it would be. Your sister will be relieved you are safely returned.'

And you? Did you wish my return to be safe, or did you wish me to the ends of the earth and back again?

Darcy ran a hand through his hair. 'Er…quite. Excuse me, Miss Bennet.' He gestured at his state of attire. 'I must make myself presentable.'

He started up the stairs but was unable to resist another glimpse of the lady.

Elizabeth remained where he left her, her fine eyes fixed upon him, and Darcy acknowledged the heaviness of his heart.

Out of sight, out of mind was a fallacy. Of all the ineffectual, trite sayings there were, absence clearly did make the heart fonder.

✣

Frustrated by the fluctuations of her spirits upon Mr Darcy's sudden appearance, Elizabeth returned to the cottage, where she reprimanded herself over the unfathomable nature of her behaviour.

For heaven's sake, Lizzy Bennet! You fully comprehended the gentleman was due to return to his home today. Why are you so unsettled by it?

With a rueful smile, Elizabeth walked to the window to look at the house. She had badly misjudged Mr Darcy. It was bound to disturb, as was the recollection of all she had ever thought or said of Wickham.

After a half hour of reasoning with herself, she felt sufficiently composed to return to the main house and found her friend in the drawing room with the Darcys.

The gentleman was in quiet conversation with his sister, and Elizabeth hurried to join Anne beside the hearth.

'Do not let me interrupt you.' Elizabeth indicated Anne's book as she put it aside, but her friend shook her head.

'I am merely attempting to keep occupied.'

'Where are the captain and the colonel?'

'Together somewhere. Colonel Fitzwilliam has been overseeing more of Frederick's exercise and has managed to coax him down the stairs.'

'Heavens!' Elizabeth smiled widely. 'That is a good deal of progress.'

'I think Frederick was keen to leave his room. The colonel indicated they would go to the conservatory, as it is cool in temperature and has space for exertion.'

Elizabeth looked longingly at the window, avoiding the chaise where Mr Darcy and his sister sat. She missed the frequent exercise she had been used to taking at home.

Unable to help herself, she coolly turned her head to where Mr Darcy sat, only to find him regarding her, and Georgiana reading her book. She turned back, warmth filling her cheeks, not aided by the smirk on Anne's face.

'Stop it,' she hissed, but Anne merely raised a questioning brow.

'Perhaps he is reflecting upon the feelings he cannot suppress.' Anne spoke softly, but the heat in Elizabeth's face and neck deepened as her friend picked up her own book.

Staring into the flames in the hearth, Elizabeth drew in a shallow breath. If only Mr Darcy had stayed away longer.

Foolish girl. Your first thought upon espying the gentleman was quite the contrary, was it not?

Elizabeth lowered her head to her hands in her lap. Confound the man! How was it she had been pleased to see him?

A light tap came on the door, and Mrs Reynolds entered and approached her master.

'There is a gentleman at the door, Mr Darcy. He seems most anxious to see you. It is a reverend, Mr Wentworth.'

Anne threw Elizabeth a frantic look, all colour fading from her face, and as Mr Darcy left the room, the two friends rose from their seats.

'Will you excuse us, Miss Darcy?'

Georgiana raised her head from her book and smiled. 'Of course.'

They hurried from the room and across the hall to the foot of the stairs, where the sound of a man's voice carried to them from down the corridor to Mr Darcy's study.

'...was so gratified to receive your letter, sir.'

They heard a door close, and Elizabeth turned to Anne.

'It is the captain's brother, yes? He must have battled the conditions in his determination to get here.'

Anne drew in a shallow breath. 'I must go to Frederick. There can be no further delay.'

They both walked swiftly along the corridor to the conservatory, but it was empty.

'Where is he?'

'There!' Elizabeth pointed to the terrace at the back of the house. Captain Wentworth walked with the aid of his cane, his head down. He appeared to be talking to himself.

'Go to him, Anne. Speak openly, tell him of the constancy of your feelings. He will hear you out.'

If only it were so simple. Her throat tight with emotion, Anne hurried over to the doors into the garden and stepped outside, gasping as the cold air swept through her clothing.

'Frederick!' Her voice failed to reach him, and she hurried along the terrace, thankful a path through the snow had been cleared, and as she drew nearer, he heard her approach and turned around.

'What are you doing out here without your shawl?' The captain unbuttoned his coat before she could forestall him. 'Here.' He placed it about her frame, and Anne shivered, despite its warmth and her present agitation.

'Frederick, it is vital I speak to you immediately.'

If her air and countenance were insufficient to forewarn him, her urgent manner of speaking would have alerted him, and Captain Wentworth frowned, taking her hand in his.

'What is it? What has happened?'

They both spun around at the sound of firm steps coming from the far end of the stone terrace.

'Father!'

Sir Walter strode towards them, and Anne gripped Captain Wentworth's hand fiercely. Had her father come to remove her personally?

Fetching up before them, Sir Walter disregarded Captain Wentworth's short bow as he glared at his daughter.

'Miss Anne Elliot! What are you about? You have repeatedly ignored my orders to return to Kellynch Hall. Did I not expressly forbid you from visiting this man.' He gestured at the captain. 'Some days ago?'

Anne was conscious of the captain's rigidity at her side, of his need to rest heavily on his cane as he spoke with clipped tones.

'I resent your manner of speaking to the lady, sir. She is under my protection, not yours, whilst in this house.'

Sir Walter's look was scathing as he took in the captain's walking cane, which shook slightly in its efforts to support him.

'Protection? What an amusing concept.'

Anne drew in a sharp breath, but Captain Wentworth held her back as she went to step forward, whispering in her ear, 'Let him have his moment. It will not affect us.'

Though Frederick's voice was calming, the closeness of his form beside her bringing a hint of reassurance, Anne could not be so at ease.

'If you will excuse us, Sir Walter, your daughter has been standing in the cold for too long. She must return to the warmth of the house.'

'You will hear me out, Wentworth.' Sir Walter glared at the captain's exposed sleeves, then turned on Anne. 'You, Miss Anne Elliot, are a disgrace to the family.'

Captain Wentworth took an unsteady step forward, and Anne held onto his hand, conscious of the anger radiating from his body.

'You will not speak to Anne in that manner. As my wife-to-be, she is—I repeat—under my protection, and I will not have it.'

Anne's frantic gaze fastened upon her father, her hand gripping Frederick's as tightly as ever. She felt sick, her insides swirling as though a storm had struck, and she swallowed hard, trying to suppress her fear.

'How dare you refer to my daughter by her given name?' Sir Walter drew himself up. 'You are in need of a timely reminder, sir. You evidently recall setting your sights on Anne—a penniless sailor aspiring to the hand of the daughter of a baronet, no less?'

'I do.' The captain's voice was firm, his fury detectable in his bearing and the tight grip he maintained upon Anne's hand, even as the cane supporting him continued to quiver precariously.

Sir Walter sneered at him.

'Then you must also recall the end of the engagement and being sent on your way.' He pointed a finger at Anne. 'At my daughter's very own choice *and* by her doing.'

The captain's skin paled rapidly as the cane fell to the ground, and his expression was unreadable as he released Anne's hand. Her heart pounding, she shuddered under the warmth of his coat. This was the moment; the last one of Frederick loving her.

How would she ever recover a second time?

CHAPTER THIRTY-ONE

Anne's chest clenched so fiercely she could scarce draw breath. She recalled all too easily the disgust and anger on the captain's face all those years ago. After such a felicitous period, she could not bear to see them claim his features once more.

'Captain Wentworth suffers from a form of amnesia, Father. He has no recollection of our separation.' Anne's voice broke as tightness gripped her throat again, and she raised eyes brimming with tears to the captain. His face was white as the snow surrounding them, his countenance blank. 'Please try to forgive me, Frederick.'

Turning away, Anne moved as fast as her skirts would permit, but within a few steps her arm was firmly gripped.

'Wait. We are not done here.'

Anne took in the captain's pallor and the rigidity of his frame. His voice was strained, and she could tell he struggled to maintain his physical strength.

Unable to utter a word, her throat closed tightly in her anguish, Anne could only nod.

'Come with me.'

Captain Wentworth retrieved his cane, and Anne followed him to stand before her father once more.

For a moment, both men eyed each other with contempt. Then, the captain straightened and raised his chin.

'I recall full well my departure from this county in the year six. How could I not?'

Anne gasped and made to take a step backwards, but Captain Wentworth placed her hand on his arm and she held onto it tightly, conscious of the coldness of the captain's skin through his shirt as he turned back to face her father.

'But this has little relevance. I asked Anne to be my wife a second time, and she was minded to accept. Thus, *sir,* I think you may be mistaken, for we are, most assuredly, engaged to be married.'

Anne's mind reeled as her father's mouth opened, emitted no sound, then closed with a snap. Had Frederick truly recalled the past or did he claim it to be so in the face of her father?

'Preposterous!' Sir Walter's complexion turned an unflattering puce.

'On the contrary, sir, it is the first sensible thing to happen in recent memory.'

'I—this is—' Sir Walter stopped, drew in a breath, then glared at Anne. 'This is not the end of the matter!'

With that, he turned his back on them both and stalked back across the terrace, disappearing round the corner of the house.

Anne could scarce move, her mind reeling.

'I need your help.'

The captain's abrupt voice roused her. He was paler than ever, and with the aid of the cane and her arm, she led him over to a bench against the wall, onto which he dropped heavily.

'You cannot remain out here, Captain. We must get you inside.'

He drew in a long breath, then exhaled, struggling to his feet and wielding the cane again as they made their way slowly back towards the doors to the conservatory.

Once inside, Captain Wentworth sank onto the nearest chair, and Anne hurried to pull the bell. With no hearth, it should have felt extremely chilly, but after being outside for so long, it was a welcome relief from the biting December air.

Anne was uncertain what to do. The captain leaned his head back against the chair, his eyes closed, and she removed his coat and walked over to drape it across his chest, hoping she could return the warmth he had earlier given to her.

The captain's eyes remained closed, his features drawn, and Anne felt quite choked up. The strain had been too much for him, and she was torn between staying or going in search of a servant to send for Mr Robinson. She looked around the room for a cushion to put behind his head. Much of the furniture had been pushed aside, so the colonel could make use of the area in aiding the captain with his exertions. He would not be impressed with his charge overreaching himself today.

A light tap came on the door, and Mrs Reynolds entered, her brow creasing as she took in the pale and dishevelled captain.

'What has happened, Miss Elliot? Has he collapsed?' She spoke quietly, but Anne felt reassured by her presence.

'I think the captain may have done a little too much. Would it be possible to send some hot tea?' Anne chewed on her lip. 'Do you think we ought to ask Mr Robinson to call?'

'No, do not.'

The captain opened his eyes as the housekeeper hurried to his side.

'Do you not think, sir, being restored to your room, where a fire burns in the grate, would be beneficial?'

The captain lifted a hand. 'My head is tempted, but my legs argue against it at present. Tea would be most welcome though, Mrs Reynolds.'

The lady nodded and left the room, and Anne found she could not look at him.

'Sit by me.'

Startled, Anne raised her eyes to Frederick's. His voice was gentle, and as she took in the expression upon his face, she could not hold back a sob, a hand flying to her mouth.

'All is not as it seems. Come, sit with me.'

Pulling forward a chair, Anne positioned herself beside him and he held out a hand, which she grasped willingly, disturbed by its coldness, and she began to rub it between her own. The captain's eyelids dropped again, and silence fell until Mrs Reynolds returned with a servant bearing the tray of tea, some biscuits and a couple of thick woollen shawls, which she passed to Anne before leaving them alone again.

The captain roused at the disturbance, and Anne held up the shawls.

'Can you sit up?'

Captain Wentworth obliged, his coat falling into his lap. 'I should appreciate the brown one, if you please. Lemon does not favour my complexion.'

Anne smiled as she tucked the darker toned shawl around him.

'You must wear it, Anne.' He gestured at the other shawl as he leaned back in his seat.

She obliged before turning her attention to the tray of tea, bringing him a cup, along with a biscuit, then doing the same for herself. Surely nourishment would aid the captain in bringing some colour back into his cheeks? Or was she simply delaying the conversation that hovered tantalisingly in the air between them?

Taking courage from his earlier declaration to her father, Anne resumed her seat, cradling her cup in her lap. 'Did you truly know we parted, and on unpleasant terms—or was that to thwart my father?'

Captain Wentworth looked a little evasive, taking a sip of his tea, but Anne was on tenterhooks. What, of all that had passed recently, was real?

He placed the cup on a side table and turned to face her. 'Do you forgive me, dearest Anne?'

Forgive *him*? Anne blinked.

'For what, pray?'

He smiled ruefully. 'This is not how I would have told you. We have become adept at deceiving one another, have we not?'

The captain raised a hand and touched her cheek. 'For a brief and wonderful moment, when I woke up after so much darkness to your dear face… I knew you and thought: God has not forsaken me. Consumed though I was by the loss of so many men, knowing you were there was all the solace I required. I had no memory of us parting, only of the happiness of being with you.'

'And did you believe it to be the year six?'

He frowned. 'At first. It is strange. I could recall some of the storm, the ship going down and had some vague memory of my first command, the Asp.' The captain regarded her intently. 'Beyond that, the only thing I could recall was our love for each other.'

Anne drew in a shallow breath. But what of now? 'And when did that alter? I do not understand how I would not know.'

'Do you not?' The captain drew in a long breath. 'Reality crashed in on me the second night after I awoke. Memories bombarded my head, the pain was excruciating and liberating at the same time.' He leaned his head back against the chair, and Anne hesitantly took his hand in hers. 'I still could not comprehend how I came to be in Somersetshire, at Kellynch, of all the damned places.'

Anne squeezed his hand. 'You asked to be brought here.'

'And thus, the heart speaks without the mind's consent. His eyes raked her features. 'I was half agony, half hope. Such pain and pleasure as I had experienced... yet I felt resentment, even after all this time, only to realise it was tempered twice-fold.'

'Oh. And in what ways?'

He grimaced. 'The first is no compliment. I was unable to move, so I had no choice but to remain where I had been brought.'

Anne could not help but smile. 'And the second? Will it be more to my liking?'

He leaned towards her, raising a hand to her face again. 'Then there was you. My Anne, piercing my soul with eyes full of love, with no sign of bitterness or distrust upon your sweet features. Could such precious feelings have endured, ones I had long assumed gone forever? It was as though the five years I recalled had not happened, and how I wished they had not.' He drew in a shallow breath. 'You went along with my mistake over our still being engaged, and at first, I struggled to understand you, to give you credit for such an action. I wondered how long you might persist in the charade, whether you would continue when next I saw you.'

Captain Wentworth eased forward in his seat, taking up Anne's other hand to hold both in his. 'It was as though one of my dreams had stepped from inside my head to stand before me, to ease my recovery, to mend my heart. The loss of you in the year six almost broke me, yet I have loved none but you. My attachment is fervent and undeviating, and you gave me such hope as I had never dreamed of. Could such precious feelings remain? I feared learning otherwise and chose to bask in the affection that flowed so freely from your eyes and prayed you would forgive me when you learned the truth.'

'As did I. There were many times I intended to tell you, but I did not want my happiness to end. I knew all the pain of parting from you, felt I had been given a second chance to love you, and I could not bear to see you as you were when we separated back then.'

A spasm crossed his features.

'What is it?'

'Will you forgive me also, for a small deception I played upon you that day?

Casting her mind back, Anne's eyes widened as realisation fell upon her. 'The letters!'

'Indeed. I expected your pretence to last but a moment, that I misinterpreted your compassion for affection, that you could not love me as you had once said you did.' Anne went to protest, and he placed a gentle finger against her lips. 'You know that was what I believed back then. That you did not love me sufficiently to stand up to those who persuaded you against me.' He dropped his hand, leaning back in his seat again but retaining his hold on one of her hands. 'To my swiftly concealed amazement, there you were, declaring you had saved every word I ever wrote to you.'

'They were so few. I worded my response so carefully, but you knew all along you had never written to me when at sea. All my collection consisted of was the poem we composed together and the two letters you wrote when you were obliged to go to Southampton for a few days.'

'And the rose and pebble you claimed you would keep forever?'

'Those too.' Anne could scarce believe the conversation passing between them. 'And…and what you said to my father…'

'You know it to be true. I asked and you answered, oh so carefully, my dearest Anne, but I knew your purpose.' He leaned forward to place a soft kiss upon her mouth, and she felt she must surely drown in the flood of delight sweeping through her body. 'I have loved none but you. I bore you resentment, refused to understand you, but my heart remained constant. Tell me,' he hesitated. 'I was ashore in the year eight. It was just before I was promoted and gained the Laconia…' His expression darkened for a second, and Anne squeezed his hands. 'I considered writing to you. I had not forgotten you.'

'Why did you not write?' Anne's eyes were moist. Such a missed opportunity, of which she had known nothing.

Captain Wentworth seemed surprised. 'Would you have renewed the acquaintance, despite the acrimony of our parting, my angry words?'

'I would.'

His astonishment was obvious. 'I wanted to do so, to ask you again for your hand, but I was too proud.'

Full of love for him, and secure in its return, Anne raised his hands and placed a kiss upon each one. 'We must put it behind us.'

The captain frowned. 'What was your urgency in speaking to me earlier? Did you foresee your father's arrival?'

Anne blinked as she remembered. 'Your brother, he is here!'

Captain Wentworth sat forward quickly. 'Edward? Here?' He made to get up and Anne aided him to his feet.

'I feel a little stronger. Where is my trusty cane?'

'There.' Anne passed it to him. 'I knew you would learn to rely on your new friend given time.'

The captain leaned down to kiss her, his spare arm holding her close and emotion filled Anne's being as she returned it, so much so that when he drew apart from her, a tear rolled down her cheek.

'What is it, my love?' The captain wiped it away, placing a kiss where it had been.

'I do not know. Everything.' Her voice hitched. 'Almost too much happiness to bear.'

Captain Wentworth tossed the cane onto the chair and wrapped her in his strong embrace, and she leaned her head against his chest, listening to the steady beat of his heart and despite her best efforts, the tears fell thick and fast in gratitude for their being blessed with a second chance.

CHAPTER THIRTY-TWO

'Your brother went into Mr Darcy's study.' Anne and the captain made their slow way to the entrance hall. 'Do you think you ought to rest by the fire for a while? Mr Wentworth could come to you.'

Captain Wentworth leant heavily on his cane again but before he could answer, a shout came from the adjacent corridor.

'Fred!'

'Brother!' The captain released Anne's hand, steadying himself with his cane as Mr Wentworth came towards them.

'My God, Fred. I thought you were gone.' The reverend's voice broke on the last word and his face convulsed as he reached his brother and threw his arms around him.

The cane fell to the floor as Captain Wentworth clung to him, and Anne's throat tightened with compassion. She brushed a tear from her cheek as they drew apart, but when she saw the raw emotion on both their faces she struggled to suppress a sob.

'Thank the Lord you were spared.' The reverend's voice was hoarse as Captain Wentworth slapped him on the back, and Anne bent to retrieve his cane. What should she do? Ought she to leave them alone?

Before she could move, however, Captain Wentworth looked over and smiled at her, holding out his hand as she passed him the cane.

He turned back to his brother. 'Anne has told me of your grief when intelligence first arrived of the ship's fate. I am sorry for it, but I have been well cared for here.'

Mr Wentworth appeared a little confused, but then a wide grin appeared.

'You are reconciled. It gladdens my heart, Fred.'

'There is more good news, Edward.' He held out his other hand to Anne, and she grasped it willingly. 'Miss Anne Elliot and I are to be married.'

An equal measure of surprise and pleasure filled the reverend's face, and he took Anne's free hand and kissed it before shaking his brother's.

'I cannot believe it. After all these years!'

'It has been a long road, I will not deny it, and we will brook no delay in securing the date.'

Conscious she must let Elizabeth know how the situation had altered, Anne reached up to whisper in Frederick's ear. He looked at her lovingly, and full of emotion, unable to speak, Anne touched a hand to his face, smiled tremulously at his brother, and hurried to the door.

Once Anne found Elizabeth, they repaired to the conservatory, where they could speak freely and the former could keep her eye on the captain's progress as he walked on the terrace once more—warmly attired, his brother supporting his elbow.

They were cosily wrapped in thick woollen shawls, a blanket across their laps and some welcome cups of hot chocolate on the tray before them as Anne spoke of all that had been said.

Elizabeth listened in astonishment. 'I still cannot believe your father behaved as he did.'

'Nothing my father does surprises me, though I will own to a moment of despair when he first began to speak.' Anne turned in her seat to face Elizabeth. 'Dear Lizzy, how can I bear such happiness? If only my father realised what a favour he did, releasing us both from our pretence.'

Elizabeth embraced her friend impulsively, then tucked her hands back underneath the blanket on her lap. 'I cannot believe he concealed his returned memory from you!'

Anne laughed. 'Nor I. And to think how I fretted. He did own he was in dread of what my father might reveal. Like myself, he wanted to be the person to tell the truth, not for it to come through another.' She smiled at Elizabeth. 'Little did Father realise he would be the means of reuniting us sooner than had it been left in our dithering hands.'

Elizabeth's eyes lit up. 'I am so happy for you both. The only fitting end for such constant and genuine affections.'

Picking up her cup, Anne sipped the concoction. 'Mr Darcy's cook makes the best hot chocolate.'

Extricating her hands, Elizabeth picked up her own cup, inhaling before tasting the drink. 'I suspect the addition of a dash of whisky helps.' She took another sip, appreciating the warmth of the liquid. 'I shall miss her cooking, too. The meals here have been delightful.'

The thought of returning home saddened Elizabeth, and she frowned. Was she not homesick, longing to see Jane again?

'Is the chocolate not to your taste?'

Elizabeth shook her head. 'It is delicious. I am just surprised to realise in how little a hurry I am to return home.'

Anne smirked. 'How remarkable. Has Mr Darcy's company grown upon you?'

Elizabeth chose not to answer. 'I shall miss my new friends, you in particular, dearest Anne.'

'And you do not consider Mr Darcy a friend also?'

'You are persistent!' Then, Elizabeth's brow furrowed. 'Friendship with Mr Darcy…it is a singular notion; I had not considered it.'

Anne sipped from her cup again, then placed it on the table before them. 'I believe your resentment has faded, Lizzy, and I am thankful for it, because Frederick and I have a deal of gratitude for Mr Darcy and all he has done for us.'

'My astonishment at his kindness towards the captain, and by extension, yourself, has long passed. The gentleman has shown himself to be a good man.' Elizabeth blinked. Had she truly accepted that at last?

'Frederick suggested moving to The King's Arms in Montacute, but Mr Darcy insists on his remaining as his guest, saying there are rooms aplenty and that an inn is no place to complete a recovery.'

The evening passed swiftly, and though Darcy was conscious of Elizabeth's gaze upon him far more than usual, he had done his best to keep his attention on the party gathered to the table. To be certain, with the reverend joining them, the conversation throughout the meal and afterwards in the drawing room had mainly centred around the newly engaged couple and Captain Wentworth's recovery.

Everyone had lately retired, however, and Darcy had barely exchanged a word with Elizabeth. Turning from watching

Georgiana make her way up the stairs, he was drawn to one of the windows overlooking the garden.

There were lights shining from the cottage windows, and he wondered how Elizabeth felt since his return. She must have enjoyed the respite from his company, surely? And what of her friend? Anne and the captain would be leaving as soon as he was fit to travel, and Elizabeth would go home.

'Darce? Come on, man.'

Looking over, Darcy noted his cousin striding with purpose towards the study and with one last glance at the cottage, he followed him.

'That was an interesting meal, was it not?'

Darcy glared at the colonel as he entered the room. 'You push the boundaries too far sometimes, Cousin.'

The colonel seemed unconcerned as he walked over to the drinks tray. 'You had experienced a long and arduous journey. All I intended was to keep you sufficiently alert so as not to fall asleep in your soup.'

He picked up the decanter of port and a glass, and Darcy nodded. Perhaps it would help him comprehend why Elizabeth's eyes seemed so often cast in his direction.

'What do you take from Sir Walter's demand of an audience tomorrow?'

Darcy shrugged. 'No pleasure, to be certain. I am sure my absence was not approved of.'

'What will you do?'

'Play my role for now.' Darcy stretched in his seat, thankful to be by his own hearth. 'Did you discern aught of significance during my absence, a glimmer of hope that might be of service?'

'I did not, but I have been constrained by the weather and unable to speak to anyone beyond the most immediate neighbours.'

'I trust you used your discretion well?'

'I am flattered you feel I have any.' The colonel smirked over at Darcy as he filled two glasses. 'My instinct remains the same, that finances are the root to dig for. The intelligence I have been able to drum up so far supports your impression from when you met Sir Walter in Town in the autumn: they are slow to settle bills, and in some instances, there are whispers the payment never comes. None of this is sufficient influence, however.'

'We need an insider who is willing to help us.' Darcy frowned, recalling his recent trip to Town. 'I saw Shepherd when I was at the Guildhall—you recall Sir Walter's legal man?' Discomfort trickled through him on recalling the man's assessing stare across the room. 'He was cryptic when we spoke briefly.' Darcy waved a hand. 'Something about consequence having its tax, and how difficult it is to keep the actions and designs of one part of the world from the notice and curiosity of the other.'

The colonel raised a brow. 'He is verbose. Do you think he knows of Sir Walter's hold over you? One has to wonder what his purpose was in Town in these conditions.'

'Perchance Shepherd attempts to raise funds for the estate? He is known hereabouts as Sir Walter's confidential friend.' Darcy waved an unconcerned hand. 'Sir Walter will have to involve him in the discussions about settlements…'

He paled. What if it went that far, or worse? Then, he pushed the notion aside. He would not give up so easily. 'I have enough to contend with, without becoming consumed with Shepherd and his movements.'

'Miss Bennet seemed quite engrossed by *you* over dinner. What have you done this time?'

Darcy stirred in his seat, trying to rid himself of any thought of the Elliots, then took the glass of port from his cousin, who settled into the chair next to him, placing the decanter on the table between them.

'How can I have done anything, Richard? I have been absent for days and only back in the house a matter of hours.'

The colonel laughed and took a sip of his port. 'Long enough to put a foot wrong if I know you. Would you care to satisfy my curiosity?'

'Experience tells me your curiosity is never satisfied.'

'It should also tell you, Darce, that being evasive will not suffice either. Come on, out with it, man. You went to Town to talk to Bingley. What was the outcome?'

Darcy was in no mood for relating his meeting with his friend, but his cousin was unlikely to let the matter drop, so he quickly ran through the gist of his conversation with Bingley.

'He was shocked, you say, to learn of Miss Jane Bennet's engagement?'

He reflected on the difficult few hours he passed with his friend.

'Not entirely. In Bingley's eyes, she always was an angel, both in appearance and nature. He was not surprised to learn someone else had recognised her charm. But he was…'

Devastated? Inconsolable? Darcy recalled the charged moments when he had truly seen the full weight of the despair he had brought upon his friend. Was it any wonder Elizabeth hated him?

'Darce?' The colonel clicked his fingers in front of Darcy. 'Where have you gone to, old man?'

Draining his glass, Darcy placed it on a side table. 'He was desperate to find a solution.'

'Bingley accepted your apology? Did he question how you understood matters to be different from how you had perceived?'

'You know Bingley, Richard. He is easily led. Too easily. Despite my failings towards him as a friend, he was willing as ever to take my word on the matter.'

'To what avail? The lady is engaged.'

Darcy shifted in his seat again, and the colonel refilled their glasses.

'From what Eliz—Miss Bennet told me when we'— Elizabeth's angry visage flashed into his mind—'talked.' Darcy took another sip from his glass.

Talked? Such a mild description of an angry conversation that ended all his hopes. The colonel snapped his fingers again, and Darcy blinked.

'As you said at the time, Richard, who am I to assume a better knowledge of Miss Jane Bennet than her sister? Eliz—' *Damn it.* 'Miss Bennet's conviction of her sister's deep attachment to Bingley carried weight, and he knew it as much as I did.'

The colonel raised a brow. 'You told Bingley of your argument with Miss Elizabeth Bennet?'

'I merely said we had spoken, and Bingley was far too taken up with the portent of the message, that the lady had only allowed herself to become engaged to that hapless parson because of Bingley's perceived desertion.'

Colonel Fitzwilliam reached for the decanter again. 'Why we must conform to such small glasses for the consumption of port is beyond me. Why can we not simply pour a hefty tumbler full and be done with it?' He splashed the dark liquid into his glass and offered the decanter to Darcy, but he shook his head.

'And I imagine he bounded about like a puppy, straining at the leash to get out of the door and off to Hertfordshire?'

Darcy laughed reluctantly. 'Indeed.' He met his cousin's amused look. 'I suspect he would have leapt into Miss Bennet's lap, had she been present.'

The colonel gave his usual bark of laughter. 'So, *his* wishes remain unchanged.' He drained his glass. 'And what next?'

'Bingley plans to return to Netherfield. What can be achieved, bearing in mind Miss Jane Bennet's current obligation, I know not, but it is out of my hands.'

Darcy made to get up. 'It has been a long day. I am for bed.'

The colonel held up a hand.

'Before you go, you ought to know Miss Elizabeth Bennet is now aware of the true nature of Wickham's connection with this family.'

Darcy's skin went cold as he sank back into his seat. What the devil happened in his absence? Had that scoundrel been here?

'Do not fear. Georgiana let slip something to the lady.' The colonel grinned. 'Miss Bennet is easy to talk to, is she not, Darce? One finds one sprouts all sorts of inanities whilst gazing into those fine, intelligent eyes.'

Darcy almost gritted his teeth.

'Precisely,' the colonel continued. 'I took it upon myself to enlighten her as to Wickham's true nature. She took the revelation admirably. She is quite the lady, Darce. Quite the lady.'

Throwing his cousin a speaking glance as he stood up, Darcy walked to the door and opened it as the colonel breezed past him into the hall, chuckling.

'I know, I know. I preach to the long converted.'

There was little Darcy could add to that, and he followed his cousin silently along the hall, wishing his mind was as weary as his body felt. What with the difficulty of Sir Walter's threat and the ever present possibility of having to wed Miss Elliot to save his sister's reputation, and the stark reality of Elizabeth's opinion of him—much of which he had come to own—there was no likelihood sleep would find him any time soon.

When Elizabeth woke the following morning, her first thoughts were of Anne and her captain and the happiness they displayed at dinner the previous evening.

Rolling onto her back, she hugged her pillow, a smile touching her lips. The happiness shining from Anne's warm brown eyes and the looks exchanged between her friend and the captain at the dinner table assured Elizabeth of their mutual happiness and devotion.

The memory faded, however, and Mr Darcy soon displaced it as a strange sensation gripped Elizabeth.

Nonsensical girl. Think of something else.

Shuffling onto her side, Elizabeth stared at the shutters. Sunlight filtered through a gap, and she closed her eyes. Hopefully, it would help thaw the icy conditions outside. She ought to be thinking about her packing. After all, she ought to return to Longbourn now all was resolved for Anne. Christmas was almost upon them, and if she did not begin her journey on Monday, she would not arrive in time. Jane should have arrived the previous day, along with the Gardiners and their brood. Distraction in familiar company was surely all she required to put the gentleman firmly from her mind once and for all.

Elizabeth threw back the covers and lifted her legs out of bed, walking over to stare at her reflection in the mirror on the washstand. She would have to request the use of a carriage from the gentleman. He would accede of course. She had learnt that much about him.

Her eyes were troubled, as well they might be. Mr Darcy was quite the conundrum. Proud as she had ever been of her ability to judge a character, she failed spectacularly over Wickham. How much more severe a disservice had she done Mr Darcy?

Dissatisfied with herself, Elizabeth turned her back on the mirror and walked over to the washstand just as the door opened, and Elise entered with a bowl and a pitcher of water.

'Morning, miss.'

'Good morning.' Elizabeth smiled weakly and reached for a towel as the maid poured the water into the bowl.

It was no good. Mr Darcy was firmly entrenched, and as Elizabeth prepared for another day, she accepted the need to apologise for defending Wickham as she had. She had grown fond of the family. Georgiana was a darling and the colonel both charming and amusing. One felt he would be a good friend to have in one's corner, something his cousins no doubt comprehended full well.

And Mr Darcy?

The gentleman's image entered her disobedient mind again, and as Elise left the room, Elizabeth walked over to the window and stared across the snow-covered grounds towards the main house.

There was a time when suffering was all she ever wished upon Mr Darcy. Now, her heart clenched in her breast, and she felt inexplicably sad.

'Unfathomable,' she muttered, pushing away from the wall. It was time for breakfast, fortunately a meal the gentleman tended to indulge in earlier than the ladies. All she needed was some company and then a good walk, during which she would take herself to task over her impossible musings.

Darcy prowled restlessly in the drawing room, unable to settle. His sister had called upon him in his study before she headed to the breakfast room, full of plans for decorating the principal rooms for the season, but he agreed to her proposals without heeding them. The mention of the impending Yuletide was sufficient to place Elizabeth firmly at the forefront of his thoughts.

He saw her only briefly that morning as they passed in the entrance hall, but she seemed a little subdued. Or did he imagine it? Darcy walked over to the basket beside the hearth and reached for a log, tossing it onto the fire in the grate and picking up the poker. Was it the impending alteration in their circumstances here at Meadowbrook House?

Mr Wentworth spoke over dinner as though it was settled. Although he left that morning to return to his new wife in Shropshire, the man's expectation was that his brother and Anne would join them for Christmas—as it happened, his wife's older cousin planned to travel up from Lyme with her son and could collect them on her way.

It was already the twenty-first, and once the lady left, Elizabeth had no reason to remain…

Darcy thrust the poker at the logs, causing them to spit and spark.

You are a damned fool, Darcy. Remain? The lady will be relishing her chance to escape, and if you truly care for her, you will aid her in the endeavour.

'Is this to be it, Elizabeth?' Darcy straightened up, addressing his own reflection in the large, gilded mirror above the mantel. 'The end of our laboured acquaintance?'

The ache in Darcy's breast made itself felt once more. He could not bear to let her go, but what choice had he? Elizabeth was not his, nor would she ever be, even if he managed to release himself from the trap he had fallen into with Sir Walter.

It was a sobering recollection, and Darcy turned his back on his unsettled countenance. He may have lost his chance with Elizabeth, but he would fight against the supposed obligation to Miss Elliot with his entire being, with his last breath, if he had to. To live out the rest of his life alone would be preferable to such an alliance.

This welcome reminder roused Darcy's ire, and some fire returned to his gut as he strode over to the door. Reflection did not serve him well. It was time for action.

Darcy glanced at the clock in the hall as he passed it. It was too early for the planned call on Sir Walter, and with his cousin busy with Captain Wentworth, he crossed to pull open the front door, staring out onto the snow-covered driveway.

Though it was a fair day, the sun shining weakly from a pale blue sky, there was little strength in its rays. There would be no rapidity to the thaw, and closing the door, Darcy leaned against it. He was in need of diversion; something, *anything*, to dislodge this taut band across his chest, one that tightened with every thought of Elizabeth.

CHAPTER THIRTY-THREE

'There is a letter for you, Miss Bennet.'

Elizabeth looked up as she emerged from the breakfast room, then took the offering from the housekeeper.

'Thank you, Mrs Reynolds.' To her surprise it was another from Aunt Gardiner. 'The cart did well to make it along the lane today with all this snow.'

The lady was sorting through a variety of post. 'Yes. Some of the farmhands have been out with their shovels.' She raised the remaining letters. 'Excuse me, ma'am. I must put these on Mr Darcy's desk and pass a note to Miss Elliot from the Hall.'

She turned away, and Elizabeth, who had left Anne talking to Georgiana and Mrs Annesley whilst they consumed yet another cup of tea, walked over to a settle against the wood-panelled wall and opened her letter. There were two sheets, covered on both sides, in her aunt's neat hand.

Elizabeth started to read, curious as to what warranted a second letter so soon after the last. Anticipating an entertaining tale of trying to harness the children and get them packed ready for the journey to Hertfordshire, but scarcely had she skimmed the first paragraph when a name leapt out at her from the page: *Mr Darcy* had called in Gracechurch Street!

A hand shot to Elizabeth's chest, and she almost dropped the letter. What on earth could Mr Darcy have been doing in Cheapside? Rising from the settle in astonishment, her attention was suddenly drawn to the corridor leading to the conservatory. Voices approached—the captain's, and then the colonel's familiar bark of laughter—and Elizabeth grabbed her shawl and left the house, crossing over to the cottage as fast as she could and hurrying up to her chamber.

Sinking onto her bed, Elizabeth read the entire letter through, then drew in a sharp breath, but it hitched in her throat. Why did she feel like crying?

Stuffing the letter inside her writing case, she stood, sank back onto the bed, then rose to her feet again, her mind reeling with her aunt's news. If Mrs Gardiner seemed a little vague as to Mr Darcy's true impetus for his unanticipated call, she did not seem concerned, expressing praise for his purpose in coming, and paying a compliment to 'the rather agreeable-looking young man.'

Elizabeth paced across her room, then back again. She had to get out of the house, walk off her interminable speculation. She had thought her biggest obstacle this day would be finding a suitable moment to apologise to Mr Darcy for her accusations regarding Wickham. It seemed she had a myriad of questions for him too.

Donning her warmest pelisse and scarf and snatching up her gloves, Elizabeth hurried down the stairs and emerged from the cottage, pausing on the doorstep to inhale the crisp morning air, welcoming its caress upon her cheeks. It was like the gentlest of stings on her skin, rousing her in exactly the manner she hoped. Everything seemed so still. There was no bird song, but Elizabeth could hear the chopping of wood over by the service area at the back of the house, and the rhythmic sound of a shovel against gravel.

Tugging her gloves on, Elizabeth set off along a cleared pathway, eyes on her feet to ensure she did not stumble on the still icy surface, her mind engrossed with the letter's content.

On rounding the corner of the house, she espied a workman expertly wielding a shovel. He worked with great energy, piling snow into a mound just outside the gates, but Elizabeth hardly noticed as she made her way down the driveway.

According to her aunt, Mr Darcy had called to speak in confidence to her and Uncle Gardiner. What *could* have persuaded the gentleman to pay a call not only in Cheapside, surely a place well beneath his notice, but further, to initiate an introduction to some of the same connections he disparaged? His professed purpose she knew, of course, for that is why her aunt had written, but what could have motivated such a call?

The workman paused and leaned on his shovel, surveying his labours. Then, Elizabeth halted, her skin growing warm as she recognised the man's familiar breadth of shoulder, the length of leg, and the dark hair curling over his collar.

Suddenly, he turned, and the shovel fell from his grasp.

'Miss Bennet!'

'I—er…' Elizabeth dropped a curtsey, heat rushing into her cheeks and her heart racing. What on earth was wrong with her? 'Mr Darcy. I did not expect—'

'I needed to…exercise, to be active.' The gentleman swallowed visibly. 'Winters at Pemberley bring a vast deal of snow. I am used to helping in the clearing of it.'

Silence fell upon them, but Elizabeth could not help noticing his attire. This was a Mr Darcy she had never seen before, sporting no coat but instead a leather jerkin, which exposed his shirt sleeves. His neckcloth had been removed, and she tried not to stare at the open collar of his shirt.

Conscious the heat in her face was increasing, Elizabeth raised her eyes to his, unsurprised to discern equal embarrassment in his countenance.

'Please forgive the informality of dress. I had not expected...I did not imagine anyone would be out so early.'

'Yes, of course.' Elizabeth cleared her throat. Part of her wished to hurry away, but she was conscious of the opportunity before her, and before she could question her motives, she took a step closer, that she might speak more quietly.

'Sir, may I ask a question?'

With a look of surprise, the gentleman bent to retrieve his shovel. 'Provided it is not to enquire who my tailor is.' Elizabeth laughed, and he gave a self-deprecating smile. 'My cousin was obliging in the loan of this.' He gestured at the leather jerkin.

The ease of tension between them encouraged Elizabeth to step a little closer again. 'I have received a letter from my aunt, Mr Darcy. My aunt in Cheapside.'

He stilled, and Elizabeth pressed on.

'It seems you called there to speak with her and my uncle about my sister's situation.'

Mr Darcy held her gaze for a moment. 'I did. I am surprised at Mrs Gardiner. I asked her to speak no word of it.'

Elizabeth arched a brow. 'My aunt is about as good at following orders as I am, sir.' Then, she relented. 'She has told me why you called.'

'It was the least I could do.' Mr Darcy hesitated. 'I am not certain it will alter matters. But I had to do something.'

'My sister seems to be a law unto herself of late, and I have no idea whether it will affect any improvement either. But your making the attempt...' Elizabeth's voice hitched. She felt quite overcome. 'I am grateful.'

'It should never have been necessary, and had I not interfered in the first place, it would not be.'

Elizabeth's eyes raked his face. 'I cannot account for your taking such a step.' Her brow furrowed. 'How did you discover the address?'

Looking a little sheepish, Mr Darcy waved a hand at the house. 'You left some letters on the salver in the hall.'

'Oh!' Elizabeth said nothing further, but waited, and then he drew in a long breath.

'If you will hear it, then so be it. Until we spoke the other day'—Mr Darcy's face clouded for a moment—'I only knew what I believed I had perceived. You were quite correct to defend your sister's feelings. It brought enlightenment—I was in error, making such a judgement. My going to Town to see Bingley was thus essential. I had a duty to confess my interference.' He sighed. 'My friend is prone to falling in love at the drop of a hat, Miss Bennet. I had no reason to suspect this was not another case of his appreciation blossoming and then fading like a summer flower.'

'And you wished to believe Jane indifferent.'

'I did.' Mr Darcy said no more for a moment, and Elizabeth tried to define the expression in his dark eyes as he whispered some unintelligible words.

Strangely, her insides swirled, and she clutched her midriff.

'Forgive my bluntness, Miss Bennet. Honesty is vastly important to me, but if I have erred, I wish to own it.'

'It is an admirable trait, sir.' There. Elizabeth finally managed to pay the man a compliment! Who would have thought it but a few weeks ago?

'You are smiling.' The edges of the gentleman's mouth twitched, as if he too would do so, but then he continued. 'When I saw the letters addressed to your sister and aunt at the London address, it occurred to me there was an endeavour I could at least attempt. Before calling on Bingley, I went to Gracechurch Street and, as luck would have it, saw Miss Bennet leaving the house with some young children.'

'My young cousins.'

'Indeed. Then, I presented my card. Mr and Mrs Gardiner—though a little surprised by my visit—were extremely welcoming. They are both charming.' He seemed a little conscious. 'You would know that, of course.'

Elizabeth could not help but laugh. 'I do indeed, sir.'

'I explained who I was, that you and I had spoken of your sister's current situation, and I merely wished to ascertain the lady's present sentiments in the matter. I used the connection of being nephew to Lady Catherine, Miss Bennet's betrothed's patroness, as a reason for my interest. Mrs Gardiner was most obliging, and I was sufficiently encouraged to proceed on to see Bingley. His unhappiness was obvious. We had an honest discussion, as a result of which, he plans a return to Hertfordshire.'

'Then I did not err? Mr Bingley was strongly inclined in favour of my sister?'

'Very much so, and still is. My friend knows of her circumstances and though he took some comfort from knowing Miss Bennet had truly held him in affection, it was little consolation.'

'You did not think to simply call at Gracechurch Street with him in tow?'

Mr Darcy shook his head. 'As an engaged young woman, it would not be entirely proper for Bingley to call upon your sister. Besides, I tried to put myself in your sister's shoes.'

Elizabeth eyed his snow-covered boots, then laughed. 'You do like to present yourself with difficulties, sir.'

He shook his head again. 'From what you had told me, Miss Bennet was deeply affected by what appeared to be Bingley's defection; her heart broken. Even had my assumption of your sister's indifference been correct, to turn up in either circumstance would have brought either pain or embarrassment. Had Mrs Gardiner cautioned against it, I would not have spoken to Bingley of your sister's sadness in her situation—for her sake.'

An inexplicable rush of feelings swept through Elizabeth as Mr Darcy spoke these words, his countenance indicative of his sincerity. How she had misjudged this man!

'I believe my aunt made her opinion of Jane's situation clear?'

Darcy smiled. 'She did. I think Mrs Gardiner felt that, as a representative of the family, I might carry some sway over what she referred to as a coercive situation.'

'My mother,' muttered Elizabeth.

'Quite. Miss Bennet, I do not know that I achieved anything by my call, but I felt honour bound to do what little I could to assess if there was any chance for my friend—and your sister—to rebuild the happiness I was instrumental in destroying.'

Elizabeth's heart was full. 'You have left me much to ponder.'

Mr Darcy inclined his head. 'If you will excuse me, ma'am. I must attend to my duties.' He gestured at the remaining snow.

'Then I shall leave you to it, sir.' Her earlier desire to speak to Mr Darcy regarding Wickham, to apologise, never even entered Elizabeth's head, reeling as she was from all she had learned.

They exchanged acknowledgements, a little awkwardly in the gentleman's circumstances, but instead of continuing on her way, Elizabeth turned back. She no longer wished to escape and had no desire to clear her head. She wanted to find a quiet corner somewhere and go over every single word Mr Darcy had said.

CHAPTER THIRTY FOUR

It was some two hours later before Darcy emerged from his chamber, suitably dressed for the impending visit to Kellynch Hall, but though his appearance had been restored to order, a myriad of thoughts gambolled through his head like spring lambs in the fold at Pemberley.

He had not anticipated Elizabeth's finding out about his cautious call upon her relations, but he had to own his relief. Disguise of any sort sat ill upon him, though her gratitude was not what he wished for. No, what he longed for was beyond his reach, and no amount of atonement would bring it closer.

'Darce! Wait up, man.'

Darcy watched his cousin as he all but ran along the landing to join him.

'You know I will always be your second, whatever the circumstances.'

'I do, Richard, but this I must deal with alone for now.'

They headed down the stairs in silence, but as they reached the bottom step, the colonel stayed Darcy with his hand.

'Keep your eyes and ears at the ready for any hint. We must find some influence over the man.'

'And until then, I have no choice but to imply I am considering this farce of an engagement.'

The colonel's expression darkened. 'If you are not careful, it will become a farce of a marriage.'

Darcy threw the colonel a speaking look as they walked down the hall to his study, but once the door was closed and they had taken a seat either side of Darcy's desk, he blew out a breath.

'This is damned ridiculous, Richard. What the blazes am I to do if I cannot find anything on Sir Walter to counter with?'

The colonel shrugged, raising both hands to emphasise the futility of the situation. 'I will own to being at a loss, my friend. Perchance you had best prepare yourself for the worst. Or you take a gamble.'

Reluctantly, Darcy shook his head. 'I cannot. I will not bring pain and disgrace down upon Georgie, under any circumstances.'

A snort came from the colonel. 'You think her living at Pemberley with Miss Elliot as mistress will be painless?'

'Thank you, Richard.' Darcy stirred restlessly in his seat. 'You cannot feel it any more deeply than I.' He leaned his head back against the leather chair. 'I may have to resign myself to it.'

'To be fair, Darce, before Miss Elizabeth Bennet came into your life, you sought only a mistress for the estate and an heir to carry it on.'

'Is that not the way with most of our class?'

'Ha!' The colonel grinned. 'Unless they are second sons like me. We seek a hefty dowry too.'

Darcy reluctantly owned the truth of the matter. Had he ever anticipated an alliance borne of love and admiration? Though his parents had been happy, he comprehended full well the marriage had been considered a joining of two influential families of consequence, and a sound financial transaction for the Darcy estate. Any feelings of respect and affection had come later.

The thought of ever gaining either for Miss Elliot drove him from his seat, and he strode over to stare out of the window, his heart sinking even lower in his breast.

The colonel came to join him. 'Miss Elliot is also hale and hearty and stands a good chance of surviving childbirth.'

'Do not be crude, Richard.'

'It is not crudity, it is honesty, which is more than you practise upon yourself.'

'Perhaps.' It did not bear considering, yet Darcy must. If there was no counteraction to Sir Walter's coercion, he may well have to go through with the marriage. If only he had not made so many mistakes in what he believed was his courtship of Elizabeth...if only she had heard him out, accepted him...but then he would not have been able to save Georgiana...

'On a more fortuitous note,' the colonel interjected, 'the ladies sharing a name will hide any blunders.'

Perchance if Darcy closed his eyes, he could be able to imagine a different Elizabeth?

'You would have to close your ears and all your given senses as well.'

Darcy frowned. 'Did I say that out loud?'

'No—your countenance did.'

Elizabeth found little chance for the exploration of her feelings after her conversation with Mr Darcy, for Anne waylaid her and encouraged her to accompany her friend over to Meadowbrook House.

'My father has asked me to call on him. It was a curiously conciliatory note.'

'Would you like me to come with you?' Elizabeth took her friend's arm as they made a circuit of the drawing room, where Georgiana sat with Mrs Annesley, their heads each engrossed in a book.

'I would not risk subjecting you to my father's ill humour, Lizzy.' Anne's brow furrowed. 'I cannot understand his no longer being angry with *me*, but he claims it to be so.'

'I wonder what could have affected such an alteration. Forgive me for saying, Anne, but your father is quite mercurial in his temperament.'

'It was not always so. I wonder what has made him so changeable?' Anne appeared thoughtful as they reached the windows and turned about. 'My father's antipathy for Captain Wentworth was profound, yet this latest request was quite unlike the earlier notes demanding my return to Kellynch.'

'What time do you intend to go?'

'Directly. I know my father's schedule, and it will definitely be the most inconvenient time to arrive.'

Elizabeth laughed as they moved to the door. 'I see I am beginning to affect you.' They both paused by Georgiana, agreeing to meet with her in the music room on their return, and escaped into the hall.

A footman lurked near the staircase, and they approached him.

'What are the conditions like in the lane? Is it accessible on foot now?'

'It is icy, ma'am, but passable.'

'Where is it you wish to go?'

Elizabeth tried not to stare at Mr Darcy as he walked over to join them, the colonel on his heels.

As Anne explained her mission, Elizabeth covertly examined the gentleman. He wore a dark blue coat that thoroughly became his tall figure, and she could not help but compare his appearance with that of the supposed labourer she encountered earlier. No matter what he wore, there was no denying his attractiveness.

Elizabeth blushed. Why had she never noticed how pleasing he was to the eye?

'Lizzy?' Humour filled Anne's face.

'Forgive me. Shall I see you back at the cottage later? I will make haste to return. The colonel is to take some exercise with Frederick, and Mr Darcy is also Kellynch bound. We are to walk together.'

'You are not riding?' Elizabeth looked from Mr Darcy to Anne, but it was the colonel who replied.

'Hereward is still recovering from his last foray on the icy roads.' He grinned. 'I think his fellow mounts would rather not be put through more of the same.'

'Shall we set off in a half hour, Miss Elliot?'

'Yes, of course.'

Heading for the door to the garden with Anne, Elizabeth peered back down the hall. The colonel had gone, but Mr Darcy remained where he was, and she frowned. Why did his countenance suddenly bespeak a tortured man?

Elizabeth smiled tentatively, and he bowed before turning on his heel and disappearing from sight. Hurrying to catch Anne up, she pushed away the nonsensical notion.

There could be little to cause a man of Mr Darcy's consequence such torment.

'Ah, Darcy, there you are.'

The butler led him to the great hall, where Sir Walter held his hands out to the fire in the grate. The gentleman caught sight of his daughter as she too entered the room, and he frowned.

'Your timing is not fortuitous, Anne. I am due to speak with Mr Darcy.'

'I am at liberty, Sir Walter.' Darcy interjected. 'The lady has a greater claim. Perhaps there is somewhere I could await you?'

Sir Walter straightened his waistcoat, then consulted his watch. 'So be it. You recall where the study is, Darcy? I shall join you directly. Come, Anne.' He took the steps up to the drawing room, and the lady followed behind.

Darcy was thankful to reach the study without coming across Miss Elliot, and as the door closed behind him, he sank back against it, floundering over how to hinder Sir Walter. If only a solution would present itself.

There was an open ledger on the desk, along with the estate terrier and several other papers. The lid of the ink well was raised, a pen resting on the blotter, a glistening spot of ink below it.

Surveying the room, Darcy noted the many cabinets and drawers. The colonel would probably be tapping the panelling by now, on a mission to seek out hidden compartments. Whatever the circumstances, however, he could hardly ransack Sir Walter's study when the man was to join him.

Darcy pushed away from the door, surveying the room as he crossed it. Was Georgiana's letter in here somewhere? A rush of anger filled him as he scrutinised the many cupboards, drawn slowly to the desk. There was a small pile of letters to one side, the top one marked both 'personal' and 'confidential', and Darcy almost picked it up. Then, he stepped away. Much as he wished to gain a mark on Sir Walter, browsing his correspondence went against his principles.

As does marrying against my will…

He walked to the window, feeling hollow inside and completely at a loss to see a way forward.

'How the devil am I to outwit a man who has no compunction in applying coercion to attain his goal?'

The clearing of a throat drew his sudden attention. Sir Walter's trusted advisor and lawyer, Mr Shepherd, stood in the doorway.

'Shepherd. I…er, I did not hear you come in.'

The lawyer approached the desk, sending Darcy an assessing look as he straightened the pile of post.

'Clearly, sir.'

An awkward silence ensued, but before anything further could be said, Sir Walter arrived.

'Leave us, Shepherd. You can return to your books in due course.'

Shepherd closed the ledger and placed the pen in its stand.

'As you wish, Sir Walter. Mr Darcy.' He bowed, the same speculative look on his face, and Darcy watched him leave the room with relief.

'You have been in Town, so Shepherd says.'

Darcy almost rolled his eyes.

'I was surprised to see your man in London.'

Sir Walter waved an unconcerned hand, walking to a large plan pinned to the far wall. 'I had some business for him to carry out. The original estate boundaries.' He tapped the plan, and with little choice, Darcy joined him.

He studied the map, his alert eyes taking in the extent of the estate. 'The *original* boundaries?'

Sir Walter blustered. 'Well, we all have to retrench at times, do we not, Darcy? As master of an estate, you must comprehend the trials we face.'

Darcy said nothing, continuing to look at the plan. It was dated 1585, which tied in with the construction of the main parts of the Hall. Shutting out Sir Walter's blustering about having to dispose of this farm and that block of woodland in recent years, Darcy tried to rein in his disgust. He would never sell off parts of the Pemberley estate. He was proud of it, of keeping it in good stead, and worked hard to ensure it could sustain the costs of managing it. He was damned if it would be anything but fully intact and ready to hand over to its next guardian.

The reminder of his need for an heir brought Darcy's current predicament to the fore again, and he straightened and turned to face Sir Walter who, although he now stared out of the window, continued to witter on about his need for a cash injection into the estate funds. Well, he could go whistle. Darcy was not about to be his source.

'Why did you wish me to look at this?'

Sir Walter tsked as he glanced at him. 'As a reminder. You have been presented with an opportunity to join an esteemed family, Darcy. A titled one at that. I insist upon you becoming well-versed in the magnitude of the estate you are connecting yourself with.' He turned back to face the window. 'There is no point in glaring at me. It may not have been your intention, but you could do far worse than attach yourself to a family of our rank and standing.'

So distasteful was the thought of being connected to the Elliots—much as he respected Miss Anne Elliot—Darcy felt bile rise in his throat.

'May I?' He gestured at a tray of spirits, and Sir Walter met him beside it.

'I shall join you. We are due a toast. Perhaps I should send for Elizabeth before—'

Darcy raised his hand. 'I would prefer not just now, Sir Walter. Besides, I believe Miss Anne Elliot proposed to seek out her sister after speaking with you.'

'Hmm, Anne…' Sir Walter splashed brandy into two glasses and handed one to Darcy, who took a slug, desperate to wash the bitter taste from his mouth. 'It is fortunate I am of a forgiving nature or I would not take kindly to you harbouring not only my daughter but also Miss Bennet.'

How the devil had he…

'My housekeeper saw the lady in the grounds of Meadowbrook House when walking up the lane.' He took another mouthful of drink and swallowed. 'As for this naval man. He is recovering, as I saw for myself.'

'Thankfully, yes. Captain Wentworth is making excellent progress and becomes stronger by the day.'

Sir Walter pulled a face. 'He may become whatever he chooses. I am resigned to the match, however. Anne is of age, and it would be futile to attempt to discourage her this time.'

Unwilling to comment, Darcy took another sip of his drink as Sir Walter sent him a frustrated look.

'I would not take well to your overruling me, sir, with regard to Miss Bennet remaining on the estate and supporting Anne in her defiance, had we not more important matters in hand.'

'We must choose our battles, Sir Walter.'

'Quite.' The gentleman moved to the desk. 'Now, on to business. You know my proposal and what the danger is, should you refuse to accept it. What is your decision?' He drained his glass.

'You understand, Sir Walter'—Darcy came to stand in front of the man—'that I do not concede willingly to your coercion? You have a hold on me, without which I would never consider your demand. It cannot surprise you to know that I will do all I can to resolve the matter before I am forced to marry against my will.'

Sir Walter raised a brow. 'You know the stakes, Darcy. It is your choice. I have already made the only concession I am prepared to, and that was to give you a little time to become attuned to it. My patience is thin.'

As was Darcy's.

He drained his glass and put it on the tray. 'If you wish for my willing agreement, sir, I suggest you rein in your impatience.'

For a moment, Sir Walter said nothing. Then, he huffed. 'Yes, yes. We can each aid the other, can we not? But I would appreciate you expediting your efforts. I have already applied to the archbishop for the necessary license.'

Darcy assumed an inscrutable mask, concealing the dread filling him at such a notion. Time was indeed running out.

CHAPTER THIRTY-FIVE

Anne was disconcerted by the depth of her relief on leaving Kellynch behind, so much so, she and Mr Darcy passed the gateway and emerged onto the lane before she took in the demeanour of the man walking by her side.

Mr Darcy often presented an inscrutable mien, but his troubled countenance left Anne in little doubt that, whatever his purpose in calling on her father, it had not been of a pleasant nature.

She cast about for a topic to distract the gentleman from wherever his thoughts had taken him, but just then, he turned his head.

'I trust the call was to your satisfaction, Miss Elliot?'

Her father certainly surprised her. 'I am of two minds, sir. It is a relief my father knows of my engagement to the captain and, even though it is not entirely to his liking, he is accepting of there being nothing he can do about it.' Her mind drifted to the brief conversation that had taken place. 'But he has asked me to return home. He has promised no objection to my meeting with Frederick but believes I should no longer trespass on your kindness.'

'You are welcome to stay in Willow Cottage for as long as suits you, ma'am, though I believe you are for Shropshire soon?'

'I am not certain.' A notion struck Anne and, curious as to the response it may provoke, she added, 'Whether I leave for Shropshire or return home, of course, my friend cannot remain. Her sister returns from Town today, and I am sure she is longing to see her. Indeed, Lizzy was originally to have left last Thursday, and once Frederick and I depart, she will be anxious for Hertfordshire.'

The gentleman's pace slowed, his complexion paling, and Anne smirked. It was entirely as she supposed.

'Miss Bennet knows her own mind.' His voice was flat.

'But I do not think she does, Mr Darcy.' He threw her a puzzled look, and Anne pressed on. 'At least, not yet.'

The gentleman looked unsure of her meaning, as well he might.

'Since speaking to my father, there is some likelihood Frederick and I may stay in Somersetshire for Christmas. If it be so, is it truly no inconvenience if I remain at the cottage? I should much prefer to pass the Yuletide season in such convivial company, and I do not wish to lose Lizzy until I must.'

Anne looked away to conceal her notice of the emotions filtering across Mr Darcy's face. She long suspected he held an interest in Elizabeth, but this was clearly more. Now, if only her friend would open her own eyes to what afflicted her, then—

'I—er, you are most welcome. I know that Georgiana is gaining so much from having…young ladies in the house.'

'And you, sir?' Goodness, Elizabeth's boldness had begun to rub off on her! 'Do you gain much from the additional company?'

They reached the entrance to Meadowbrook House, and turned their steps down the drive. There was no answer from the gentleman at first, but as they reached the door to the boot room, he turned to Anne.

'It has been enlightening, Miss Elliot.'

With that, Anne had to be content.

Restless, Elizabeth prowled back and forth in her room at the cottage, her anxiety for whatever Anne's audience with her father might bring tussling with her inability to remove Mr Darcy from her mind.

His features swam before her. It was as though he had been shrouded in veils, the removal of each successive layer disclosing more of his complex character.

What was she to do with these revelations…and had Mr Darcy truly held her in high regard, as Anne alleged? Was Charlotte correct in her surmising, that the gentleman had shown interest in Elizabeth all those months ago?

Impatient with herself, she turned on her heel and strode back across the room. Mr Darcy was clearly respected…no, more than that; the servants who accompanied him to Somersetshire revered him. An excellent master, they said, and an esteemed landlord, renowned for the care of his estate and its loyal tenants.

How had Elizabeth perceived him so wrongly?

Because you were blinded by wounded pride.

Elizabeth owned the truth of it. Yes, he had been rude on first acquaintance, but since then, his perceived offences had been directed towards anyone *but* her.

Her steps slowing as she neared the window, Elizabeth stared across to the main house. How was it the man had begun to affect her so?

🎕

Anne and Mr Darcy parted at the boot room door, with the lady heading for the cottage, but then her eye caught a movement. Captain Wentworth was some distance away, walking on a stretch of cleared path, his pace steady as his strength continued to improve, the walking cane nowhere in sight.

Treading carefully along the path, conscious some icy patches remained, Anne emerged onto the paved area where she had seen the captain, but he had disappeared.

She looked to the left and then the right, her breath forming icy swirls, and then shivered.

'Eek!'

A low laugh came from behind and Anne turned quickly, a hand to her neck where she had felt the pressure of the captain's mouth. Frederick smiled in such a way, her heart almost fluttered as he wrapped her shawl more closely about her, taking both ends in his hands to pull her closer.

'Were you, perchance, seeking a lost soul, ma'am?'

'Perchance.' Anne cast a quick look about, then turned back to him.

'We are quite alone, dearest Anne.' His grin widened. 'I am glad you are come to rescue me.'

Captain Wentworth leaned down and placed a firm kiss against her cold lips, and she closed her eyes, savouring the moment as she returned it.

'How did it go with your father this morning? I would not have hesitated, should I have needed to come to your rescue.'

Anne shook her head. 'He was remarkably civil.'

'Are you warm enough to walk with me a while?' The captain offered his arm, and she took it willingly.

'My father was surprisingly stoic about our engagement. To be certain, there is little he can do to prevent it, but he was strangely...' She hesitated, unsure how to describe Sir Walter's manner from earlier. 'It is as though he had more important matters on his mind. There is something, though.'

She stopped walking. 'Would you consider postponing our journey to Shropshire? The annual St Stephen's ball is taking place on the twenty-sixth, and my father has asked me to attend.'

A shadow crossed the captain's face. 'And insists I do not?'

'No! Quite the contrary.'

A sceptical brow rose, but the captain placed Anne's arm on his own again as they fell into step once more.

'You must believe me, Frederick. I was quite astonished, but he was not in jest. Even my sister, when I saw her afterwards, mentioned it.' Anne held onto his arm more tightly. 'Are you willing to delay our visit to your brother? Will he mind if you do?'

'I doubt it. Edward is quite wrapped up in his new wife and busy getting to know his parishioners. We can travel there once the ball is over, though we will have to arrange for an alternative chaperone. So, should I ask you to reserve the first place on your dance card for me?' The edges of the captain's mouth twitched. 'What amuses you so?'

Anne reached up to place her gloved hand against his face. 'It is a long time since we danced, Frederick. I shall anticipate the first set with more pleasure than you can likely imagine.'

Taking her hand, the captain pressed a kiss upon it, then leaned down to capture her lips with his, and for a while they were wrapped in a world where only they existed.

When the embrace drew to a close, Captain Wentworth retained Anne in his embrace, and she rested her face against his coat, relishing the strength of his arms holding her safe, her heart so full she could hardly breathe. Then, a rumble came from the captain's chest, and she raised her head.

'Why are you laughing?

'I fear I am become quite the magpie, my darling. Once again, I must ask to borrow garments from Darcy, for I have nothing fitting for such an occasion.'

'It is a blessing you are of similar height and frame.'

The captain took her hand as they turned their steps in the direction of the cottage. 'Aye, and it is also fortunate there is a skilled valet in want of some occupation.' He regarded his smart attire. 'I must order some clothing directly.'

Once they were returned to the pathway running from the cottage to the main house, the captain stopped again, taking both Anne's hands in his.

'Will you marry me soon, Anne? There is much for me to resolve, not least where we can stay until I am able to take command of another ship—assuming the Admiralty condones it.' He raised her hands and kissed each one. 'But I am no poor naval officer now, and I will provide a home for us as soon as I am able to seek one. Have faith in me.'

'I do have faith in you.'

'It would mean a vast deal to have my brother perform the ceremony.' His expression was earnest. 'We can arrange for the putting up of the banns at Kellynch church before we depart, and then—once we are resident in Shropshire—we can have the banns read there, after which we can set a date. Would you mind if you did not marry in the church here?'

Anne studied his face, one she thought never to see again.

'All I wish is to never be parted from you again, and the sooner we are wed, the more content I shall be.'

The captain expressed his happiness on hearing these words as any gentleman deeply in love would, but then Anne, flushed and a little breathless, leaned back in his arms.

'We are in full view of the house, Frederick!'

'And everyone in it knows we are engaged.'

Elizabeth curled up in an armchair by the fire, her mind a jumble of thoughts. Was it really just a matter of weeks in which Mr Darcy had changed from being the last man on earth she wished to be in company with to the one whose face she persistently sought?

My feelings will not be repressed…

What if those words meant, as Anne suggested, that he had developed an affection for her?

Elizabeth almost laughed. It was a ridiculous notion. Yet how much did she wish he might care for—

'Lizzy, I am returned.'

With a start, Elizabeth looked up as Anne crossed the room.

'I did not hear the door. How was it?' She observed her friend's demeanour as she took the seat opposite, relieved to detect her calm demeanour.

'I passed no more than ten minutes in my father's company but then I had to call upon my sister, and Mary was present. It took me some time to extract myself.'

'And did Mr Darcy come back with you?' The words were out before Elizabeth could stop them.

'Yes, but I have much more to tell you.' She leaned forward. 'You recall there was…there *is* to be a ball at Kellynch? On St Stephen's Day?'

'I had forgotten.' Elizabeth bit her lip. 'But are you not Shropshire-bound for Christmas? I have written my father to say I will return before the sacred day—indeed, with the distance I must leave on Monday at the latest.'

'I spoke to Frederick, and we are to visit his brother a few days later than planned. We are to be married in Shropshire once the banns have been read.' Anne was most earnest. 'My father wishes me to return to the Hall, but Mr Darcy is more than willing for me—for us—to remain here, and we intend to do so until the Monday after Christmas—the thirtieth. But beyond this, Father insists upon my attending the ball. He says it will look bad if I am not present. You know how appearance is everything to him.'

'I am surprised, but grateful that he can overlook all that has happened to present a united front. But what of the captain?'

'It is most singular. Though my father remains a little disgruntled over my engagement, he can do naught about it, and was even open to Frederick attending the ball with me.'

'I am pleased for you. It is certain to be less of an ordeal with Captain Wentworth by your side, and perhaps Sir Walter intends to publicly acknowledge his connection.'

'But there is more, Lizzy. My father came after me when I left him and extended the invitation to you. If you will stay. Please say you will remain here until I leave and come to the ball.'

Elizabeth stared at Anne in disbelief. 'I thought Sir Walter did not wish me to darken his doorstep ever again?'

Anne shook her head. 'I comprehend your feelings. I do not know what has precipitated this change in him, but he was most adamant that you should be there. Though I know not his reasons, I would be grateful for your support.'

Unease filtered through Elizabeth. What game was Sir Walter playing? She rose from her chair and walked to the window, turning to lean against the sill, trying to comprehend her relief at the potential reprieve over her imminent departure.

'And the captain has agreed?'

Anne's eyes shone. 'He is going for my sake rather than his own. You cannot imagine how I long to stand up with Frederick once more!'

'His attention will be for none but you.' The muffled sound of voices drew Elizabeth's notice, and she looked out of the window.

Mr Darcy walked with his cousin at the back of the house. Whatever they discussed, it did not please them, but suddenly, the colonel barked a laugh, making a gesture with his arm, and Mr Darcy laughed.

Elizabeth clutched her midriff as a whirl of sensation whipped through her. What was happening to her?

'What is it? Lizzy, you have gone quite pale.' Anne hurried over to take her friend's hands in her own.

'No, no, no…' Elizabeth intoned, her voice only just audible.

This could not be happening to her…

'Speak to me. You look…' Anne hesitated, her attention drawn to the window. 'Come.' She tugged on Elizabeth's hand and urged her on. 'Let us take some air.'

Darcy soon related the gist of his meeting with Sir Walter, along with his encounter with the lawyer.

'I should not have been so unguarded, but the words were torn from me.'

The colonel shrugged. 'Shepherd may not have heard you.'

'Of course he did. You should have seen the considering look on his face.' Darcy berated himself for not having enough care to avoid it.

'Well, there is nothing to be done. Sir Walter knows you are not happy. It is what it is, Cousin. The man's suggestion of having you await him in his study was singular.'

Darcy's pace slowed as they approached the boot room door, then he faced the colonel, but before he could speak, he espied Elizabeth, walking along the path from the cottage with her friend.

'Darce?' The colonel snapped his fingers.

'I suspect Sir Walter thought Shepherd was at work in there.' Darcy lowered his voice as the ladies stepped up onto the terrace. 'There were open ledgers on the desk and a pile of post, but I was hardly going to risk getting caught examining the man's correspondence.'

His notice was drawn once more to the approaching ladies, but then he frowned. Anne spoke urgently to Elizabeth, who seemed as though she would turn back.

The colonel rapped him on the arm with his cane.

'Ow!' Darcy rubbed his arm. 'What was that for?'

Rolling his eyes, the colonel spoke quietly. 'You have the attention of a gnat just lately. So, there were letters?'

'Yes. Unopened, on the desk.'

'Hmph.' The colonel muttered as the ladies approached, then hissed in an aside, 'Your adversary has no such compunction. Did you not discern a single thing?'

'One letter was marked confidential.' Darcy frowned. Did the postmark not trigger a memory? Then, he stiffened as the ladies neared and added, 'And I have the strangest notion the hand was that of a lady.'

CHAPTER THIRTY-SIX

Elizabeth's mind was all confusion as they joined the gentleman, and she found she could not look at Mr Darcy.

'How went your visit to the Hall this morning, Miss Elliot?' The colonel beamed at both ladies in his usual genial fashion.

'As well as one might hope, Colonel.' Anne turned to address Mr Darcy.

'My father has extended an invitation to the St Stephen's Day ball to myself and Frederick, and also to Lizzy, sir.'

Elizabeth's discomfiture deepened, but some courage returned, and she raised her eyes to Mr Darcy's.

'I have trespassed unduly on your hospitality for many days now.'

Why did the notion of leaving tear at her senses?

The gentleman seemed lost for words, and the colonel offered Anne his arm.

'Come, Miss Elliot. I am in need of intelligent conversation, and it is far from forthcoming in my cousin.'

Conscious of Anne's smirk as they passed them, Elizabeth swallowed quickly. 'I—er. The invitation was unexpected.'

Why were her hands feeling so warm? Flexing her fingers, Elizabeth tugged off her gloves.

'You—' Mr Darcy stopped and cleared his throat. 'You are not for Hertfordshire on Monday, then, Miss Bennet? It is…I did not expect you to remain for the festive season.'

Elizabeth's embarrassment was profound. 'I would have spoken to you, but I only this minute heard of it.'

He shook his head. 'I spoke badly. You must know you are welcome to stay, should you have a mind to accept the invitation. Why not remain until Miss Anne Elliot leaves for Shropshire?'

'I am grateful to you, sir.' Elizabeth could say no more, and she continued to fidget with the gloves she held. If she was to remain in his temporary home for a little longer, then she had better cease her endless speculations about the gentleman.

Her heart was not so obliging. It pounded in her chest, yet she could not remove her eyes from Mr Darcy's face. Nor did he seem inclined to look away. What did he think? Was he recalling her poor judgement of his character, her harsh words to him? He did not seem displeased. His habitual inscrutable mask was nowhere to be seen, and Elizabeth felt warmth stealing into her cheeks again.

It was not until Mr Darcy offered her his arm and, tentatively, she rested her hand upon it, that realisation dawned. Strength emanated through the fine cloth of his coat, and she wished she might never have to let go. As he stepped forward to lead her to Anne and the colonel as they walked back along the terrace, Elizabeth's breath caught in her throat. This could not be! Was she, or was she not, in danger of falling in love with the gentleman?

Agitated, she dropped her gloves, bending to retrieve them but not quickly enough.

'Allow me.'

Elizabeth raised cautious eyes to Mr Darcy's as they both straightened. 'Thank you,' she whispered, taking them from him. He said nothing, merely beheld her. The moment seemed to linger forever, and she drew in a shallow breath, clutching the gloves tightly to her chest.

No, she was not in danger of falling in love with Mr Darcy. It was too late. She already *was* in love with him.

Struggling with this realisation, Elizabeth appealed to Anne as they joined them. 'I must go to my chamber.' Her voice was hoarse, and Anne took her arm as they excused themselves, urging her friend onward to the cottage.

Elizabeth dared not look back.

Darcy's attention followed Elizabeth as he ignored his cousin's voice. The ache in his breast, which accompanied all and any thought of her for some time, deepened during the last few moments. What passed through the lady's mind, he could not tell, but her confliction was apparent. How he longed to ask for her confidence, find a way to alleviate what troubled her.

'I am for the stables, Darce.'

Darcy started, then frowned. 'You are hardly dressed for riding, Richard. Nor are the conditions conducive.'

The colonel rolled his eyes, and he tried to focus.

'Do you not listen to a word I say? I just said I wished to see about Hereward and also let the groom know you have suggested the bay mare for the captain's use.' He smirked, eyeing Darcy with noticeable amusement. 'That was quite the impassioned exchange you had with Miss Bennet.'

'We did not speak.'

With a snort, the colonel turned away. 'Precisely.'

Darcy watched his cousin head for the stables, then returned to the house, a tumult of emotion in his breast. He had not imagined it then, that conscious look from Elizabeth? Why had her colour been so high, her vivacity so subdued? Was it down to the delay in her return home...or another matter entirely?

'Sir.' Darcy looked up as Mrs Reynolds came along the corridor. 'You have a caller. He arrived but five minutes ago and would insist upon awaiting your return. I have put him in the drawing room.'

Peering out of the window, Darcy's scrutiny fell—as it so often did—upon the cottage, but then, with a sigh, he turned back to his housekeeper.

'I shall be there directly. Did he leave a card?'

'No, sir. Just his name. It is a Mr Shepherd.'

Anne closed the door to her friend's room and headed back down the stairs. Whatever inflicted her, Elizabeth was in no mood to speak of it.

Emerging from the cottage, she set off along the path to the house, but she had only reached the terrace, when the captain came out of the house.

'I kept watch for you.'

His attention was drawn to the cottage, and Anne looked over. Elizabeth stood by the window.

'Is Miss Bennet not coming?'

Anne shook her head as she took the captain's arm, and they turned their steps back in the direction of the house.

'She wished to be alone.'

Captain Wentworth raised a brow. 'Your friend does not strike me as someone who prefers her own company to that of others.'

'No, it is not Lizzy's way, but I think there are times when we all seek a little respite.' Anne hugged his arm to her. 'Not from you, of course.'

Before anything further could be said, footsteps crunched on the gravel behind them, and they turned to see the colonel approaching from the direction of the stables.

'Good afternoon, Captain, Miss Elliot.'

'Colonel Fitzwilliam.'

'There is a fine mount at your disposal, Captain, should you have a mind to use it.'

Captain Wentworth's gratification was clear. 'Darcy is a kind and generous man.'

'He is indeed.' The colonel blew on his hands and rubbed them together. 'Have you seen him?'

The captain pointed at the door into the house. 'I saw Mr Darcy in the hall but five minutes ago. Mrs Reynolds advised him of a caller.'

The colonel raised a brow. 'I will seek her out, find out who it is.'

Darcy considered the man opposite without comment. His trepidation, on first hearing who the visitor was, had been powerful, and Shepherd's silence as they walked to the study brought little reprieve.

Yet Darcy realised he had no scruple in owning the truth of the matter to Sir Walter's man. Yes, he did seek to find a hold upon the gentleman, but his reasons for doing so, he was at liberty to keep to himself. As it was, he had no intention of letting Shepherd detect his apprehension.

'You are reserved, sir.'

Darcy stirred in his seat. 'Is it any surprise?'

Shepherd inclined his head. 'As I have said, I appreciate your seeing me without prior notice. I believe we have dealt with the niceties inherent on any business meeting, and it might be pertinent for a certain matter to be discussed.'

'Perhaps you had best describe in general terms what it is, sir.' If the man wanted to play games, he needed to show his hand. Without that, Darcy would not know how to lay his own cards upon the table.

Shepherd cleared his throat. 'My father worked for Sir Walter Elliot for many years, Mr Darcy, from when he came into his majority until he retired in the year two. Since that time, I have been privy to all his dealings of a legal and financial nature...' Shepherd's voice faltered. 'That is to say, there is much I comprehend about his actions.'

Still uncertain of the man's intent, Darcy leaned back in his seat, pretending a nonchalance he did not feel. It was as though he stepped out upon a tightrope suspended high in the air. Was Shepherd going to be his safety net, or would he be the one to topple him from his carefully balanced perch?

'Sir?'

Darcy blinked, then sat forward. 'Go on.'

To his surprise, Shepherd stood up, and Darcy rose slowly to his feet as well.

'I would not generally take such steps, you understand?' The lawyer paced to the window, then turned to face Darcy again. 'But—as you know full well—I heard your comment, and one must snatch at life's chances, eh?'

Darcy remained silent, waiting, and Shepherd gestured between them. 'I believe we can be of service to one another, sir.'

Anger trembled through Darcy as he stepped out from behind his desk, intent upon showing the man the door.

'I will not give you money in exchange for silence.' Sir Walter could hardly be surprised to find Darcy sought a way out of his trap. 'I have had sufficient of the machinations—'

Shepherd held up a hand. 'You misunderstand me, sir. I ask for the aid of your influence, not your pocketbook.' He walked back across the room to stand before Darcy. 'I seek the benefit of your connections. That is all the recompense I require.'

Darcy's mind was dark with frustration. Was the lawyer to exercise coercion upon him, as well as the baronet?

'Recompense in exchange for what? I will not be managed, nor will I introduce a man bent upon extortion to any of my acquaintance.'

Shepherd all but wrung his hands. 'I do not desire to extort anything from you, Mr Darcy. It is a request for your aid. In exchange for mine.'

Darcy observed him intently for a moment, his burst of anger receding as quickly as it came.

'Sit down, Shepherd.' He waved him back into his seat as he took his own. The man looked as if he would expire if he did not sit. Besides, the direction of the interview roused Darcy's curiosity. 'You came here with a purpose. Speak openly or depart, and keep your own secrets.'

Shepherd inclined his head. 'I believe you to be an astute and honourable man.'

Darcy frowned. 'And?'

Clearing his throat, Shepherd met Darcy's firm stare guardedly. 'You must understand, I am in Sir Walter's employ. So much so, I have little time for other clients. Yet it is this position that has pushed me to the boundaries of legality at times.'

'Why have you stayed? Surely there must have been opportunities to ease away from him?'

Shepherd shook his head dolefully. 'Believe me, sir, I have tried before now to step down from being Sir Walter's legal advisor, but he spoke in such a way—'

'He threatened you?' Distaste stirred Darcy's insides.

Has the man no morals at all?

'Let me say, his words were sufficient to have me fear for my livelihood if I ever spoke out of turn. I had a daughter to think of, Mr Darcy. Responsibilities.'

Though this picture of Sir Walter was hardly gratifying—indeed, it painted an image far worse than Darcy imagined—it brought with it a glimmer of hope. Lowering himself to the man's level did not sit easily upon Darcy, but with nowhere else to turn, and Sir Walter unlikely to be held at arm's length for much longer, he had no choice but to hear Shepherd's offer and see where it took him.

'So'—Darcy paused for a moment—'how do you believe you can help me? I cannot—'

'Say nothing, Darcy!'

Both men started as the colonel strode into the room, and Darcy stood.

'Cousin! Do not—'

'No, no.' The colonel held up a hand as he faced Shepherd, who slowly rose to his feet, his countenance reflective of his alarm. 'We will not be cowed by—'

'Richard! Stand down.' Darcy waved Shepherd back into his seat.

The colonel's mouth settled into a firm line, and he pulled a chair to the end of the desk and sat.

'Shepherd offers me a barter. I am of a mind to hear it.'

CHAPTER THIRTY-SEVEN

'A barter, you say?' Colonel Fitzwilliam's attention settled on Shepherd, who fidgeted under its scrutiny. 'And what would this exchange consist of?'

The man said nothing.

'Shepherd?' Darcy prompted.

'It is as I hinted, sir.' The man cleared his throat again, and Darcy resisted the urge to tell him to get on with it. 'If you are willing to assist me in finding an equally lucrative position, that I may finally be free of Sir Walter's hold, then I may have information which might aid you equally in being released from your...obligation.'

Darcy exchanged a look with the colonel, who gave an almost imperceptible shake of his head. This was no time to reveal his hand. 'And precisely what is it you believe I need to free myself from?' Damn the man if Sir Walter had been liberal with his words about this farce of an engagement.

'The gentleman has already instructed me to prepare the marriage settlement between yourself and Miss Elliot. It is why I was in Town.'

'And I suppose you paid a call at Doctors' Commons.'

A hint of culpability filled Shepherd's features. 'Indeed, sir.'

Another lightning glance passed between Darcy and his cousin, tension gripping the former as Sir Walter's net tightened.

'And?'

Shepherd had gone quite pale. 'Forgive me if I speak out of turn, sir.'

The colonel snorted. 'I think we must *insist* upon your doing so, or we shall still be here when the cows are due their next milking.'

The man looked at Colonel Fitzwilliam with consideration, then turned his notice upon Darcy. 'Sufficient words were spoken between the lady and her father in my hearing for me to ascertain you are not a willing party to this transaction.'

An understatement. Darcy drew in a short breath, trying to curb his impatience with Shepherd's slow exposition.

'Continue.'

'Sir Walter harbours a secret. Whatever he is hiding, it is obvious he does not want it discovered.'

The colonel rolled his eyes. 'Hence it being a secret.'

Darcy threw his cousin a warning look. 'And you have uncovered it, Shepherd?'

The man hesitated, then said, 'I believe I am on its tail, and it may be to your advantage.'

'You are prepared to share this information in exchange for my assistance? You understand I will need proof, unshakeable evidence of whatever it is?'

Shepherd almost quivered in his seat. 'I do, sir.'

Hope rose steadily in Darcy, though he knew he might well be clutching at straws. The colonel was uncharacteristically silent.

'When will you share what you know?'

Shepherd raised his chin. 'If you will do your part, Mr Darcy, and use your influence and connections to secure me a position of comparable recompense, then I will impart what I have discerned. I am not particular as to where the position is. My wife has passed away and my daughter is newly married. I am prepared to settle elsewhere.' He shuddered, and Darcy could well imagine why. Sir Walter's wrath when he discovered Shepherd's actions would be fierce.

'So be it.' He got to his feet. 'Are we agreed?'

Shepherd rose quickly, alongside the colonel. 'I must know I have security before I can reveal my findings.'

Darcy studied the man for a second. It was a tenuous offer, but he would grasp it willingly. His side of the bargain was the easy part.

'Understood. I shall send word by express to some of my connections.'

Shepherd held out his hand, and Darcy shook it. 'I will offer my findings immediately upon a successful outcome, sir.'

After the lawyer closed the door behind him, Darcy and his cousin said nothing for a moment. Then, the colonel shrugged.

'It is hardly promising, but as it is all we have…'

Opening the ink well, Darcy picked up a pen.

'And I have little time to squander.'

Pulling a piece of parchment from his desk, he set to, penning letters to several of his close acquaintance. If Sir Walter had a secret, and Darcy could find it out, it might pave the way out of this damnable predicament.

Elizabeth had been unable to sit since returning to her chamber, her spirits too agitated for any form of repose. The ignominy of having fallen in love with a man she once detested she accepted, but for a fleeting moment, she wondered if she ought to depart for home on Monday as planned.

This notion was swiftly countered. She had no desire to leave the gentleman; she wanted, in truth, to seize every possible moment in his presence before common decency demanded she remove herself from his home.

Walking listlessly to the bedside table, Elizabeth was conscious of an ache in the back of her throat, and she tried to swallow it away, to no avail. Then, she noticed the books on the table, and she picked them up, holding them to her chest as emotion gripped her throat even tighter. Had she not selected these particular volumes because Mr Darcy recommended the first to his sister and had been reading the second the next day?

How had she not detected the hints of a turn in her regard? And what of the gentleman?

The suggestion of his once having feelings for her returned, and Elizabeth's brow furrowed as a faint hope rose within. What did Mr Darcy truly think and feel at this moment? Would he speak, perchance, or would he refrain, because of their argument?

A light tap on the door roused her, and Elizabeth tucked the books under her arm as she opened it slightly.

'It is time to go across, Lizzy.'

Elizabeth summoned a weak smile. 'I beg you would ask Mr Darcy...' She hesitated. 'Please pass on my apologies. I have an aching head and must excuse myself this evening.'

Anne's mild, dark eyes were not as sympathetic as Elizabeth expected. 'You have never struck me as someone who would give in to so trifling an indisposition as an ache in your head.'

Her friend's astuteness would have amused Elizabeth in other circumstances. 'It is true, I am the object of my own scorn right now.' She stepped back. 'Come in.'

'What is this about, Lizzy?'

Elizabeth could not help but laugh. 'If you only knew!'

Anne all but rolled her eyes. 'Do you think I do not see? You cannot keep from turning to Mr Darcy time and again, and your air and countenance when you are near him in recent days is in stark contrast to what it once was. Is this merely because of what your aunt has told you?'

'Not wholly.' Elizabeth recalled vividly the colonel's revelations about Wickham.

'Your aversion seems well overcome.' Anne's satisfaction was evident. 'I am pleased, for it pained me when you did not like him.'

Not like him?

Those feelings felt so distant now, Elizabeth could scarce recall them.

'Lizzy?'

Elizabeth shook her head and said nothing at first, but her feelings could not be contained. 'It is…' She placed the books on a small side table and straightened to look at her friend. 'It is quite unfathomable, but I seem to have developed an…an attachment—a most profound one—to the gentleman.' She threw Anne a helpless look. 'What am I to do?'

'Oh my dear Lizzy!' Anne swept her friend into a brief embrace. 'Why such despondency? I remain confident Mr Darcy has affection for you, and you yourself have puzzled over the words he spoke, of his feelings.'

Elizabeth drew in a shallow breath as her heart clenched in her breast. 'I thought I hated him. How could I have fallen in love?' Her voice broke on the last word, and Anne regarded her with sympathy.

'Because you have come to understand what an exceptional man he is.' She patted Elizabeth on the arm. 'I will send Elise to you.'

With that, she closed the door. Elizabeth was not proud of herself for almost succumbing to her inclination, but the realisation of her feelings was so new, it threatened to consume her.

An evening of pretence, of talking trivialities, and not being caught looking at Mr Darcy with her heart in her eyes, would be quite the trial.

※

His duty discharged and the express rider on his way, Darcy approached the drawing room before dinner that evening uncertain how he felt. Though Shepherd's offer brought some hope, it was sufficiently vague. Cautioning himself to put it aside for the present, as the likelihood of a reply from his associates before the forthcoming festivities was slim, Darcy's mind filled swiftly with thoughts of Elizabeth.

What was on her mind? Her distraction earlier had been evident, as had been the fact that, whatever pressed upon her, it did not bring her pleasure. Was he the cause?

Darcy fetched up by the door to the drawing room.

Of course it is, you dunderhead.

Though their dealings with each other since his failure to propose had been civil—even cordial at times—he hardly distinguished himself, despite making an attempt to reconcile Elizabeth's sister with Bingley—which had its limits, in the light of the lady's dispiriting obligation.

One you will be sharing if you are not careful.

Darcy pushed away the reminder as a footman opened the door. Careful had nothing to do with it.

To his disappointment, Elizabeth had yet to appear in the drawing room, but then he realised none of the ladies had arrived, and he joined the gentlemen, who both seemed in excellent spirits. Taking a glass of brandy from the colonel, Darcy knocked it back, savouring the burn of the liquid in his throat. Ignoring his cousin's amused look, he refilled the glass and stood by the hearth, from where he had an excellent view of the door. A little Dutch courage would not go amiss if he were to try and engage Elizabeth in conversation, and…

Darcy blinked. Was that truly his intention? Then, he shrugged, placing his glass on the mantel and grabbing the poker and giving the logs a fierce prod. Though Elizabeth's departure had been delayed, she would ultimately return to Hertfordshire once Anne and the captain left. Why should he not grasp any remaining chance to hear her voice, see the liveliness of her countenance, and indulge in the intelligence of her fine eyes? After all, she seemed far from antagonistic towards him since his return from Town.

'I am indebted to you once more, Darcy.'

Welcoming the intrusion to his endless speculation, he regarded Captain Wentworth. 'To what end?'

'Your loan of evening dress, sir. I have already been subjected to a fitting by your talented valet and am assured it will be ready in time.' The captain grinned. 'The poor man will have to unpick it all once I have left, along with everything else you have kindly loaned.' He waved a hand at his present attire.

'Nonsense. It is his profession, Wentworth. He lives for it.' The colonel joined them, and he indicated the captain hold out his glass and topped it up.

Darcy drained his glass, his eye instinctively seeking the clock on the mantel. Where were the ladies?

'Much as I am not looking forward to an evening in Sir Walter's home, it is worth it for the chance to stand up with Anne after all these years.'

Staring into his glass, Darcy reflected on the last time he asked Elizabeth to dance. It had hardly been the experience he had anticipated, but now...yes, damn it. He *would* ask her.

He looked up as the colonel tugged his empty glass from his hand. 'Will you do the honours, Wentworth?'

The captain headed for the decanter, and Colonel Fitzwilliam spoke quietly to his cousin. 'I would exercise caution regarding the ball, Darce.'

'It cannot be frowned upon, to stand up with the ladies in our own party.'

'No, but do not let your high regard for Miss Bennet escape you for the duration of a set.'

Darcy watched the captain refill their glasses. 'Thankfully, my will remains my own. I shall be under good regulation, but do not censure me for indulging in a simple pleasure before I am obligated to give it all up.'

Elizabeth took herself to task as she and Anne, warmly wrapped against the falling temperature, walked briskly along the path to the house. An obliging footman relieved them of their cloaks, and she placed a hand to her too-warm cheeks, willing the colour to fade.

Anne took her hand as they approached the drawing room, and before Elizabeth knew it, the footman opened the door and they were amongst the company. With conversation flowing and drinks being served, it was a moment before she discerned Mr Darcy's position, but when she detected his eyes upon her, she took a hasty sip from her glass.

Was Anne correct in her surmising? Did the gentleman's look hold approval? Slowly, Elizabeth returned her attention to him. He spoke to his sister and Mrs Annesley, but suddenly, he turned his head and their eyes locked across the room.

'And how do you fare this fine evening, Miss Bennet?'

With a start, Elizabeth tore her gaze from Mr Darcy's. 'Quite well, thank you, Colonel Fitzwilliam. And yourself?'

'Better than my mount. Poor Hereward remains incapacitated.'

'Oh, I am grieved to hear it.' Thankful for the ease of the colonel's conversation, Elizabeth could feel the tension receding as her cheeks cooled, and she took another sip from her glass. 'What is the prognosis? I trust he will recover?'

The colonel beamed at her. 'Indubitably. It is merely rest he requires, and I must therefore rein in my impatience or use another mount.' He waved a hand at the windows. 'Assuming the weather permits a gallop across the fields on the morrow. Do you ride, Miss Bennet?'

'If I must.'

Laughing, the colonel took a drink from his own glass. 'But you are fond of walking?'

'Very much so. The horses at home are more often wanted on the farmland than for country pursuits, so I grew up not relying on them.'

'Darcy is a fine horseman.'

Elizabeth followed the direction of his attention, unsurprised to see it on his cousin. Thankfully, Mr Darcy was in conversation with Captain Wentworth, Anne having taken a seat beside Georgiana, and she was able to study his noble features without fear of detection. She would have to commit them to memory, for she was no artist and could hardly ask his sister if she could spare a likeness!

'This amuses you?'

The colonel observed Elizabeth with humour, and she gave a self-deprecating smile. 'Not at all. How soon must you return to your regiment, Colonel?'

'Not until the New Year, though my mother laments my not spending some of my leave with them in Town this year. They meant to be returned to the estate by now, but with the weather conditions, it simply was not feasible.' He indicated Elizabeth's almost empty glass. 'May I fetch you some more sherry?'

Generally, Elizabeth would decline, but this evening she felt in need of it, but as the colonel headed off to refill her glass, she became aware of someone behind her.

CHAPTER THIRTY-EIGHT

'Oh!' Suddenly wishing the colonel would hurry back, Elizabeth stared up at Mr Darcy, desperately seeking a more intelligent response.

'Are you quite well, Miss Bennet? Forgive me for noticing, but your colour was rather high when you arrived.'

A little mortified, Elizabeth shook her head. 'Not at all, sir. I am certain it was merely the brisk walk from the cottage.'

The gentleman frowned. 'It is not practical in these inclement conditions for you to be constantly going from heat to cold to heat. You will catch a chill.'

'You are not condemning your kindness in offering Willow Cottage to us, sir?'

The notion was gallantly contested but feeling once again the imposition of being an unanticipated and—at the time, surely unwelcome—guest who was extending her stay yet further, Elizabeth's eyes searched his face. Did Mr Darcy seek a polite way of enquiring whether she intended to remain until next Easter?

The gentleman smiled slightly. 'You have an expressive countenance, Miss Bennet.'

Elizabeth bit her lip. She hoped he could not deduce *everything* her face might portray just now.

'Forgive me,' he continued. 'I would not customarily say it of you.' He stopped and Elizabeth could imagine the direction of his thoughts. He certainly had not read her well in the past. Then, he cleared his throat. 'Quite.'

Elizabeth's amusement was clear, and the edges of his mouth twitched.

'Here we are!'

The colonel handed Elizabeth a fresh glass of sherry and looked from her to his cousin.

'Did you ask the lady, Darce?'

The gentleman looked blank, and Elizabeth raised a curious brow.

Colonel Fitzwilliam rolled his eyes. 'Miss Bennet'—he gestured at Mr Darcy—'this is my cousin. He is fond of neither balls nor dancing, claiming the latter is a futile exercise, requiring far too much effort and conversation with those he does not wish to pass time with.'

'Richard!'

To Elizabeth's amusement, Mr Darcy's retort was ignored as the colonel continued. 'Consequently, he is monstrously ill-suited to request a lady stand up with him.' Colonel Fitzwilliam shook his head in exaggerated fashion. 'It is shocking to be so unaccomplished after such an expensive education, do you not think, Miss Bennet?'

Elizabeth could not help but laugh, despite the glare Mr Darcy bestowed upon his smirking cousin, but she sobered as the gentleman turned to behold her.

'If you will excuse me.' The colonel winked at Elizabeth, then walked away, and silence embraced them once more.

Then, Mr Darcy cleared his throat. 'For all his waffle, my cousin speaks the truth, Miss Bennet. Would you'—he swallowed visibly, and Elizabeth held her breath. 'Would you do me the honour of dancing the first set with me? At the ball, I mean…not now…'

Laughing, Elizabeth's heart was full of anticipation. 'I would like that a vast deal, Mr Darcy. My memory of the last…or should I say, the only time we stood up together does not serve me well. I welcome the chance to improve upon it.'

Nothing more was said as they were called into dinner, but Elizabeth sent a tremulous look in Anne's direction as she took her seat.

St Stephen's Day could not come soon enough.

Darcy was thankful when the time came to retire, as Elizabeth continued to consume his mind.

'Will that be all, sir?'

Raworth watched him cautiously from across the room, as well he might. Darcy had hardly been himself for days, and tonight his introspection must have been writ clear upon his countenance.

'Yes, thank you.'

He turned away as the valet left the dressing room and walked into his chamber, throwing his bed a cursory glance. There was little point in attempting sleep. Taking a fireside chair, Darcy stared unseeingly into the flames, his thoughts mired in the complexities of his dilemma.

Paying marked attention to Elizabeth with all that hung over him was perhaps an indulgence he could ill afford, but he had been unable to resist.

Stirring in his seat, Darcy laced his hands. Concealing his feelings was ingrained within him.

Keep yourself under good regulation.

It had been his father's strict edict, and it was one he lived by. Until Elizabeth came whirling into his life on an autumn breeze...

Leaning back in the chair, Darcy reflected on how enjoyable an evening it had been, both during the meal and afterwards, when the colonel had taken it upon himself to ensure both Anne and Elizabeth had the three gentlemen of their party on their dance cards. Darcy laughed at the memory of Captain Wentworth's face when Elizabeth teasingly suggested Miss Elizabeth Elliot may expect him to stand up with her. He hurriedly begged Anne to fill the rest of her card with his name, but for Darcy, the best moment of the evening had been the warm look Elizabeth bestowed upon him as they all said their goodnights.

His contentment lasted but a moment, falling away as soon as his true situation came to the forefront again.

'Set it aside, man,' Darcy muttered, getting to his feet.

He was sufficiently encumbered by Sir Walter's entrapment. This was no time to dwell upon Elizabeth.

The following morning, Elizabeth studied her reflection in the looking glass. She appeared much as usual, belying the turmoil of emotions, hopes and dreams flowing through her.

She padded to the window to examine the extent of the thaw. It promised little in terms of a walk, and she leant back against the sill, considering the same thoughts as had plagued her through the long night.

Why was Mr Darcy being so...so kind? Had he not claimed, at Netherfield, his good opinion, once lost, was gone forever? Yet he did not appear to begrudge Elizabeth the damning of his character.

Then, she recalled the gentleman asking her to stand up with him for the first set. It was an attention she could never have imagined. Perhaps they could at least attempt a friendship, further their acquaintance, whereby she might be able to show him her opinion had improved?

'I do not know who you think you are fooling, Lizzy Bennet,' she muttered as she picked up her writing slope. 'Would "improved" not be the grossest of understatements?'

She headed down the stairs, intent upon writing yet another letter to her father, explaining she had decided to remain in the West Country with her friend for the festive season. What Mr Bennet would make of it, she knew not.

The following two days passed swiftly as the Yuletide season approached, with the ladies secreted away from each other as they prepared gifts to exchange. Thus it was that Elizabeth saw very little of Mr Darcy, other than when partaking of the evening meals, and in some ways, she preferred it, for she remained a little overwhelmed by the newness of her feelings.

As for the gentleman, she struggled to ascertain the direction of his thoughts. His gaze continued to rest upon her, and it was far from censorious. The conversation they managed seemed wrapped in unspoken meaning, yet Mr Darcy's reticence was also apparent, as was his occasional distraction—despite the company—his face darkening with unknown thoughts. Whether it stemmed from the lingering memory of all she had accused him of, or was down to the suffering his sister had implied he would undergo, Elizabeth knew not.

Tuesday soon dawned, and though the weather continued to cast doubts upon any activity in the fresh air, it was Christmas Eve. As Elizabeth and Anne had agreed to help Georgiana decorate the house, there would be occupation enough.

'Miss Bennet, there is a letter for you.'

Elizabeth smiled at the housekeeper as she and Anne approached the drawing room after breakfast, reaching out to take it as Mrs Reynolds addressed Anne.

'This was sent down from the Hall, ma'am.'

Both girls studied their letters as they headed to the drawing room.

'It is from Jane.' Elizabeth was filled with anticipation over what intelligence it might bring from Hertfordshire. She looked at the second. 'And *another* from my aunt.'

'I trust they both bring good news, Lizzy. This is not a time of year for vexations.'

Elizabeth threw Anne—who studied her letter in puzzlement—a quizzical look. 'Is your own letter not to your liking? It is not from your father?'

'Not at all.' Anne pushed open the door and they crossed to a couple of comfortable chairs near one of the windows. 'It is unusual, that is all. I told you of my mother's maid, Mattie?' She waved the unopened letter. 'It is rare I hear from her above once a year, usually near my birthday in the summer. I am hoping there is nothing amiss.'

Elizabeth placed her aunt's letter on the circular table between them. 'The sooner it is opened, the quicker your concerns will be allayed.'

Anne laughed. 'Ever the pragmatist, dear Lizzy.' Then, she sobered. 'How shall I ever do without you?'

'All will be well, for you will have the good captain at your side.'

'For which I could not be happier. But I will still miss you.'

They turned their attention to their correspondence, Elizabeth's eyes skimming Jane's letter. When she raised her head again, Anne watched her.

'I cannot detect whether you are pleased or not!' Anne laughed. 'Does your sister have anything promising to report?'

Elizabeth was a little uncertain how she felt. Was this good news? She placed Jane's letter on the table and picked up her aunt's.

'They arrived back at Longbourn last Saturday, and Jane speaks mainly of the household but there is a marked alteration in the tone of her writing. She is much more like the sister I knew, and she has mentioned one thing of significance: Mr Bingley has returned to Netherfield. Mr Darcy had not been certain when it might be, but it is now confirmed. He is already in residence, and Jane says Mama is all a flutter again.' Elizabeth rolled her eyes. 'How thankful am I that I do not have to bear witness.'

'But with your sister engaged to your cousin, what can your mother hope to achieve, especially in light of her supporting their match?'

Laughing but with little amusement, Elizabeth broke the seal on her aunt's letter. 'You must not underrate Mama, Anne. There are still three unwed daughters at home.'

Anne smirked. 'And one who will return after Christmas.'

'Which makes me tempted to refuse to go home until I am safely wed of my own choosing!' Warmth immediately filled Elizabeth's skin, but she ignored Anne's pointed look. 'Was your letter reassuring?'

'Oh, yes. Mattie is in Montacute for the season with her husband and young daughter, making some stay with old friends. She expresses the hope we shall meet up before she returns to Cornwall.' Anne looked at the clock. 'Will you excuse me, Lizzy? I wish to send a note to her directly.'

'Yes, of course. I have yet to read Aunt Gardiner's letter. Miss Darcy said she would come to the drawing room shortly, so I will await your return here.'

After Anne left the room, Elizabeth settled more comfortably into her seat to peruse her second letter. Aside from a brief report on their journey, it was a much more satisfying missive. Not only had Mr Bingley returned to the neighbourhood, but Jane had seen him more than once.

Elizabeth's eyes could not read the words fast enough, and when she finished, she began again at the beginning, eager to consider every word. Then, she lowered the letter to her lap, her throat tight with emotion.

It seemed Mr Bingley had come across Jane when out walking. What was more, he had called at Longbourn to pay his respects and had already been invited to dine there twice over Christmas. Jane, of course, would have considered it inappropriate to mention the gentleman overmuch in her letter, being an engaged woman, as well as wishing to discourage any resurgence of hope in Elizabeth, but Aunt Gardiner spoke openly.

Mr Bingley was charming and pleasant, much as she supposed, but in unguarded moments it was obvious his esteem for Jane had not abated. As for her sister, she presented a calm manner when the gentleman called but had been less composed after she encountered Mr Bingley in the lanes adjacent to Longbourn a second time.

This intelligence was sufficiently encouraging to raise Elizabeth's spirits vastly, though she knew not what was to come of it, and she folded the letters and tucked them up her sleeve, getting to her feet as the door opened and Georgiana entered, followed by a footman bearing several branches of greenery.

🌼

'Are you sure about this, Georgie?'

Darcy waved a hand at a footman, who obligingly dropped some bundles of hawthorn and laurel onto the large cotton sheeting spread out across the entrance hall.

Georgiana looked up from where she was neatly threading ribbons through a bough of evergreens. 'Quite certain, Fitz.'

Mrs Reynolds came through the service door carrying a wooden, circular frame—the base for the wreath that traditionally graced the main entrance at Pemberley.

'We brought this with us, sir, but it is perhaps a little large for here.'

Darcy walked over to take it from her. 'And a little heavy for the door. It will have to be fitted to the portico at the front of the house.'

Mrs Reynolds walked over to sit beside Georgiana as Darcy set the frame aside.

'Do you require reinforcements?' He took in the piles of greenery waiting to be made into garlands, along with the gossamer ribbons and the dried fruits already neatly fastened into bunches. Surely Elizabeth would be a willing helper, and then he could—

'Miss Bennet and Miss Elliot are obliging me, Fitz. They are trimming the drawing room as we speak. Miss Elliot says she is used to decorating the Hall—under her sister's instruction, of course—and assisting at Uppercross Cottage too.'

'And is she not welcome this year?'

Georgiana shrugged lightly as she picked up a piece of ivy to lace through her garland. 'Apparently, Sir Walter has secured the services of a flower merchant, his own team of gardeners and the chandler to supply candles for the ball. They are dressing the house accordingly.'

The colonel raised a brow and said quietly, 'More expense.'

Darcy was disinterested in anything happening at the Hall, his attention fixed upon the closed door to the drawing room, his mind full of Elizabeth. He saw so little of her in recent days, and—

'Ow!' The colonel nudged him hard in the ribs. 'What was that for?'

The colonel waved a hand at Georgiana. 'Your sister is waiting for your answer.'

Georgiana did indeed regard him speculatively, but her quick peep over to the drawing room did not go amiss, and Darcy pulled himself together.

'Forgive me, Georgie. What did you say?'

'Have you time to spare to assist us, Brother? We have far fewer servants on hand to help prepare the wreath and all the garlands for the staircase and mantels.'

Darcy could not help but laugh as his amused housekeeper shook her head.

'And we have far fewer mantels to decorate than Mrs Reynolds has to oversee at Pemberley, dearest.'

'But you have been for your ride! There is no fishing to be had in this weather, and no billiard room in which to hide yourself.'

'Do not press him, Georgie.' The colonel scooped up some evergreens and holly, settling on a bench, his spoils balanced in his lap. 'He will soon recall he has a library, if you do.'

'I am no shirker.' Darcy looked from her to his housekeeper. 'Tell me what I am to do, and it shall be done.'

'If you could tie the ends it would help, sir.' Mrs Reynolds held up a ball of string and a sharp knife. 'It requires some strength of wrist to ensure they are fully bound.'

'Over here, Darce.' The colonel waved the branch ends he grasped. 'I trust Captain Wentworth has been duly employed as well, Georgie?'

'Of course. He has gone to gather more holly from the garden.'

'And Mrs Annesley?'

Georgiana rolled her eyes at her cousin. 'She is preparing lengths of ribbon, Richard. Must you account for everyone before you are prepared to pull your weight?'

They worked in silence for a half hour, with Darcy making short work of fastening the ends of the garlands already prepared, laying them out on the floor for the footmen to take up, his attention moving time and again to the drawing room door.

When the colonel stood and stretched, claiming he needed a tot of brandy to keep him going, Darcy willingly followed him across the hall.

CHAPTER THIRTY-NINE

Elizabeth was attempting to fasten some silk roses into a bough of greenery destined for the mantel, but she looked up when the door opened, expecting the captain to be returning from his foray into the garden.

'Miss Elliot, Miss Bennet.' The colonel bowed to them each in turn. 'I see Georgiana has you hard at labour too. We have been enlisted as reinforcements.' He turned for the sideboard. 'Once I have taken a restorative draught, that is.'

We…? Elizabeth observed Mr Darcy as he entered the room, but the instant his eyes met hers, a familiar sensation from the past few days assailed her. He did not break the connection, and she swallowed quickly, then blinked as he finally turned to join his cousin.

'Stop it'—she cautioned her heart silently as its beat picked up—'for heaven's sake. Be calm or you will be as red as the berries on Anne's garland.'

'May I?'

Elizabeth's head shot up. Mr Darcy stood beside her chair, his hand held out. She offered the rose to him, and it trembled in the air between them.

Then, a smile slowly formed on his face. 'I meant the twine.'

Feeling foolish, Elizabeth offered him her other hand as she rose from her seat.

'If you would be so kind, Miss Bennet.' The gentleman held up a piece of twine. 'With the rose?'

Staring at him as though wishing to charge every nuance, every feature to her memory for safekeeping, Elizabeth had no words.

'Shall I?'

Should he *what*? She blinked as he took the hand holding the neglected rose and raised it between them.

'Oh! Yes. Forgive me.' His warm dark eyes held hers and, flustered beyond measure, Elizabeth hurriedly pressed the rose upon him, trying not to quiver as his skin brushed hers. This was ridiculous, and she would surely laugh herself out of it, if it would not raise all manner of curiosity amongst the gathered company.

Mr Darcy placed the rose on a nearby table and bent to scoop up some greenery from the floor.

'If you would be so kind as to direct me.'

Amusement tugged at the corners of his mouth, making the gentleman all the more adorable in her eyes, and Elizabeth pulled herself together. 'Yes, of course. If I hold the bough, would you be able to fasten the roses to it? It pains my fingers, for the twine is stiff to work with.'

They continued in silence for a while, and the methodical routine helped calm Elizabeth, so much so she began to softly hum a carol as two more roses were added to the greenery.

Holding the bough as Mr Darcy tied the final flower into place, she looked over to see the colonel busily untangling some strands of ivy, and Anne engaged in fastening some ribbons to her garland. It was such a calming, domestic scene, and she stopped humming and released a soft sigh.

The gentleman looked up. 'Is it not to your satisfaction, Miss Bennet? Have I failed to deliver to your high standards?'

With a laugh, Elizabeth shook her head, admiring the neatly fastened roses. 'Not at all, sir. You may add floristry to your list of accomplishments.'

Mr Darcy straightened and took the bough from Elizabeth, holding it up for her inspection. 'Is that a compliment?'

'It is long owed, sir.'

He smiled warmly, and Elizabeth's heart resumed its customary dance.

'I have not seen these before.' He pointed to one of the silk roses as he laid the bough gently on the floor.

'I made them, Mr Darcy, in recent days. I often make such small offerings for the Christmas decorations at Longbourn. Your sister kindly obliged with providing the fabric, so I am pleased they have come to be useful here at Meadowbrook House.'

This reminder of home recalled her aunt's letter, and Elizabeth spoke quickly. 'I wish to thank you once more, for your call upon your friend.'

He raised a brow. 'There is news so soon?'

Elizabeth shook her head. 'Not entirely, but Mr Bingley seems to have returned to Hertfordshire with a new-found purpose, not least that of imposing his company as often as he can upon my family.'

Mr Darcy's eyes narrowed. 'But that was not my recommendation. He may just as well have called upon your aunt and uncle in Town if he was to be so unsubtle.'

Elizabeth turned her head to one side. 'You are unhappy he did not follow your advice, sir?'

His lips twitched. 'You misunderstand me, Miss Bennet.'

'Surely not?' Elizabeth laughed, and he joined in.

'I suggested he would be better served in returning to his estate to seek out Miss Bennet by accident, not design.'

'Then he has circumvented your guidance rather than ignored it.'

'How so?'

'Mr Bingley seems to have recalled my sister's favourite haunts and has managed—twice in as many days—to come across her by chance. My aunt believes the gentleman is succeeding in raising some doubts in Jane over her recent decision.' Elizabeth was warmed by this recollection. 'I am grateful for what you have attempted to do. It brings long awaited ease, thus, I must repeat my thanks to you, sir.'

'Then I hope you will excuse me if I also thank myself?'

Elizabeth was amused. 'It is a strange concept, Mr Darcy. For *what* do you thank yourself?'

He said nothing for a minute, and an indefinable silence hovered in the air between them. Then, he lowered his voice. 'For bringing you comfort, Miss Bennet.'

Emotion swirled within Elizabeth as he held her gaze. Then, they both started at the scrape of a chair as the colonel stood and stretched.

'Darcy?'

The gentleman looked over to where his cousin raised his empty glass. 'Not for me, thank you.'

Mr Darcy picked up one of the unused roses from the table beside Elizabeth and studied the intricate creation before raising his head. 'Such beauty to behold. Henceforth, it will adorn...' He hesitated, then added: 'I shall take much pleasure from them at Pemberley next Christmas.'

'Lizzy?'

They both looked over towards the hearth.

'I believe your friend is seeking your attention.'

Anne beckoned, and Elizabeth excused herself and hurried across to join her.

'Forgive me for dragging you away.' Anne extended her hand as Elizabeth joined her. 'Did you take the opportunity to speak to Mr Darcy about Mr Bingley?'

Elizabeth placed a hand to her cheek. 'A little. I think I need some air.'

Anne threw her an arch look. 'You are flushed, to be certain. Her expression sobered. 'Frederick received word from the Admiralty this morning and must attend a hearing in January.'

'About what happened to the Laconia?'

'Yes. Apparently, of the few men who survived, there are two who have sufficiently recovered to attend and bear witness to events.'

'There is no fear of repercussions?' Elizabeth could hear the murmur of Mr Darcy's voice as he spoke to his cousin. It was truly no aid to calming her erratic heart beat!

Anne shook her head. 'Frederick says it is a formality.' She smiled. 'I was about to go in search of him. He has been gone almost a half hour, which is time enough to bring us every piece of holly remaining, and I am not certain we have enough mantels and sills to accommodate it.' She eyed the lingering colour on Elizabeth's cheeks. 'Perhaps you should go?'

Relieved for the opportunity to pull herself together, Elizabeth was determined to return to the room in a more poised and collected manner.

'Of course. Though if I do not come back within a few minutes, you had best send reinforcements. I do not have your art of persuasion where Captain Wentworth is concerned.'

Elizabeth laughed at Anne's expression and slipped from the room, refusing to look in Mr Darcy's direction.

There was an alteration between them; the gentleman's reserve seemed to have receded, and she needed time to think about its possible implications whilst not under his searching eye.

The captain and Elizabeth soon returned, the former laden with more holly, and the latter relieved to find her heart under better regulation for her brief foray into the cold air.

A busy hour followed, with Georgiana and Mrs Annesley joining Anne and Elizabeth in putting the final touches to the garlands and boughs, and then there was nothing to be done but for them to be fastened into position, a job which required the assistance of the footmen, and once they were summoned, the ladies excused themselves to attend to their appearance, for their hands were dirty and their garments littered with leaves.

The gentlemen welcomed the completion of their duties, and with Captain Wentworth excusing himself to deal with his correspondence, the colonel stretched his arms above his head.

'Darcy, cease that infernal humming. This is no time for carols. A word if I may.'

Relinquishing his position beside the window, through which he watched Elizabeth return to the cottage with Anne, Darcy viewed his cousin wearily. He recognised that tone.

'I comprehend your desire for Miss Bennet's company— and I am glad you will at least have the first set at the ball with the lady—but remember your need to be more circumspect when not in this house. You must take care.'

'In what way?'

'Sir Walter expects you to be engaged to Miss Elliot, yet you do not seem to be able to pay attention to aught beyond Miss Bennet.'

The recollection of helping Elizabeth earlier was sufficient for Darcy to immediately be lost in the memory.

'Darce! For pity's sake, man!'

'Forgive me.'

'I do not blame you for paying Miss Bennet attention, when you had such hopes of her, but with all that is at stake, you must take care not to raise her expectations *or* the suspicions of Sir Walter and his daughter.'

'I do not think raising Miss Bennet's expectations is a risk, Cousin. She has made it abundantly clear what she thinks of me.'

'You are not being honest. Is it with me, or with yourself?'

Damn his far too astute cousin. 'Fine. Yes, I am well aware of the quandary, and that there seems to be a change in…'

What? What *did* seem to be happening between him and Elizabeth?

'Precisely. There is a stark alteration in the lady this past four and twenty hours. She can hardly take her eyes from you. Miss Bennet is a confident young woman with both courage and conviction, yet she is notably lacking in her usual flair for conversation these past few days.'

Darcy drew in a short breath. 'What would you have me do? You know all that has passed between me and Eliz—Miss Bennet. Will you censure me for deriving what pleasure I can from her company before she leaves for Hertfordshire? I thought I must say goodbye before Christmastide. To have these precious extra days is a gift, and one I will not easily forego.' If he failed to extract himself, these memories would be his only comfort henceforth.

'Old man. My dearest friend.' The colonel placed a hand on Darcy's rigid frame for a moment. 'I comprehend full well your predicament, but there is much at stake. I believe you have reason to hope where Miss Bennet is concerned, but unless you can turn this situation, it will, nay, it *can* come to naught.'

The small flames of anticipation within Darcy's breast—ones which began to take hold and burn more fiercely in the past four and twenty hours—were reduced to smouldering ashes in an instant.

'You are right, Cousin. I am on a knife-edge. My focus must be upon thwarting Sir Walter's designs. Whatever hopes remain, should I be successful...'

'I will be your second in whatever comes your way. You know that, Darce.'

He stopped as the door opened.

'This has come by express, sir. The rider is awaiting a response.' The footman handed over a letter, then walked over to stand by the door, and Darcy turned his back on him as he broke the seal, perusing the contents before handing it to his cousin to read.

'Tell the man the reply will be with him in a quarter hour. Ask Mrs Reynolds to offer refreshment before he begins the return journey.'

'As you wish, sir.' The footman bowed and left the room, and Darcy turned back to his cousin, who refolded the letter.

'Quite fortuitous. A vacancy with immediate effect.' The colonel handed the letter over, and Darcy headed for the door.

The colonel followed in his wake. 'And Shepherd? Do you think this will suffice? It is a good position and suitably distant from Sir Walter.'

'If the man is as set upon leaving Sir Walter's employ as he implied, then the terms look more than adequate. Lord Renishaw is a fair man, but his lands and business dealings are extensive. Sad though the sudden demise of his current legal man is, I believe Shepherd will be just the person to aid him.'

They walked out into the entrance hall, Darcy bent upon reaching his study and penning a suitable response, but they were waylaid by Georgiana, who stood in the middle of the hall, surveying the efforts of the footmen in attaching a garland to the balustrade of the staircase.

'There you are! You must come and admire the dining room, and then help with—'

'Georgie, it will have to wait. Besides, can the ladies not provide a willing audience?'

His sister frowned. 'I do not know where they are. You will both have to do!'

Colonel Fitzwilliam snorted. 'Flattering!'

Darcy concealed his amusement, for Georgiana fixed them with a stern eye. 'How often is it that I request a favour of you? Especially you, Richard?'

The colonel exchanged a look with Darcy.

'She is reminiscent of your mother, is she not, Darce?'

It was uncanny how true the likeness was in that instant, and Darcy was torn between amusement and sentiment as he joined his sister.

'Forgive us, Georgie. I have an urgent letter to write, but then we will be at your disposal once more.' He dropped a kiss on top of her head, and she beamed up at him.

'Thank you, Fitz.'

The two men made their way down the corridor to the study in silence.

Once inside, however, Darcy drew two sheets of paper from under his blotter and took a seat.

'What the devil are you proposing to send Renishaw, Darce? A novel?'

Selecting a pen, Darcy flicked open the ink well before raising his eyes to his cousin.

'I think a second note—to Shepherd, to wait on us at his earliest convenience—would not be inappropriate in the circumstances. As soon as he has agreed to Renishaw's terms, he will be obliged to fulfil his side of the deal.'

CHAPTER FORTY

Elise soon restored both Anne's and Elizabeth's appearance, and the latter was in the sitting room, attempting to write a reply to both her letters. The one to Jane was quickly penned, but as Elizabeth began a second side of parchment to her aunt, she stopped writing, the pen falling onto the blotter. What a fool she was!

She skimmed the first page, torn between humour and despair. Mr Darcy's name was liberally scattered across the page: words praising his conduct, his character and…Elizabeth blinked. Had she truly shared her appreciation for Mr Darcy's fine-looking features with her aunt?

Scrunching the paper into a ball, Elizabeth stood up and hurried to the fireplace, disposing of the incriminating words instantly.

'There,' she said softly. 'No one must ever know.'

She returned to the desk, but her inclination to write further dwindled. Nothing interested her but a certain gentleman, and—

'Are you done with your letters?'

Anne came into the room, and Elizabeth pointed to the one addressed to Jane. 'Not quite.' Are you going out?'

Her friend picked up a warm cloak.

'Frederick and I are to walk in the grounds. We have much to discuss regarding the wedding. Will you return to the main house? I am sure Miss Darcy will welcome your company.'

'I think I shall remain here.'

'To what purpose?' The corners of Anne's lips turned up. 'Mr Darcy can have no objection to your company.'

'You do not know it for certain, despite our suspicion of what he may once *have* felt.'

Anne shook her head at her friend. 'And I believe he is in love with you yet.'

Tears pricked the back of Elizabeth's eyes. If only it were true. 'Then why does he not speak?'

'Perhaps he once made the attempt and now needs encouragement.'

It was a sobering but heartening thought, and Elizabeth's eyes brightened.

'Should I...?' She stepped to the window to view the house. 'Ought I to make an attempt? Strive to let Mr Darcy comprehend how much my feelings have changed?'

A small laugh came from Anne again as she came to stand beside her friend.

'Dear Lizzy, it is plain for all to see. He may struggle to accept it, bearing in mind your argument, but I am certain he will come to understand. Only you must become you again.'

Elizabeth threw Anne a confused look. 'Become me?'

'You have lost the ability to converse or pay anything but Mr Darcy any mind.'

A hand shot to Elizabeth's face. How mortifying!

'You mean everyone has noticed.'

Walking over to retrieve her cloak, Anne eyed her friend with sympathy. 'If it is any consolation, I think the stable lad has yet to discover it. Come, Lizzy. Get your wrap and find Miss Darcy. You are in want of distraction!'

It was early evening when Darcy was disturbed in his study by the arrival of a visitor.

'Show him in please, Mrs Reynolds, and could you ask my cousin to join us?'

Getting to his feet, Darcy could sense the return of his tension, but before he could speculate too far, the door opened.

'I appreciate your coming on Christmas Eve, Shepherd.' Darcy waved the man into a seat just as the door opened again to reveal the colonel.

Greetings were exchanged, and the offer of employment with Lord Renishaw discussed. Thankfully, Shepherd was not only agreeable to the terms but was determined to begin his new position as soon as was feasible.

'Capital,' exclaimed Colonel Fitzwilliam. 'Shall we drink to it?'

'Not yet, cousin,' Darcy cautioned. There was more at stake.

Silence settled on them for a moment, and Darcy exchanged a look with the colonel. Shepherd's demeanour was not encouraging.

'I have completed my share of the bargain. What have you to tell us, Shepherd?'

So much hinged upon this, Darcy could barely breathe.

The man clasped his hands. 'Sir Walter's spending since his wife passed away has reached new heights, so much so, he is having to divert funds from the estate to support his lifestyle, and that of his daughter Elizabeth.'

'This much we have noted for ourselves.' Darcy drew in a breath. The man better not be wasting their time. 'What else has he been doing?'

'He has cancelled any existing retainers, cashed in whatever assets he can that exist beyond the entail. There is, however, one payment that continues. He refuses to discuss it, and I have never seen any records appertaining to its being set up. I looked back through the ledgers to trace the commencement of the payment, which is shrouded in secrecy. It is made in the name of Williams—'

The colonel harrumphed. 'Conveniently common name.'

'The name is what it is, Cousin.' Darcy looked back at Shepherd. 'What are the payments for?'

'I cannot say precisely at this moment, but—'

Getting to his feet, the colonel glared at the lawyer and threw Darcy a warning look before walking over to the tray of spirits.

Darcy raised a brow. 'Cannot, or will not, Shepherd?'

'Bear with me, sir. The commitment has been on-going since before I began working for the estate. It is remitted every quarter day, and the sum is always the same. Sir Walter has never divulged the reason for the payments.'

Colonel Fitzwilliam returned to his seat, a glass in his hand. 'And you have discovered an item of interest in relation to this?'

The man looked from the colonel to Darcy. 'There are two matters that raise questions for which there are no obvious answers. With regard to this payment, I can only add this at present: I suggested an end to it, as had happened to all others. If Sir Walter does not retrench, he will be in dire straits in a year or so. He blustered, agreeing he wished he could, but that it must endure until the duty was fulfilled.' Shepherd knit his brows. 'He did add that he had plans to ensure it was close to seeing an end.'

'I do not see how this is of any use.' The small ball of hope unravelled, and Darcy cast his cousin a hopeless look.

'The payments date from the year one, about a year after the death of Lady Elliot, sir, and that brings me to another oddity, which I have recently come to suspect is connected.'

Darcy's eyes snapped to Shepherd's. 'What is it?'

'Last December, Miss Mary Elliot, as she was then, married Charles Musgrove. It was an extravagant affair, with no expense spared.'

The colonel drained his glass. 'As Mrs Musgrove delighted in telling us.'

'Yet the estate coffers are all but dry, and not one account came through Sir Walter's books. I saw no transactions, nor could I identify whence the funds came to cover the costs. Sir Walter brushed the matter aside.'

'Curious,' added the colonel.

Shepherd looked from him to Darcy again. 'I suspect Mrs Musgrove obliged.'

Darcy was confused. 'Charles Musgrove's mother?'

'Nay. Mrs Mary Musgrove. From her own reserves.'

'How is that possible?'

'Before the marriage, when the usual settlements were drawn up, Sir Walter instructed me to meet him in London at a legal firm, Knight & Dey.' He waved an airy hand. 'I arrived late due to inclement weather and Sir Walter was alone in the office, the clerk having left to arrange for some coffee. But I digress. The purpose of the visit was down to James Stevenson—Sir Walter's late father-in-law—having set up a separate estate trust for his daughter's use after the marriage had taken place. This fund, upon Lady Elliot's death, so Sir Walter told me, passed in equal shares to his daughters, each sum payable to the lady on her marriage.'

He named the amount made over to Mrs Musgrove a year ago, and the colonel released a slow whistle.

Darcy looked to Shepherd in surprise. 'Mr Stevenson was an extremely generous man. A separate estate trust is not uncommon, but do you know why it was set up after his daughter's marriage had taken place?'

Shepherd shook his head. 'As I have said, Mr Darcy, I did not begin my service until many years later.'

'You suspect Sir Walter persuaded his daughter to use some of her trust to fund the wedding extravagance?' If Darcy's opinion of the man could sink any lower, it would have done.

'Though Miss Elliot favours her father, Mrs Musgrove, too, has a predilection for connections of consequence and a desire to impress with opulence reminiscent of Sir Walter.'

The colonel raised his hands. 'All the same, persuading someone to spend their own funds is not an offense.'

'No, but there is still the hint of a connection to the matter I mentioned earlier, Colonel.' Shepherd reached for the leather case at his side and withdrew some papers. 'Sir Walter asked me to obtain a copy of the separate estate trust document when I was lately in Town.' He eyed the papers he held, then raised his head. 'The clerk was surprised, as it is recorded on the file that Sir Walter was furnished with a copy in 1800, when his wife died, and the trust passed to the girls. He was the sole guardian by then, and his daughters had not reached their majority. I have never seen a copy at Kellynch, and I suspect Sir Walters wishes to pass this copy to Miss Elliot on the occasion of her marriage.' He sent Darcy a conscious look.

'The document is fairly standard, set up for Lady Elliot's exclusive use, should she need it, and upon her death, to be distributed in equal shares to any female offspring upon their marriage. I have seen it once before, of course, last winter—at the meeting I just mentioned—but I only just noted a peculiarity in the wording.'

He set the document on the desk, and the colonel got to his feet to join his cousin in studying it.

'The addendum, as you would expect, lists the three Miss Elliots.' Shepherd flicked to the back of the document where it was attached.

'What is odd about that?'

'Nothing. It is the wording at the top of the addendum.' Shepherd pointed to it, and both Darcy and the colonel read it before raising their heads in unity to stare at the lawyer, who retrieved the document and read aloud.

'This trust, upon the death of Lady Elizabeth Elliot, to be divided equally, upon their marriage, between any surviving *legitimate* female offspring.' Shepherd lifted his head. 'Mr Stevenson must have known—or at the very least, suspected—something to word it so carefully.'

'Diverting,' murmured Darcy, but the colonel shrugged as he sat again.

'And what of it? The aristocracy is no stranger to side-slips. They weather it with arrogance and rank in a way the gentry could not hope to achieve, or they pretend it has not happened.'

'There is much truth in it.' Darcy's mind grappled with this new information. 'But then, you must ask, Richard, what hold might this Williams have upon Sir Walter that brings him to his knees, forces his hand to commit to longstanding payments?

Payments, I would remind you, that Shepherd here is adamant he can ill afford.'

Who was this person, and what did Sir Walter hope to protect?

Splinters of thought whirled through Darcy's head. 'Thus, Williams may well be a woman.'

'Indeed, sir.' Shepherd resumed his seat.

Furrowing his brow, Darcy stared into the flames in the hearth. 'An affair and an illegitimate child makes for a weak ultimatum.' He looked over to his cousin. 'Is it enough?'

'I doubt it, though at least we can see Sir Walter's motive in trapping you into marriage, Darce. He probably hopes he will be able to persuade his eldest to oblige with some funds, much as his youngest did, only more to fill his own pocket than provide for a lavish celebration.'

Darcy was torn between hope and despair. 'May I?' He held out a hand, and Shepherd passed the document over. He flicked to the signature page. 'This is dated 1785, and the payments to Williams only began in 1801.' A sudden thought came to Darcy. 'Shepherd, how far back did you go in the ledgers?'

'To 1800, sir. I traced the quarterly Williams payment to the year one, and in the preceding twelve months, there was nothing, so I stopped looking any farther back. Those records are archived and not kept in the study.'

'What if they were in a different name?' Darcy looked to Shepherd, then back to his cousin.

The colonel's eyes narrowed. 'Whose name?'

'Think, Richard.' Darcy paced over to the window, then turned. 'Stevenson had this document drawn up in the first year of his daughter's marriage. If a woman is involved, as appears to be the case from how he asked the addendum to be worded, what is not to say she was unmarried at the time, and perhaps now she is?'

Enlightenment dawned on both men's faces, and Shepherd's expression became eager.

'I can make use of the ball. With Sir Walter committed to his guests for the evening, I will have ample time to explore the archives to see if the same regularity of payments occurs in another name.' He looked from the colonel to Darcy. 'Only the most recent years' ledgers and documents are kept in Sir Walter's study.'

It was agreed as the only chance accessible to them, and Shepherd placed the document back in his leather case and walked to the door as Darcy recollected the last time he had been in the study.

'Wait.'

The man turned around.

'What is the Northamptonshire matter?'

Shepherd frowned. 'I do not follow, sir.'

Darcy waved a hand. 'A while back, you were in the study when Sir Walter and I came in the other day, and I am certain I recall you mentioning the county in relation to a problem of some sort.'

Enlightenment dawned on Shepherd's features, but he shrugged. 'Just a begging letter, Mr Darcy. As a wealthy man yourself, you will comprehend how many he has received over the years.'

The colonel raised a brow. 'What is its content?'

'Oh no, sir.' Shepherd shook his head. 'I have never seen it. I am Sir Walter's man of business. He alone deals with personal correspondence.'

'So why is it a problem?'

'It is more a little singular, to be certain,' Shepherd agreed. 'Despite Sir Walter ignoring the initial request, the letters have continued for about seven years. They are always marked 'personal and confidential', of course. A clever notion to ensure it reaches no one but its target. I have suggested he write back in strong terms, but he seems disinterested, claiming that if they wish to waste the ink and postage, that is up to them.'

With that, Shepherd left them in peace, but the colonel studied Darcy with curiosity.

'Why the interest in that county?'

'No particular reason.' Darcy noted the time. The ladies would be gathering in the drawing room, and he indicated they join them. 'That letter I mentioned on Sir Walter's desk the other day—the one in a lady's hand—the postmark was Northamptonshire.'

The colonel raised a brow as they left the room.

'Could be any number of female relations.' He rubbed his hands together as they made their way along the hall. 'Shepherd may be on to a clue, though. It seems you have received an unexpected Christmas gift, Darcy.'

CHAPTER FORTY-ONE

There was little time to speculate further on Shepherd's findings thus far, or what he might yet uncover, as the Christmas Eve festivities took precedence, with a superb meal provided by the household servants and then an evening of music and—in all but Darcy's case—games.

Before the evening ended, they all gathered by the largest hearth—that of the fireplace in the spacious and elegant entrance hall—to sing Christmas carols in the glowing light of the Yule log, delivered earlier that day with great ceremony.

Once everyone retired, however, Darcy and the colonel returned once more to the study, going over word-by-word all they had learned.

'I am not confident this will be sufficient, Richard. Whatever this secret is, it is well-concealed, and all we have is supposition.'

The colonel topped up their glasses. 'Unless Shepherd can deliver more'—he shrugged—'there is little to be done for a few days, with Christmastide upon us.'

Darcy opened the doors onto the garden, relishing the cold night air, his breath forming swirls drifting into the darkness. His mind resisted a return to the task of unearthing Sir Walter's secret, full as it was of Elizabeth, whom he could picture in the dancing glow of the Yule candle whilst dining, laughing with his sister, sparring with his cousin, speaking fondly with Anne and her captain, but most of all, falling uncharacteristically silent at times, her dark eyes upon him. If only he could trust what he believed he saw in them—what his cousin hinted at.

The colonel joined him, then leaned forward to pull the doors closed and faced Darcy. 'Let Shepherd do what he must.'

Darcy took a drink, pushing away his hopes and dreams of Elizabeth Bennet. There was another Elizabeth to deal with first.

'Distasteful though it is to search another man's papers, I fear we have no choice.'

'If we are to beat Sir Walter at his own game, Darce, morals will have to be put aside.'

Draining his glass, the colonel retrieved Darcy's from his grasp and placed them on the tray before gesturing at the door.

'Come. Let us rest. There is much to enjoy in the coming days before we must face what lies ahead.'

They climbed the stairs, Darcy's weary mind full of the information they had received. At the top of the staircase, he faced the colonel. 'If there *is* a woman involved, how are we to find her? And if we do, what then? Surely she will cling to her secret?'

The colonel shook his head. 'I have no answers, Darce, but what choice is there but to put our faith in Shepherd?'

They continued to their respective chambers in a heavy silence, but as Darcy bade his cousin goodnight and entered his room, he acknowledged the truth of it.

What else could he do? Time was running out.

There was a severe frost when the household awoke to Christmas Day, and Darcy ventured from room to room before any of the other occupants rose, pleased with the tasteful festive displays. The hard work of the previous day, under Georgiana's direction, had been beneficial.

Garlands adorned every mantel; boughs of holly, laurel, and ivy were intertwined along the balustrade of the staircase and—thanks to the early rising servants—fires glowed brightly in every hearth.

'Good morning, Mr Darcy.'

Darcy smiled. 'Good morning, Mrs Reynolds. I wish you the blessings of the season. I hope we shall not make too much work for you today, with our additional guests?'

Mrs Reynolds shook her head as she came to stand before her master. 'Not at all. Is it acceptable for the servants to attend morning service, sir?'

'Most indubitably. We shall only require cold refreshments this afternoon.'

'That is as may be, sir, but as a result you and your guests will be in need of a nourishing meal this evening.' She looked on Darcy with the familiarity of an old servant. 'Christmas it is, but someone must prepare a suitable repast. Besides, we have the morrow to recover from our exertions, do we not?'

'Indeed.' They turned to walk to the dining room. 'And the morning after the ball, please utilise as few of the household servants as possible. I am told it runs well into the early hours. I doubt anyone will be about before noon, and if they are, then they can fend for themselves.'

Mrs Reynolds shook her head as they entered the breakfast room. 'You are becoming quite the radical, sir. What would your father have said?'

'My father was an excellent man, as well you know. He gave me good principles, but I am less certain of late that his encouragement of my pride—in myself, of my standing in the world—was the wisest of counsels.'

The lady said nothing, merely placing some napkins on the table as Darcy poured himself some tea, but then she came to stand before him.

'There is much you should be proud of, sir, not least your management of the estate, your dealings with your tenants and the exemplary guardianship of Miss Georgiana.'

Darcy winced. He felt all his shortcomings where his sister was concerned. To his surprise, his housekeeper rested a gentle hand on his arm.

'She is safe, is she not?'

'I—er…' Did she know? Did the entire Pemberley household know how near Georgiana had come to ruin at Wickham's hands? A chill descended upon Darcy's skin, despite the roaring fire.

Mrs Reynold's expression softened even further. 'It is known only by me. Miss Georgiana confided in me one day. You were not at home, and she had become distressed. I did not press the confidence from her.'

Darcy swallowed hard. Yet again, he had been absent when needed. 'Of course you did not.'

'And it goes without saying—though say it I shall—no word will ever be spoken of the matter by me, Master Fitzwilliam.'

Amused by the use of his childhood name, the coldness dwindled. 'Your loyalty is a great comfort.'

'You will always have it, as will those who are dear to you.' She turned to survey the array of dishes spread across the sideboard. 'Now, where is the honey we know Miss Bennet to be fond of?' She tsked. 'Excuse me, sir. I must go down to the kitchen and find some.'

Darcy shook his head. If he was that obvious, it was no wonder his cousin cautioned him!

Picking up a slice of toast, Darcy took a seat, just as the door opened and his cousin entered, followed shortly afterwards by the ladies and Captain Wentworth.

They all exchanged seasonal good wishes, and Darcy tried not to follow Elizabeth's every move as she selected her breakfast.

He failed miserably.

Once the meal was over, Elizabeth and Anne flew back to the cottage to collect the gifts they had made for the ladies of the house, and they entered the drawing room to see a footman pouring sherry into small glasses before bringing them round on a salver.

Taking a sip, Elizabeth observed the room. It was tastefully dressed for the season, and she could not look at the bough containing the silk roses without recalling the pleasure of working on it alongside Mr Darcy.

'Will you join us, Miss Bennet?'

She looked to the colonel, who gestured to where the rest of the party gathered in the seating arranged either side of the hearth, a fire burning merrily in the grate as a few small gifts were exchanged.

Elizabeth and Anne soon handed over their offerings to Georgiana and Mrs Annesley, and the latter smiled warmly at them both.

'That is kind of you.' She raised a brow at their empty hands. 'Did you not bring a token for each other?'

'Anne and I exchanged gifts before coming over for breakfast.' Elizabeth's mouth curved in pleasant recollection. 'I am the happy recipient of a small watercolour of my home in Hertfordshire, which Anne took some sketches of whilst staying there.'

'And Lizzy made me a beautiful pin cushion, trimmed with the sweetest of tiny flowers.' Anne sent Elizabeth a fond look. 'You are deft with a needle. One can hardly discern the stitches.'

'What spoils do you have, Georgie?'

Mr Darcy's voice was sufficient to draw Elizabeth's attention, and she looked to where his sister showed him the bookmark she made for her, along with the small box decorated by Anne.

Georgiana came across the room to where Anne and Elizabeth sat.

'I shall treasure all my gifts. I have been so fortunate. Richard has procured some books for me and my brother gave me some music I have long been desiring.' Georgiana smiled at Elizabeth. 'I hope to try the airs on the morrow.'

'We will look forward to hearing them.'

Anne turned to answer a question from the captain, seated to her other side, and Georgiana leaned in to whisper in Elizabeth's ear.

'There is something I wish to give you, Miss Bennet. Would you come with me?'

Surprised, Elizabeth rose from her seat. 'But you have already given me a fine set of embroidery silks, Miss Darcy.'

Curious, she followed the girl from the room, conscious of Mr Darcy's fixed attention, but when they reached the hearth where the Yule log continued to burn, Georgiana reached up her sleeve and extracted a small flat box and handed it over.

'I do not know what to say.' Elizabeth considered the box on the palm of her hand, quite bewildered.

'You may not like it. It is just...' Georgiana grasped Elizabeth's free hand and squeezed it gently before releasing her. 'You have been so kind, listening to me and speaking so kindly. It is truly like having a sister.'

To Elizabeth's dismay, easy tears filled Georgiana's eyes.

'Dear Miss Darcy, today is no time for sadness. Come, let me inspect your offering. There now, you hold the lid for me.'

Georgiana took it from her, and Elizabeth removed the small pouch from the box. A miniature slid out onto her palm, and she stared at it: a portrayal of both the young girl before her and her brother.

'I cannot accept this.' Elizabeth's startled gaze flew to Georgiana's eager one, but it was swiftly drawn back to the treasure she held. 'How did you...I mean, when was this likeness taken?'

'You must take it, Miss Bennet, as a thank you. I did not wish to present it to you in front of others, but it means a vast deal to me for you to have it. Mrs Annesley painted it last summer, but it is not the only one she has done. I wish for you to have it, that you will always remember us.'

Touched beyond measure and thrilled more than Georgiana could possibly know to be able to have such a precious keepsake to take home with her, Elizabeth embraced her quickly.

'I think I can truly say, Miss Darcy, that I will never forget you...or your brother.' Her brow furrowed. 'Is Mr Darcy aware of your generous gesture?'

'Oh yes, indeed. I was at a loss at what to get for you—though I had already ordered the silks—and Fitz suggested it.'

✣

The party from Meadowbrook House walked to Kellynch Church for morning service, lending to the festive air. The lane was firm after such a hard frost and in no danger of muddying the ladies' clothing, and although the clear skies portended a cold night ahead, everyone was well-wrapped against the chill and in excellent spirits.

Anne and the captain led the way along the lane, with Georgiana and the colonel following in their wake, and Elizabeth walked with Mrs Annesley.

Darcy followed behind, his mind agreeably engaged in reflecting on the pleasures of watching the lady's delight over the small gifts bestowed upon her that morning. He had yet to speak to Georgiana about how her additional offering had been received, but his attention was suddenly drawn back to the figures in front of him as Georgiana called for Mrs Annesley to join her.

Increasing his pace slightly, he fell into step beside Elizabeth.

'Do you feel as though you are herding sheep, Mr Darcy, bringing up the rear to ensure none of us strays?'

He laughed. 'I think the hedgerows are sufficiently tall here to keep everyone in order.'

They walked in a companionable silence as the church came into view, but then, Elizabeth threw him a lightning glance. 'I seem to spend an inordinate amount of time expressing my gratitude to you, sir. I was moved beyond measure by the miniature given to me by Miss Darcy earlier, and I believe I have you to thank for the notion?'

If she only knew how strongly he debated with himself over it. Knowing he was unable to give her a gift directly, it seemed the perfect compromise, but he made a huge assumption in hoping she might wish for a memento.

'Mr Darcy?' Elizabeth cast him an amused look. 'Is it so difficult a question, sir?'

He shook his head as they reached the lych gate into the churchyard, and they stopped beside it as the rest of the party walked in.

'These have been unprecedented times, Miss Bennet.' He studied her leisurely for a moment, drinking in her lovely features. The bright eyes he had long appreciated sparkled, her cheeks flushed from the cold air, and he only wished someone was there to capture the image on a miniature for his own keeping. How he would cherish it henceforth.

'I will never forget…them, sir.'

'Darce! Come on, man!'

They both looked over to where the colonel stood outside the church, and offering his arm, Darcy drew in a contented breath as Elizabeth took it, and they turned their steps up the path to the open door.

✦

The notion of attending church on Christmas morning with Frederick by her side gave Anne more pleasure than she imagined. The captain, having less affinity with the estate than Anne, was simply thankful to no longer need the walking cane.

Once inside, they lingered not far from the door, and she greeted a few neighbours as they filled the aisle in search of a seat with a good view of the pulpit, and then spoke to some of the estate tenants before they filed into the rear pews. The remainder of her own party moved down the aisle too, and she took the captain's arm as he led her forward to follow the stragglers.

419

'Poor Darcy has been waylaid by Miss Elliot.' Captain Wentworth leaned to whisper in her ear. 'Does your eldest sister always dress quite so extravagantly for church?'

Anne perceived her sister, then sighed.

'You know how she is. It will not matter that this is a small country parish, not St George's in Mayfair.'

They skirted past Elizabeth Elliot and Mr Darcy, and sending Georgiana a smile, where she had been invited to sit with her companion in a pew near the front, Anne walked with the captain to those on the right-hand side.

As they reached them, however, Captain Wentworth turned to face her. 'Here? Do you think it wise for me to enter the family pew?'

Though Anne comprehended his uncertainty—when had he ever received a civil look or word from her father or eldest sister—she was determined to do right by him.

'You are soon to be family, Frederick, and—'

'Ah, Anne. There you are.'

Anne exchanged greetings with her father, her insides in knots over how he would behave.

The gentlemen acknowledged each other, and Frederick squeezed Anne's hand. 'I will leave you to speak with your father. Sir.' He bowed once more to Sir Walter and eased along the pew in the second row to await her.

On tenterhooks over what her father might say, Anne was surprised when he merely spoke of the morning at the Hall—Mary and Charles had apparently stayed the night—and then reminded her to not be late arriving for the ball on the following day.

He turned away to greet someone, but then came back to Anne, his regard drifting to Captain Wentworth.

'I am becoming accustomed to this alliance, Anne.' He made no attempt to lower his voice, and she was certain Frederick heard him. 'The captain's rank is an improvement on that of commander, and his appearance is not unfairly balanced against your superiority of rank. All this, assisted by bearing such a well-sounding name. I am inclined to consider him worthy of the association, and it encourages me to offer my blessing.'

A sound emanated from Captain Wentworth, but Anne knew not what to say other than, 'Thank you, Father.'

'Yes, yes. Quite right.'

With that Sir Walter moved away, and releasing a relieved breath, Anne edged along the pew to sit beside Frederick.

The captain said nothing at first, his notice remaining with the service sheet, but then she realised his body heaved, and looking a little closer, she saw he struggled to contain his amusement.

'It would seem we must both be thankful I was not named Scapetrough or Dungbottom or some other such un*worthy* name.'

Anne laughed quietly. 'It is so like father to be impressed by physical appearance, Frederick. We must be thankful the blow to your head did not land upon your nose.'

His hand closed over her own, resting on the pew between them. 'And I am simply thankful for that blow, and for my mind taking direction and sending me back to you.' The captain raised her hand and placed a kiss upon it, but then someone tapped Anne on the back.

'Anne! Anne, I am here.'

She turned in her seat to behold Mary.

'I did not know if you would be well enough to come. The season's greetings to you. And to you, too, Charles. Did you not wish to spend the day with family at Uppercross? Are your sisters home from school?'

Charles Musgrove beamed affably. 'Henrietta and Louisa returned some days ago, but Mary's desire was to be at Kellynch, and as she is close to her confinement, I wished to accommodate her wishes.'

Mary ignored her husband and scrutinised the captain—who rose from his seat—pointedly, and Anne joined him to perform the introductions.

'Captain Wentworth, allow me to present to you my sister, Mrs Mary Musgrove and her husband, Charles. This is Captain Frederick Wentworth.'

Mary's generally querulous expression was quite eager as her eyes darted from Anne to the captain. 'Father says you are engaged! You sly thing, Anne, to hide such an acquaintance from us all.'

'Mary,' her husband cautioned, but his wife—as was her wont—ignored him.

'Is your acquaintance of long duration?'

'Since the year six, ma'am.' The captain took Anne's hand. 'But I have been away at sea.'

'You were at school when first we met, Mary.'

Congratulations were offered by Mr Musgrove, but Mary looked plaintive once more, and Anne was thankful to see the congregation taking their seats, Sir Walter leading his eldest to the front pew as the vicar led the choir down the aisle. There was no time for further discussion and, with relief, Anne turned back to face the front, grateful the morning exceeded her expectations, and welcoming the chance to worship the saviour's birth with a clear mind.

Darcy had not given the Christmas service the attention it deserved. Sitting in the pew beside Georgiana, he was achingly conscious of Elizabeth sitting behind him with his cousin, and the words in the hymnbook were unreadable when all he could do was relish the sound of the lady's voice.

His annoyance over Miss Elliot accosting him and talking utter nonsense was nothing, however, to Sir Walter urging him to join them in their pew.

Darcy studied the gentleman across the aisle. He was ridiculously over-dressed, his hair fashioned as though he were about to be presented at Court rather than attend a country service, and his face was quite red, though whether from cold or over-indulgence Darcy could not tell. Nor could he care less. Today, he intended to enjoy every moment in the company of…his own family party.

After services, the congregation gathered in the churchyard as they spoke to the vicar, each other and paid their respects— some with noticeable reluctance—to the occupants of Kellynch Hall.

Conscious of his cousin's warning against letting any preference for Elizabeth Bennet slip in front of Sir Walter, Darcy distanced himself from the lady.

'Darcy, a word, if you would be so obliging?'

With reluctance, Darcy joined Sir Walter as they walked a little apart from the general melee. He said nothing, waiting on Sir Walter's purpose. Surely, he would not speak of what lay between them in public?

'Your attention should be with my daughter, sir. I am displeased to learn you have only asked her for the third set at the ball.'

Considering the man before him, Darcy was only restrained from walking away by the knowledge of how much damage Sir Walter could do.

'I am surprised, sir, that you think so.'

Sir Walter's eyes narrowed. 'You know the cards I hold.'

'I am well aware, but you also need my compliance as much as I desire your silence. We will serve each other best by remembering that. Standing up with the ladies of my own party first is what will be expected.'

Sir Walter looked as though he would protest, and Darcy, sure of his ground, added. 'The—' He would be damned if he would refer to it as an engagement. 'Promise you seek on my part is not yet sealed. Paying such public attention might encourage gossip. I trust you wish to protect the lady's reputation, sir, from misinterpretation?'

Sir Walter's skin paled. 'I will not have such talk!'

Then, he glared at someone beyond Darcy, and he glanced over his shoulder, his eye drawn instantly to where Elizabeth stood in conversation with Anne and the colonel, surrounded by chattering parishioners.

He turned back to Sir Walter. 'If you will excuse me, I must join my family. I wish you a pleasant remainder of the day.'

Trying not to let the man rile him further, Darcy strode over to his sister and Mrs Annesley. It was time he gathered his party and returned to the sanctuary of Meadowbrook House.

CHAPTER FORTY-TWO

'Miss Anne!' An elegant woman, with a young girl in tow, approached where the lady stood. 'I had so hoped to see you at church today!'

To Elizabeth's surprise, Anne embraced the smartly dressed older lady.

'How well you look, Mattie. How long is it since last we met?'

'Oh, miss, it must be some years since I was in the district. Thank heavens for correspondence!'

'Indeed!' Her pleasure evident, Anne turned to Elizabeth and the colonel. 'This is Mrs Williams. Mathilde was my mother's personal maid, and I have known her all my life.'

The colonel studied the lady with marked attention, and Anne hid her amusement. Mattie was extremely well looking and oft drew a gentleman's appreciation.

'I prefer Mattie, Miss Anne.'

Anne almost rolled her eyes. 'I have told you before to call me Anne. You are a married woman now, and it is many years since you were in service.'

'Old habits are hard to forego. I was present for Miss Elliot's arrival, and'—she smiled fondly at Anne— 'Miss Anne and Miss Mary's births.'

'It is no wonder you are attached to the family.' Elizabeth liked the lady. Her countenance was filled with good sense. She must have been a good influence for Anne in her youth.

'And who is this young lady?' Colonel Fitzwilliam clicked his heels together and bowed to the child, who clung more tightly to her mother's hand and seemed to want to merge into her skirts.

'This is my Betty, sir.' Mathilde leaned down. 'Say happy Christmas, dearest.' A whispered sound came from the girl, but she kept her head lowered. 'She is shy yet in company, but then, she is but eight years old.'

'I had a nurse called Betty once,' mused the colonel, and the child looked up. 'She had a lazy eye.' He made a comical expression, and Betty giggled. 'Kept one on my brother, one on me. Invaluable to my mother, of course.'

Colonel Fitzwilliam placed a hand behind his ear, then brought forth a coin, and Betty's eyes widened.

'Here, child. A gift for Christmas.'

With her mother's encouragement, Betty reached out to take the coin, a barely audible 'thank you' falling from her lips, and the colonel took his leave of the ladies, strolling to join his cousin.

'Have you seen Mary and Elizabeth, Mattie?'

Elizabeth was quick to note the pleasure vanish from the lady's face.

'Miss Mary entered church as I arrived. She seems to be delighting in her situation as a married lady, if not in her condition.'

Anne laughed. 'Yes, she has been wild to get married since being of age.'

'And Miss Elliot?' Mathilde observed the throng outside the church. 'I have not greeted her, though I saw her in church with your father. I am surprised she is not yet wed. Is there no suitor?'

'My sister shares so little with me, Mattie, but I do not think so.'

The notion of anyone attempting to court such a woman as Miss Elliot amused Elizabeth.

'I had supposed Sir Walter would be eager for it to happen.' Mathilde looked thoughtful.

'It is true, she is now six and twenty, and my father has seemed intent upon her securing someone sooner rather than later.'

Mathilde sent Anne a tender look. 'And you, dear Anne?'

A becoming pink filled Anne's cheeks, and Elizabeth nudged her friend. 'You must tell her.'

As Anne shared her good news with Mathilde, Elizabeth's attention wandered across the churchyard to the Darcys. Colonel Fitzwilliam appeared to be entertaining both his cousins and as Mr Darcy had his back to her, it permitted Elizabeth the luxury of admiring his tall form. It was only as she caught Georgiana's eye watching her that she hastily looked away. Captain Wentworth was in conversation with the vicar, but Elizabeth's attention was drawn back to the ladies as Mathilde said her goodbyes.

'Will you not call upon us, Anne, before we return home? And you know you are always welcome to visit us in Truro.'

Anne's eyes lit up. 'I would be delighted. Frederick is sometimes in Plymouth, which must only be a half day's journey from Truro.' She turned to Elizabeth. 'Mattie was born in Brittany but moved here as a child. She has lived in Cornwall since her marriage.'

'It reminds me of home, Miss Bennet, for the scenery is not dissimilar.'

With that, Mathilde took Betty's hand once more and departed, and Anne and Elizabeth moved closer to the rest of their party.

'She has done well for herself, Anne.'

'Mattie made a respectable marriage to a physician she met in Exeter, about a year after she left service.' Anne's face was shadowed for a moment. 'My father was unable to employ her once Mama passed away.'

Elizabeth's heart went out to her friend. It seemed every bond Anne made was taken from her. Thank goodness the tide had at last turned for her.

And you? What of your fortunes?

Not wishing to think on it, Elizabeth summoned a smile and within minutes of joining the others, they were off for Meadowbrook House.

As soon as they reached the house, the colonel all but marched Darcy to the study.

'What is so urgent, Richard? We are meant to be going with the captain for a ride, and I thought you were eager to test out Hereward now he has recovered.'

Colonel Fitzwilliam quickly related his meeting with Mrs Williams, but Darcy was unimpressed.

'You said it yourself yesterday, Cousin. Williams is a common enough name. I even have two unrelated tenants called such.'

'Yes, but this is a personal maid who worked in Sir Walter's household until his wife died.'

Darcy walked over to the full-length windows and pushed them open, letting a cold blast of air into the room. Was his cousin right?

'So, if the lady married after she left service...'

'It tallies with the payments to Williams commencing a year after that time.' The colonel scratched his head. 'Though we can hardly ask Miss Anne Elliot about it. It has the potential to become rather delicate.'

Darcy continued to survey the gardens. 'I am of a mind to tell the captain what is afoot. Not,' he added hastily, 'about Georgiana and the letter, just that duress is being applied.'

The colonel shrugged. 'We need all the trustworthy assistance we can get. Captain Wentworth as good as owes you his life, and I think he will do anything to repay the debt.'

Ten minutes later, the captain entered Darcy's study to find both gentlemen staring out of the French doors into the garden. They looked up as he came to join them, and all three viewed the scene.

'Are we looking at anything in particular?' the captain asked.

'Seeking divine intervention.' The colonel closed the doors. 'We are tardy.'

'Not at all.'

Darcy attempted to marshal his thoughts.

'Are you amenable to delaying our ride for a half hour, Wentworth? There is a matter I wish to put before you.'

The gentleman threw Darcy a shrewd look. 'Of course.'

They made their way to the chairs grouped beside the fireplace, talking of the previous evening's meal until a tap on the door heralded a tray of tea and a plate of biscuits.

'Shall I serve, sir?' Mrs Reynolds picked up the pot.

'We will look after ourselves, thank you.' She took her leave, and Darcy turned to his cousin. 'Richard? You are most practised in pouring.'

With an exaggerated sigh, the colonel stood up. 'As you wish. I will wait upon you.'

He deftly poured the drinks and handed them over before grabbing the plate of biscuits and resuming his seat.

'I must bind you to secrecy on this, Wentworth.'

The captain took a sip of tea. 'I am all ears, Darcy.'

It took but a few minutes for Darcy to explain the situation, and the captain looked from him to the colonel and back in astonishment.

'You will not go through with it?'

'I may have no choice. We are hoping to discover a hold upon Sir Walter, but time is running out.'

The colonel turned to the captain. 'What do you know of Mrs Williams, Wentworth?'

He looked surprised. 'I only met the lady this morning. Why do you want to know?'

'Just a suspicion she may have information of interest to Darcy.' Colonel Fitzwilliam looked expectant, but the captain shrugged.

'I know very little of the lady. Anne may have mentioned her during our short acquaintance in the year six, but if she did, I do not recall it. I was introduced to her at church earlier. She has been married for about ten years, has a daughter—Betty— aged eight, and they live in Truro. That is all I know.'

'What of her employment at Kellynch?'

'It was not discussed.' Captain Wentworth looked from the colonel to Darcy. 'She is a respectable lady now, married to a physician, I understand. Her days in service must be a distant memory.'

'She has a slight accent,' mused the colonel. 'From the continent.'

'Mrs Williams is French by birth, that I do know.' The captain leaned forward to select a biscuit from the plate. 'And she was personal maid to Anne's mother from before her marriage to Sir Walter. Do you genuinely believe she may have knowledge that might help you escape this?'

Darcy leaned back, his cup cradled in his hands. 'Not so much genuinely, as tentatively. All we have is a mystery payment to a Williams, on-going since a year after the lady left Sir Walter's employ.'

The colonel drained his cup and stood up. 'You would not happen to know the lady's maiden name?' He walked over to the tray and refilled his cup before resuming his seat.

'As it happens, I do. Aubert. We spoke to the Musgroves after church, and Anne mentioned Mattie, and her sister went on to refer to the lady as Aubert. When Anne objected, saying Mattie was married now, Mrs Musgrove stuck her nose in the air, much as her father is wont to do, and declared Aubert was all she would ever be to her, and then began a complaint about servants wishing to be known by their given name over their surname.' The captain paused, then added. 'I will own to having engaged her husband in conversation at that point, as there seemed no way of shutting the woman up.'

Silence fell upon them, and Darcy stared at his cousin.

'You may have given us a further clue, Wentworth.' Getting to his feet, Darcy placed his empty cup on the salver, then picked up a pen.

'A note to Shepherd at home will hopefully point him in the right direction in the archives tomorrow.'

The remainder of the day passed with little incident. The gentlemen returned in high spirits from their ride, the colonel pleased by Hereward's return to fitness, and Captain Wentworth relishing the chance to be active once more.

The ladies awaited them in the drawing room, where Mrs Reynolds and her servants had done them proud with a wonderful array of cold refreshments. The wine flowed and they played a few noisy hands of speculation.

They dined sumptuously under the glowing lamplight of the beautifully dressed dining room, followed by the ladies taking turns to play the pianoforte, before there were more carols beside the Yule log, and Elizabeth could not recall passing a pleasanter Christmastide.

As the day dwindled, however, she found herself yearning for a moment's conversation with Mr Darcy. The colonel had been entertaining her with his nonsensical commentary, but he had gone to secure a refreshing of his drink from an obliging footman, and Elizabeth studied the room's occupants.

Anne and the captain sat together on a chaise beside the hearth. He held her hand and spoke earnestly, and Elizabeth bit her lip. His eyes shone with such love whenever he beheld Anne. How she envied them. Instinctively, she sought Mr Darcy. He stood—as he so often did—by one of the windows, staring out at the ink-black sky, and Elizabeth admired the broad shoulders in the well-fitting coat. Ought she to go talk to him?

'I think I shall retire for the night.' Georgiana rose from her seat, bade Anne, Mrs Annesley and the captain goodnight and walked over to Elizabeth, just as her cousin returned.

'Though I am not attending, I know the morrow will be quite arduous. Miss Bennet. 'You ought not delay in taking your rest.'

The colonel laughed as he handed Elizabeth a refreshed glass of wine. 'We are to attend a ball, Georgie.'

'Which will last for some duration, Richard.' Georgiana returned her attention to Elizabeth. 'It will be a busy day of preparation for Miss Bennet and Miss Elliot. I can easily spare Tilly if Elise wishes for assistance in readying you both.'

Colonel Fitzwilliam harrumphed. 'It is beyond me how it can take a young lady all day to prepare for a mere evening of dancing.'

To Elizabeth's amusement, Georgiana sent her cousin a patronising look. 'There are many things that are beyond you with regard to our sex, Richard.'

Colonel Fitzwilliam opened his mouth, but no sound came out, and Elizabeth hid her amusement as Georgiana walked over to say goodnight to her brother, her cousin striding after her.

Putting her glass aside, Elizabeth rose from her seat and wandered to the small pianoforte in the far corner of the room, picking up some music, and ostensibly perusing it before raising her eyes to where Mr Darcy was in conversation with his cousin, Georgiana having left the room.

She had lost her opportunity. Glancing at the clock, Elizabeth sat on the stool and began to play a melody from memory. Perhaps tomorrow would present the chance she sought. After all, she was to dance the first set with Mr Darcy, was she not? It would provide a full half hour for her to find the words she wished to express to him.

The tune ended, and Elizabeth looked up as Anne approached.

'Will you join us, Lizzy? We wish to speak to you and Mr Darcy.'

Curious, Elizabeth followed her friend across the room to where the captain stood with the colonel and his host.

'I have explained to the gentlemen, Miss Bennet.' Captain Wentworth smiled at her. 'We leave for Shropshire next Monday, as you know—in the company of two of Edward's former parishioners, a couple to whom he became close during his years in the neighbourhood—and once we reach my brother's, the banns will be read and a date set for the wedding soon after.'

The captain drew Anne to his side.

'It will be a small wedding, Lizzy, with little ceremony, and once the breakfast is over, we will journey to Plymouth to spend some time before Frederick's future is determined.' Anne held out her other hand to her friend. 'Say you will come to Shropshire? Be one of our witnesses?'

'Oh, I cannot. I mean, I would love to be there, but I must spend some time at home. My parents expected me to return long before now.'

'I am to be their other witness.'

Against her will, Elizabeth looked at Mr Darcy. His warm regard was little comfort. How she longed to go.

The colonel rolled his eyes. 'Overlooked again for my cousin. 'Tis always the way of it. Perhaps you could pass a few weeks in Hertfordshire and then journey over, Miss Bennet.' He gave an exaggerated sigh. 'So many departures. Our little company will be quite split up.' Then, he smirked. 'Of course, once I am gone on my way, my cousins will be quite despondent, nay, inconsolable.'

Elizabeth could not help but laugh. 'You are a presence hard to replace, sir.'

The colonel inclined his head. 'Indeed. It is a stretch, I grant you.'

'Lizzy? Will you come?'

'Miss Bennet.' Elizabeth's gaze flew to meet Mr Darcy's. 'You cannot desert your friend at such a time.'

'So be it.' Elizabeth smiled tentatively at him, then more warmly at Anne and her captain. 'Thank you for asking me. It will be an honour, though what my parents will think of all this travelling, I know not!'

With that, the conversation turned to the engaged couple's plans for the future, and before long it was time to retire for the night.

CHAPTER FORTY-THREE

Though he slept until the early hours, peace eluded Darcy and, frustrated with the turn of his thoughts as they careered from the pleasure derived from simply passing time in Elizabeth's company to the predicament he faced, he kicked aside the tousled sheets and stood.

The fire had long burned low, and cold permeated his skin. He lit a candle from the embers, noting the face of the clock on the mantel with resignation. It was almost four o'clock. Grabbing his banyan, Darcy donned it and headed out onto the landing. He was in need of a cup of tea.

Wincing as his bare feet touched the tiles in the hall, Darcy strode through the service door and down the stone stairs. There were a couple of lamps burning low when he entered the parlour adjacent to the kitchen, and Darcy inspected the room. Mrs Reynolds was used to him seeking tealeaves and hot water at Pemberley and always had a small box set aside for him and a kettle upon the stove ready for warming. Where might the special supplies be at Meadowbrook House?

A faint clatter came from the kitchen, and Darcy ceased his perusal of the cupboards. The servants were due the day off, so—

Darcy almost started as the door opened and someone came through bearing a tray. Not a servant girl, but Elizabeth!

Even in the dim light, he discerned deep colour flooding her skin. She was dressed—or rather, undressed—much as he was, in nightclothes topped with a robe, her long hair in a plait hanging over her shoulder, and he swallowed hard. Never had she seemed more beautiful to him.

'Mr Darcy…I did not expect…I…'

He recalled himself and stepped forward. 'Why are you carrying that?'

He grasped the tray but Elizabeth, being Elizabeth, held fast.

'I find it an efficient way of transporting more than one thing at a time, sir.' Elizabeth tugged at the salver, and the crockery tinkled in response. Her colour remained high, and Darcy's lips twitched.

'Touché. Please, allow me. This is no time of day for a repeat of the battle of the basket.'

With a small laugh, Elizabeth relinquished her hold on the tray and Darcy studied its contents as he placed it on a side table: a pot of tea, a cup, spoon, some milk and a plate bearing a large slice of cake.

'There are no proper facilities for storing food in the cottage. I wished for some of the delicious fruit cake and decided tea would be a fitting accompaniment.'

'The cottage is most horribly deficient.'

'Oh no, sir. Not at all. I have been so—' Elizabeth stopped as Darcy's lips twitched. 'You are in jest.'

'I believe so.' Then, he raised a brow. 'What were you saying you have been, Miss Bennet?'

'Nothing, sir.' Her attention drifted to the discarded tray.

'Forgive me. I am depriving you of your night-time feast.'

Elizabeth shook her head. 'It is simply I prefer my tea piping hot.'

'Then you had best make haste. Let me carry the tray to the drawing room for you, though there will be no fire lit.'

'Oh, I did not intend to intrude. I could not make use of the drawing room uninvited.'

'Did I not just invite you to do so?'

'Yes. But no. I mean, I had intended to return to Willow Cottage with my spoils.'

Staring at her in disbelief, Darcy took in the heavy salver. 'You intended to carry this across the lawn in this weather and in the dark?'

'I left a lamp burning outside the cottage, and though I grow older in years, my eyesight has yet to fail me.'

Reluctantly, Darcy laughed. 'No, indeed. How did you gain access to the precious tea caddy in Mrs Reynold's absence?'

'Your housekeeper gave us a supply, which is kept over at the cottage in this.' She indicated the small wooden box on the tray. 'I simply brought it with me. You are welcome to join me, sir.' She gestured at the tray.

The temptation was too much. Darcy picked up the teapot and followed Elizabeth, who took the box of tea from the tray, into the kitchen.

She opened the door to the stove and gave the coals a fierce prod with a poker. 'The kettle has not long boiled, it will soon be hot enough.'

Spooning more tea into the pot, Elizabeth returned to the stove, but when the time came, Darcy stepped forward, lifting the heavy iron kettle to pour the hot water, and soon they sat at the small parlour table, two cups of hot tea before them.

Elizabeth clasped her hands around her cup, and Darcy looked at the darkened grate.

'Let me get this fire going.'

The first cup of tea had been consumed almost in silence as the kindling smouldered and flickered, and as the flames began to take, Elizabeth raised the pot.

'Another, sir?'

Darcy held out his cup. He would savour the memory of this moment forever, whatever the future held for him. His curiosity was piqued, however.

'I do not wish to pry, Miss Bennet, but why *are* you so awake at this hour as to need to leave the cottage in the dark of night?'

Elizabeth peered at him over the rim of her cup as though considering his words. 'Can there be boundaries to conversation in a setting such as this? There is a mystical air about this hour, Mr Darcy. Do you not agree? The half-night between darkness and light, where all is not as it seems.'

'The world of dreams, perchance.' Darcy spoke softly, his eyes upon Elizabeth.

'Perhaps. It makes me feel all things are possible.'

'You have not answered my question.'

Elizabeth sipped her tea. 'I could ask the same of you, sir. Do you make a habit of visiting your kitchen under the cover of darkness?'

'Not a habit, no, but Mrs Reynolds knows my preference when I am unable to sleep and has always left the necessary at my disposal should I have need of it.'

'She is clearly devoted to your needs.' Elizabeth's brow furrowed. 'As are all your servants. Is it true they are all from Pemberley?'

'Yes—they did not expect the snow so far south.'

'Nor did I.' Elizabeth looked over to the window, and Darcy took the opportunity to study her profile, the thickness of her dark lashes, the curve of her cheek, and the fullness of her lips. How could he ever have called her tolerable, when he considered her one of the handsomest women of his acquaintance?

'Sir?'

Blinking, Darcy realised Elizabeth had turned her head and was watching him.

'I think it is time we tried to find some rest.' He drained his cup, and they had reached the door when he looked back. 'I keep forgetting the servants are at leisure tomorrow.'

'Should we wash them?'

'No—one of the servants volunteers each year to be the one to light all the fires on this day, and whoever it is will deal with it, but that is no excuse for leaving it out here.'

Having soon returned the tray and its contents to the kitchen, they walked in silence back to the entrance hall, where Elizabeth paused by the door to the garden to scoop up a thick wrap from a chair. She stared at Darcy's bare feet, and he could feel warmth flood his face.

'I did not expect to see anyone.'

Raising her eyes, Elizabeth held his solemnly. 'Nor did I.'

Ludicrous though it was in the circumstances, Darcy bowed. 'Goodnight, Miss Bennet, for what remains of it. I hope you are able to gain some rest.'

To his surprise, she laughed. 'Oh, I doubt it, sir.'

Before she opened the door, she paused on the threshold, looking over at him. 'Thank you for such a lovely day, yesterday.'

He said nothing for a moment, his dark eyes fixed upon her own. 'I am pleased you found it so. It was perhaps a little quiet, for all the company.' Darcy would cherish the memory forever.

Elizabeth looked a little hesitant, then she raised her chin in a familiar gesture which tugged at his heart. 'May I ask you a question, Mr Darcy?'

'I think we agreed, there are no bounds to conversation at this hour.'

She drew in a noticeable breath. 'You once said that your good opinion, once lost, was gone forever?'

Darcy made a small sound. 'There are many things I have said that might not fare so well if re-examined.'

Elizabeth stared at him. 'In this you are not alone.'

Did she mean she regretted some of her words, that she better comprehended his character?

Before he could reflect further, Elizabeth took a step closer.

'I shall miss...the company here at Meadowbrook House when I return to Longbourn.'

In the light of Darcy's solitary candle, it was difficult to detect her expression, but her tone was warm, and he had not missed the pause. Did it mean what he hoped, or was he muddled in this half-night, as Elizabeth called it?

'I would not prevent you from doing whatever you wish, Miss Bennet, but I am glad you were persuaded to linger a little longer.' The light that temporarily filled his heart glowed. 'For myself, I do not wish you to leave. Ever.'

Bold of you, Darcy, in the circumstances.

Boldness be damned. The colonel's words of caution rang in Darcy's ears, and he acknowledged their wisdom. He may be in no position to speak of his affections, to test the lady's response, but he would not have her think for one more moment he did not care.

Before he could rationalise himself out of it, Darcy reached for her hand, placing a kiss upon her palm.

A small gasp escaped Elizabeth as her eyes flew to meet his. In the candlelight, he could not quite discern the message they held, but before he could commit any further madness, she offered him a small smile, dropped a curtsey, and fled through the door.

Darcy stood in the open doorway, watching her slight figure until it reached the cottage. He saw her lift the lantern and open the door, and then she was gone.

'You slept late, Lizzy.'

It was true. Elizabeth had fallen asleep after leaving Mr Darcy, her head full of hopes and dreams. Charlotte's words from months ago merged with Anne's as she tried to recall the man she had thought she knew, the proud, arrogant gentleman who had affronted her pride and stirred both her anger and dislike.

'Lizzy?' Anne's voice held amusement, and Elizabeth roused herself.

'Forgive me. My night was disturbed at first, hence my tardy awakening.'

They walked across to the house for breakfast, and Elizabeth could not help but dwell upon Mr Darcy's appearance from the night before. He was a perpetual revelation to her.

'You are quite pink.' Anne laughed. 'And do not say it is the cold. We have been out in it but five seconds.'

Elizabeth stopped as they reached the terrace and faced her friend.

'I am flummoxed and know not what to think.'

'About a certain gentleman?'

'Mr Darcy made it plain last night he does not wish me to go home.'

'For which I am eminently grateful.' They slowly resumed their steps. 'And this is a puzzle to you?'

Elizabeth raised her hands helplessly. 'Daily, I fall more deeply in love and, though I now perceive his admiration, I will be forever beneath his notice.'

'You do not strike me as someone who believes that of yourself, Lizzy.'

They came to a halt by the door.

'It is true, I do not. But I cannot see a gentleman of Mr Darcy's station—no matter his goodness or his compassion...or, indeed, his persuasion in someone's favour—stepping outside the boundaries of his position in society.' Aware of her dampening spirits, Elizabeth drew in a short breath. 'Let us be done with such thoughts. Talk to me of aught else. Your anticipation of dancing once more with your captain!'

Anne opened the door and Elizabeth followed her into the house.

'Frederick seems to be anticipating the ball with some relish, which I cannot bring myself to do. My father's changeable nature of late means I cannot rely on his seeming acceptance of the situation. Frederick, of course, fears nothing. His confidence was one of his many charms when I first met him.' Colour rushed into Anne's cheeks, but the edges of her mouth lifted. 'Frederick is extremely...'

'Charming? Fine-looking? Persuasive?'

Anne laughed. 'All of those and more.' Then, she sobered. 'There is nothing I do not love about him, but I do not trust my family. Why is Papa being so accommodating now, when he would not have a dying man in his home but a fortnight ago? Why is he…' Anne bit her lip, her anxious eyes upon Elizabeth.

'Why is he allowing your lowly friend to attend the ball when I was never to darken his doorstep again?' Elizabeth shrugged. She could not comprehend it, but the notion of dancing a whole set with Mr Darcy overruled all questions she may have.

Anne paused as they approached the breakfast room. 'My father seeks to gain from every situation, never to give. His largesse is out of character and unsettles me.'

'I will own I was of two minds about going to the ball.'

'Because of my father? Or Mr Darcy?' The warmth that had eased from Elizabeth's cheeks returned in full measure. 'You need give no further answer.'

'Did we not agree to speak of other things? Are you satisfied with your wedding plans?'

Anne opened the door and faced Elizabeth. 'I did once dream of being wed at Kellynch. Since Frederick returned, I have happier memories of Meadowbrook than I ever did up at the Hall. Shropshire will be as good as anywhere, and the day cannot come soon enough.'

Elizabeth laughed. 'I am surprised you are waiting for the banns to be read!'

Anne grinned. 'It is true, as a baronet, my father could approach the archbishop for a special license, but it is an unnecessary expense, and I have waited so many years for Frederick, a few weeks further will matter not, when we have the rest of our lives to share.

Suppressing her envy, Elizabeth followed Anne into the room. If only she too could anticipate such happiness in marriage.

✤

With no shoot or hunt taking place, the gentlemen opted for a gallop over the fields, and the ladies filled their time attending to their accessories for the ball, with the aid of Elise and Georgiana's maid, Tilly—who both willingly offered their services in exchange for taking the following day instead. Though unable to attend, Georgiana was vastly interested in what they might wear and persuaded Elizabeth a few days earlier to hand over her gown, that her maid might make some small modification to it.

After the gentlemen returned and made the necessary improvements to their appearance, the afternoon progressed in similar fashion to the previous one, except—with the servants at their leisure—Mr Darcy, Captain Wentworth and the colonel took it upon themselves to wait upon the ladies, the latter providing much amusement by donning a footman's apron and incessantly performing exaggerated bows.

✤

Several hours later, Elizabeth stared at her reflection as Tilly left the room. Used as she was to having Jane help with her hair, there was no denying how stylishly (in the hands of a skilled maid) her tresses could be dressed.

She smoothed the folds of fabric on the gown she had worn for the Netherfield Ball. When her mother had pressed it upon her, insisting she pack it, she had held no notion of needing it. She was thankful for the foresight, for there were bound to be only the latest fashions on display at the ball. At least no one there would know the gown had been pressed into service for a second time in but a month, and the embellishments exquisitely stitched into place by Tilly only enhanced it.

The maid, under Georgiana's eager instruction, had sewn rows of beads beneath the bust line of the dress and along its hem, giving it a weight, which caused it to swing against Elizabeth's legs in a satisfying manner. Delicate ribbon had been threaded along the bodice and through the edging of the sleeves, and pins bearing the same beads adorned her intricately fashioned hair.

Even with her own simple jewellery added, she had to admit that the ensemble was a triumph. Would Mr Darcy think so?

'Nonsensical.' Elizabeth silenced the thought, though a frisson of anticipation whispered through her.

'You look beautiful, Lizzy.'

Anne came to join her before the mirror. The rich cream of her gown contrasted well with the pale green silk of Anne's.

'As do you. Captain Wentworth will be quite lost for words.'

Anne pulled a face. 'I hoped my father would be.'

Elizabeth laughed as she picked up her cloak and reticule and followed Anne to the door, but her friend hesitated on the threshold.

'I am a little nervous, Lizzy.'

'As am I, though I suspect for different reasons.'

Anne followed her onto the landing. 'I truly do not think standing up with Mr Darcy is to be feared, Lizzy.'

Elizabeth laughed reluctantly as they made their way down the stairs and into the cottage's sitting room. 'You did not see us at the Netherfield ball. I declare our mutual air and countenance would have made a warrior quail!'

'Frederick will have to be my warrior this evening. Thank heavens he is all but returned to full strength.'

As they waited for the carriage to draw up, Elizabeth kept her own counsel. She did not trust Sir Walter Elliot, but her pre-occupation with Mr Darcy, and the anticipation of standing up with him for the first set, was far too prevalent in her mind to permit anything else to linger.

What would this evening bring?

CHAPTER FORTY-FOUR

The gentlemen soon joined the ladies in the carriage, and as it travelled the short distance to Kellynch Hall, Darcy permitted himself the luxury of watching Elizabeth.

The lady sat diagonally across from him, dressed in a long velvet cloak with a hood resting atop her curls, her gloved hands in her lap and her head turned to the window. Leaving the gentle tide of conversation to the engaged couple and his cousin, Darcy beheld the curve of Elizabeth's cheek, grazed by the soft glow from the carriage lamps. What did she think of? Did she anticipate their dance as highly as he?

He lowered his head. It was the only pleasure he could foresee in these next few hours. The mere sight of Sir Walter Elliot was sufficient to put him in all manner of foul moods, and the obligation to stand up with Miss Elliot would surely be the longest half hour of his life.

Thankfully, the carriage turned in through the gates, and there was plenty of distraction from such sobering thoughts as the ladies were assisted from the conveyance and they all made their way into the house.

Divesting themselves of their outer garments, Darcy straightened his dress coat, his attention instinctively drawn to Elizabeth as they proceeded to the great hall, and he all but caught his breath. She was a vision this evening, her gown shimmering in the glow of the chandeliers, her hair—adorned with small, jewelled pins—elaborately dressed, exposing the creamy skin of her neck.

Insensible to his veneration, Elizabeth took in the elaborate decorations, her entertainment evident, and he longed to go and stand beside her and, indeed, took a step forward, but a hand restrained him.

'Not now, Darce. Best not to antagonise Sir Walter further.'

'You must allow me some compensation, Cousin.'

'Dancing the first set will have to suffice, old man.'

They both looked over to where the gentleman held court, Miss Elliot at his side, as he received each guest in turn. Then, with a last glimpse of Elizabeth, who laughed with her friend, her eyes sparkling with good humour, Darcy moved towards Sir Walter.

'Come, we had best do our duty.'

The room had been over-dressed, as Darcy anticipated, but most of those present gawped at the vast tree in the centre of the room—some in awe, the majority in amusement.

The colonel said nothing as they made their way through the throng, but once they exchanged greetings with Sir Walter and Miss Elliot, they eased away, walking to the far side of the room. Darcy looked for Elizabeth, but the crowd seemed to have swallowed her. Anne and the captain were currently being presented to her father, but Sir Walter seemed to have maintained his preference from the day before, and they were soon free of his notice and walking rapidly away.

'Good evening, Mr Darcy. Colonel.'

The lawyer appeared at their side.

'Shepherd.' Darcy flicked a look at Sir Walter, to where he held court, and the man urged them into an adjacent corridor.

'It is best we are not seen in protracted conversation.'

The colonel spoke quietly. 'You received Darcy's note?'

'Yes, sir. It is the first name I will look for.'

This reminder of the precariousness of his situation struck Darcy anew. 'What if you find nothing of import?'

The colonel rolled his eyes. 'You approach things in completely the wrong fashion, Darce. Have some faith. Besides, what else is there for us to do?'

It was a fair point. Darcy observed his watch. He ought to head to the ballroom.

Shepherd bowed. 'I am away to the archives, but first I must collect the keys from Sir Walter's desk. There is little chance of anyone venturing along that corridor tonight. He will be fully occupied, and the servants are over-stretched as it is.'

Watching him walk away, Darcy was filled with trepidation. If this did not deliver, what hope was there? He followed his cousin back into the great hall. Sir Walter had taken up a position by the tree, talking loudly to a couple of gentlemen about the necessity for titled families to emulate the Royal Family by following their new traditions, but beyond a few stragglers, most guests seemed to have moved on to the ballroom, and following the sounds of the musicians warming up, Darcy and the colonel joined them.

As it was, from the moment Elizabeth placed her delicate hand in Darcy's, and they made their first steps across the dance, all thought of Shepherd's stratagem disintegrated. He only wished the lady was not obliged to wear those confounded gloves, for the memory of taking possession of her hand in the early hours—the softness of her skin, the warmth of her palm as he placed a kiss upon it—lingered, and he longed for the liberty once more.

Suddenly conscious of their mutual silence, another memory forcibly intruded—that of the beginning of their dance at Netherfield, but though Darcy still lacked some conviction over the lady's true feelings, he felt sufficiently confident they were more cordial than those of the previous month.

'It seems a long time since the ball at Netherfield, does it not, Mr Darcy? It is but a month ago, to the exact day, but I feel as though I have lived a lifetime since then.'

Darcy threw Elizabeth a conscious look. 'You read my mind, Miss Bennet.'

She did not respond as they turned full circle and took their places in the line again. Then, she added: 'I believe we struggled to find topics of shared approval back then, sir. I hope we shall do better this evening.'

There was a note of question in her voice as they stepped forward once more to take hands.

'Perhaps we comprehend each other better than when last we stood up for a set. I am striving to improve those aspects of my character, which have been so lacking. I remain a little unsure as to the level of my success.'

The edges of Elizabeth's lips curved upwards.

'I believe you do quite well, Mr Darcy. Besides…'

They were obliged to turn away, but Darcy raised a brow as they returned to the line.

'Besides?'

Elizabeth hesitated, and his curiosity was roused. Besides *what*? What else might he have done...or not done...or—

'Forgive me if I speak openly, sir.' They took hands again, and as they turned about, she spoke. 'You are not the person I believed you to be—or that I was led to believe by others. Misinformation and...' Colour flooded her cheeks, and Darcy willed her to continue as they resumed their places in the line. 'And, if you will forgive my honesty, your own air and countenance at times, prevented me from seeing the gentleman I have discovered you to be.'

Darcy almost missed his step as they proceeded through the next movement. Had he truly succeeded in redeeming his character in Elizabeth's eyes, and in so short a time? A rush of relief consumed him, swiftly followed by a wish for it to be so much more, which he quickly stifled. This must be sufficient. Besides...he smiled slightly. *Besides*, he had other matters to deal with before he could even contemplate any furtherance of his acquaintance with Elizabeth.

Silence settled upon them as they continued the dance, but it held no awkwardness. Then, Elizabeth laughed.

'Dancing—though you may have little patience with the activity—features rather prominently when I reflect upon our acquaintance, Mr Darcy.'

'Will you enlighten me?'

'I may.' She laughed again as they followed the movements of the dance. 'Though you may regret it.'

Watching Elizabeth's light and pleasing figure as the ladies performed a few steps, Darcy felt he could regret nothing about this moment. The fine eyes he had long found pleasing were bright with vivacity and delight in the dance, and as she resumed her place opposite him, he observed with pleasure her smooth skin glowing in the candlelight, the swell of her breasts rising and falling from her exertions.

When next they clasped hands, Darcy had to forcibly reject the desire to hold on and never let go; to walk from the room and pull her into his arms. Thankfully, the lady was not privy to his unruly thoughts, and a smile touched Elizabeth's mouth as their eyes met, and Darcy returned it.

'You talked of dancing, Miss Bennet?'

'I recall you once saying balls were a subject which always make a lady energetic.'

Darcy had not forgotten the moment when Elizabeth first drew his interest, nor his inability to extricate himself from the alluring web she began to spin around him.

'You speak of the evening at Lucas Lodge.'

Elizabeth inclined her head as the gentlemen performed their part in the dance.

'I feel I am improving,' he then continued, 'in the art of requesting a dance with you.'

'Or not being persuaded to do so, sir?'

The impish look Elizabeth sent him as she turned away enticed him, despite the discomfort he experienced at the memory of his rudeness at the Meryton assembly.

'Perhaps I preferred to watch you perform, Miss Bennet. After all, as I once observed before, a man can appreciate a lady's charms far more easily from a near distance than by her side.'

An arched brow was the only response at first, but then humour tugged at her mouth. 'I suppose it depends upon where the gentleman's eye is resting, sir.'

He was caught out! Warmth invaded his neck, but Darcy could not help but laugh at the lady's expression.

'Touché, madam.'

'I was much surprised by your application at Netherfield, Mr Darcy.' Elizabeth smiled wryly. 'Though Charlotte—Miss Lucas—believed I would find you an agreeable partner.'

Recalling the opening dance of the ball, throughout which Darcy debated with himself over asking the lady to stand up with him, he grinned.

'Though you may not have regarded me with approval then, I trust I performed more adequately than your first partner that evening.'

Elizabeth shook her head, the delicate earrings dancing beside her flushed cheeks. 'My cousin. Such mortification during a miserable half hour.' She looked serious as they once again joined hands. 'It would not be difficult to better him, sir, though I will own to thinking it would be a misfortune to find you agreeable at the time.'

This was unsurprising intelligence, and Darcy merely inclined his head, but Elizabeth continued.

'I believe it is important to speak the truth, Mr Darcy, and I will thus conclude my statement by saying it has taken me a month to fully comprehend my friend's meaning.'

The closing movement of the dance separated them for a moment, and the music faded, but Darcy's heart pounded to the rhythm of its own beat. It seemed he understood her correctly, after all. Then, his expression sobered as reality took a firmer grip. If only they did not have the barrier of Sir Walter and his coercion between them, the uncertainty of what the next few days might bring.

The second dance soon commenced, with Darcy wishing it might never end, and they soon fell into conversation again.

'You once told me, Mr Darcy, of your abhorrence of disguise.' Elizabeth raised a brow as they stepped forward to exchange places.

'I have little patience for it.'

'Then in the spirit of openness, will you permit me to ask you a question?'

If she only knew that which he most wished to ask her! He met her inquiring look with a smile.

'Is that your consent, sir?'

He inclined his head.

'Then it will have to be sufficient, and you must heretofore absolve me of any impudence.'

'I have always appreciated your ability to speak your mind.'

Elizabeth laughed as they stepped forward and then back again. 'You may make a virtue of it if you wish, sir. I shall raise no objection. Yet I know impertinence when I hear it, especially from my own lips.'

They returned to the line, Darcy's eye instantly drawn to the lady's mouth, but she no longer seemed pleased. 'Then speak, Miss Bennet. Ask me what you will.'

'What troubles you so this evening?' Elizabeth spoke firmly but quietly, that only Darcy might hear her. 'And do not pretend, or say "nothing of consequence", for that will be disguise of the highest sort.'

Darcy blinked as the couples either side passed before them. What on earth could he say? The ballroom was no place to speak of the duress he was under!

'Mr Darcy? Is it so difficult, sir?' Elizabeth bit her lip. 'Forgive me. I am thoughtless. Your business is your own, and I should not speak so.'

'No—not at all! I am bound to silence at present...I hope to be able to shed its veil at the earliest opportunity, but for now, I cannot.' He held her gaze, his heart, his mind, willing her to understand. 'It prevents me from speaking as openly as I would wish.'

As they crossed the dance once more, this time their hands clasped, Darcy put some pressure upon Elizabeth's and though she did not look at him, he felt a return of the gesture. The tendrils of hope, so quick and easy to ebb and flow, took firmer hold as they wrapped themselves about his heart.

'Do I have your trust, Miss Bennet?'

They stepped beyond the other dancers before coming back together, standing as close as was permissible.

'Most indubitably,' the lady whispered, her cheeks flushed and her eyes bright. 'I would trust you with my life.'

Darcy swallowed hard on the rapidly rising emotion gripping his throat, saying nothing as they took their positions back in line.

'You make me quite uneasy, sir.'

'It is not my intention.' The dance drew to a close, and as the movements ceased and the last note drifted away, Darcy bowed along with all the other gentlemen, then raised his eyes to meet Elizabeth's. Her faith in him meant everything, and though these precious moments in her company were exquisite, his mind could not help but turn to the morrow once more and to his doing all in his power to get out of this ridiculous bind.

He offered Elizabeth his arm, which she accepted with pleasing alacrity, and—unable to resist—he placed his other hand over hers as he escorted her from the floor, repeating the pressure he earlier bestowed upon her fingers. She did not raise her eyes to his, but the grip upon his arm tightened in response, and he knew more than ever that he must free himself from the Elliots, and then nothing would stop him from making his feelings and intentions clear to the lady.

As they reached the edge of the dance floor, Darcy sought sight of his cousin.

'Darcy. There you are.'

Damn the man. Darcy turned to face Sir Walter, Elizabeth still upon his arm.

'Miss Bennet.'

The gentleman looked a little self-satisfied, and Darcy frowned, but then Miss Elliot joined them.

'I believe this is our dance, Mr Darcy?'

Darcy shook his head. 'Ours is the third, Miss Elliot. Miss Anne Elliot is my next partner.'

'Nonsense, Darcy.' Sir Walter blustered. 'Besides, I have told Anne to step aside, she is gone over there with her captain.'

He waved an airy hand, and Darcy looked across the room. Anne and Wentworth met his gaze, and the lady sent him a reassuring nod.

The musicians were warming up again, and with little choice, Darcy bowed as Elizabeth's hand slipped from his arm.

He faced her. 'If you will excuse me, ma'am.'

Sir Walter moved to the dais where the musicians were seated, and Miss Elliot followed him, but Darcy beheld Elizabeth solemnly for a second, and a smile touched her lips.

'Will you keep the supper dance for me?' he asked softly, that only she might hear.

The lady's regard remained fastened upon him, a faint colour tinting her cheeks, her eyes holding a message he could not quite fathom. 'It will be my pleasure, sir.'

Darcy bowed and turned on his heel, willing himself not to look back, and praying the half hour with Miss Elliot would soon be over.

❦

Elizabeth's heart sprung like a new-born lamb, and she placed a hand against her breast, willing it to calm. What was

Mr Darcy's purpose in being so markedly attentive? Was it possible he could truly be in love with her?

Was it really so inconceivable that two people who had known so little about each other would reverse course from enemies to become so much more? There must have been stories of love far stranger than this.

'Miss Bennet.'

She looked up, taking the colonel's arm.

'I think we will join the line forming at the back. My talents have not been put to the test lately, and I would hate to embarrass you.'

Elizabeth laughed as they took their places, conscious of Mr Darcy in the line forming before the dais, Miss Elliot opposite him.

The sudden and reverberating bang of a gong drew the guests' attention. Sir Walter had taken to the dais and bore a self-satisfied air.

'If I could have your attention, my lords, ladies, and gentlemen. Before we commence the second set, I have an announcement.'

An excited murmur arose from those gathered before him, with more people flooding into the ballroom from the card room and the conservatory, the ladies fanning themselves in the heat of the crush.

Elizabeth sought Mr Darcy, but his eyes were fixed upon their host, and she could see Anne and the captain standing further down the line.

'Firstly, and with great pleasure, I wish to announce the engagement of my daughter—'

Elizabeth stared over to where Anne stood. A public acknowledgement would be the final seal of approval. Pleased at such a happy outcome for her friend, Elizabeth observed

Anne's astonished attention upon her father as she gripped the captain's arm.

'Elizabeth, to Mr Fitzwilliam Darcy of Pemberley in Derbyshire.'

CHAPTER FORTY-FIVE

There was a loud buzzing in Darcy's ears, a combination of dread and anger thrumming through him, as people offered felicitous words and—in the case of some of the men present—slapping him on the back.

Desperately, his eyes sought Elizabeth in the lines of dancers and, being tall, he had no difficulty in finding her. Her cheeks were pale as the frost from earlier that day, the conflict in the lady's countenance smote him, and though Darcy knew he had a role to play in the farce Sir Walter had enforced upon him, he began to make his way through the throng of people to reach her.

By the time he reached where Elizabeth had been standing, she was nowhere in sight.

'Darcy.' The colonel grabbed his arm as he made to rush past him. 'Heed my warning. You must remain under good regulation, especially when we may be on the scent of the hunt.'

Distraught though he was, Darcy comprehended the sense of his cousin's caution. He drew in a short breath, conscious of the tautness in his chest as the colonel released his hold.

'What a damnable disaster, Richard!'

'Now, my lords, ladies, and gentleman…' Sir Walter paused as his eldest daughter joined him, and he kissed her on the cheek before turning back to face his guests, who had their rapt attention upon him.

Looking as satisfied as he could conceivably be, Sir Walter, beckoned Darcy.

'Darcy, come here. Let us raise a toast to you and Elizabeth before you commence your dance.'

What choice had he? If he were to turn and walk away, Georgiana would be doomed. Sir Walter's wrath at such a public rejection would know no bounds. What if Shepherd discovered a way out for him?

'Darcy!' Sir Walter flashed his teeth at the gathered company, but when his notice returned to Darcy his countenance was fierce. 'If you please?'

Assuming his mask of inscrutability, Darcy moved slowly back to the dais, unable to stop his fists from clenching and conscious of the astonishment of Anne Elliot.

'I do not understand. How can this be?' Anne turned to the captain, eyes wide with concern.

'If ever there was evidence you ought to be under my protection, not your father's, this is it.' She took in the loving expression upon Captain Wentworth's face. 'The sooner the banns are read, the better.'

Tears filled her eyes, and the captain lowered his head, speaking softly only to her.

'This is no time for sadness. We will be the happiest of couples.' He sent a guilty look in Mr Darcy's direction, but

Anne knew he spoke the truth. There would be no happiness in marriage for the gentleman shackled to her sister.

Blind to the truth, the guests held up the glasses being distributed by a team of liveried servants and toasting the engaged couple merrily.

'I must find Lizzy.'

The captain beheld her for a moment as understanding passed between them.

'I had suspected as much.' Captain Wentworth's countenance expressed his sympathy as he looked over to where Mr Darcy stood beside Miss Elliot, his face devoid of any emotion, his eyes staring blankly over the heads of the gathered company. 'Where is the colonel?'

Anne's eyes skimmed the room. 'I have no idea.'

'Then, go. Find your friend, and I will be on hand for Darcy.'

Elizabeth had no plan when she fled the ballroom, unheeding of the colonel's call after her; indeed, she had no thought for anything except she must escape the scene she had just witnessed.

Mr Darcy's coachman happened to be with the carriage, and though he was clearly surprised at the request to return to the house so soon after the ball commenced, he obliged, and they rattled along the lane before Elizabeth could consider what she might do next.

As soon as Meadowbrook House came into view, Elizabeth's frame drooped. Her heart lay heavy in her breast, a taut band gripping her insides, but the realisation she must leave, and as soon as possible—and perchance never see Mr Darcy again—brought a despair she had never before experienced.

As the carriage turned about, in order to return to the Hall, Elizabeth stepped into the house, unaware of Boliver closing the door behind her. She looked around the familiar space, dressed for the season, and as she recalled the happiness of Christmas Eve, the moments of almost intimacy with Mr Darcy, emotion took hold of her throat. How could he have been so attentive, knowing of his obligation to another? And what a person to choose!

'Miss Bennet! Are you unwell?'

Vaguely, Elizabeth looked to where Georgiana stood in the doorway to the drawing room. The girl frowned, then hurried over.

'Where is your cloak?' She touched Elizabeth's arm above her glove. 'You are frozen. Come by the fire.'

Images spun through Elizabeth's mind as she stared at Georgiana: dancing with Mr Darcy, the significant looks they had exchanged and then the shock of the announcement.

'No, I—' Her voice sounded distant, unlike her own. 'If you will excuse me.'

'I insist, Miss Bennet.' Georgiana was surprisingly firm as she led Elizabeth over to the drawing room. 'Shall I summon Mrs Reynolds? If you are unwell the last thing you should be doing is going out with no cloak again.'

Elizabeth did not answer, sinking onto a chaise with little concept of where she was. How could this be? Why had it not been openly spoken of, and why had Mr Darcy paid such attention to *her* in recent days if it were so?

'What has happened?' Georgiana's voice was wary as she took a seat beside her. 'I am anxious. Is my brother all right?'

Her brother...Elizabeth drew in a calming breath, wiping away a solitary tear.

'I believe he is quite well, Miss Darcy. I offer my congratulations. I did not know of the engagement.'

'Oh no!' Georgiana paled, a hand shooting to her throat. 'How did you find out?'

Elizabeth's mind raced. Had they both chosen to keep it secret from her? But *why*? If only she had known…

'Miss Bennet?'

With a sigh, Elizabeth raised hopeless eyes to Georgiana. 'It was announced at the ball.'

To her surprise, the girl burst into tears, burying her face in her hands. 'No! I cannot believe it.'

Concerned, Elizabeth placed a comforting arm about her. This was somewhat irregular; such singular behaviour!

Georgiana's distress showed no sign of abating and pushing aside her own hurt and confusion for a moment, Elizabeth removed the girl's hands from her face.

'Dear Miss Darcy, please do not cry. I am grieved to have brought distress upon you, but I cannot see how.'

Georgiana stilled, and she wiped her eyes with her fingers before raising tear-stained cheeks to Elizabeth. 'Forgive me, Miss Bennet, you must think me such a child.' She pulled a handkerchief from her sleeve and mopped ineffectually at her wet face.

Shaking her head, Elizabeth struggled to balance her own ragged emotions with her curiosity to understand what she was missing. Why would such a thing cause this level of upset?

'Not at all, but it is now my turn to ask if you are unwell? Shall I find Mrs Annesley?'

Georgiana shook her head as she dabbed at her eyes with the prettily embroidered handkerchief.

'I am simply an anchor on the heel of my family. This is all my fault, and now Fitz will suffer for the rest of his days because of me.' Her voice broke on the last word and the tears fell anew, and Elizabeth got to her feet, drawing Georgiana to hers and placed a comforting arm about her as she wept.

When the storm of emotion had fully passed, they remained in a quiet embrace. Having comforted her younger sisters in such a manner on many an occasion, Elizabeth remained silent, allowing the girl time to become calmer.

'Please forgive me.' Georgiana finally raised her head, and Elizabeth released her hold. 'Pay me no mind, Miss Bennet. I am being self-indulgent, but I love my brother so much.' She frowned. 'But why have you come home so precipitously and in such distress?'

To Elizabeth's dismay, the question found its answer in the air between them as she saw Georgiana's eyes widen.

'Oh Miss Bennet…' Georgiana's voice was hoarse.

'Do not distress yourself further. There has never been anything between your brother and me. It is merely my own folly, a secret I must keep. I simply desire to retreat as fast as I possibly—'

'No! You must stay. I cannot bear it, and nor will my brother.'

In the circumstances, there was nothing to add to this.

'I believe it best I return to my family directly.'

'But my brother needs you! Oh, I cannot bear it! I have brought this upon him—upon all of us.'

Concerned by Georgiana's ashen complexion as she sank back onto the chaise, Elizabeth tried not to take comfort from her words. Whatever Mr Darcy may have needed was irrelevant now.

Elizabeth studied Georgiana's hunched form, her hands almost shaking as she gripped the ends of her shawl, then walked across the room. So be it. They would soon consume the evidence. She poured two small glasses of wine and returned to Georgiana to offer one.

'Here, Miss Darcy. Sip this. It will help.'

The girl accepted the glass and took a generous gulp, then started to cough. Elizabeth patted her gently on the back. 'Sip, my dear.'

Georgiana tried again, this time with a small sip, and Elizabeth settled in the chair opposite, cradling her glass in her hands.

'You must wonder at the extremity of my response, Miss Bennet.'

Elizabeth hesitated. What would serve the girl best, a polite negation or an honest reply?

'Indeed, I do, Miss Darcy. You knew about the engagement?'

'I knew of its threat.' There was silence for a moment, other than the crackling of logs in the grate, but then Georgiana continued. 'I cannot disclose it all, but it would be a comfort if you would listen to what I *can* say.' She drew in a short breath. 'Fitz is a true gentleman. He is also the most loving b-brother anyone could imagine.'

'We should be careful how we speak, Miss Darcy."

'Yes, I know. But there is a…there has been an occurrence beyond what I told you of Mr Wickham.'

Elizabeth shuddered involuntarily, forgetting her own pain for a moment. 'Wickham has not been in touch? He has not threatened you?'

Georgiana shook her head vehemently. 'Not at all. It is not his error this time, but mine. I have acted…or rather, failed to act as carefully as I should have, and as a result it has brought us here.'

Elizabeth remained silent; her eyes fixed upon Georgiana's troubled features as she swallowed visibly. But before anything else could be said, the door opened, and they both looked over in trepidation. Thankfully, it was Anne.

'There you are!' Her features filled with relief as she took in the scene. 'Is there another glass?'

Elizabeth pointed to the decanter and Anne poured a measure before joining them.

'Forgive me for leaving the ball in such haste, Anne.' The memory of Sir Walter's words returned in an instant, and Elizabeth flinched. What had happened since she fled the scene?

'I asked Frederick to escort me back. He has gone to the kitchen to beg a cup of tea. He will not disturb us.' Anne embraced her friend before taking the seat beside Georgiana. 'I am as astounded as you must be, Lizzy. I cannot understand it at all.'

Against her will, tears pricked Elizabeth's eyes, but Georgiana's attention was fixed upon her.

'I am oft reprimanded for speaking too unguardedly, but this is important. I believe Fitz has been in love with Miss Bennet for some time. You can imagine his pain over this.'

Elizabeth was conscious of the ache in her breast deepening at Georgiana's words. What had she lost?

'But I did not know.'

'Fitz fully comprehended your poor perception of him. He was humbled by it.'

'That is all undone. I think extremely highly of him.'

The front door opened and banged with great force. Colonel Fitzwilliam's voice could be heard, the words indistinguishable, followed by Mr Darcy's, though in a tone Elizabeth had never heard.

Georgiana looked between the two women and held out the glass blindly.

'I must go to him. Miss Bennet…please…do not leave tomorrow.'

'Here, let me take that.' Elizabeth stood up and held out a hand for the empty glass, and handing it over, Georgiana hurried from the room.

Anne's face filled with sadness. 'Leave tomorrow? Oh please, Lizzy, no.'

'It is but a few days ahead of my planned departure. I cannot remain here. You are well chaperoned with Mrs Annesley and Miss Darcy in the house until you leave as arranged.'

'It is not a chaperone I seek, Lizzy, but a friend. Take a little time to think about it. Please?'

Elizabeth was torn. Much as she desired to escape seeing Mr Darcy again, she could not bear the notion of *not* seeing him. Beyond that, she did not wish to fail her friend for Anne lacked them.

'I will think about it. I promise.'

'Thank you.' Anne pointed to the empty glass in Elizabeth's hand. 'Let me refresh these.'

They were soon settled on the chaise, whilst Anne relayed to Elizabeth all that happened when she left the ballroom.

'They danced the second set. Mr Darcy's mien was impossible to read, but happiness in his situation was clearly missing. I saw little of him after that, as Mary and Charles came over to express their delight over the connection, but as soon as we could excuse ourselves, we left. Frederick believes he saw Mr Darcy striding down a corridor after my father, but he cannot be certain.'

Elizabeth sipped her drink. 'Did you know?'

Anne's eyes widened. 'Of the engagement? Of course not. I would never have kept that from you.'

'But you anticipated an incident.'

'I was wary. It did not make sense that my father was so willing to extend his hospitality to you...or either of us. When he began to speak, I was surprised, it seemed as though he would announce *my* engagement. It came to me as he spoke the words, how desperately he wants my elder sister married and how much Mr Darcy fits the mould. I find it difficult to believe the gentleman could pay you so much attention whilst he has been courting my sister.'

Elizabeth opened her mouth, then closed it.

'What? What is it?'

'Miss Darcy, upon hearing of the engagement, was extremely distressed.'

'I cannot say I blame her.'

'No, it was more, Anne. She was devastated and said it was all her fault.' Elizabeth hesitated. 'It was as though she felt a deed she had done had brought it to pass, that it was not Mr Darcy's choice.' She frowned as she acknowledged the time on the mantel clock. 'And if he was willing, why is he returned so early?'

'How singular. What could it mean?'

With a sigh, Elizabeth put her unfinished drink aside. The meaning was irrelevant.

'It does not matter. They are betrothed. That is all there is to it.'

Anne placed an arm about Elizabeth. 'My heart shatters for you, Lizzy. It seems both you and Mr Darcy have been dogged by the most unfortunate timing.'

They got to their feet. It was not quite ten o'clock, but Elizabeth felt she had lived a lifetime in the hours since they departed for the ball.

'Will you excuse me, Anne? I wish to go to my room.'

Anne accompanied her to the door. 'You do not wish to see anyone else this evening.'

Unable to stop herself from casting a look of longing down the hall to Mr Darcy's study, Elizabeth's throat closed as once more the reality of the situation swept through her.

Tears hovering on her lashes, she shook her head and, with one last embrace from Anne, she slipped through the door to the garden and hurried across the frost-covered lawn to the sanctuary of Willow Cottage.

CHAPTER FORTY-SIX

'Well, at least Hartwright has earned his keep this evening—three separate journeys to return five people to the same residence. He will be demanding pecuniary satisfaction on this St Stephen's Day, Darce, or at least a se'nnight of rest.'

The colonel strode over to the drinks tray and splashed brandy into two glasses before turning to face Darcy, who had sunk back against the closed door to his study and not moved, unimpressed with his cousin's attempt at a joke. How could he ever be amused by anything again? There were no words to describe his present feelings. The anguish upon Elizabeth's features had been sufficient to confirm what he had longed to comprehend, what he had wished for, dreamed of. Could there be any stronger indication that the lady's feelings had changed?

Darcy's chest was taut with emotion, his mind full of suppressed anger for Sir Walter's actions, yet all he wished for was the freedom to seek out Elizabeth and tell her why this had come to pass; confess that she, and only she, would ever hold his heart. He was but eight and twenty, yet he felt his life was over.

Forcing his legs to move, Darcy stepped forward. How the hell could he extricate himself from this plight *now*?

A tap came on the door, and he turned back to swing it open.

'Georgie!' Darcy frowned as she walked into the room. 'What is wrong?'

Georgiana's eyes filled with tears again as she grasped his hands. 'I saw Miss Bennet.'

Darcy's heart faltered. 'And she told you.'

'She was distressed. How can it have come to this?'

The colonel walked over to join them. 'Because Sir Walter Elliot is a shallow, scheming, unpleasant man.' He offered Georgiana his handkerchief and handed a glass of brandy to Darcy.

'Here, take this, man.'

'But Miss Bennet...' Georgiana looked from her cousin to her brother. 'She is talking of leaving us on the morrow.'

This was little comfort to Darcy, and he took a slug of brandy, then coughed, wiping his mouth with his hand. How he longed to beg Elizabeth to stay those few extra days, but to what end? He was a betrothed man, with no way out before him.

'Georgie, I need to speak with your brother. We will come to you when we are done.'

'Yes, yes of course.' Georgiana reached up to kiss Darcy's cheek, then slipped from the room, and Darcy sank into one of the chairs beside the hearth. Despite the roaring fire, he shivered. He felt like he would never be warm again.

'We have to act, Darce.' The colonel sat opposite him, then took a slug from his own glass before leaning forward. 'Though I do have a token for you from Shepherd.'

Darcy's head shot up. 'When did you see him?'

'Hmph.' The colonel leaned back in his seat, cradling his glass. 'Good to see the medicine is rousing you. I went out into the great hall during your dance with Miss Elliot, having lost my partner, and he appeared out of the shadows.'

Darcy placed his glass on a side table and leaned forward. 'Tell me it is a good token, Cousin. I beg of you.'

'I shall do more than that.' The colonel placed his own glass on the floor and reached inside his coat, pulling out two letters, tossing one over to Darcy.

Darcy unfolded it, then looked up at the colonel. 'This is the missing letter. The one Georgie kept as a reminder.' He eyed the second in his cousin's hand.

'This is a copy. An expensive education is not synonymous with intelligence. Who has a copy made and then keeps it with the original?'

Darcy's skin grew even colder. 'There is another who is aware of its content?'

The colonel shook his head. 'Be not alarmed. Shepherd confirmed he made the copy under Sir Walter's instructions. It is how he so fully understood the duress you were under and knew where to find them. There is a small safe in the study, apparently.'

Darcy studied the letters in his hand. 'This will not save Georgiana.'

'I know. He may no longer have the proof, but Sir Walter will only have to mention what took place in all the right places. The gossip column will have its day. People will have faith in anything they are told if it is said with sufficient conviction.'

'What if he notices they are missing?'

The colonel shrugged. 'Shepherd says he put two folded pieces of paper back in their place and wrote the direction out much as it is on the original. Unless Sir Walter chooses to pick it up to read the contents again—which is unlikely—he may never notice. It is a risk, but you would not have had him leave them there?'

'No, of course not.' Darcy tucked the letters inside his waistcoat. 'Was that all?'

'Shepherd says the safe only ever holds bank notes and blank cheques.' The colonel settled more comfortably into his seat. 'But Sir Walter had asked him to place both the letter and the copy in the safe the other day.'

'He has not found anything on the name of Aubert?'

'Not yet. He told me he had made a start, but then recalled these letters and decided to collect them whilst there was no chance of being caught. As far as I know, he is still in the archives now.' The colonel gestured at Darcy's glass. 'Have you finished?'

There was no answer, and he got to his feet and walked to his cousin.

'Has love addled what was once an agile brain, man? Here.' Resignedly, he held out a hand for Darcy's glass. 'Darce?' The colonel snapped his fingers. 'Rouse up, man. Let us find Georgiana.'

'Yes, yes, of course.' Darcy followed his cousin out into the hall.

'What was Sir Walter's response when you confronted him?'

Anger returned in an instant. 'That my cooperation was the only way to silence him, and if I cared for my sister, I would'— Darcy bit back on an expletive—'I would do my Christian duty and put her needs above my own interests.' The trap had all but closed. Soon it would be padlocked, and Sir Walter would be the one to throw away the key. 'He said the announcement will be in *The Times* tomorrow.'

The colonel released a string of profanities. 'I want to run him through.' He made a lunging gesture with his arm as they crossed the entrance hall. 'Though I would hate to stain my sword with his blood.'

Noting the door to the garden, Darcy tried not to think about Elizabeth's interpretation of all that had taken place, hoping she managed to find rest.

He doubted he would.

Anne passed a restless night, torn between memories of dancing the first set of the ball with Frederick on the previous night, the shock of her father's announcement and the despair of her friend. Would Elizabeth truly leave for Hertfordshire today, or could she be persuaded to stay?

She flung back the covers and got out of bed, padding over to the window. There had been no further snow, but the scene was shrouded in the pale grey that precedes the dawn.

Donning her dressing robe, she went out onto the landing and up to the door of Elizabeth's room, pressing her ear against it. There was no sound from within, and she cautiously opened it.

'I could not sleep.'

Pushing it further open, Anne looked over to the hearth. Elizabeth was curled up in a large armchair, her shawl tucked over her toes.

'Nor I.' Anne hurried over and took the seat opposite. A fresh fire had been set in the grate, but no attempt made to light it. 'Shall I?' She gestured at the hearth, and Elizabeth shrugged.

Taking that as acquiescence, Anne lit a taper and soon the kindling caught, and although it would be a little while before conspicuous heat would be felt, the sound of the crackling wood was a comfort.

Elizabeth stared into the flames, and Anne watched her for a moment, uncertain whether she would rather be left alone. It was certainly how she felt when it was feared the captain had been lost at sea.

Then, her friend roused herself, swinging her feet to the floor and facing Anne with a smile that almost reached her eyes.

'Forgive me for being so feeble last night, Anne. It was all rather a shock. I have done much reflecting and whilst I will find it difficult to be near Mr Darcy, for the sake of a few days, I will stay until you leave. Our friendship will long outlive any foolish notions I had regarding the gentleman.'

Elizabeth's voice was firm, and Anne longed to believe she meant every word. Getting to her feet, her friend stretched, then donned her shawl. 'Of course, Mr Darcy may not be happy with my remaining. If my attachment has become so obvious, I might bring him embarrassment.'

'I suggest you let the gentleman make his own decisions on that, Lizzy. Besides, he may be busy in the interim. He seemed as surprised by this announcement as the rest of us.'

Walking over to the window, Elizabeth pulled back the shutters, and Anne came over to join her. There were a few lamps lit over at the house as the servants made it ready for the day ahead, and her eyes instinctively travelled to the room she knew to be Frederick's.

The clock on the mantel chimed just as a tap came on the door and Elise's head appeared.

'Shall I bring hot water up, Miss Bennet? And for you too, miss?'

'Yes, please, Elise. And some tea.' The maid left and Anne pushed away from the sill and walked to the door, turning to look over at Elizabeth.

'I am going to call on Mary later. Would you like to come with me? It will give you some occupation.'

Elizabeth shook her head as she walked over to the dresser and opened a drawer to extract a towel.

'Let us see what Mr Darcy's verdict is on my remaining first. It may be that I have plenty of occupation in packing my things.'

Not wishing to speculate, partly because Anne had no notion of what Mr Darcy's thoughts might be as an engaged man, she returned to her own room to make preparations for the day, hoping and praying the gentleman would be as reluctant to forego Elizabeth's company as she was his.

Elizabeth was on tenterhooks upon entering the breakfast room, but to her relief, only the colonel and Georgiana were within when she arrived. Mr Darcy, apparently, had broken his fast early and was out on a solitary ride.

As this made it impossible for Elizabeth to establish the gentleman's thoughts on her remaining, she hovered all morning between whether to start packing or not, declining again the offer to join Anne and the captain on their visit to Uppercross. She had even gone so far as to tug her trunk out from the wardrobe and thrown open the lid but dissatisfied with her own company and the sadness consuming her thoughts, she sought distraction over at the main house.

There was no one in the drawing room other than Mrs Annesley, who said Georgiana had chosen to practise her music. Elizabeth was halfway along the corridor to the music room when the door to the study opened and Mr Darcy stepped out.

'Oh!' Elizabeth's head lowered to her feet, and she studied the toes of her shoes with great interest. How did one start the conversation she needed to have?

'Miss Bennet.'

She raised her head, her heart pounding in her chest and her throat tightening as she took in his agreeable features. How could she have fallen in love with him so deeply?

Conscious of wetness forming on her lashes, Elizabeth curtsied hurriedly and made to move away, but Mr Darcy stayed her with a hand on her arm.

She stared at his firm but slender fingers as he removed his hand and swallowed quickly as her eyes met his.

'Sir?'

'Do not leave.'

Elizabeth looked at Mr Darcy, uncertain how to respond, a tear escaping from her lashes and rolling down her cheek, and she brushed it away with impatience.

Pull yourself together, girl, she admonished silently.

'I do not wish to, but—'

'There are no "buts" to be had.'

Drawing in a short breath, Elizabeth clasped her hands together. 'Anne is desirous I remain for the next few days, but…' She stopped as he shook his head.

'Then do so. It was already your intention, why alter it?'

Because I cannot bear to see you, to love you, knowing you are to wed another. And yet likewise, to leave you will tear me apart.

Emotion gripped Elizabeth so fiercely, she could not speak. Nor could she look away as he beheld her with warm regard.

'Miss Bennet…Elizabeth, if I may, on this one occasion.' With an intake of breath, she realised he had taken her hand in his, and warmth flooded her skin at his touch. 'There is little I can say, as I mentioned last night.' He lowered his voice. 'What I can tell you is this: I had no notion Sir Walter would act as he did. He has put me under an obligation, and I fear I must stand by it, at present, but I wish you to comprehend that it is not of my choosing.'

Elizabeth's throat tightened with sadness over whatever his predicament was, but then she held her breath as Mr Darcy raised her hand and placed a firm kiss upon it.

'Promise me, you will stay until your planned departure? If not for me, then I know you will wish to do so for your friend.'

He released her hand, and Elizabeth's skin tingled from the pressure of his lips. 'I believe I understand you perfectly, Mr Darcy. And I will stay.' She hesitated, then added, 'And not only for Anne's sake.'

A small smile touched his mouth, and Elizabeth summoned one in return. Then, he bowed.

'If you will excuse me.'

Elizabeth watched Mr Darcy walk away from her, then slowly made her way to the music room as she attempted to comprehend all the gentleman had said.

CHAPTER FORTY-SEVEN

The remainder of the day after the ball was a quiet one at Meadowbrook House, with Darcy continuing in his study, sometimes accompanied by his cousin or Captain Wentworth—upon his return from Uppercross—often alone.

There were two visitors, the first being Shepherd, who confirmed he had found payments of the exact same amount, payable on the quarter days, to someone called Aubert, commencing in early 1785 and ceasing the quarter before the payments to Williams began. Mr Robinson followed soon after, paying a call of courtesy to ensure the captain remained in good health, having been summoned to Kellynch Hall to attend Sir Walter.

Much as the colonel hoped the latter had fallen down the stairs and broken his neck, he had to be satisfied with his having tripped over the ornate foot of one of his full length looking glasses and badly spraining his ankle. As he bore a compression on said ankle and could wear neither shoe nor boot and, what is more, had to make use of a cane for support, he remained confined to his apartments. In truth, Sir Walter refused to be seen in public using a walking stick as it smacked of infirmity.

Though Darcy's suspicions had been confirmed, that Williams and Aubert were one and the same person, he still had little faith in an illegitimate child being sufficient to silence Sir Walter and free Darcy from his ties.

What illegitimate child, though, and where in the world was it?

He did his best with the company over dinner, but most of the liveliness came from the engaged couple and his cousin, with Darcy, his sister and Elizabeth all frequently drifting away into their thoughts. It was a release when they all retired for the night, and though Darcy went in search of tea at two in the morning, he was relieved not to encounter the lady on this occasion, for fear of what he might share with her.

The following morning, Darcy left his chamber just as dawn broke, though he spent the hour before staring out into the blackness of the grounds. Somehow, he needed an audience with Mrs Williams, in the hope she would be prepared to talk.

Darcy walked across the entrance hall to stare out of the door facing the cottage. Had Elizabeth slept? He was about to turn away when a light caught his eye, and pulling the door open, he stepped out onto the terrace to peer over at an upstairs window, backlit by the glow of a lamp.

Then, his heart reeled in his chest as the window was pushed up to reveal Elizabeth, wrapped in a thick shawl, her hair about her shoulders, though it was not possible to read her expression.

Darcy's heart clenched harder and he raised a hand, gratified when the lady reciprocated. Tearing himself away, he turned on his heel and returned to the house.

To his surprise, he was not the first person in the breakfast room.

'Morning, Wentworth.' Darcy poured some coffee and took a place opposite the captain, who put aside some papers and picked up his cup.

'I could not sleep.' The captain gestured at the papers. 'For the hearing next month.'

'When is it set for?' Darcy savoured the fragrance of the coffee before taking a sip.

'Eleven in the morning on the seventeenth. I am to see the admiral beforehand, and it will be an opportunity to meet with a couple of the men who survived who will be in attendance. Three are still bed-ridden, but the process should be a formality.'

'And what of another command?'

Captain Wentworth stirred in his seat. 'We are at war, which is both a blessing and a curse. The likelihood is a vessel will be offered directly.' He considered his attire for a second, 'I shall be certain to stock up on my wardrobe whilst in Town, that you may have your own returned to you.'

They talked of the forthcoming nuptials briefly, with the captain confirming he was also under instruction from Anne to order a new dress uniform for the wedding.

'It was kind of you to offer your London home, Darcy, but I will be comfortable at a hotel. No need to disturb your household for the sake of two nights. It is good of you to put the carriage at my disposal.'

'The household servants would have been delighted to have someone to fuss over.' Darcy doubted they would find much delight in a mistress such as Miss Elizabeth Elliot.

'How has it come to this, Wentworth?' The tension gripping Darcy made itself felt.

The captain raised his hands. 'Do not give up hope. Even when the darkest hour approaches, there is sometimes reprieve. I will do all in my power to aid you in finding a way out of this. All I seek is a direction.'

'As do I.'

They discussed in subdued tones the findings of Shepherd, with Captain Wentworth offering to speak to Anne to ascertain Mrs Williams' movements.

'If she is one and the same as the person receiving the payments, the lady may be our only hope.' The captain rose from his seat. 'I will seek Anne out directly.'

'It is good to have you on side, Wentworth.' Darcy studied the man opposite, whom he had come to like a great deal. 'If there is any compensation for what I am facing, it is that I shall have you and Miss Anne Elliot as kin henceforth.'

The captain inclined his head. 'Small recompense, I suspect, Darcy.'

⚜

Elizabeth huddled beside the fire, which had begun to take hold, rubbing her hands together, her mind consumed yet again by attempting to decipher the message Mr Darcy had tried to convey.

What could be amiss with this engagement? Even had she not fallen so deeply in love with Mr Darcy, she could not have believed him developing respect or affection for Miss Elliot. Yes, a man of his standing required a wife, but she did not believe Mr Darcy would enter into a lifetime of suffering simply for duty's sake.

A memory whispered through Elizabeth's mind, of the day they met in the snow near Uppercross and she asked him outright whether he would always put duty to his family before his own happiness.

The gentleman's image swam before Elizabeth's eyes as he replied: "If I had forsaken my duty, I do not think I could find peace or contentment."

Georgiana came immediately to mind. Mr Darcy would do anything for her—had already, in saving her from Wickham— and the girl had already implied her brother was in some sort of predicament, due to an error on her part.

With an impatient sigh, Elizabeth sank into the chair beside the hearth, loosening her shawl as the heat from the fire began to make itself felt, only for a small item to fall to the floor. Scooping it up, she studied the miniature given to her on Christmas Day—a time when she had been filled with dreams and anticipation. She touched Mr Darcy's face with her finger, then raised the precious gift to place a kiss upon it.

So much remained unfathomable, with no answer to be had. Stretching her legs and wriggling her toes in the warmth of the fire, Elizabeth leaned back in her seat. Should she attempt to coax the truth from Georgiana? She did not like to force a confidence from her, though the young girl had already shown a propensity for coming out with things that ought, perhaps, to have remained private. Who knew what a small amount of encouragement might do.

Then, she sighed. What difference did it make? Whether Elizabeth comprehended the reasons for Mr Darcy's present situation or not, it would remain unaltered.

'Let it be,' Elizabeth cautioned herself, getting to her feet and throwing the shawl onto the chair before placing the miniature in a drawer.

She must make the most of these few days in Anne's company and accept that the blessing of her friendship was compensation for her own disappointment. Elizabeth would recover from her loss one day, but the bond formed by herself and Anne would endure, she was certain.

They were wise words, and Elizabeth tried desperately to believe them as she welcomed Elise into the room and prepared to face the day.

To Darcy's surprise, Shepherd appeared on the doorstep near midday, and he went out to greet him.

'Boliver says you wished to see me out here?'

'If you will, Mr Darcy.' He gestured at a carriage pulled up to the bottom of the steps. 'I wish to introduce you to someone.'

Curious, Darcy followed Shepherd down the steps to the conveyance, whose door was open, a footman standing to attention beside it.

Peering inside, Darcy nodded at the extremely elderly gentleman seated on the bench.

'Mr Darcy, permit me to introduce you to Mr Boneshaker. Sir, this is Mr Darcy, whom I explained to you is about to enter into an alliance with the Elliot family.' The old man inclined his head, and Shepherd turned to Darcy.

'Mr Boneshaker was a partner at Knight & Dey, the legal firm which represented Mr James Stevenson in London, and it was he who drew up the original separate estate settlement for him.'

The ever-present glimmer of hope swelled as Darcy met Shepherd's confident expression. 'I was able to discover, but two days ago, that the gentleman now lives near Crewkerne, and he kindly responded to my request to call upon me this morning. I will leave you to your questions.'

Shepherd walked back to stand at the top of the steps, and Darcy studied the gentleman with interest. 'Forgive the intrusion upon your leisure, sir.'

'Leisure, you say?' Mr Boneshaker shook his head. 'I am surplus to requirements, Mr Darcy. Even when I call at my old office now, there is rarely a face I recognise, and no one to indulge in memories of the good old days.'

'Then will you not come inside, take some refreshment in return for your time?'

'It is a kind offer, sir, but you will have to indulge me and enter my carriage, for I cannot stand for any length of time and those steps are beyond me.'

Darcy did as he was bid, taking the seat opposite.

'Now, how may I assist you, young sir?'

Knowing he would have to give convincing evidence as to why he wished to ask questions, Darcy explained his forthcoming marriage to the eldest Miss Elliot.

'Ah, yes. Mr Stevenson's daughter and the separate estate trust. I recall it well, one of the last cases I worked on.'

'I was curious as to why it was not set up when the marriage settlements were prepared.'

Mr Boneshaker said nothing for a moment, but then inclined his head. 'I have been retired these many years, sir, and my client, Mr James Stevenson has long paid the debt of nature, as has his daughter. I cannot see the harm in sharing the document's origins. The late gentleman and his wife did not think they would be blessed with a child, and when the daughter, Elizabeth, was born to them, late in life, they worshipped her. When she married that fop, Sir Walter Elliot, Mr Stevenson was seriously displeased, but his daughter would have her way, and they were not in the nature of denying her.'

His voice was not strong, and Darcy leaned forward to catch his words.

'Then, a few months into the marriage, it came to light Elliot had a mistress of long standing, and she was with child.

Mr Stevenson was beside himself, until I suggested a separate estate settlement be put in place, providing financial stability for his daughter, should she need to free herself of the marriage. Determined to protect Lady Elliot and any female offspring she produced within the legal boundaries of the marriage—sons, of course, have other means of supporting themselves—and, importantly, avoid any claims from other sources, the addendum was created, with a strict directive specifying Mr Stevenson himself as the only person able to request the name of a child be added.'

Unsurprised by Sir Walter's behaviour, Darcy felt deeply for the late Lady Elliot, his mind wrestling with this new information.

'So, there *is* an illegitimate child out there?' And perhaps not only one.'

With a shrug, Mr Boneshaker pulled out his watch and studied it, then looked back at Darcy.

'If it arrived safely into this world, who knows what happened to it? It may well no longer be living, though if it is, Elliot may have made some provision for it.'

Trying to effect nonchalance, Darcy asked, 'Did you know the name of the mistress?' Was this a chance at finding the secret? 'Was it Williams, or Aubert?'

Boneshaker frowned. 'Definitely not.' Then, he brightened. 'It was Ward. A Miss Ward. That was the name.'

'You have an exceptional memory, sir.'

The gentleman assumed a complacent air. 'Not at all. It was my late wife's maiden name, which is why I recall it. Mr Stevenson did not, I am certain, mean to mention the name, but he was so angered by the affair, he made an unguarded comment, not dissimilar to "Miss Ward can go rot in…" Now where was it?' Boneshaker shook his head. 'It is gone.' He tucked the watch away. 'If you will excuse me, Mr Darcy. I am due at my club. I hope I have been of some assistance in helping you understand the generosity of your intended's late grandfather. An admirable man.'

Darcy thanked him and wished him well, emerging from the carriage almost as confused as when he entered it.

Mr Boneshaker lowered the window as they exchanged farewells, but as Darcy was about to turn away, he called him back.

'Northamptonshire, sir.'

'Pardon?'

'I have remembered. That was the county Mr Stevenson wished for Miss Ward to rot in.'

Having come across Georgiana in the breakfast room earlier that day, clearly under an oppression of spirits, Elizabeth invited her to walk with her to Montacute. She wished to avoid Mr Darcy as much as possible, knowing full well the evening would mean them being in company. With Anne busy at Kellynch Hall with Elise, overseeing the packing and removal of the garments and possessions she wished to take into her married life, Elizabeth needed occupation.

They enjoyed the walk to Montacute, calling in at the bookshop and the haberdashery to make a few purchases, before turning their steps in the direction of Meadowbrook House.

'I am grieved you will be leaving so soon, Miss Bennet.' Georgiana turned a woeful face to Elizabeth. 'I shall miss you so.'

'Dear Miss Darcy, for dear you have become to me.' Elizabeth took one of Georgiana's hands in her own as they walked. 'You know I cannot remain, especially once your brother…and I must return home to my sisters.'

Georgiana's countenance was despondent. 'But they all have each other, do they not, your sisters? I have none, at least until…'

The conviction of how awful a sister Miss Elliot would be to Georgiana was countered by knowing how superb Anne would be.

'I am so sorry to leave you. I truly am. But Mrs Annesley will be adequate company, will she not?'

Georgiana lowered her head. 'She is a kind lady, but she could never be as a sister to me.'

Elizabeth squeezed the hand she held gently as Georgiana raised sorrowful eyes to her. 'We have correspondence. I will write to you as often as I possibly can.' It was not what she wished. Continually receiving intelligence of Mr Darcy was the last thing she wanted, but she could think of nothing else to offer.

The young lady, however, seemed satisfied. 'Then I must take comfort from that. And'—she hesitated—'do I ask too much, but Miss Bennet, should I feel….if I find that my life is…' She drew in a short breath as Elizabeth held hers in trepidation.

Please do not ask me to call upon you in Town or to stay at Pemberley!

'Would you—or do I ask too much—invite me to stay a while with you at Longbourn?'

Unable to help herself, Elizabeth laughed. 'Do you comprehend what you ask? My family is quite different to yours. My home is pleasant enough, but it is smaller even than Meadowbrook House.'

'Provided your family is vastly unlike the one further down the lane, I shall be more than content. Please, Miss Bennet, I beg of you. If I need to escape for a while, will you take pity on me? I promise to be no trouble at all.'

Elizabeth chewed her bottom lip. The last she heard the regiment was still quartered in Meryton. Wickham had been a regular caller at Longbourn—though recent news from home indicated he had become engaged to a Miss King. Knowing what she did of the man, Elizabeth's sympathies were with the lady. Yet she could not knowingly draw Georgiana into a situation whereby she might encounter the man.

'I promise, should you feel the need for respite, you can ask me for assistance.'

That was as far as she could commit at present, and as Georgiana had little reason to suppose that this did not mean she *could* go to Longbourn, the girl was content.

CHAPTER FORTY-EIGHT

Elizabeth and Georgiana walked in a comfortable silence for a while, but then the latter slowed them to a halt.

'I can no longer bear it in silence.' She clasped her hands together. 'I must speak, though I know I should not.'

Suspecting where this might lead, Elizabeth all but held her breath, as Georgiana added. 'My brother is being forced to wed Miss Elliot.'

Unsurprised by this, after what the gentleman himself had disclosed, Elizabeth was nevertheless awash with curiosity.

'It would be a difficult thing to impose, Miss Darcy. Your brother knows his own mind and is well able to make his own choices. The duties of a gentleman can seem unfair—harsh even—but is it not the way for those with duty to an estate?'

Georgiana shook her head. 'You do not know...there is a reason behind it, and it is my fault. I cannot help him, nor can my cousin. He is trapped against his will.'

It sounded highly improbable, yet Elizabeth knew the situation was absurd, not simply because the notion of Mr

Darcy considering Miss Elliot as a suitable wife was laughable, nor down to her own desire to see him freed of the obligation.

'In what way, Miss Darcy? How can an intelligent, respected gentleman of your brother's standing be forced into anything?'

Swallowing visibly, Georgiana's face dropped. 'I told you I had made a mistake, was taken in by someone.'

'Yes, I recall.'

'And Fitz saved me from making a big mistake, but if it were to come out—what I almost did—it would ruin me. Sir Walter—' She stopped and drew in a long breath. 'Miss Elliot and her father found out about it.'

Elizabeth's heart went out to Georgiana, and she placed a comforting arm about her.

'They…he threatened to expose my past to the world unless Fitz took Miss Elliot as his wife.'

Elizabeth's mind reeled, but her heart swelled with an indefinable emotion. She was beginning to understand Mr Darcy's recent behaviour. 'Come, let us find some place more conducive to conversation.'

Georgiana took the arm Elizabeth offered and they walked briskly along the lane, slipping through a gate in the wall bordering Meadowbrook House. It was too cold to sit outside, but knowing Anne was at the Hall, Elizabeth led Georgiana over to Willow Cottage.

Soon ensconced by the glowing fire in the sitting room, Georgiana began to talk, spilling all her anxiety, her distress and her shame to Elizabeth, unaware she already knew what happened with Wickham.

Anger stirred within her breast. How could Miss Elliot stoop so low as to read and then take another's private letter? What kind of man was Sir Walter, to threaten and coerce a man of Mr Darcy's ilk into a loveless marriage with his daughter?

When Georgiana's tale of woe had drawn to a close, Elizabeth got to her feet, too agitated to remain seated. She walked over to the window and stared across at the main house. What agony must the gentleman be going through? His determination to protect his sister's reputation was admirable, but at what sacrifice?

'I have displeased you.' Georgiana's voice was tremulous, and Elizabeth hurried back across the room.

'No. There are others who anger me in all this, Miss Darcy. You are not one of them. You are incredibly brave. Your secret shall be safe with me, and I thank you for telling me this. I have been...' Her voice faltered as she recalled Mr Darcy's expression as he pressed a kiss upon her hand, and a tear pricked her eye.

'I was right, you do love my brother.'

Elizabeth managed a watery smile. 'How could you not guess? I believe I failed miserably to conceal my feelings.' Once, this would have mortified her, but she wanted Mr Darcy to be in no uncertainty. Whatever he truly felt for her, he deserved to know it.

'You had a right to know the truth, Miss Bennet.' Georgiana sighed. 'Fitz has long held you in the highest esteem.'

'I had not anticipated...' Warmth filled Elizabeth's cheeks. 'I am proud of my heritage, Miss Darcy, but I am hardly a catch when it comes to marriage. Miss Elliot, for all her failings, has the dowry and connections to make her a suitable wife for someone of your brother's position in society.'

Georgiana sank back in her seat, her forlorn gaze upon Elizabeth. 'And she will become mistress of Pemberley, and'—her voice hitched, and she wailed—'*my* sister!'

What was there to say? Having seen ample evidence of how poor a sister Miss Elliot could be, it seemed it would not only be Mr Darcy who would suffer henceforth.

The colonel joined Darcy and the captain in the study as they contemplated all they learned from Boneshaker.

'So, we now know, from Boneshaker, that Stevenson found out about the mistress—and her being with child—in the first few months after the marriage.' The colonel clapped his hands. 'What now?'

Darcy looked from his cousin to the captain.

'Is Northamptonshire the connection? That letter on Sir Walter's desk—the one dismissed by Shepherd as a begging letter—held the county's postmark and a lady's hand.'

'Could be a request for funds for herself, or for the child?' The captain shrugged.

'But how does that relate to the payments to Williams and Aubert?' None of it added up, and all Darcy gained was an ache in the head to balance the one he bore permanently in his breast.

It was as though he had come close to uncovering the secret, but it remained tantalisingly out of reach, as though shrouded in veils.

'We need to speak to Mrs Williams.' Darcy looked from his cousin to the captain. 'Is she likely to acquiesce?'

'Not if she is being paid for her silence.' The colonel looked sceptical. 'It is no inconsiderable sum. If Mrs Williams *is* the recipient, she will not want to lose it.'

'But what choice do we have? We have no other trails to follow.'

The tendrils of hope swirling through Darcy disintegrated. 'It still makes no sense. How can a Miss Ward in Northamptonshire be in any way connected to Mrs Williams, or Mademoiselle Aubert, as she was back then?'

'There is only one way to find out.'

Darcy was weary of the debate. It went round in circles, when all he wished to do was seek out Elizabeth. He had yet to see her today.

Captain Wentworth stood up. 'I spoke to Anne earlier. She sent a note to Mrs Williams to find out her plans. She may not know whatever we might discover about her father, but there is no love lost between them. I doubt it could lower her opinion of Sir Walter any further. Let me see if she has received word.'

It was almost a half hour later before the captain returned, Anne by his side.

'Forgive me, Darcy. I had to explain some reasons for your present circumstances to justify requesting an audience of Mrs Williams. Anne will respect the confidence.'

Anne walked up to Darcy, her expression solemn and her colour high.

'Suspicious though I was of how your engagement to my sister had come about, sir, I had no notion of its being so bad. I cannot believe—' Her voice was indicative of her emotion, and the captain stepped forward to hold her hand. 'Mattie is to leave Somersetshire on the morrow. They are returning to Cornwall.' She regarded Darcy seriously. 'Frederick will not tell me why you wish to speak to her, other than she might be able to assist you. Mattie has the kindest, most generous disposition, and I am certain she will oblige, if you will give me permission to explain a little of your present situation?'

What other consideration was there? 'You may tell her what you wish, Miss Elliot. I do not want to cause her distress, but if there is anything she feels she can share with me, I will be eternally grateful.'

Anne studied him for a moment. 'I made a promise, Mr Darcy, when you were so kind to me in my moment of need, to repay you in kind. It is the least I can do.'

An hour later, Boliver appeared in the doorway to the study.

'There are some callers, sir. A Mrs Williams, accompanied by her husband.'

The colonel and the captain got to their feet. 'We will wait in the conservatory, Darcy.'

'Does Miss Anne Elliot wish to be present, Wentworth?'

He shook his head. 'Apparently, Mattie requested that she is not.'

As they left the room, Darcy turned to stare out of the window, his heart pounding in his chest. What would this meeting deliver?

Within a few minutes, Darcy welcomed the couple, offering them tea or coffee, both of which were politely declined.

'I am grateful for your time, Mrs Williams.'

'I would do anything Anne asked of me, sir. She was her mother's dearest child and is thus equally dear to me.' The lady reached out and grasped her husband's hand. 'My husband knows all I am about to share with you, from him I have no secrets.'

Their close bond was almost palpable, and Darcy envied it. There was no likelihood his marriage to Miss Elliot would produce such a one.

'You understand my situation?' Darcy looked from the lady to the gentleman.

'Miss Elliot gave Mattie to understand there is some duress in the matter, that you are unable to free yourself because of a threat of exposure that would damage a family member.' Mr Williams held Darcy's regard openly. 'We are not privy to any details, and you can trust my wife. She is well able to keep her silence when it is warranted.'

Mrs Williams fixed Darcy with a firm eye. 'I cannot promise anything I share will be of worth, for though I have a tale to tell, it is merely one as old as time.'

'Please, ma'am, begin. Let us hope your information will guide me.'

When the afternoon post came, Elizabeth escaped from the drawing room and hurried over to the cottage. Thankful for the distraction of news from home and praying Jane's letter continued in the same vein as the last, Elizabeth sank onto a sofa and broke the seal, her eyes scanning the opening lines. Then, her breath hitched in her throat and tears stung her eyes.

Tugging a handkerchief from her sleeve, Elizabeth dabbed at the wetness, that she might more clearly read the words. Jane had much to say, covering both sides of the paper and writing, as was often their fashion, across the lines as well.

Despite the turmoil in her breast, relief consumed Elizabeth. It had been months since Jane had filled anything more than a single side with her news, and she turned her full attention to the letter's content. Scarcely had she reached the end, when a sound drew her attention, and she looked up to see Anne entering the room.

'Are you well, Lizzy? You left so precipitously, I feared—'

'There is nothing to concern.' For what felt like the first time in ages, Elizabeth felt true happiness. 'It is the best of news, Anne. Jane is free of her engagement to Mr Collins!'

'Good heavens! How did it come about?'

Elizabeth scooted along the sofa so Anne could sit beside her.

'My father wrote by express to Mr Collins as soon as Jane confessed that she could no longer stand by her engagement.' Elizabeth laughed. 'Apparently, Mama was unhappy about Mr Bingley's constant presence at Longbourn, and demanded my father instruct him to stay away. She feared Jane would give up Mr Collins, only for Mr Bingley to head for the hills once more.'

'So how was it resolved?'

'My mother has taken the pressure off, because someone— and I suspect I know who—previously suggested to Mr Bingley that he remind my mother of the fine dower house he could offer her, when the time came. Not only did it reassure of his future intentions, but she well comprehends all the Longbourn estate can offer the widow is a small cottage, not even as spacious as this, and with much inferior decor. '

Anne smiled widely. 'Oh, Lizzy, I am so pleased for you, and for your sister.'

'There is no formal engagement yet, for I think Jane feels it is too soon and fears it will damage the gentleman's reputation, but Mr Bingley has persuaded Jane to consider his suit, telling her they will move to Timbuktu and begin a new life as camel merchants, if it will make her happier.'

'I like the sound of this Mr Bingley.' Anne sighed contentedly. 'He will be a fine brother-in-law for you.'

This brought an unwelcome recollection, however. Such a close connection when the gentleman was a firm friend of Mr Darcy...

'You look saddened, Lizzy. Too much so for these happy tidings.'

The gentle voice roused Elizabeth, and she shook her head. 'How can I be unhappy? You are finally to wed your captain, and now my sister is released from a bind she should never have put herself in.'

Anne placed a hand on Elizabeth's arm as they got to their feet. 'Other people's happiness, no matter how much you love them, is always harder to bear when you are grieving a loss.'

Elizabeth sighed. How true it was, yet she summoned a smile all the same as they walked to the door.

'It is strange how our positions have almost reversed since I came to Somersetshire.' Her brow furrowed as they went out into the hall. 'There is an anomaly regarding Mr Darcy's engagement to your sister.'

Anne's countenance was filled with compassion, and Elizabeth shook her head.

'You doubt my words. It is not because of my feelings for the gentleman.'

'I do not question them. I know them to be true, and I am certain I comprehend the gentleman's feelings all too well. I would say, 'I told you so', but I know such sentiments are both unwelcome and unnecessary. Let us go back to the house.' Anne tugged the front door open. 'You are better to have company, and I would not have you stay here on your own.'

'I am perfectly well. Jane's good news after all these weeks of worry has been a happy release.' Elizabeth meant it. Though her heart remained heavy regarding Mr Darcy, knowing the joy Jane could anticipate was a balm to her fraught emotions.

Darcy stared thoughtfully over at Willow Cottage as Anne and Elizabeth emerged. Mrs Williams's tale had been absorbing. It was indeed as old as time in its origins, but it was also an extraordinary story of darkness and light. A notion, however, troubled him, and he was frustrated he could not discern what it was.

The door opened and Colonel Fitzwilliam and Captain Wentworth entered, their faces expectant, and waving them into the comfortable chairs either side of the hearth, Darcy came to the centre of the room.

'That was an interesting experience.'

An understatement, Darcy.

The colonel exchanged a look with the captain, then rolled his eyes at his cousin. 'Well, come on then. Out with it. Do we have hope?'

'Did you not say, Wentworth, there is always hope?'

Captain Wentworth inclined his head at Darcy. 'So long as you hold onto it.'

'Then I shall attempt to do so.'

He leaned against the edge of his desk and began.

'Mrs Williams—Mathilde—was, as you know, employed at first by James Stevenson as his only child's personal maid. The young ladies were close in age and, notwithstanding the bond that can develop through the intimacy of such relationships, with Miss Stevenson having no brothers or sisters, they quickly became confidential friends.'

The colonel gestured at the clock on the mantel. 'You will be challenging Shepherd for slowness of exposition if you are not careful, Darce.'

Darcy threw him a frustrated look. 'Do you want to hear it or not?'

Assuming an attentive expression, the colonel grinned, and Darcy continued.

'When Miss Stevenson became Lady Elliot, in the summer of 1784, Mrs Williams accompanied the lady to her new situation at Kellynch Hall.'

'Whatever induced Lady Elliot to marry an idiot like her husband?' The captain looked from Darcy to the colonel.

'According to Mrs Williams, youthful infatuation with the man's appearance, quite out of nature in her mistress, whom she claimed was of an extremely superior character, and generally both sensible and amiable.'

'No wonder Boneshaker claimed Stevenson to be unimpressed.' The colonel stretched out his legs. 'Carry on, Darce.'

'Hardly had the New Year turned, when it came to light Sir Walter had been having an affair of long-standing—'

'With this Ward woman, like Boneshaker said?' The colonel regarded the clock again. 'Is it time for a drink yet?'

'Most indubitably, and no.' Darcy settled more comfortably against the desk, trying to keep the facts in order in his mind.

'Why did Elliot not wed this lady, if the affair had been long-standing?' Captain Wentworth folded his arms on his chest. 'He must have been taken with her, or even attached, especially to continue it after his marriage.'

'Mrs Williams was able to give some background, for Lady Elliot had confided in her once she knew the truth. Apparently, Miss Maria Ward, Miss Ward's younger sister, wed a baronet, Sir Thomas Bertram of Mansfield Park in Northamptonshire.'

'Ha!' The colonel beamed. 'The Northamptonshire connection!'

Darcy ignored him. 'Miss Ward had aspirations of achieving the same, setting her sights on Sir Walter Elliot, and she had some success, in that they entered into a relationship. Her wishes may even have come to fruition, had an incident not occurred that turned the gentleman away from her. Her other sister, Miss Frances Ward, made an extremely poor alliance, marrying the low-born, ill-educated and highly undistinguished Mr Price. Balking at the connection, Sir Walter distanced himself, turning instead to pay his attentions to the wealthy Miss Stevenson, who lived in the neighbouring county of Gloucestershire.'

'Seriously, Darce. I am not doing all the talking, and *I* am parched!'

Darcy glared at his cousin, then looked at the clock. If it would silence him, then they had best all take a drink. 'Go ahead.'

The colonel strode over to the tray and filled three glasses liberally with brandy, handing them out as he returned to his seat.

'Continue.' He settled back contentedly.

'Somehow—neither Mrs Williams nor Lady Elliot seemed to know—the affair recommenced soon after Sir Walter married, and although Miss Ward was cautioned by her family to end it, she did not, and within a few months, discovered she was with child.'

Darcy took a long drink of his brandy. 'Under Lady Bertram's persuasion, Sir Thomas agreed to stand by her sister but refused to take on the child if it was safely delivered. He would only allow Miss Ward to remain under his protection on the condition it would go to an orphanage.'

The colonel made a sound. 'How noble of him.'

'Indeed.' Darcy drew in a breath. 'Someone of a more charitable nature intervened.'

The colonel's eyes narrowed. 'Who was he? Come on, Darce, out with it!'

Darcy considered all he had so recently learned. Would his cousin be as astonished as he had been?

'It was the late Lady Elliot.'

CHAPTER FORTY-NINE

The colonel shot up in his seat, brandy sloshing over his hand.

'Damn it!' He put the glass down and pulled out a handkerchief. 'Go on, man, do not mind me!'

Captain Wentworth looked as astonished as Darcy felt on learning of it.

'When the prospective fate of the unborn child became known to Lady Elliot, she was distressed. Mrs Williams said that, as an only child, conceived with difficulty, she had no confidence in producing offspring herself. The marriage was already more than six months old, with no sign of success. She made the proposal that the child, once delivered, be brought to Kellynch and passed off as her own.'

The colonel stared at Darcy in disbelief, but the captain seemed discomfited. 'Anne knows nothing of this, I am certain.'

'How was such a deception carried out?' The colonel laced his fingers and rested his hands on his chest. 'I am thoroughly diverted.' He eyed Darcy seriously. 'Assuming there is some promise in all of this rather than the plot for a crowd-pleasing novel?'

'With the help of Mrs Williams. A personal maid was in the perfect position to assist Lady Elliot in a pretence at pregnancy, being so intimately acquainted with her dress and toilette. Miss Ward's child was due in the summer, and when the time came, an express was sent to Kellynch and shortly after, the baby was brought there, under cover of darkness. Mrs Williams took delivery of the child, taking it by way of the servants' staircase to Lady Elliot's chamber, where it was widely reported her confinement had come a little early.'

'And henceforth, the child became Miss Elizabeth Elliot.'

'Yes, though Sir Walter wished to give his first-born another name. Lady Elliot, according to Mrs Williams, stood her ground, insisting it be named after her.'

The colonel released a low whistle, but the captain drained his glass.

'What am I to tell Anne? I do not know how she will take this.'

'That she is the eldest daughter?'

'Hmph. The eldest legitimate daughter'—snorted the colonel as he too drained his glass.

Darcy returned to his place, leaning against the desk. There it was again, the notion he missed something.

'Will it silence Sir Walter?'

Looking over at the captain, Darcy shrugged. 'I have no idea. He is desperate for his daughter to be wed.'

'If only we could have the success he has with Mrs Williams. She has kept her secret a long time.'

'Sir Walter paid her well for the silence, initially when she was in his employ as Aubert, and when she left after the death of Lady Elliot, he continued to pay. The agreement was she would be paid until Elizabeth Elliot was safely wed and financially secure under a husband's protection.'

'Why was she prepared to speak out now?'

'She has been anticipating the termination of the payments ever since Miss Elliot reached marriageable age. Having learnt what she recently had from Miss Anne Elliot, she wished the association over directly. The money was useful when she left service, enabling her to establish herself, even saving to provide a small dowry. The funds have been utilised over the years for good causes, charitable institutions, and to support medical research.'

The colonel blew out a breath. 'Quite the woman.'

'Indeed.' Captain Wentworth shook his head. 'What a story. It makes me thankful Lady Elliot had such a friend through difficult times. What a man Stevenson was!'

Darcy's head shot up as he realised what escaped him.

'So, this begs the question: Why is Miss Elliot listed on the addendum as a legitimate child? Boneshaker said only Stevenson had the distinction of being able to notify them to add a name.'

Shrugging, the colonel leaned back in his chair. 'I think the question is more *how* than why, Darce.'

Darcy's mind spun. 'There is no way Sir Walter could have requested it be added. Stevenson would never have allowed it—it would contradict the entire purpose of the addendum.'

Captain Wentworth shrugged. 'The man has covered his tracks well. Have you seen his copy of the *Baronetage*? Miss Elliot is formally listed therein.'

The *Baronetage*…a shadow of memory floated towards Darcy, and as his mind grasped it, he straightened from his position against the desk.

'I know not how it was perpetrated, but I would put my own money on Sir Walter adding that name.'

'But the legal firm had strict instructions.' The captain looked to the colonel, then back to Darcy. 'It would be impossible, for only this Stevenson could add names.'

'You would be surprised the value of an annotation.' Darcy spoke firmly. 'The first time I saw the book up at the Hall, I noticed all the additions Sir Walter had made to the printed text. Those were the words he used. Somehow, I think he managed to annotate the document held in Knight & Dey's office.'

The three men exchanged a look.

'I think we need to talk to Shepherd, Darce.' The colonel got to his feet. 'An attempt to defraud the trust is exactly the weapon we sought, but without proof, it holds no ammunition.'

Once a note had been dispatched to Shepherd, the captain left them alone, expressing the desire to speak to Anne, though he owned to having no notion of what he could or should share with her. It was, indeed, a delicate matter.

For the following hour, Darcy and the colonel settled in seats beside the hearth and went over all they had uncovered, considering the best way to present these astonishing findings to Sir Walter.

Then, the colonel stretched in his seat. 'When will you go up to the Hall?'

'First thing in the morning. I waver between hoping Sir Walter will wish Miss Elliot's lineage kept hidden and fearing he will brush it aside, question my feint, so I wish to understand all I can about the annotated document.'

The colonel rubbed his chin thoughtfully. 'Is there any merit in approaching this Bertram chap? He knows about it, after all, and has harboured his sister-in-law's secret these many years. Can you not threaten Sir Walter with this Bertram's wrath being brought down upon him if the lady is revealed as having given birth to Miss Elliot?'

Darcy shrugged. 'It is worth a try, perhaps, but Northamptonshire is a long way from here, and one can hardly send the request in a letter.' He walked over to stare out into the garden. Would this torture ever end? 'How is one to achieve anything in the time left? The marriage license is no doubt already winging its way to Sir Walter as we speak, and—'

A knock on the door heralded the stately arrival of Boliver.

'Mr Shepherd is here, sir.'

'Show him in, please.'

Darcy waved the man into a seat.

'Thank you for coming so promptly, Shepherd, and so late in the day. I have a question I hope you can answer, but first, let me tell you all we have learned.'

He related as succinctly as possible the facts emanating from the interview with Mrs Williams, and for a moment, Shepherd simply stared at Darcy, astonishment writ clear upon his countenance. His mouth opened, then closed, and he looked to the colonel, then back at the gentleman opposite.

'I know not what to say, Mr Darcy. Though we had suspicions of there being a child, I had no notion of the complexity of the truth.'

'Nor did we.' Darcy stirred restlessly in his seat. 'I mean to confront Sir Walter directly, but wanted to ask about the addendum. How could Miss Elliot be listed if only Mr Stevenson had the power to add names?'

Shepherd frowned. 'An excellent question, sir. I have only seen the document exactly as shown to you the other day. It was thus when I joined Sir Walter at the legal firm and—' He stopped, his eyes widening. Then, he shook his head. 'No, surely not.'

The colonel threw Darcy a frustrated look.

'What is it, Shepherd?'

The lawyer got slowly to his feet. 'The meeting at Knight & Dey—to establish Mrs Musgrove's trust, prior to her marriage—you will recall I found Sir Walter alone in the office, having arrived late?'

Nodding, Darcy shifted in his seat again. Were they finally nearing the prize?

'The original documentation for the trust, set up in 1785, was on the desk. I did not have sight of it, of course, until the clerk returned, and the meeting commenced.' Shepherd narrowed his eyes, clearly trying to remember. 'Sir Walter bore an air of complacency, which I put down to his supposition he would be able to persuade the lady to share some of the money. But—'

There was a pause, and Darcy leaned forward. 'But?'

'After we left the offices, Sir Walter spoke to the effect of the fund bringing financial benefit. At first, I assumed he meant as I have just suggested, that his daughter would be open to handing some of the money to her father.' Shepherd's expression remained serious. 'Might he have made the alteration to the document on that day?'

Darcy's brain whirred. 'But would you not have noted the familiar hand?'

'I did not look for it, sir. It has only just occurred to me. Besides, each entry was in the hand of a different clerk, as you would expect, and he would surely have made some effort at concealment.' Shepherd looked astounded. 'It explains the disparity in the spacing on the original. I had noted it but thought little enough of it. There was a gap between the names of Miss Anne Elliot and Miss Mary Elliot. Sir Walter must have fitted Miss Elliot's name in *above* the former, thus emphasising the larger space remaining between the other two names.' Shepherd looked from Darcy to the colonel. 'I cannot believe it, but it is the only way.'

'Could it have been done at any other time?'

Shepherd shook his head. 'As far as I know, the only other time Sir Walter was in that office was after his wife died. My father would have attended him on that occasion.'

'Then there is a chance he did it back then.' Once again, hope faded, and Darcy sank back against the chair consumed with disappointment. 'Whichever it was, he has successfully added it to the original copy, which makes it appear legally binding, and no one will ever know it was not there all along.'

'Unless we can *prove* Sir Walter made the alteration.' Shepherd's expression was more animated than Darcy had ever seen, his eyes bright and his air agitated. 'And there may be a chance of that. Do you recall, sir, it was noted on the file that Sir Walter had been given a certified copy of the document, including the addendum, when the separate estate settlement passed into the hands of Lady Elliot's children, back in 1800?'

Darcy raised a brow. 'I do.'

'I have no idea where this is going,' murmured the colonel, 'but I am more engrossed than if I watched the most riveting of plays on the stage.'

Shepherd walked back across the room to stand before Darcy. 'I know where the older copy is. Sir Walter may have forgotten it exists or where it is.'

Darcy's interest was profound.

'If the annotation was done last year, then there should only be two names on this older copy.'

'And if it is so,' Darcy drew in a sharp breath. 'We have him.'

'Yes, by god.' The colonel slapped a hand on the desk, and Shepherd jumped. 'He has attempted to cheat the Trust, and that would be the proof.'

'Then he has committed more than one offense. Not only has he falsified a legal document, he has perpetrated a crime, that of fraud.' Shepherd looked to the colonel, then back at Darcy. 'Mrs Musgrove, you see, has received only a third of her entitlement, instead of a half share of the funds, and the same can be said for Miss Anne Elliot upon her marriage. Miss Elizabeth Elliot is not eligible for a single penny.'

'This is grand larceny.' Darcy's heart pounded through sheer relief.

'And the gentleman is a coward, Mr Darcy. Make him aware of your comprehension of his fraudulent actions. Tell him you will see him convicted and sentenced, if he does not comply with your terms.'

'Where is the older copy, Shepherd?'

'I came across it by chance when going back through the archives during the ball. I started with 1800. As well as soon identifying the pattern of payments in the other name, I came across several files, one of which pertained to Lady Elliot's passing. I gave it a cursory look. It was mainly receipts for the funeral costs, mourning jewellery and so on, but there was a copy of the separate estate trust in there. I did not bother to examine it because I had the copy I had recently collected, but now I think it needs retrieving.'

'Shepherd, I have done you a disservice.' The colonel got up and slapped the man on his back. 'Well, what are you waiting for?'

'Dawn, Richard. Shepherd can hardly go barging in at this hour to raid the archives.'

'The Sabbath?' The colonel's brow rose. 'Of course. Sir Walter will not attend church because he cannot. You will have him captive, Darce.'

'And that is all I require, and I will not delay.'

'You can always attend evensong Cousin.' The colonel looked to Shepherd. 'Let us hope it is to give thanks rather than pray for your soul.'

Darcy rose to his feet. 'I do not know how to thank you, Shepherd.'

'It has been my pleasure, sir. Truly.' The man smiled, a rarity, and Darcy returned it. 'We cannot be confident until we see the earlier copy, but you have more than delivered on my part, and I am hopeful I am about to reciprocate. I only wish it had not been at the eleventh hour.'

The hour be damned. Finally, Darcy had hope.

CHAPTER FIFTY

After so many disturbed nights, Elizabeth woke late on Sunday morning. She blinked her tired eyelids, then rolled onto her side, emitting a soft sigh. Such strange dreams haunted her, and it took a few moments for the effects to recede and reality intrude.

'The water is ready, miss.'

Sitting up, Elizabeth pushed her hair back over her shoulders.

'Thank you, Elise.'

'I shall return to help you dress directly.'

She disappeared through the door, and Elizabeth threw back the coverlet with a heavy heart.

This was her last day at Willow Cottage—for on the morrow she must tear herself away from Mr Darcy and, much as she longed to see Jane, no hint of homesickness could penetrate the deep sadness she felt over her imminent departure from Somersetshire. Her only solace would be the memories she held dear, of spending Christmas with Mr Darcy in his home, and of those few moments between them when she had truly felt his regard for her. They would remain with her forever, and she would cherish them.

Standing up, Elizabeth stretched and walked over to the dressing room and began to prepare for the day, determined to think of better things, and of all she gained from her stay, the friendship of Anne Elliot—so soon to be Mrs Wentworth—would be the most prized henceforth.

A half hour later, Elizabeth inspected her appearance in the looking glass, doubting her hair would ever look quite so sophisticated again.

She surveyed the room wistfully. How uncomfortable she had felt, that first night in the cottage. Yet now, how she loved it.

And the gentleman who gave us sanctuary.

'I will always love him,' she whispered as she walked to the window to take in the expanse of Meadowbrook House. 'At least I shall always have the comfort of knowing what it is to truly love, to comprehend that a man such as Mr Darcy once held me in the greatest esteem.'

In danger of her spirits sinking, Elizabeth raised her chin. She had to make the most of today, and with that in mind, she hurried from her room in search of Anne.

At ten in the morning, Darcy strode from his study and into the entrance hall, where Boliver assisted him into his great coat, but as he tugged on his gloves, a movement caught his eye, and he espied Elizabeth on the terrace at the back of the house.

Pressing though his call was, he could not depart without speaking to her, and he walked swiftly to the door and stepped out.

'Oh!' Perceiving his approach, Elizabeth stopped her pacing. 'I did not expect to see you.' She gestured with a hand at the cottage. 'I am waiting on Anne.'

Darcy walked to where she stood, then took her hand in his, studying the paleness of her skin. 'You will take cold out here with no gloves on.' He raised his head, concerned. 'And no shawl to protect you.'

'It is only for a moment, sir. We are coming into the house to sit with Miss Darcy.'

Though the outcome of his call on Sir Walter was not yet determined, Darcy's anguish over Elizabeth's departure was insurmountable.

'I have a duty to carry out, and I must go directly to the Hall.'

Elizabeth's gaze held his. 'If I could relieve you of whatever agitates you so, I would, Mr Darcy. Must you truly go to a place from which you appear to derive little solace?'

Touched, he placed his other hand over hers. 'God-willing, this may be the last time. Hold that hope for me.'

She said nothing for a moment, and he all but held his breath, but then she raised her chin. 'I will pray, in your absence, for the outcome you most desire, sir.'

There was little else to be said, and with a gentle squeeze of her hand, he bowed and turned on his heel.

The ride to Kellynch Hall passed in a flurry of memories—of Darcy's first sight of Elizabeth, the tortuous early days of their acquaintance, to the increasingly intimate encounters of more recent days. Somehow, he had to make this work.

Shepherd awaited him on the doorstep, and Darcy handed the reins to a waiting groom and followed him into the house. He never feared confrontation, but so much hinged on this meeting, his future hanging so perilously in the balance, and tension had a firm hold on his rigid frame.

'I shall join you directly, sir.' Shepherd set off for the lower floor, and Darcy paced to and fro in the great hall. For all the agony Sir Walter had put Darcy through, when it was finally the time to face him, he mostly just wanted to be done with it, that he might be able to seek out Elizabeth and finally tell her the truth. It was time to make Fate swing in his favour.

Within five minutes, he was shown into the drawing room, where Sir Walter reclined with a newspaper, his injured ankle still bound tightly and resting on a stool. Thankfully, Miss Elliot was nowhere in sight.

'Ah, Darcy. Fortuitous timing.' He put the paper aside and straightened, gesturing at a piece of parchment on a side table. 'The license arrived this morning. The date is set for this coming Friday.'

'May I?' Darcy pointed at the document.

'You may, but do not think of tearing it up.'

'I have no need to destroy it.'

Darcy spoke with confidence, but he did not feel it. He briefly noted the wording, before folding it up and returning it to the table. His heart pounded in his breast. He only hoped the earlier copy addendum would deliver what Shepherd suspected.

'Sit down, man.' Sir Walter waved an impatient hand. 'I shall gain a crick in the neck from looking up at you.'

This was more than adequate inducement for Darcy to remain standing.

'It is a shame you went to the expense of obtaining a special license. I have come to advise you that I will not be marrying your daughter.'

Sir Walter looked a little surprised, but then he laughed. 'I think you will, Darcy. Oh, you must consider yourself so clever. I do not know how you did it but removing your sister's letter from my safe will not save her. I have not forgotten the content and will not hesitate to repeat it loud and far if you so much as hint at deserting my daughter.'

Darcy clenched a fist at the self-righteous expression on the man's face.

'I am not forsaking Miss Elliot by stepping away from an obligation *you* forced upon me, against my will, and announced without my consent. I told you I would consider your terms, but I never agreed to them.'

Sir Walter's face turned red. 'I will not have my daughter humiliated!'

'Then you should not have announced an unconfirmed engagement to all your acquaintance. It is also the epitome of self-centredness to condemn the mortification and potential damage to Miss Elliot's reputation whilst simultaneously threatening my sister with the same.' Darcy opened the leather folder. 'I am not here to fight, Sir Walter. I am here as a courtesy, to explain why *you* will not dispute the dissolution of this fallacy of an engagement.'

Sir Walter smirked. 'You attempt to intimidate me with your airs. That might work on the weaker sex, Mr Darcy, but it does nothing for me.'

Ignoring him, Darcy removed a copy of the estate settlement trust from the leather folder he held.

'Permit me to persuade you to my way of thinking. You asked Shepherd to obtain this, I believe, from the legal firm representing the interests of the late Mr James Stevenson.'

His eyes narrowing, Sir Walter stared at the document in Darcy's hand. 'What of it? Elizabeth's share is due to her upon the marriage date.'

'Perhaps you have forgotten all that it contains?'

Sir Walter's face blanched. 'I know not what you mean.'

'This,' Darcy placed the folder on the seat behind him, and flicked through the pages to the back, holding it up to show Sir Walter. 'Is the addendum, documenting the offspring legally entitled to a share of the Trust.'

'What of it?'

Darcy raised a brow. 'There is a discrepancy, Sir Walter. You have two legitimate children, yet there are three names on here.'

His face as white as the binding of his ankle, Sir Walter made to get up, but fell back with an exclamation of pain. 'Damn you, Darcy. What game are you playing?'

'Not the same one you are, thankfully.' Darcy took a step closer, holding the page out to Sir Walter and pointing to the word 'legitimate'.

'Somehow, Miss Elliot's name is on this list.'

Sir Walter began to breathe rapidly, his skin fluctuating from white to red, a film of wetness appearing on his brow.

'How dare you speak so of my daughter,' he hissed.

'How did you do it? How did this name become added to this document?'

'I do not know what you are insinuating, Darcy.'

'But you will admit to Miss Elliot not being a daughter of your late wife? There is little point in denying it, for I know the whole sorry story of Miss Ward.'

Still breathing rapidly, Sir Walter pulled out a handkerchief and mopped his sweating brow. 'Aubert! She will receive no more funds from me! How dare she?'

Darcy's anger built rapidly. 'How dare *you*, sir. Mrs Williams has done all and more than was asked of her. You wished your eldest wed so you could stop making the payments—money you can ill afford to pay, but more than that.' He held up the addendum again. 'You hoped to gain access to some of the funds set aside by Mr Stevenson, by having a share illegally paid to Miss Elliot.'

Sir Walter's regular colour returned, and he shifted in his position, drawing himself up as best he could when seated. 'Prove it. You cannot. Once you are married to my daughter, the payments to Aubert cease naturally, and the meeting Shepherd attended in London set things in motion for Elizabeth to receive her share of the fund. There is the end of the matter.' He assumed an arrogant expression. 'That document you hold is certified as a copy of the original document in Knight & Dey's office—a *legal* confirmation of my eldest daughter being born within wedlock.'

The man's arrogance was extraordinary.

'Let me be clear, Darcy, I will not—'

They both looked over as the door opened, and Darcy released a taut breath as Shepherd entered.

'What the devil are you doing here again, Shepherd? I thought you finished this week's business yesterday?'

'I had one last service to perform, sir.' Shepherd stepped forward and held out a document to Darcy with a momentous look.

Relief almost swept his breath away.

'What is that?' Sir Walter snapped, pointing a hand at the document. 'Shepherd!' Rage filled the man's face as he tried to reach his lawyer, only to end up prostrated across the couch, his bad ankle falling heavily from the stool, and he emitted a howl of pain.

Darcy made to move forward to assist him, but Shepherd stayed him with a hand as the door opened and two footmen came rushing in.

'I think Sir Walter requires a little assistance.'

They hurried to set him up again, but as soon as they had done so, he waved them away impatiently. 'Get out of here!'

The footmen scurried from the room and Darcy turned the pages to the addendum of the certified copy he held, dated 1800. There it was, just as Shepherd surmised—the proof.

'Not only is your daughter guilty of theft, but you, sir, have committed a most serious crime, and we now have that all-important proof.' Darcy raised the second document. 'You know full well what this is, do you not?'

Sir Walter's fierce stare landed on Shepherd again. 'You…you…how *dare* you enter the archives without my express permission!' His roar could probably be heard down in the kitchens. 'Get out of my sight and out of my employ! Your services are no longer required. You are dismissed!'

'I am afraid you cannot do that, Sir Walter.' Shepherd withdrew a piece of paper from his waistcoat and placed it on the couch beside the gentleman. 'You see, I have already resigned my position.'

He turned to Darcy and handed him a letter bearing a familiar hand 'You may wish to ask about this too? I will await you outside, sir.'

Once Shepherd left the room, silence descended as Darcy studied the lettering on the letter he held.

'Would you care to explain what these letters are? From Miss Ward, I suspect? Or shall I read it for myself?'

'You will not read my personal correspondence!' Sir Walter tried to get up again and failed, and he almost snorted in his frustration. 'You have no right to do so.'

Darcy merely raised a brow, though the irony of Sir Walter's words were lost on the man as he struggled to sit up without disturbing the lay of his coat.

He made as though to unfold the letter.

'Fine, fine!' Sir Walter gestured at it, and Darcy handed it over. 'That damned Norris woman—Miss Ward as was—became a widow some seven years ago, and since then has been on reduced means. She has been writing every so often to try and get my sympathies roused—had the preposterous notion of suggesting we renew our acquaintance. Never had any other children either, and wanted to meet Elizabeth.' Sir Walter screwed the letter up and threw it across the room.

'Does Miss Elliot comprehend the truth?'

Sir Walter said nothing for a minute, then glared at Darcy. 'She found out last year.'

Darcy raised a brow. 'Did you tell her?'

'No, damn it, I did not!' Sir Walter growled, gesturing to where the ball of paper lay. 'She happened to come across'—he gestured to the ball of paper on the floor—'one of that woman's letters.'

'Your daughter has a talent for coming across other people's correspondence, sir. You would do well to tame her predilection.'

Satisfied there were no more secrets, Darcy placed both copy documents into his leather folder and sealed it, before walking over to retrieve the marriage license.

'I believe we are agreed, then, Sir Walter? I will not have your daughter charged with theft and will keep her illegitimacy—and the proof of your crime—to myself, as a result of which, you will not face the gallows or worse. In return, you will maintain your silence over anything you may have assumed from reading my sister's private correspondence. You will never mention the letter.'

A myriad of expressions flit across Sir Walter's face, his eyes darting from left to right as he clearly sought a way out. Then, he wilted.

'What letter? I saw no letter.'

'Precisely.'

Darcy turned on his heel, but Sir Walter called out frantically. 'What am I to tell Elizabeth?'

Having reached the door, Darcy shrugged. 'Thankfully, sir, that is none of my business. I will begin my withdrawal from Meadowbrook House as soon as possible but will not be calling at Kellynch Hall again. You may consider our acquaintance at an end.'

Having said his farewells to Shepherd, along with expressing his gratitude once more, Darcy sped along the lane on Gunnar, the cold winter air sweeping aside the tension and anger from the past few weeks, his heart finally accepting he was free.

Free to address Elizabeth at long last.

Darcy entered the house quietly, making his way to the study without encountering anyone, to find his cousin and the captain deep in conversation by the hearth.

'Well?' The colonel stood up, as Darcy looked from him to the captain with an inscrutable expression.

Then, unable to conceal his relief any longer, he broke into a wide grin, and the colonel whooped and stepped forward to clap him on the back, and Captain Wentworth rose from his chair to shake Darcy's hand vigorously.

'I am freed of my obligation, and Georgiana's secret is safe.'

Just being able to say the words brought a restriction to his throat, and Darcy turned away for a moment, conscious of his cousin's comforting hand on his back.

Then, he blew out a breath. 'I must speak to Georgiana, and then I wish to seek out Miss Bennet.'

The colonel smirked. 'Yes, but first you must enlighten us as to how the conversation went.'

Darcy obliged, then added his thanks to both men for supporting him over the past difficult days. The colonel was all for raising a toast, but Darcy declined. Until he was completely sure of Elizabeth, he could not celebrate, and leaving both gentlemen to their deliberations, he headed back down the hall in search of the ladies.

There was no one in the drawing room, and he walked along to the music room, only to find Anne in there, practising an air.

'I believe Miss Darcy went up to her room for a while.' She sent Darcy an amused look. 'And Lizzy went over to the cottage for her pelisse. She wished to take some air. May I ask, sir, if your call at Kellynch delivered all you hoped for?'

'You may, and yes, it did. I regret any embarrassment it will cause your sister, but I am now free of my obligation.'

'I could not be happier, Mr Darcy. For you and for…your loved ones.'

Acknowledging her kind words, Darcy turned for the door.

'Oh, and Mr Darcy?'

He looked back at Anne.

'Lizzy intended to walk in the rose garden.' With that, the lady returned her attention to the keys of the pianoforte, and Darcy set off in search of his sister, after which he would take a good long walk—and preferably not alone.

CHAPTER FIFTY-ONE

In the hour since Mr Darcy had ridden up to Kellynch, Elizabeth had all but worn a hole in the cottage floor, such was her pacing. She was currently in danger of doing the same to the stone path weaving through the barren rose garden.

What could be happening up there? Was there any chance Mr Darcy had found a way to extricate himself from his enforced engagement?

He seemed quietly confident before he left, but what if it did not proceed as he hoped?

Elizabeth assessed the skies. The clouds were low, and the temperature had plummeted. Were they in for more snow? She shivered, but not just from the cold air brushing the skin of her face.

Turning on her heel, she trod briskly in the direction of the rose bower at the end of the walled garden. She had only gone a few paces, however, when she heard a step behind her. Mr Darcy was coming towards her.

Desperately trying to read his demeanour, Elizabeth all but held her breath as he neared. His countenance was unreadable, but his eyes were full of warmth as he fetched up before her.

'And sir?'

The gentleman's gaze raked her features. 'And now, I may do this.'

He leaned down and pressed a firm kiss upon Elizabeth's mouth, leaving her lips tingling from the touch and her cheeks glowing with hope.

'Is that a farewell, Mr Darcy, or a beginning?'

A smile caught the edges of his mouth, then formed fully. 'I am released from the binds of my engagement, such as it was.' Mr Darcy held out his hand, and she stared at it for a moment. 'Will you take my hand, Elizabeth?'

'If I do so, sir, then you will have to come with it, wherever I go.'

'Gladly.'

Such joy filled Elizabeth, as she had never known, wetness forming on her lashes as she took in the loving expression on his face. How she had inspired such feelings, she knew not. Her breath hitched, and with a laugh, Mr Darcy drew her to him.

'Is that a yes?'

'It is, sir.' Elizabeth rested her head against his chest. Suddenly, she did not feel the cold, despite the occasional flake of snow drifting down from the wintry sky.

'I made a foolish promise to myself when I was about thirteen. Nothing would persuade me into matrimony other than the deepest of affection. As I have grown, I began to realise how vain a desire it was.' She raised her head. 'You have proved me wrong, Mr Darcy. I could not love you more than I do now. At least, I do not believe I could, but perhaps you will prove me wrong as the years pass.'

'It will be my solemn duty.' He leaned down to kiss her, and words suddenly mattered little as they were able to finally express their true feelings for each other.

When they parted, Elizabeth drew in a calming breath. Blood pulsed through her veins as sensations she had never before experienced assailed her.

Conscious of the gentleman's affectionate attention, she studied his features. 'You have lost that drawn look I have discerned upon your face for far too long.'

Mr Darcy raised a hand and placed it gently against her face. 'It is the relief of being freed from my obligation.'

'Only to enter into another. Are you quite certain? You have had but the blink of an eye between them.'

He raised her hand and placed a kiss upon it. 'I have wanted to marry you for some time, Elizabeth. I even prepared a speech once.'

'I suspected as much, though not until later. Yet it seemed so incredible, I found it hard to believe.' She shook her head. 'We did not get on in Hertfordshire.'

Mr Darcy took her arm and placed it upon his own, turning their steps back along the path. 'I felt quite the contrary. I was enchanted by you from the earliest days of our acquaintance.'

Elizabeth laughed. 'But not on the first, when I believe I was not handsome enough to tempt you.'

He drew her to a halt. 'Can you ever forgive me? I was in a foul mood, having been dragged out by Bingley, tired of his sister's fawning attention and you know, by now, how much I enjoy a ball. I suspected you had overheard me, but such was my arrogance, I never considered the offence it might cause.' He sighed. 'You have humbled me, Elizabeth, made me see that although I had good principles, I sometimes followed them in pride and conceit.'

'Now, sir, you take too much on yourself. I believe you enjoyed concealing your true self from others, that it was armour of sorts. But I have found you out, seen your kindness and compassion for your fellow man, observed how important your family is to you.' It was Elizabeth's turn to reach out a hand and rest it against his face. How she relished being allowed the indulgence. 'I was in love with you before I even realised I had begun. When I thought I had lost you to another...'

She could no more put such pain into words as reach the moon.

Sweeping her into his arms, Mr Darcy held her close, then lowered his head to kiss her in thorough fashion, wiping away all thoughts of loss and pain.

'Dearest, loveliest Elizabeth. I suspect I have been falling in love since the first day we met, and once I had fallen, there was no going back. You have filled my every waking thought and haunted my dreams these past few months.'

'Heavens, that sounds positively exhausting. Who knew true affection could be so—'

'Incredible?'

'Sleep deprived.'

'At times, but no longer. Come.' Mr Darcy offered his arm again. 'Let us return to the house to share our news.'

They walked swiftly as the snow began to fall more steadily, and once in the boot room, the gentleman helped Elizabeth from her pelisse, then took her hand.

'You look rather pretty with snowflakes adorning your hair.'

Elizabeth's impish smile appeared. 'As do you, sir.'

Anne was in the drawing room alone when Elizabeth entered, and she hurried over to sit beside her.

'I have news. Mr Darcy and I are engaged to be married.' She was filled with such joy, it was hard to sit still, and when Anne quickly embraced her friend, Elizabeth laughed. 'I am struggling to contain my happiness. I cannot believe I have gone from sorrow to delight in a matter of minutes.'

'Oh, Lizzy! I am so happy for you. Frederick told me Mr Darcy had successfully gagged my father. I am ashamed to bear his name, cannot wait to relinquish it and become Mrs Wentworth.'

Elizabeth's mood sobered a little. 'And what of your sister, Miss Elliot?'

Anne assumed a thoughtful expression. 'I have oft wondered why we are so different. You would think, being half-sisters, we might share some commonality, but beyond the shade of hair colouring, I see nothing. I do not care if I ever see her again.' Anne squeezed Elizabeth's hand. 'I am so pleased, Lizzy, for you both. What will happen now? You will not depart on the morrow?'

'Mr Darcy wishes to call at Longbourn to speak to my father. He believes he can be ready to travel the day after.'

'Your family will be surprised.'

Elizabeth got to her feet, then hesitated. 'I am a little concerned for Mr Darcy's reception in Hertfordshire. You know how he can be perceived, Anne. He will be lucky if my mother lets him cross the threshold.'

The delight of securing Elizabeth's hand was all consuming at first, and Darcy found the unpleasantness of the preceding weeks fading rapidly, enhanced by a note from Kellynch Hall early the following morning.

'Here, Richard. Read this.'

He passed the note to his cousin as they broke their fast. What Anne would make of it, he had no idea.

Colonel Fitzwilliam raised a surprised brow. 'I had not supposed Sir Walter's brain capable of making such speedy decisions.'

Darcy laughed, taking back the note and skimming his eyes over it once more. 'Leasing out Kellynch Hall will have its merits, not least for his pocketbook.'

Getting to his feet, the colonel pointed to Darcy's empty cup. 'The estate and neighbourhood are also likely to benefit from having a steadier hand at the helm. To be certain, whomever it may be, they could not be worse.'

'He clearly plans to take no leave of anyone.' Darcy tossed the note aside, thankful for the postscript confirming a retraction of the engagement announcement would appear in *The Times* within eight and forty hours.

The colonel returned with two full cups of tea and retook his seat. 'I doubt either he or his eldest will be missed. I am surprised he is heading to Town, though. Surely his expenses will be more excessive than if he had chosen somewhere like Bath.'

Darcy assumed a thoughtful expression. 'I suspect he feels there will be more pickings for Miss Elliot to choose over.'

'You think this is about getting her married off, then, rather than skulking away and disappearing into the crowd?'

Darcy viewed his cousin over his cup. 'I do not think Sir Walter Elliot has the ability to feel shame. His desperation for public approval and admiration are what will keep Georgiana's secret safe.'

A snort came from the colonel. 'In addition to which, he is an inveterate coward, and would hardly fare well in the prison cells awaiting trial for grand larceny, let alone its outcome.'

'True. I am certain we shall read of Miss Elliot's engagement within a few months. Never have I encountered a man more determined to see a daughter wed.' Then, Darcy laughed again. 'Though I have observed one such mother. You must do your utmost to attend the wedding in Hertfordshire, Cousin, once the date is set. I shall enjoy watching Mrs Bennet's attempts to matchmake you with one of her remaining daughters.'

Though it remained cold, the precipitation that day was rain rather than snow as a thaw set in, and Anne and Captain Wentworth chose to delay their departure a day to ensure the last of the snows had cleared.

Darcy spent the remainder of the morning in discussion with his housekeeper and butler over the removal of the household servants back to Pemberley, after which he repaired to his study, writing various letters to notify the necessary persons of his intentions.

By the following morning, the house was a hive of activity. The carriages and horses had been prepared for long journeys on behalf of Darcy and the captain. The colonel's man, Mackenzie, busied himself loading a cart to transport their possessions to Blandford, whilst Colonel Fitzwilliam intended to ride Hereward back to camp.

Trunks were soon stacked in the entrance hall, the footmen scurrying to and fro under Boliver's orders, with the departing company all in their respective chambers preparing for the day ahead.

Anne and Elizabeth passed a sentimental final morning in the cottage, packing and sharing Elise between them as they dressed for travelling. It took an inordinate amount of time, because they kept dashing into each other's rooms to discuss a random thought, or share a memory, or simply for a quick embrace before returning to their own.

Finally, Elizabeth took her time visiting each room of the cottage, fondly touching the furniture and frequently drawn to the view of the main house from the window and recollecting her many mixed emotions throughout her unanticipated stay. Then, knowing Anne was busy giving Elise her instructions for when she and James arrived in Shropshire, Elizabeth picked up her pelisse and, clutching her reticule, left the cottage to hurry over to the house.

'There you are.' Mr Darcy was by the open front door as she crossed the entrance hall. 'I began to think I must drag you away.'

Elizabeth reached up to kiss his cheek. 'It is hard to say farewell to a place where I have lately been so content and to someone I have become most attached to.'

Darcy pretended to pout. 'I thought I was the person you were most attached to.'

Laughing, Elizabeth took his hands in hers. 'You, sir, comprehend full well you are the most important person in my life.'

Observing the room was empty, Darcy leaned down for a kiss, meaning for it to be brief, but as Elizabeth's pelisse and reticule fell to the floor as she held onto him, he allowed himself the indulgence of her soft mouth.

The clip-clop of hooves and wheels turning slowly on the gravel sweep slowly intruded, however, and Darcy raised his head. Elizabeth's eyes remained closed, and a smile tugged at his lips. Placing a final kiss on her nose, he released her, and she opened her eyes.

'Must reality intrude?'

Darcy bent to retrieve her things. 'We have but a few weeks to endure, my dearest, and then we shall go to Pemberley and be blissfully quiet, just the two of us.'

'And Georgiana, of course.'

Musing as he straightened, Elizabeth's pelisse over one arm and her reticule in the other, Darcy grinned. 'I do not find her particularly noisy.'

Laughing, Elizabeth held out her hand for her pelisse, but he shook his head and, dropping the bag onto a side table, held the coat up and helped her into it.

As Darcy fastened the clasps, he was conscious of Elizabeth's dark gaze upon him, but he refused to meet it. If he looked once more into her loving eyes, he would embrace her again, and this time they would likely be caught out.

'Yes, yes. I am quite able to use the steps unaided, young man.'

Darcy's hand froze on the last clasp, his startled look meeting Elizabeth's curious one, before they both turned as one to face the open door.

CHAPTER FIFTY-TWO

'It is my aunt,' Darcy whispered to Elizabeth, striding out the door to find Lady Catherine de Burgh arriving on the top step, a hapless footman standing to attention by the carriage pulled up at the front of the house.

'Aunt Catherine. This is an unexpected pleasure.'

'Do not attempt to humour me with pleasantries, Darcy. I desire an explanation.' She marched past him into the house, only to fetch up short in front of Elizabeth as she fastened the ribbons of her bonnet. 'Who is this?'

Darcy sent Elizabeth a regretful look. He knew this would not go well but there was no point in avoiding it. 'This is my betrothed, Miss Elizabeth—'

'Preposterous!' Lady Catherine's eyes took in Elizabeth's pelisse and simple bonnet. 'This is no baronet's daughter. We need to talk, Darcy. You cannot get engaged without so much as the courtesy of a by your leave. What of *my* daughter?'

'Excuse me a moment, Elizabeth.' Darcy sent her a warm look but then turned a steely look on his aunt. 'Your daughter and I have never been engaged, nor did either of us have any intention of becoming so. It was a delusion you laboured under in isolation.'

'And where is this Bennet person? That family! I know it all, Darcy. One of the daughters is a hussy and has thrown over Mr Collins, and now I learn you are harbouring another of the girls under your roof. It is all things inappropriate. Have you no consideration for Georgiana's reputation?'

Darcy had plenty to say on that subject, but before he could answer, the door to the garden opened and Anne entered, just as Captain Wentworth came down the stairs.

Turning her indignant face on Darcy, his aunt gestured at them. 'And who are *these* people?'

Ignoring her rudeness, Darcy smiled warmly at the couple as they linked arms and approached.

'Aunt Catherine, let me introduce Miss Anne Elliot and Captain Wentworth, who are engaged to be married. Miss Elliot's father is my present landlord. Captain, Miss Elliot, this is my aunt, Lady Catherine de Burgh.'

A begrudging curtsey was his aunt's only response to this, and she stalked into the centre of the hall. 'This house is entirely too small. Have you taken leave of your senses, Darcy, being tenant on another man's estate?'

'It has turned out to be the most sensible thing I have ever done, Aunt.' Darcy noted the confused expressions on Anne and the captain's faces. 'We are, in fact, about to depart. Would you care for some tea before you continue on your way?'

'Continue on my...' Lady Catherine glared at him. 'Where is my niece? What are you thinking, Darcy? I shall write to your uncle and then we shall see what he has to say on the subject.' She looked around the space, then made for the drawing room door.

Knowing Georgiana was in there, awaiting the instruction to come out to the carriage, Darcy was about to set off after his aunt when Elizabeth spoke.

'Fitzwilliam. I think someone else has arrived.'

Darcy's attention was drawn to the open door, and then he put a hand to his head. What was going on? Before the carriage came to a halt, however, the colonel flew down the stairs.

'What the devil is my father doing here?'

Torn between going to follow his aunt and greeting his uncle, Darcy threw Elizabeth a desperate look, but she sent him a reassuring smile.

'I will go to your sister.'

His momentary gratitude was soon swept away by the implications. Elizabeth knew not the wrath of his aunt, but before he could stop her, his uncle and aunt entered.

'Darcy! There you are!' Lord Matlock caught sight of his son. 'Richard. We planned on coming over to Blandford to see you once we have sorted this situation here.'

Situation?

'Uncle, Aunt.' Darcy greeted them. 'This is unexpected.'

The gentleman snorted. 'As was that damned announcement in the paper, Darcy. What the hell is going on?' He seemed to notice Anne and the captain then. 'Forgive me, ma'am.'

'What about me?' The lady accompanying him reached up to kiss Darcy's cheek. 'Do I have to put up with your bad manners without apology?' Lady Matlock smiled warmly at Anne and the captain. 'Do forgive the intrusion. My impetuous husband insisted we leave Town.' She walked over to her son and embraced him. 'Are you losing weight, Richard? I cannot believe how you survive on those paltry rations.'

'Do not be ridiculous, my dear. The boy is of sufficient rank to be served a decent portion.' Lord Matlock walked over to his second son and patted his midriff in the way only a parent can. 'See. Solid as Hereward's flank.'

Exchanging an amused look with Captain Wentworth, Darcy made the introductions.

'Well, Darcy. You surprised us all. Why the secrecy? And where is this young lady to whom you have become engaged?'

Ah. Darcy's heart sank. 'Excuse me a moment.' He strode over to the drawing room and flung open the door.

Georgiana sat on a sofa, staring at Lady Catherine, her mouth slightly open as she clutched Mrs Annesley's hand.

'Obstinate, headstrong girl! Are the shades of Pemberley to be thus polluted?'

Elizabeth stood opposite his aunt, her bonnet in her hands, chin raised and eyes flashing, and Darcy took a moment to admire her, before stepping forward.

'That is enough, Aunt Catherine. You will not insult my future wife, and you will not cause a scene in my home.'

Lady Catherine all but stamped her foot. 'This is *not* your home. It is time you returned to where you belong. How can you contemplate marriage with someone of Miss Bennet's station? Yes, I know it all. Mr Collins told me I would find this person here.' She pointed at Elizabeth. 'But I had no idea of her wiles. She has no dowry to speak of, and her family connections are with tradesmen!'

'I do not propose marrying Elizabeth's connections, Aunt. I wish to marry her.' Unwilling to be cowed by such a display of ill manners, Darcy walked over to stand beside Elizabeth, taking her hand in his. 'I care little for what material gain Elizabeth brings. Her value to me is beyond riches.'

A soft pressure on his hand came from the lady, who said nothing, but Lady Catherine had not finished.

'Ridiculous. What possible distinction can she bring to a marriage with a Darcy of Pemberley, whose connections include the aristocracy? Who is her mother or her father?'

'*I* am her father.'

Darcy's attention whipped to the door. Mr Bennet stood on the threshold, his countenance stern as he looked from Lady Catherine to his daughter, then the hand clasping hers.

'And I demand to know what is going on.'

'Does no one use the post anymore?' Elizabeth whispered as she passed Darcy to greet her father.

Laughing despite the situation, Darcy met his aunt's furious eye. 'This is no time for amusement, Darcy. *Do* something!'

'On the contrary, Aunt, this is the most ludicrous moment in recent months, and that is quite the achievement.' He strode over and tugged the bell. 'Now sit down and I will arrange for some tea.'

He turned his back on her, sending Georgiana a reassuring look. His sister eyed him warily, before looking back at her aunt, who glared after her nephew.

Where had Elizabeth gone? This was no way for Mr Bennet to find out, there were already too many aware of his daughter's engagement.

He emerged into the hall. His aunt, uncle, and cousin were in conversation with the captain and Anne and—surprisingly, Jane Bennet—but Elizabeth and her father were nowhere to be seen.

'Darcy, there you are.' His uncle approached him. 'Were those my sister's dulcet tones?'

'Would you do me a favour, Uncle? Please go and calm her down. I have rung for some tea, though I think we are all going to need a stronger remedy shortly.'

'I can deal with that,' chimed in the colonel as he followed his father to the drawing room.

'Lizzy took Papa into the garden, Mr Darcy.' Jane smiled at him, and he thanked her for the direction, and made to go after her, but his aunt stayed him with her hand.

'I know not what is happening, my dear.' Lady Matlock raised a brow as the sound of Lady Catherine's voice reached them again. 'And you seem a little busy at the moment, but I want you to know that whatever you are doing—if it brings you happiness—I will support it.'

Full of thanks for his one sensible aunt, Darcy kissed her cheek. 'Thank you,' he mouthed.

She touched a hand to his face, then turned back to the captain, Anne and Jane as Darcy walked rapidly over to the door into the garden.

He could see Elizabeth standing opposite her father and it did not look as though things went well.

Elizabeth, meanwhile, was eager to establish why her father had come such a long way.

'What else would you have me do, Lizzy? You ask if you can stay with a friend you have known but a short while. You claim you will be away a fortnight, but it is almost a month since you left.'

'I am sorry, Papa.'

'I receive an express from this Sir Walter chap, saying you are to return directly, followed immediately by your own saying you will not and, what is more, you are moving to another property on the estate with your friend!' He regarded her sternly. 'Your new direction, I will confess, I kept to myself.

Your mother's delight in telling the entire neighbourhood she had a daughter staying as guest of a baronet kept her perpetually out of the house. It was blissfully peaceful.'

A laugh escaped Elizabeth, and she was relieved to see her father's lips twitch.

'I did not know, however, you and your friend had become guests of that proud Mr Darcy until two days ago.'

Elizabeth was astounded. She had not written to anyone in the last few days, there had simply been too much going on!

'How *did* you find out?'

'That hapless pup, Bingley, is how.'

'Oh dear.' Catching a movement from the corner of her eye, Elizabeth realised Mr Darcy approached them.

'Papa, there are things you must know about Mr Darcy.'

Mr Bennet's eyes narrowed. 'I think I know him well enough, mainly due to your opinion, Lizzy. I cannot understand what would induce you to stay in his home.'

'I have not been in the main house, Papa.' She gestured behind. 'Anne and I have been staying in this cottage and taking our meals over there.' She was thankful when the gentleman joined them.

'There has been little chance to explain yet.' She spoke quietly, and Mr Bennet's sharp eyes moved from her to the gentleman by her side.

'Mr Darcy.' His expression was uncompromising. 'Who is that angry lady in your house, and why did she insult my daughter?'

'That, sir, is my aunt, Lady Catherine de Burgh. She is inordinately fond of the sound of her own voice.'

A short laugh came from Mr Bennet, much to Elizabeth's relief.

'Papa, we were about to leave, to take the carriage home. To Longbourn.'

Mr Bennet's brows rose. 'A remarkable piece of timing. You have promised to make the journey more than once, and then have broken it each time—the last of which was a choice to not come home for Christmas—which is why I decided, as soon as your aunt and uncle left, to come and fetch you.' He raised his chin. 'Your sister refused to let me leave without taking her along. It is quite singular, but I can only assume your company has been missed.'

Elizabeth was not blind to the softening of his expression as he held her gaze.

'Will you come inside and take some refreshments, Mr Bennet?' Mr Darcy gestured back whence he had come. 'We seem to have amassed quite the gathering.'

'A cup of tea would be welcome, but it is fortunate Lizzy is already packed. We must be on our way if we are to reach an inn by nightfall.'

Mr Darcy and Elizabeth exchanged a look as they fell into step behind Mr Bennet. Once returned to the now empty entrance hall, however, she turned to her father.

'I must speak to you, Papa, but Mr Darcy would—'

She broke off as the drawing room door opened and then closed and the colonel approached, beaming in his usual fashion.

Quickly introducing them, the colonel then inclined his head in the direction of the room he had just left.

'My father is successfully talking over Aunt Catherine, and Miss Elliot is keeping Georgiana calm. I think—'

What the colonel thought, however, had to be kept to himself. Footsteps could be heard echoing on the steps outside as, through the still open doorway, their faces full of curiosity, came Mr and Mrs Gardiner.

Eyes wide in surprise, Elizabeth threw Mr Darcy a placating look and hurried forward. 'Aunt! Uncle! Whatever are you doing here?'

'I could well ask you the same thing, Bennet.' Mr Gardiner's confusion was obvious as he greeted his niece, his eyes on his brother-in-law.

'The children wished to stay at Longbourn a while longer, so we took the opportunity of travelling west.'

Mrs Gardiner smiled around at the others. 'We decided to make use of the quiet period between Christmas and New Year to explore the West Country and also call upon our niece.' She turned to Elizabeth. 'You were much missed over Christmas, my dear.'

The colonel looked at Darcy. 'This is quiet?'

Darcy greeted the Gardiners graciously. 'It is a pleasure to see you both again.' He turned to Elizabeth. 'Eli—Miss Bennet, would you take your family into the drawing room? I will join you directly.'

'Of course.'

Watching them go and trying not to see the intense scrutiny of Mr Bennet as he passed Darcy, he walked over to look out of the door at the four carriages assembled on the driveway.

'I do not think we will be starting our journeys today.'

The colonel shrugged as he looked at the line of conveyances. 'It is not as though we can get the carriages round, anyway. Come on Darce. Let us go and see what entertainment there is to be had.'

CHAPTER FIFTY-THREE

As always, Darcy was ever grateful for Mrs Reynolds and Boliver, who—once apprised of the unanticipated guests—set to marshalling the maids and footmen to arms. There were fires to set in all the unused guest chambers, lodgings in the attics required for the accompanying servants, and Darcy's coachman, groom and stable boy soon directed the newly arrived conveyances to an empty stone barn. How the conversation went with the cook and kitchen servants, Darcy had no idea, but he suspected there would be a substantial raiding of the stores that afternoon.

Lady Catherine, however, refused the offer of a bed and hot supper. So incensed was she by Darcy's engagement to Elizabeth, especially in the light of her being from the exact same family which had recently disappointed her parson, she could hardly speak as the colonel assisted her with little ceremony into the carriage and saw her on her way.

Once his cousin returned to the drawing room, Darcy walked over to stare across the lawn to Willow Cottage. He and Elizabeth should have been on their way to Hertfordshire. When would they ever get some time on their own?

As soon as you are wed, you dunderhead. Get on with it.

He walked into the drawing room to find the gathered company settled into small groupings consisting of Elizabeth, her aunt, Lady Matlock, Georgiana and Anne, on the sofas by the hearth, whilst the colonel, his father and Mr Gardiner all debated the merits of which conveyance Captain Wentworth should order as he was to be a married man.

Darcy looked over at Elizabeth.

'Where is he?' he mouthed, and she tapped a small pile of books on the table beside the sofa.

Approaching the small library a few minutes later, Darcy tried to keep his trepidation in hand. After all, what was this to everything he had been through in recent weeks?

Mr Bennet nestled comfortably by the fire, a book in his hand, and he peered over when Darcy entered the room, then rose to his feet.

'An eclectic choice of reading matter, sir.' He raised the book he held. 'I hope you do not mind. Your sister obliged in showing me your library. I am indulging myself with a ladies' novel and assume it did not come from your own collection.'

'No, sir.' Darcy waved a hand at the bookshelves lining the walls. 'The room was established by the late Lady Elliot, and the selection is more to Georgiana's taste, though there are some excellent volumes of poetry.'

'Did you wish to make use of the room? I can easily vacate.'

Darcy shook his head, finally pushing away from the door and approaching the gentleman.

'Please, Mr Bennet, stay.'

Taking the armchair opposite, Darcy drew in a short breath, in confusion over how to begin. It did not help that Mr Bennet had put the book aside and sat, hands steepled on his chest as he beheld Darcy.

'You are a surprising young man, sir.' The gentleman turned his head to one side a little. 'I have heard such contradictory reports of you.'

Suspecting how the populace of Meryton viewed him, Darcy was not surprised. 'I have learned one must not believe all one hears, sir.'

Mr Bennet made a small sound. 'Nor all one sees, apparently. My astonishment is all the greater for the conflicting reports being from the same source: my daughter, Lizzy.'

Stirring in his seat, Darcy waited, uncertain where the gentleman was headed.

'You do not ask what these are?' Mr Bennet's brows rose. 'Or perchance you already know.'

It was time Darcy took the conversation into his own hands.

'I believe you refer to the fact Miss Elizabeth Bennet once hated me.'

A brow rose. 'Once?' Then, the gentleman inclined his head. 'Indeed. Even I can detect the alteration in her estimation.' He sent Darcy a searching look. 'And Lizzy is quite decided in her opinions, as well you may know.'

'Often to my detriment, sir.'

Mr Bennet gave a short laugh. 'Quite. Despite my age, Mr Darcy, my eyesight is as sound as my hearing. I did not miss your slip with my daughter's name earlier. I have watched her this past hour, whilst you were away attending to our needs. There is a glow about Lizzy, an inner happiness I have never seen before, and it increases whenever you walk into the room.' He dropped his hands and leaned forward to pierce

Darcy with his stare. 'It obliges me to ask, sir: what is this effect you have on my daughter?'

Darcy began to wish he sat further from the fire. He ran a finger under the edge of his neck-cloth, conscious of the heat in his skin. How was this taking charge of the conversation?

He got to his feet, and so did Mr Bennet. It did not help, so he walked a few paces away from the hearth and then turned.

'I have developed a deep esteem and affection for your daughter, sir, and it is reciprocated. We have spoken, and the reason we were on our way to Hertfordshire today was for the express purpose of asking your permission to set a date.'

Mr Bennet walked over to stand opposite Darcy, his face unreadable.

'Lizzy has told me of your efforts to help Jane out of her predicament. She also informed me of the service you did for Captain Wentworth, a complete stranger, which also makes you a surprising young man.' Mr Bennet folded his arms. 'Lizzy's contentment is vastly important to me, Mr Darcy.'

'Your daughter and her happiness have become significant with me, sir, in recent months. Do we have your consent?'

Mr Bennet studied him seriously for a moment. 'Though I can see Lizzy's approval in her face and demeanour, Mr Darcy, I trust you will not mind if I hear it from her own lips? Once that is done to my satisfaction, you shall have it.'

With that, Darcy had to be content, and he left in search of Elizabeth, thankful to have the moment over.

Lord, would he be that severe on any young man soliciting Georgiana's hand in the future?

Elizabeth's assurances to her father were well-received, and he conferred both his consent and blessing on the union, though he could not help shaking his head at Mr Darcy, saying he had always considered him far too level-headed to connect himself with a family as ridiculous as the Bennets. The gentleman had countered, by pointing out Mr Bennet had already met his aunt Catherine, and he acceded, agreeing that absurdity was no respecter of rank.

Once returned to the drawing room, Mr Bennet took a seat beside his brother-in-law, whilst Darcy and Elizabeth joined the colonel, who had just thrown some more logs onto the fire.

'How did it go?'

'Papa has given his consent and blessing.' Elizabeth's eyes shone with happiness as she looked up at Mr Darcy. 'We must wait only for the banns to be read before we can set a date.' She observed her aunt, then her uncle and father, before her gaze fell upon Anne and Jane. 'Once we return to Hertfordshire that is.' She turned back to look at the gentlemen. 'I am with all those I wished to see me wed. How incongruous we should be gathered together in Somersetshire.'

Colonel Fitzwilliam looked from Elizabeth to his cousin. 'Then why not do it?' He threw Darcy an amused look. 'You could always make use of one of Sunday's spoils.'

Darcy was puzzled. 'How so?'

'The special license, old man. It would only need a small annotation to the lady's name.'

'Seriously, Richard. I think we have had sufficient of half-witted schemes of dubious legality in recent days. Besides, it was destroyed when Georgiana and I burnt Wickham's letters.'

With a shrug, the colonel smiled at Elizabeth. 'Baronets are not the only aristocracy able to apply for a special license, and I am certain my father will oblige. It could be here in eight and forty hours.'

Elizabeth's heart leapt. 'Surely it is not possible?'

Darcy observed her with quickened interest. 'Would you truly consider being married directly? For myself, I have no objection. Would it pain you to not have your mother and other sisters present?'

Shaking her head, Elizabeth's eyes sparkled. 'It would pain me more to have them here.'

The colonel laughed. 'And to marry in Kellynch Church instead of your home parish?'

'All I wish is to be wed, Colonel.' Elizabeth took Mr Darcy's hand. 'Provided you are there, Fitzwilliam, it matters little where the ceremony takes place.' She looked between the two cousins. 'Besides, is it not fitting? For all its dark moments, Somersetshire is where we were reunited.'

The plan was soon put before Lord and Lady Matlock and the former, under the direction of his wife, acceded and set to in sending an express to the archbishop directly.

Meanwhile, the lady took Elizabeth aside.

'You will have no time to have wedding clothes made up, my dear.'

'I do not mind.'

'No, I am sure you do not. Yet I feel we should do what we can. Come with me, child.'

She took Elizabeth up to the suite of rooms she had been allocated and rummaged through the gowns hanging in the wardrobe.

'There.' She held up an exquisite gown of the finest silk, a warm gold in colour. 'We are of similar frame, though I am taller. My maid can easily make any adjustments in time. What do you think?'

Elizabeth touched the rich silk. It was a beautiful gown, with long sleeves, and a small train.

'There is a cloak, too.' The lady pulled it out with a flourish.

'I am touched, Lady Matlock. Are you sure about lending it to me?'

The lady placed the cloak on a nearby chair and took Elizabeth's hands. 'My nephew is incredibly dear to me, Miss Bennet. To see his happiness is more than I ever imagined. And it is not a loan. If you like the ensemble, I give it to you.'

Unexpected tears filled Elizabeth's eyes at such warm generosity. 'But I cannot—'

The lady fished for her handkerchief and pressed it into her hands. 'Hush, hush, my dear. You can. I was torn between this and another, so shall have the other made up instead. Now, let me find my maid and arrange a fitting.'

A lively evening ensued as they saw the New Year in, with Lord Matlock still convinced Elizabeth was the daughter of a baronet despite both his son and his wife trying to explain the alteration.

'It is the usual way with my father.' The colonel grinned at Anne and Elizabeth. 'I would like to say he will have worked it out by the time you and Darcy are wed, but I doubt it.'

The cook had somehow managed to acquire sufficient supplies from Montacute to enhance what remained in the stores to provide a sumptuous dinner, and there was a festive air to the ceremony of removing the decorations and burning the greenery, whilst Elizabeth was touched to observe Mr Darcy carefully unwinding the twine binding her silk roses to the boughs and placing them aside.

There followed a hectic few days, with the wedding planned for twelfth night. An express went to Netherfield, and Elizabeth sent an explanatory letter to her mother, promising her a description of the ceremony, the clothes and the breakfast at the soonest opportunity. Her father merely added a line at the bottom, declaring his satisfaction in approving the marriage and suggesting Mrs Bennet leave all future such arrangements to him.

Mrs Reynolds and Boliver consulted with Lady Matlock, who had taken charge of organising the wedding breakfast. The special license arrived in the anticipated eight and forty hours and Elizabeth's gown and cloak were soon adjusted to fit and hanging in her wardrobe, along with a bonnet supplied by Georgiana to complement the outfit.

Tilly had taken delight in redressing it, and Anne—who spent several hours at Kellynch with Elise, arranging for the packing of her possessions—presented her friend with a small, elegantly bound hymn book, which she had been given by her grandfather James, insisting Elizabeth keep it as a reminder of their time in Somersetshire.

Two days before the ceremony, Bingley arrived from Hertfordshire, and the colonel returned by dusk, given leave of eight and forty hours to attend the celebrations, and an extremely merry party gathered at table the following evening for a pre-wedding dinner.

CHAPTER FIFTY FOUR

Darcy was deep in the realm of dreams in the early hours of his wedding day—the half-night between darkness and light. Nevertheless, it was a vivid world, where he could breathe, sense and feel, and standing at the head of the aisle on his wedding day, he was assailed by a multitude of emotions.

How he had longed for this day and—much as he disliked being the centre of attention—he could think of nothing but Elizabeth.

He studied the altar, hands clasped tightly behind his back, conscious of the colonel standing to his right but he refused to look at him—he was, after all, responsible for the brandy-induced headache that made itself felt.

Just then there was a pause in the excited chatter within the church, and a breathless hush swept over the small congregation. The skin on the back of Darcy's neck tingled, and he turned to look down the aisle.

In the dimness that shrouded the doorway, it was hard to make the couple out as they entered, and a shaft of winter sunlight through the stained glass window cast a glare, so that even as they came nearer, he was unable to read the expression upon the lady's face. Absorbed as he was, he failed to notice that the person by her side was not her father.

At last, they stood beside him, and Darcy turned to look into the eyes of his bride, then gave a strangled cry, as he recognised not the face of his beloved Elizabeth, but that of Miss Elliot, leering beatifically at him.

He took a stumbling step backwards and felt himself falling…falling…

'Umph!' Darcy's eyes flew open as his back hit the floor, knocking all the breath from his body. He lay still for a second, aware that he suffered: his head pounded, his heart beat as though he had just taken Gunnar on a fast gallop across the fields, and if he did not draw breath soon, he would surely expire.

With a gasp he took in some much needed air and closed his eyes again in relief. Despite the rude awakening from his tumble out of the bed, he was mightily relieved to have been rescued from such an unpleasant dream.

He lay where he had fallen for several seconds, then upon a courteous enquiry of, 'Sir, do you require any assistance?' opened one eye carefully.

A king of discretion—although it could hardly be said to be common to find his master flat on his back, with half the bed sheets tangled about his legs—Raworth's face was a mask. Only an acute observer would have seen the spark of humour in the back of his eyes.

Darcy said nothing, but decided it was time he opened both eyes and faced the day. Holding out a hand, his valet grasped it and hauled him to his rather unsteady feet, and he winced as he probed his skull with his fingers.

A cleared throat drew his attention to where the Raworth was poised, shaving paraphernalia to hand. It was time to prepare for this most important of days.

🐝

It had been arranged for Elizabeth to eat breakfast on a tray at Willow Cottage, before preparing for the day ahead and, having risen early—unable to sleep since dawn for her eagerness—she found herself alone in the parlour.

Trays for herself, Anne and Jane—who was to join them— had been beautifully laid out, her own bearing a brief note from Mr Darcy, which she read in delight before pressing a kiss to it and tucking it up her sleeve.

She walked over to fold back the shutters and looked over at the main house, where she would be spending the night later. Warmth flooded Elizabeth's skin, but then she laughed, shaking her head, and crossed the room to where the tea things had been laid out by Mrs Reynolds.

'Good morning, Mrs Darcy!'

The warmth in Elizabeth's cheeks increased as her friend joined her.

'You are a little precipitous, Anne.' Then, she pulled a face. 'It is a peculiar emotion, that of sheer happiness mixed with some sadness. I shall miss you dearly, for we have had quite the time of it this past month.'

'We have indeed.' Anne poured tea into her cup. 'It will be strange to be with Miss Bennet in the cottage tonight, but I think it was a lovely idea for those of us who have passed the season here to remain for one last evening.' She smirked at Elizabeth. 'Though you will perhaps wish you had the house to yourselves.'

Elizabeth put a hand to her face, which remained warm, but her eyes were indicative of her amusement.

'To be certain, Anne, the apartments Mrs Reynolds showed me yesterday are as smart as any marital chamber ought to be, but I declare we could pass our first night together in a barn, and I would awaken equally content.'

'For shame, Lizzy! You will make this single young woman blush.'

Laughing, Elizabeth poured tea into her cup, and they both took a seat at the small table upon which their trays had been placed. 'You will not be so for much longer.'

Anne picked up a fruit knife and began to peel an apple. 'We are both facing a substantial alteration in our lives.'

'But for the better.'

Cutting the apple into slices, Anne smiled. 'Most indubitably.'

Elizabeth sipped her tea, her eyes on her friend. 'I shall miss you, Anne, excessively.'

'I believe we have formed a bond that time and distance cannot sever.'

'Nor shall we permit it to do so.' Elizabeth selected a piece of toast and added a dollop of honey. 'And I can anticipate seeing you at your own wedding in but a few weeks.'

They both looked up as the door opened, and Jane entered.

'I thought you would be forwarder than me.' Jane leaned down and embraced her sister. 'I am so happy for you, dear Lizzy.'

Emotion rose in Elizabeth's throat, and she gazed mistily at her sister.

'And I am so thankful you are here.' She squeezed Jane's hand as she took the seat beside her.

'To think, Lizzy, had Lady Lucas not taken ill, you would never have come to Kellynch and been reunited with Mr

Darcy.' Jane laughed. 'I cannot begin to imagine your response when first you realised he was here on the estate.'

Exchanging an amused look with Anne, Elizabeth tried to recall how she felt and was thankful to find such sentiments were beyond her memory's reach.

'I am fortunate in believing one should think only of the past as its remembrance gives you pleasure.' She grinned at her sister. 'Where Mr Darcy is concerned, that means about three weeks!'

When they had broken their fast, Jane reached into her reticule and handed a small package to Elizabeth. 'I thought you might like to wear this today.'

Peeling back the tissue, Elizabeth caught her breath. 'Grandmama's pendant!' She stared at her sister in astonishment. 'How on earth did you—'

'I am not prescient!' Jane smiled warmly. 'When Mr Darcy sent his invitation to Mr Bingley, I asked him to add a line requesting his friend call at Longbourn to collect it.'

Touched beyond measure, Elizabeth held the necklace up to show Anne. 'This was Papa's mother's. She always said she wished each of her granddaughters to wear it on their wedding day, as she had done.'

Filled with emotion, Elizabeth embraced her sister, who gave her a final squeeze before getting to her feet.

'I will come back later to help you dress.'

As Jane left the cottage, Elizabeth drew in a calming breath, then noticed her friend's wary expression. 'Pay me no mind, Anne, I am become a little sentimental, that is all.'

'It is to be expected.'

They finished their meal and were about to make their way up the stairs when the door to the cottage was tapped and opened, and in came Elizabeth's aunt and Lady Matlock.

'How are you this morning, Lizzy dear?' Mrs Gardiner smiled kindly at Anne, then looked back to her niece. 'Did you sleep well?'

'As well as any bride to be, I suspect.' Elizabeth pushed open the door to the sitting room. 'Please come in and be seated.'

'Do forgive the intrusion, my dear.' Lady Matlock regarded her warmly as they all sat. 'We will not take up too much of your time, but your aunt wished to see you.'

To Elizabeth's surprise, Mrs Gardiner opened her palm, upon which lay a small box.

'I wore these to my own wedding, Lizzy, and happened to have them with me, as I always wear them on Christmas Day. I would be so happy if you would wear them today. I think the amber droplets will compliment your gown superbly.'

'Dear Aunt, I would be honoured.' Quite amazed, Elizabeth received the box from the lady and then opened the package she already held. 'Look how well they go with Grandmama's pendant!'

'You would make a beautiful bride without any adornment, Miss Bennet.' Lady Matlock beamed at her.

'Your generosity'—she looked from the lady to her aunt and then Anne—'and your kindness—' She broke off as a tear rolled down her cheek. 'Forgive me.' Elizabeth dashed it away. 'I am a little overcome, that is all.'

Mrs Gardiner came over to embrace her niece. 'There, now.' She wiped away another tear and dropped a kiss upon Elizabeth's cheek. 'We have taken up enough of your time.'

'Yes, we will leave you to the ministrations of your friend.' Lady Matlock took Elizabeth's hand in hers. 'I never dreamed of seeing such happiness on my nephew's features, my dear girl.' She too placed a kiss on Elizabeth's cheek, and both ladies left the room.

'Come, Lizzy.' Anne picked up the box containing the earrings and the tissue-wrapped pendant. 'Let us begin to dress the bride.'

❦

'Darcy, old chap! How are you this fine morning?'

Darcy winced as Richard's voice boomed the moment he set foot inside the breakfast room, and he threw him a disgruntled look as he poured some tea. Colonel Fitzwilliam tucked into a plate loaded with breakfast food, and Darcy threw it a jaundiced look as he took a mouthful of extremely hot tea.

'So, how *is* the groom? Did he sleep well?'

Darcy gave this question some serious thought. He was not sure, in all truth, if he could remember sleeping at all... neither could he recall retiring for the night. All he could recall was the appalling dream he had awoken from so abruptly.

'No—I believe he did not, Richard. That he was unconscious he does not doubt, but sleep—the full and proper rest one should indulge in on the night before an occasion as momentous as one's own wedding—that eluded him.'

The colonel released a bark of laughter. 'Well, Darce, that will teach you to over-indulge with the brandy bottle.'

Darcy glared at him, but realised it only increased the pain in his head. 'Forgive me for pointing out the obvious, but the damage was caused not by the bottle but its contents - I merely had control of my own glass, and *I* was not the one refilling it.'

The colonel was prevented from responding to this by the opening of the door as Georgiana entered, followed by almost every one of Meadowbrook House's impromptu guests.

'Good morning, Georgie.'

Darcy managed his first smile of the morning as his sister took the seat beside him and reached out to squeeze his hand.

'How are you, Brother?' She studied his face intently for a moment, then bit her lip. 'You are somewhat pale.'

'I am a little tired, that is all.' He took another gulp of tea as people moved from the serving table to take a seat.

'Well, Darcy, here we are! The day has finally arrived. Today you will be wed.' Lord Matlock clapped him on the back as he passed by his chair and took the one on his other side.

Darcy eyed his uncle, tempted to ask him if he had any other blindingly obvious comments to make, but bit back on the retort. The fact was, it was his wedding day and much as he did not like the attention, at least it was more discreet an affair than a ceremony in Longbourn church, where no doubt the entire neighbourhood would have turned up for their own entertainment.

With that thought, he applied himself once more to his tea. Conscious of the murmur of conversation, Darcy's eye fell upon the captain, who sat across from him.

'Was your abandonment intentional last night, Wentworth?'

The gentleman pretended surprise at the accusation. 'Of course not! The good colonel seemed to have things well in hand, so I felt confident I left you to his tender care.'

Darcy suppressed what could only be described as a snort.

'Did I not beg you to not leave me alone with my cousin? He may well be standing up with me today, but he derives more amusement from my suffering than my well-being.'

Captain Wentworth, as he expected, showed no sign of remorse, merely smirking before tucking into the laden platter before him. The odour of hot food and, more particularly, coddled eggs, began to make Darcy's stomach spin in tandem with his head.

He drained his cup and pushed back his chair, and all the occupants of the table raised their heads to stare at him.

'I have need of some air,' he muttered, and headed for the doors, crossing the entrance hall to the door into the garden and stepping out onto the terrace.

It was a beautiful morning after the recent rain, which had washed away any remnants of snow. The air was cold and crisp, and Darcy inhaled deeply.

Today, the rest of his life began, and he could not wait for its commencement.

Two hours later, Darcy stood outside Kellynch Church, thankful his earlier intake of air—along with several more cups of tea and a restorative powder, courtesy of Raworth—had cleared his head. A relatively detached observer, he watched as the inhabitants of Meadowbrook House emerged from their various conveyances and slowly filled the small churchyard.

He could feel his own contentment simmering, his heart swelling with his high regard for Elizabeth. She had handled the sudden influx of people with a confidence and aplomb belying her young years, and now a day had come that he feared he would never see.

Notwithstanding the threat held over him until recently, Darcy had spent many months in torment. The hopes that rose so swiftly once Elizabeth arrived in Somersetshire had soon been dashed, and the agony of discovering her ill opinion of him had only been superseded by that of discovering her affections had changed, just as he was about to be shackled to another.

Wishing to shed the memories, Darcy roused himself. Everyone appeared to be in high spirits, but no one more so than Bingley. His friend bounded here and there like an unmanageable pup, eagerly talking to anyone who would listen, and occasionally springing enthusiastically up to Darcy to release a verbal barrage of adjectives that indicated his pleasure in the day.

Aware that he was once again approaching, Darcy amused himself comparing this confident, smiling vision with the morose, down-spirited Bingley he had seen in Town only weeks ago.

'Splendid day for it, Darcy, absolutely splendid!'

Before he could summon a suitable reply, Bingley had seen Jane Bennet arrive, along with Anne, and he bounded away. Aware this meant the bride and her father were on their way, Darcy straightened up and turned to enter the church.

'Well, my dear, we are arrived.'

The Bennet carriage had drawn up by the lych gate into the churchyard at Kellynch, and Elizabeth clutched her father's hand as the coachman opened the door and lowered the steps. Everything had happened in such a rush, she could scarce believe what she did.

'Lizzy?'

She turned to Mr Bennet with a tremulous smile. 'I am not generally so lacking in courage, Papa, but I feel as though my legs do not wish to move.'

He laughed, and Elizabeth could not help but join in. Such nonsensical behaviour.

'I have cherished being the father of such a dear child, Lizzy. You have brought much joy into my life, and I will miss you.'

He held both Elizabeth's hands in his for a moment.

'I shall miss you too, Papa, but—'

'But now, I am simply grateful for having been able to cherish you these many years, and today, as I hand you over into the care of another, I could not be more proud.'

'And you do find Mr Darcy a good man, Papa?' Elizabeth had seen him taking pains to converse with the gentleman over the last few days.

Mr Bennet stepped down from the carriage and held his hand out to his daughter, and she stood beside him by the lych gate.

'Aye. He is a fine gentleman, and there is much to like about him.' He offered his arm to Elizabeth, and she took it as they walked the path to the church door. 'Not least in his having an extensive library, a vast distance from your mother at Longbourn, and the decency to invite me to explore it any time I wish.'

Darcy stood at the head of the aisle, his eyes upon the altar, hands clasped tightly behind his back. Aware of the colonel standing to his right, he was suddenly overwhelmed by a strong sense of déjà vu.

His skin went cold as Darcy was revisited by his dream in full force. How near had he come to it being the reality? He closed his eyes, trying to recall what he had been thinking, feeling in the dream.

Richard...that was it, he refused to pay his cousin any mind because of his drink-inspired headache. His eyes flew open. Did his head ache? Darcy stilled for a moment, unblinking, attempting to discern how his head actually felt. There was definitely an ache there, but it bore no similarity to one inspired by an over-consumption of liquor. No, this was most definitely a remnant of the fall from his bed.

Vowing to break free of this ridiculous fear, Darcy forced himself to look to his right, where he met Colonel Fitzwilliam's amused expression with a wry grimace before turning back to face the altar.

Just then there was a hush of the conversation within the church, and Darcy turned slowly to look down the aisle.

The dimness shrouding the doorway made it as hard to make out the couple approaching as it had in his dream, but Darcy refused to pay it any mind. A shaft of winter sunlight pierced the stained glass windows, and he could clearly see the form of his bride, and as she came closer, he met her sparkling eyes with his own and felt a great peace descend upon him. Elizabeth was here, and the moment he longed for was about to happen.

At last, they were beside him, and Darcy took in the lady's singular beauty, all thoughts of dreams and other such tortures far from his mind.

The clearing of Mr Bennet's throat drew Darcy's attention, and he blinked, acknowledging Elizabeth's bite of her lip in an attempt to stop a laugh from escaping, as he turned to face the vicar and his future.

Some time later, as the carriage pulled away from the church, and the good wishes of the small gathering of family and friends dispersed into the winter air, Darcy took Elizabeth's slender hand in his, relishing the softness of her skin against his. Their fingers intertwined, and he stroked the back of her hand.

'You are rather beautiful, Mrs Darcy,' he said, pressing a kiss upon the curve of Elizabeth's cheek.

She turned her head to regard him, her eyes sparkling. 'And you are rather calm now, Mr Darcy.'

'How could I not be?' he countered. 'For at last I have everything I ever hoped for.'

Elizabeth sighed deeply, her contentment evident, squeezing his hand tightly before placing a lingering kiss upon it.

'Your hands are cold, Elizabeth.' Darcy unfastened his coat, and placed her hand inside, and she held him tightly, leaning her head upon his waistcoat.

'I can hear your heart beating.'

'That is a relief.'

She laughed and raised her head, her feelings writ plainly upon her endearing features.

'I cannot believe we do not have to be parted from this day forward. This is, to be sure, a dream come true.'

Darcy choked back a laugh. 'Indeed, it most definitely is *not*!'

He was amused by his wife's evident surprise, and leaning down, his purpose quite clear, said softly, 'Trust me in this, Elizabeth…explanations can wait.'

'I should like to have my curiosity satisfied.' An impish expression formed. 'But I may wait if I can be suitably persuaded.'

Could there be a more perfect invitation? Closing the final gap between them, Darcy took his wife in his arms and kissed her thoroughly, only momentarily regretting it was but a short ride back to Meadowbrook House.

EPILOGUE

Anne Wentworth writes to her friend, Elizabeth Darcy

Moorings House
The Barbican
Plymouth
Devon

Monday, 9 March 1812

My dear friend,

I am in receipt of your last and was delighted to hear of your happiness in finally being established at Pemberley, though you will have to make more of an endeavour if you truly wish to convince me that, had you seen it last year, you would have fallen for Mr Darcy all the sooner!

It seems such a while since we were together for my marriage to Frederick. I thank you for your enquiry, he remains in excellent health and spirits, as do I. You may have guessed, my husband—how I delight in penning those words—has finally relented. The captain's cabin is to be modified to accommodate a wife, and I shall thus be able to join him when he sails for Gibraltar next month.

No logical argument made a dent in his thinking, and ultimately, I had to fall back upon reminding Frederick how we both felt the last time we were divided. Though the circumstances could not be the same, this recollection hit the mark. I cannot say he is any more content with the notion of having a female on board his ship but having just been separated for five long years and more, he accepts it will save us from the pain inherent upon us having to part for an indefinable amount of time in future.

In answer to your question, I have not heard particularly from my father or Elizabeth, though intelligence comes with rapid frequency by Mary's hand, and thus I am more well acquainted with their situation than I could ever wish to be. I cannot help but feel sympathy for them, Lizzy, though I comprehend full well they do not deserve it.

Being well regarded is of paramount importance to them both, but it seems London has not been as welcoming as it once was. According to Mary, Papa is finding it difficult to hold his head above water and has to choose between spending on his appearance or his entertainment. He will not attend anything unless dressed and coiffured in the latest fashion, and when that has been achieved, he cannot afford the expense of running the carriage or the cost of attendance. Suffice it to say, he spends many an evening at home with Elizabeth, attired as if for St James's but with nothing to do but play a hand of piquet.

Of Elizabeth, there is some news, however. Mary claims she is soon to be engaged to a young gentleman who is said to be as handsome as she is and at least as proud, though I will confess to some curiosity about my soon to be brother-in-law, as he is younger than Mary. Nevertheless, I am determined to assume the best for their union.

As for Mary herself, she seems to be adjusting to motherhood, and I must own I am looking forward to travelling to Somersetshire in a few days to meet baby Charles in person at last. She remains rather querulous and does not feel she is receiving her due in attention from the Musgroves up at the great house, though there is nothing new in that.

It seems the new tenants have moved into the Hall, and my sister is well satisfied with *them*, for they paid her the due attention of an immediate call—acknowledging her to be the sole remaining member of the Elliot family in the district. I look forward to making their acquaintance when we stay at Uppercross Cottage.

I am delighted to hear Jane has accepted Mr Bingley's hand at last! How happy you must be, dear Lizzy! The description of your mother's response was vastly amusing, and whilst I understand she must be relieved to have the security of such a fine house in which to live out her life, should the time come, I could not help but laugh to hear of her visiting it already to ascertain the quality of the furnishings.

It goes without saying, I was pleased to hear of your father's continued *good* health, and highly entertained to learn he had thanked Mr Bingley for making such generous provision for his wife, so much so that she may be moving in directly with Mr Bennet's blessing.

Fredrick and I reminisce often about our time at Meadowbrook House with you and Mr Darcy. Your invitation is well received, and I hope we will be able to travel northwards after our brief sojourn at Uppercross for Eastertide.

As for your disagreement with Mr Darcy about the library, I do hope the two of you have finally found a compromise. I can easily picture the two of you in a heated debate over how to organise the books by height, so that you could reach the volumes you wished to read without scaling the moveable ladder!

I do believe the two of you argue with the most affection I have ever seen.

Give our love to Georgiana, and write soon with all your news.

Your affectionate friend,

Anne

Colonel Fitzwilliam writes to his cousin, Fitzwilliam Darcy

Officer's Quarters
Blandford Barracks
Dorset

Tuesday, 7 April 1812

Cousin,

I am duly returned from the annual visit to our aunt at Rosings and apologise for being remiss in responding to your last. Without you there to deflect her attention, it was akin to being in an interrogation chamber, with little respite.

Thus, I am quite determined, by next year, to have followed your example in securing for myself a partner in life whom I will cherish all the more for ensuring she is sufficiently offensive in Lady Catherine de Burgh's eyes to ensure a break in our relations

Speaking of which, do not be too complacent. Her curiosity as to how the shades of Pemberley are faring since acquiring a mistress is profound. Put a man on watch, or—more practically—order the construction of a moat and drawbridge directly!

I was pleased to hear the transition to Derbyshire went as smoothly as such things can, of Georgie's delight in being home, and that your wife was sufficiently pleased with the house and thus not disappointed by her decision to shackle herself to you for eternity.

Mother has written to say she will bring the latest edition of the *Lady's Magazine*, per your request, when they visit Pemberley next month, though I do not fully comprehend how it will help you win the battle of the library—as your sister and I have affectionately labelled it. Your wife is a formidable adversary, and I am not sure the bribery of selecting new items for her wardrobe will get you any closer to winning her on to your side. I swear I often wonder if you simply enjoy the way the lady's eyes flash when she is provoked!

In other news from Kent, I made the acquaintance of our aunt's parson. What an obsequious specimen! Your description was perfectly apt. You will be unsurprised to learn he has finally managed to secure a wife from amongst the local populace—whose name was *not* Bennet (apparently, that was an edict from Lady Catherine). It will likely also be no astonishment to learn this was the seventh lady he had approached in such a manner. The lady's charm and intelligence are indicative of why she now holds her present position.

Good to hear Wentworth has a new command. They are gone to Somersetshire, I understand, to meet the Musgrove heir, before journeying to Derbyshire until the ship is ready. I will do my utmost to join you during their stay, that we may all be reunited once more.

For now, Cousin, I wish you much continued enjoyment of your new life and hope to hear in your next letter that you have settled the matter of the library's shelving to your satisfaction. From all I observed when last we met, and the intelligence I have gleaned through Georgiana's correspondence, Mrs Darcy seems perfectly happy to set you up before willingly giving in to your persuasion.

I remain your loyal servant,

Richard

THE END

ABOUT THE AUTHORS

Both avid bookworms since childhood, Cass Grafton and Ada Bright write the sort of stories they love to read—heart-warming, character driven and strong on location.

Cass loves travelling, words, cats and wine, but never in the same glass.

Ada loves nothing more than a good, subtle love story… well, except cake. She also really loves cake.

Cass and Ada are close friends who enjoy writing together.

Their popular time-travel romance series featuring Jane Austen recently came out on audio.

When they are not working together, Cass writes uplifting contemporary romance and Ada writes romantic suspense.

OTHER WORKS

The Austen Adventures

Comedic tales of time travel, love and friendship

The Particular Charm of Miss Jane Austen
Canelo Escape, 2019
The Unexpected Past of Miss Jane Austen
Canelo Escape, 2019

Both titles are available in paperback, ebook and audio format

A Quest for Mr Darcy
by Cass Grafton
Canelo Escape, 2019 (originally published 2017)

A romantic mystery, inspired by *Pride & Prejudice*

A Fair Prospect - Volumes I, II and III
by Cass Grafton
Canelo Escape, 2019 (originally published 2013)

Inspired by Jane Austen's *Pride & Prejudice*, *A Fair Prospect* is an introspective, character-driven re-imagining of Jane Austen's classic told across three volumes.

All these titles are available in paperback and ebook format, with audio coming soon

CONNECT WITH CASS & ADA

Amazon Author Pages

http://author.to/CassGrafton

http://author.to/AdaBright

Blogs

www.cassandragrafton.com

www.tabbycow.com

Facebook

https://www.facebook.com/CassGraftonWriter

https://www.facebook.com/cassie.grafton/

https://www.facebook.com/missyadabright

Twitter

@CassGrafton
@missyadabright

Instagram
@cassgraftonwriter
@adacakes

LITERACY FOUNDATION

CONNECTING THROUGH LITERACY

Cass and Ada will be donating 10% of all profits from sales of *Mr Darcy's Persuasion* to the Jane Austen Literacy Foundation.

https://janeaustenlf.org

Printed in Great Britain
by Amazon

14126658R00335